Landscapes of a
MONTANA HEART

BALLAD OF THE DROVER

C. G. Eberts

Sorrow Songs   Lafayette, Indiana

2025

Cover painting:
In the White Mist by Patrick McClellan.
Cover, maps, and book design by Colter Lease.

This is a work of fiction. Names, characters, places and incidents either are products of the author's imagination or are used fictitiously.

First Printing, 2025
Manufactured in the United States of America.

ISBN 9798991898126

Library of Congress Control Number: 2025919573
Names: Eberts, Cindelyn Gray, author.

Map of Cait's Montana Country

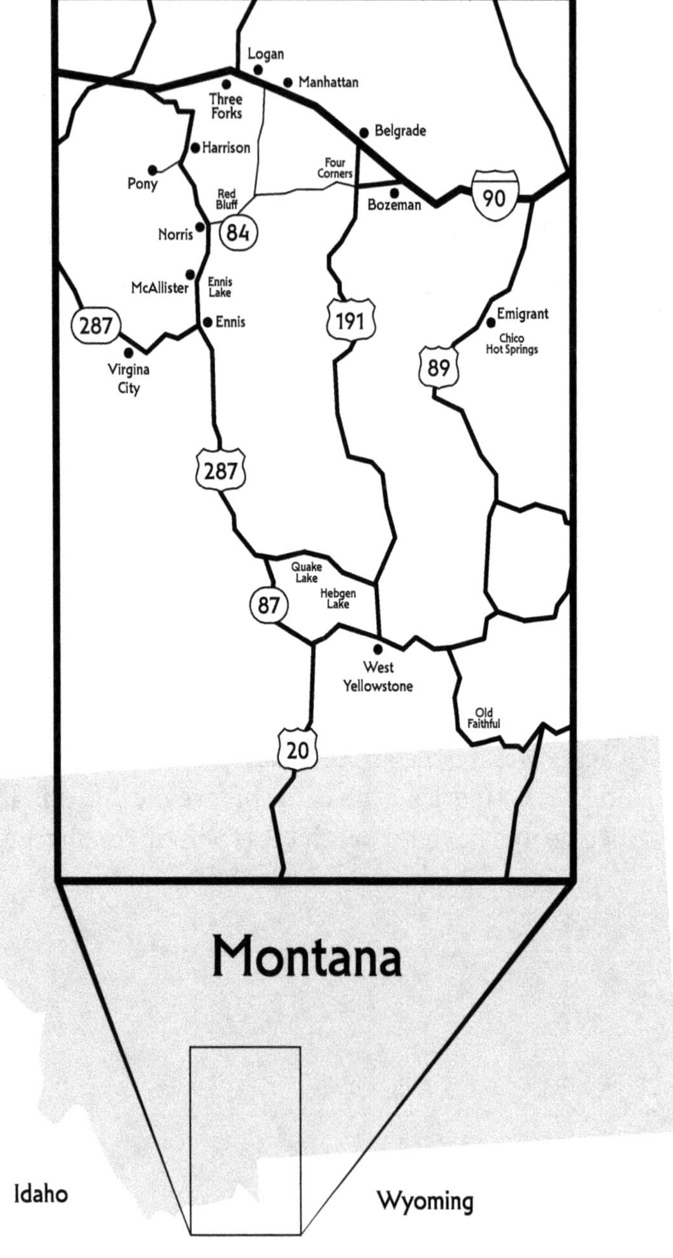

Map of Ross's Australia Country

Map of the 1866 Nelson Story Cattle Drive

~ Author's Note ~

I grew up in small town Montana reading Zane Grey, Louis L'Amour, and Norman Maclean, all sticklers for being accurate about historical details and rocks. My apologies to them and to you, dear reader—some dates of events in this story had to be shifted a few years, The *Greatest Cattle Drive* by Paul Wellman was actually published in 1964, Owen Beattie's groundbreaking work on the Franklin expedition was in 1981 and 1982. Writing about a time a quarter century ago is not without its challenges. Vita-Weats made better veggie worms than the current crackers made by Arnott's. Level 15 sunblock was all that was available in Australia 25 years ago. And Montana? The Yellowstone floods of 2022 altered the flow of the rivers—hot potting in the Gardner river is no more. Madison County has the most expensive houses in the state of Montana due to the log castles in the elite ski resorts above the Lone Mountain chapel built after WWII in memory of Nelson Story IV. The sheep ranches of my childhood? Forget it. All subdivisions. The landscape and culture of old Montana are gone forever, but this novel is my elegy to her lost empty spaces and pastoral way of life.

The brilliant skies and shining mountains remain. Indian Rocks in the shadow of South Baldy stoically still exists as described, as does the rock of Evening Star at the entrance to Bridger Canyon. A quarter century ago, the Bear Claw was a real bar at the crossroads with "*The Riders of North Meadow Creek*" painting by Larry Zabel hanging above the fireplace in their dining room and pictures of Setters and Pointers designating the toilets. The local sheep rancher did move his house off the road leaving a porch to nothing on North Meadow Creek Road. Montanans did test drive men and their rigs off road and Montanans judged their pickups by how fast they could go over the Norris Hill. I played with Nelson Story's great-great-granddaughter while growing up in Montana. I owe it to my childhood country and the people who raised me in Montana to be as accurate as possible. While the descriptions of the land—Montana or Australia—and their stories are real, the contemporary characters in this book are completely fictional. This book is for those who understand the difference between owning the land and the land owning you.

Deepest thanks to my late husband, Ray, who always understood my heart belonged to Montana and built me a cabin that kept my heart soft after he died too young. To his parents who always loved me with no conditions. To my parents, who taught me how to listen to the earth breathe and the value of our stories. To my sons, who believed in me when I didn't believe in myself. To my grandmothers who taught me how to create beauty with a needle. To my late cousin, Betsy McKinney Sweatman, for our youthful adventures, her love of family, and her laughter. To my father's cousin, Deb Ludlow on Cape Rosier, Maine, who provided a safe place for me to write where the land held no ghosts to haunt me.

I want to acknowledge my debt to my sisters in Christ. You lighted my way with your love and grace and your generous support over the years—Joni Balian, Margie Dubes, and Nancy Van Dyken. To Omer and Joy Sallee of Willow Creek, my Montana "grandparents," who loved me as a child and made sure I knew the stories of my country, and always to Harold Richardson, who taught me to make his grandmother's pie crust and watched out for me on North Meadow Creek after my husband died. Thank you, Jean Louise Wilson Thorson for your friendship, your stories of growing up in Meadow Creek, and for your role in finding a final resting place for my late husband.

My deepest thanks to my creative team: Linda Carrick Thomas for her editing, Colter Lease for his map and book design including the cover, and to Patrick McClellan for his painting of the cowboy/drover, *In the White Mist.* Thanks to Janet Watson Kruse for her technical expertise and her wisdom, to my first reader Suzanne McConville for her insightful comments, and to all my beta readers. Thanks to the friendly staff of the Madison County Library in Ennis for your kindness and support while I wrote the final draft in the summer of 2023. Thanks to my bonus Montana moms, Dr. Carol Ammons and Cecelia Goodman, who held me steady through the storm of my loss. Thanks to my Aussie mates, who taught me how to drive in Melbourne dodging street cars, schooled me in how to travel safe alone in the bush, make a proper poached egg, the importance of not letting friends drink crap beer, and demonstrated true hospitality. Thanks to all the musicians along the black snake road of my life who kept me walking after my husband was killed. Cheers to the folks of Walt's Other Pub for being the bar at the crossroads of my life. Special thanks to Tom Roll, my Montana anthropology professor. Thanks to Daniel E. Elming for our conversations at Walt's when I was uncertain about my key male characters and doubting myself. And lastly, thanks to Michael Earl Kelsey, whose wave of a purple towel and his radiant smile on August 4, 2022 as the sun was setting relaunched this book.

Dedicated to my dear friend, the late Vickie Myers,
who believed in me and challenged me to do better when
I embarked upon this difficult journey of writing.

Beannacht

On the day when the weight deadens
on your shoulders and you stumble,
may the clay dance to balance you.

And when your eyes freeze behind the grey window
and the ghost of loss gets into you,
may a flock of colors,
indigo, red, green and azure blue,
come to awaken in you a meadow of delight.

When the canvas frays in the currach of thought
and a stain of ocean blackens beneath you,
may there come across the waters
a path of yellow moonlight to bring you safely home.

May the nourishment of the earth be yours,
may the clarity of light be yours,
may the fluency of the ocean be yours,
may the protection of the ancestors be yours.

And so may a slow wind work these words
of love around you,
an invisible cloak to mind your life.[1]

John O'Donohue

~ Prologue ~

SCONE, NEW SOUTH WALES, AUSTRALIA,
AUGUST 1959

"You won't change your mind?"

Shaking her head so hard her auburn curls freed themselves from their restraints, Nora Larkin did not dare speak. Tipping her straw hat back, exposing her face to the warm winter sun and to him, he kissed away her tears, brushing her forehead so gently she hardly felt his lips. Without a word, he pivoted on the heel of his boot, moving further away from her. Each step of his leaving echoed her pounding heart.

At the top of the stairs, he turned back, taking one last look at the rolling land, the slopes of the mountains, and the woman he loved. Swooping off his cowboy hat with a gallant flourish, he bowed deeply to the woman standing statue-still on the tarmac. Folding his lanky body through the doorway of the plane, he disappeared.

Nora waited, hopefully, to catch one last glimpse of him,

but blank windows gleamed mockingly back at her. With her straw hat clenched in her hand, she waved as the plane taxied down the runway. Her arm painted broad strokes long after the tiny dot of a climbing plane vanished into a cloudless sky.

Night after night, Nora dreamed in technicolor of a green-eyed cowboy, brilliant azure skies, and purple snow-capped mountains she had never seen. When her breasts became sore and she missed her first period, then her second, Nora confided in her mum.

The silence in the kitchen lengthened with the late afternoon shadows as poured cups of tea grew cold until her mum sighed. Reaching across the table, Nora's mum took her only child's trembling hand. "Paddy did ask you to marry him and you did say no."

Nodding, Nora remained silent, tears forming and running down her face.

"Should we call him back to Australia? A man has a right to know if he's going to be a father."

"No, Mummy, please no."

"I'll speak with your father."

~ Chapter 1 ~

ILLINOIS, 1998

The ringing interrupted the movie. I pushed the pause button on the remote for the VCR and stood up. *Concentrate Cait. Answer the phone.* The distance from the chair to the kitchen seemed to increase like a stretched rubber band ever expanding. I hoped I could reach my connection to another person before the rubber band snapped back throwing me into unconsciousness. The first wave of nausea brought an intense cold, followed by the dampness of pervasive sweat. The second wave of nausea made me stagger to regain my balance. Every breath hurt, as if my lungs were pushing against some barrier. *Focus Cait.* I reached for the receiver and the movement produced a stabbing pain behind my right clavicle. *Pick up the phone, Cait.*

Ralph, my husband, was returning my earlier call. He couldn't come home until after his meeting. "No, Cait, I can't skip it; it's critical." I tried to explain how badly I felt, but he wasn't hearing me. "I'll be home at 6:00, Cait; I'll deal with you then." Deal with me, then. How typical. I was always a burden to him. He never let me forget that ours was a marriage born of necessity that matured to one of convenience, nothing more. It was as cold and barren as the wind-swept coast of the Arctic island where we had first met. We had both been college students, part of an archaeological field crew looking for decisive evidence of a lost expedition whose mission had been to find the Northwest Passage in the maze of islands and inlets that form the Canadian Polar Regions. While we helped to solve a 140-year-old historical mystery, Ralph and I never could solve the mysteries of a loving relationship. We were just as poisoned by fate and time as the men of the Franklin expedition were poisoned by lead solder. Ralph and I were as lost as the 129 men who died wandering in the barrens of the Arctic. It was no use arguing with Ralph. I never won. He wasn't coming home to help me. I hung up the phone and went back to my movie.

Fear was being replaced with a seductive calm. I was so worn from the torturous agony, the pain had started the evening before, keeping me awake all night. The emotional distress was the worst. I couldn't bear the reality of losing another child. I was ignoring the fact that this miscarriage was much worse than the previous three. The whole pregnancy had felt different, so I had been positive this one would live. Now I knew there would be no child to hold in the future. I did not care anymore.

The movie, *Cleaveth Unto the Dust* was fast becoming my sole link to humanity. Father Paddy O'Donnell, was reciting a prayer under the wide Dakota skies. His words were intermingling with my own remembrances of long ago summer days spent with my grandfather on the top of his mountain under the brilliant blue skies of Montana. My childhood skies matched the color of the priest's eyes on the glass screen before me. I could feel the warmth of the Montana sun again and the wind's cooling movement, the smell of sage filling my nostrils, the sound of stones crunching under my small cowboy boots, and vistas in all directions stretching out 30, 60, 90 miles. The priest's words were feeding the memories:

> *"I arise today through the strength in the sky*
> *light of sun*
> *moon's reflection*
> *dazzle of fire*
> *speed of lightning*
> *wild wind*
> *deep sea*
> *firm earth*
> *hard rock.*
> *I arise today*
> *with God's strength to pilot me"*[2]

Dimly, as if through water, I heard my front door bell. Father O'Donnell's deep voice was the last sound, and his compassionate azure eyes the last image, as I arose from my chair to meet the firm, hard, flatness of the floor.

My first sensation when I woke up after surgery was relief that I could breathe easily again. Sweet, deep breaths, my diaphragm moving up and down without the impediment of blood in my body cavity. Because I had waited so long, the surgeon had no choice but to open me up to repair the damage to my fallopian tube. I would have a six-inch scar across the front of my abdomen, a constant reminder of my stupidity. A sister scar to the other time in my life when I'd made a bad decision. This wound, while easier to hide, was infinitely more painful than the earlier one had been. The nurse came in and explained how the on-demand pain relief system worked. "Push this button when the pain gets too intense. The machine won't let you self-medicate too often and it regulates the dosage." She came back later that day to find me shaking, "Cait, use the medication. You'll heal faster if your body isn't in pain."

I didn't tell her I liked physical pain; it provided a distraction to the less bearable emotional pain. I knew how to handle physical pain.

My husband told me that if I'd been smart about the pregnancy, I would have gone to see a physician earlier and I wouldn't have the ugly red scar. "You'd still have a perfect body, Cait." Ralph hadn't ever wanted children. His approach to our relationship problems was identical to the approach he used on his job. Ralph engineered and implemented a solution. Without consulting with me, he had a vasectomy while I was recovering in the hospital. I was devastated when he told me. Ralph was dismissive, "I want a wife, Cait, not a corpse. I don't want to wonder every time I fuck you if my sperm is going to kill you."

"But there are other methods of birth control that aren't so final, so permanent." I countered.

"I can't trust you, Cait. Any time you want something from me, you quit using them. Just remember, Cait, you trapped me by getting pregnant, but I didn't have to marry you. You owe me. How many men do you think would want you with your past? I don't want kids. Problem solved."

I longed for the comforting structure of a ceremony, a public ritual. Our babies never could be named, never could be baptized, and worst of all never could be properly buried. My church did not do memorial services or funerals for fetuses. I asked. I wanted someone to acknowledge my pain.

When I arrived back home from the hospital, the tape of *Cleaveth Unto the Dust* was still in the video machine. Father Paddy was waiting for me. In my fourth miscarriage, I had lost more than half my blood in the explosion of tissue resulting from a life growing in the wrong place. I was facing a long stay in bed waiting for my body to regain the capacity to carry the required levels of oxygen. If I stayed up more than 15 minutes, I fainted. Ralph moved the television and the Irish priest into our bedroom, since I couldn't get out of bed. Even the elevation of a pillow made me dizzy. Lying completely flat, I watched movies while I waited.

Whenever I tried to talk to Ralph, he looked away. He couldn't or wouldn't maintain eye contact. Ralph frequently tapped while I talked to him. Ralph kept setting up barriers so he did not have to deal with me.

The second time I watched *Cleaveth Unto the Dust,* I noticed that Father Paddy listened with his entire body. I thought the way he listened was sheer poetry. I rewound the tape, studying what the priest did to create that oasis of calm. In those precious moments when people bared their hearts and souls to him, he was absolutely still, as if nothing else existed except the person right in front of him. I started watching Ralph more closely, judging him against my new standard—the priest in the movie. The more I observed Ralph, the starker the contrast became between my husband's listening style and Father Patrick O'Donnell's.

The double impact of losing a fourth baby and the finality of Ralph's vasectomy overwhelmed me. I was having nightmares. Reoccurring vivid ones. I dreamed I was frozen in hell, trapped in a tight, dark place. I could hear the pickaxes chopping at the gravel above me. The rusty nails screaming as they lost their tenacious hold in the old wood of my coffin lid. Puddles of water forming across my face. Voices marveling at my perfect form. Warm hands clutching at me for the first time in 140 years. My burial bounds breaking. My toes untied. My arms freed. My clothes removed. Strangers were caressing my emaciated limbs. When did I get so gaunt? Why couldn't I replace the dank, musty vapors in my lungs with the crisp, sweet, summer Arctic air? The firm pressure of the scalpel against my skin was tugging on my abdomen muscles as the blade created the autopsy's first incision. No pain accompanied the deep cut, only a dizzy, swirling emptiness.

I would awaken clammy and shivering, night after night, lying beside my husband in the inky darkness. I desperately wanted Ralph to wake up and comfort me, but he never did. I knew that if I woke him up, he was more apt to hit me than to ever acknowledge my suffering. I stayed quiet, trying to go back to sleep to no avail—fighting the old memories of the pale faces of the frozen British explorers staring back at us, eyelids shrunken away from their glassy blue eyes. My life was an emotional wasteland devoid of succor or grace. The discovery of the amazingly preserved bodies by our archaeological team from the University of Alberta had been wired around the planet. After the autopsy reports of the exhumed explorers, the world knew the truth about the Franklin tragedy. Ralph and I had helped tell their stories so Franklin and his men would be remembered, their sacrifices honored with the compassion and the dignity befitting their suffering.

Who would remember me and care about my suffering? Who would pass on my grandparents' stories? I lay in bed, night after night, wondering what my legacy could be without children, without love. My restless nights didn't wake Ralph from his sleep.

The panic attacks during the day continued. I couldn't bear to be in small rooms or crowds of people. The lack of open space terrified me. My therapist was in the dark about the whole story behind my panic attacks, and I didn't have the strength to tell her the entire truth. I should have confided to her about the violence in my marriage, but I couldn't. I had faced my father's actions, but I was in denial about my husband's volatile temper. She said my panic attacks were normal for someone who had come so close to dying. She gave me a meditation card with breathing instructions to carry, and told me to be patient with myself. Time would lessen the fright. I carried Father Paddy's prayer instead. The repetition of the poetic phrases eased my racing heart, slowed the shallow heaving of my tightening chest.

When I was strong enough, I went back to work at the university teaching Introduction to Archaeology. In my spare time, I was writing. My novel would have to be my legacy; my therapist had suggested it as a way to work through some of the pain and anger I felt towards my parents. One of the themes in *Cleaveth Unto the Dust* that spoke to me was that of betrayal. Father Paddy had to betray his younger brother, who was involved in the Irish Easter Rebellion of 1916, and live with the consequences after his brother died in the subsequent street fighting in Dublin. Having cleaved his soul into the dust, unable to rise above his pain and guilt, Father Paddy abandoned his verdant Ireland for the vast, arid wasteland of South Dakota. I knew something of betrayal. My father had betrayed me. My mother had allowed it to happen. I knew something about family guilt. Everyone blamed my father for my brother's suffering on the frigid Montana mountain. After my brother died, I had been pulled from my beloved Montana and taken to the far north of Edmonton, Alberta. Ralph, the father of my children, had caused my first miscarriage and my third. I understood Father Paddy's pain. It was mine.

When I was teaching again, and life seemed to be on keel, I tried to make up with Ralph by planning an elaborate 40th birthday party for him. Even keel did not last long. The week of the party was the end of the semester and my department head informed me that he couldn't hire me back in the fall. The university was hiring a tenure-track faculty member to cover my courses. I would be financially dependent upon Ralph again, which I dreaded. I hoped the party would go well and he would be pleased, because I did not want to think about how angry he was going to be when he found out I did not have a job. I decided to tell him after the party when he would be happy with me. During the party, Ralph mingled with everyone, being the perfect birthday host, but as soon as the guests had left Ralph dropped his respectable mask.

"Caitlinn, why did you waste so much of *my* money on this ridiculous party?"

I stammered a reply.

"Whatever you think I *might* like, Cait, *think* again. The exact opposite would be closer to reality, Cait."

I was on the thinnest of polar ice. If I said anything, Ralph's humiliation would escalate. If I said the wrong thing, Ralph would hit me. I was falling into the darkness of a freezing hell again when I remembered,

"I arise today with God's strength to pilot me."

The slap of a flattened hand across skin broke my nightmare as I watched the red marks darken on Ralph's cheek. A charging mama grizzly bear crossing an alpine Montana meadow couldn't move faster than me. Grabbing my writing satchel, my purse, and my jacket, I was in my car backing out of my old life before Ralph could appear at our front door to witness his wife leaving him forever.

Father Paddy had a constant in his life to heal him—his faith. I had a constant too once—Montana. With my life crumbling all around me, I went home to my safe place, the Tobacco Root Mountains of my childhood and my grandfather's cabin.

~ Chapter 2 ~

SCONE, NEW SOUTH WALES, AUSTRALIA, 1985

"Larkin Stud Farm, Ruthie Sutherland speaking."

"You out on the farm by yourself, Ruthie?"

"Yes, sir."

"Is there someone who can come over to be with you?"

"Brian will be back from town soon."

"Okay then. You might want to call your neighbor, too. I'll be out shortly."

The neighbor came first. Ruthie's brother Brian arrived second. Several minutes after Brian pulled into the yard, the constable's ute pulled in after him. When tea was made and all were seated around the kitchen table, the constable broke the news.

"The landing gear didn't lock proper when your father landed in Queensland. I'm sorry. Nora and Jacob are both gone."

Ruthie made the international call to her oldest

brother. Brian had offered, but Ruthie insisted the news come from her.

Ross was on the next plane south, leaving his wife Shelley and infant son, David, in Los Angeles. Across the Pacific, Ross's life played its own movie in his memory. Remembering working with his father training horses, how disappointed his father had been when Ross told him he didn't want to inherit the family business—he wanted to go to Sydney and study theater. Remembering the day his mum came home after a long stay in the hospital. His mum placed his sister Ruthie gently in his arms, a tiny bundle wrapped in a pink, flowered blanket, barely six pounds.

"I need your help, Ross. You know I had a hard time with Ruthie's birth." Nora's 10-year-old son nodded. Ross had listened to his father, Jacob, pacing the front hall, stifling his sobs late at night these past few weeks. Nora watched her son's eyes turning emerald green as they overflowed with tears. No need to worry Ross further. There were things her young son did not need to know.

"Your brother, Brian, will do your chores and I need you to be my little man and help me with Ruthie. You can go back to training horses with your father when I'm stronger. Can you do that for me and your Dad? Be my little man?"

Who was going to take care of Ruthie now? She was only 15. Brian could run the farm, but he couldn't train horses the way their father could. The way Ross could. Remembering his grandparents' farm—its sweeping verandas; the sound of rain on the metal roof; the faint, musty smell of the old stone house; the slope of the back paddocks; the red rocks; the stands of trees along the creek beds—Ross couldn't imagine losing his childhood home. Seven generations of his family had bred and trained horses there in Hunter Valley. He knew every rock, every tree of the place. He and Brian had been toddlers when their parents moved back to Nora's childhood home so her husband, Jacob Sutherland, could help his father-in-law. When Granddad passed, Jacob and Nora inherited the Larkin Stud Farm. Where would Ruthie go? She'd lost her parents; she couldn't lose her home, too. She had to have something constant to hold her steady. As Ross watched the dawning light dancing soft colors along the arc of the Pacific Ocean's horizon, he made the hardest decision of his adult life.

To a Child

Child do not go
Into the dark places of soul,
For there the grey wolves whine,
The lean grey wolves.

I have been down
Among the unholy ones who tear
Beauty's white robe and clothe her
In rags of prayer.

Child there is light somewhere
Under a star,
Sometime it will be for you
A window that looks
Inward to God.[3]

Patrick Kavanagh

~ Chapter 3 ~

MADISON COUNTY, MONTANA, 1999

Despite my claustrophobia, I insisted on a window seat for the flight home. I wanted to see Montana as soon as we crossed the state line. The flight attendant promised the captain would announce it for me, which he did. My first sight of Montana—the irregular shapes of fields twisting to match the contours of the land, dark freshly plowed soil juxtaposed against fallow fields, snowcapped mountains raising up to greet me—stirred a memory from my childhood. My grandpa told me one sunny afternoon on the top of his mountain outside of McAllister, Montana, "Always remember Cait, when times get bad come up here to God's cathedral, listen to His sermon delivered on the wind, and watch the majesty of His light show play across the sky, the foothills of the valley, and the surrounding mountains. This sacred place heals my soul; it will be here to heal yours too, sometime in the future. Don't forget this place.

It will never forget you, my darling girl. The land knows we are here, you and I."

Thinking about my grandfather, I saw our familiar ranges coming into view out the window of the plane from my perspective in the Montana clouds—the Crazies, the Bridgers. Maybe my grandfather was right, maybe Montana could heal my body, heart, and soul now that I needed healing. Across the aisle, I could barely see the Tobacco Roots as the plane circled to land at Gallatin Field. Memories of my family, good and horrible, flooded my eyes, and I nervously wiped my tears away on my sleeve. I couldn't be crying when I met my best friend, JoAnn, who would be at the airport with her children.

I fingered the patterns of my beaded bracelet, which I always wore on my right wrist, remembering the first bracelet Jo had given me when I was 14 and how happy I was when I received the current one in the mail last year. JoAnn was a jewelry artist and we had known each other since we were toddlers because her family had ranched next to my grandparents' place in Kelly Canyon outside of Bozeman. My parents had moved with me to Canada when I was 12, but Jo and I had seen each other enough in the subsequent summers to maintain a close friendship. All through college and the subsequent years, we wrote each other and called every few months. Jo lived on her family's place with her husband, Luke MacKinnon. The MacKinnons were another Bozeman pioneer canyon family who had been close friends with my grandparents.

Since today was Sunday, Jo's children would be with her and I couldn't wait to hug them all. I hadn't seen any of them since my grandmother's funeral 10 years ago. Elizabeth was the oldest at 18. Julia was 14. Ben, who was five, and Teddy, who had just turned two, I knew only from the photos Jo kindly tucked in her frequent letters to me. Jo's children were the nieces and nephews I would never have. I had fun remembering their birthdays and sending them Christmas boxes. Nothing had touched me more than when Jo called me and her children sang a boisterous "Happy Birthday" to me over the phone the year before I left Ralph.

Jo's enthusiastic family was easy to spot. Teddy was spinning around his father's leg. Julia started jumping up and down when I walked around the corner into the terminal. The MacKinnons swept me up in their swarm and we headed towards town. Since my last visit, Bozeman had grown like a teenage boy, sprawling ungracefully and rudely across the valley. We headed towards the Bridger Range which was part of the mountains forming the circle around the valley cradling my birthplace. Riding past the big white brand on the west face of the mountain into the mouth of Bridger canyon, I thought about how much Montanans liked to brand their mountains in addition to their livestock. The students at Montana State University had built the giant M in 1915. It took the class of 1918 two years to construct their white brand, which was visible from the college campus. Sixty sophomore men staked out the letter and placed rocks inside the determined boundary while the sophomore women cooked a big meal in the picnic area below the mountain slope. The next year, the same students, now juniors, whitewashed the positioned rocks. Subsequent teams of students maintained the brand. Years ago, the high school students had left their mark on a lower foothill in the form of a B. Even the little town of Logan down the valley had a letter L on the neighboring hill, as did Ennis with an E overlooking the town.

As a child, I had hated my name. Everyone called me

Cait, never Caitlinn. No one at school ever spelled it right. I bitterly complained to my grandma. "My name should have been Marias. Everyone thinks I'm Kate with a K and no I. That's so boring."

My mother had wanted to name me, Marias, after her favorite river far to the north near the Canadian border. My father thought naming children after rivers was stupid. He wanted to name me after his adopted mother, Kathleen. He said it was a damn good thing mother hadn't grown up over by Wisdom on the Big Hole or over in Birney on the Tongue.

I was born early and without a name. My mother was still refusing to speak to my father because of his crude river jokes. Grandpa interceded on my behalf, "Sheila, my granddaughter deserves a name. You liked the Irish variant of Kathleen when you were young. Remember how you named your doll, Caitlinn? Compromise with your husband and quit calling the child 'Baby.'" My birth certificate finally had a name in front of Burnett, but only one. My parents were tired of fighting.

One afternoon, my mother made the mistake of telling me her second choice for my name, Maria, from the song. Mother had had a promising career when she met my father. She had performed in the acclaimed *Paint Your Wagon* production back east. Then she got married and came back to Montana. My father did not like the reminder that he had failed to keep his promise to his wife. Maria wasn't going to be the name of his child. What a pity; to have a name synonymous with the wind would have been so romantic.

When I brought the name Maria to my grandfather's attention, he didn't make jokes; he frowned instead, "Wasn't meant to be, dear. Wind wasn't blowing when you were born. It didn't blow all while your mother was in labor.

Strangest thing. Absolutely still the entire time, as if the world was holding its breath. Waiting." He seemed disturbed by his recollections.

"Why does the wind matter?"

He would never tell me. Sometimes I did not understand Grandpa.

After Grandpa died, I asked my grandmother about the lack of wind the day I was born. Grandma wasn't going to explain, but one look at my face made her change her mind. "Sit down, Caitlinn. Your grandfather was a special man. He believed in the old Irish traditions, including the superstitions of his family. Dermot was like one of the old Irish bards in his passion for music, stories, and his belief in the mystical forces of this world. Honestly, Cait, I didn't always know what to do to ease his melancholy. He always found such hope in the wilderness, so I never complained when he went to his cathedral of the Tobacco Roots on a fishing or hunting trip or over into the Paradise or anywhere else he would go in Montana with Frank, Ike, Jake, or the MacKinnons. Your grandfather always came back calmer, more at peace with the world. It was as if God's wilderness healed him and gave me back the man I married. Dermot noticed things other people missed and he always had a sixth sense. Your grandfather never approved of your mother's choice of a husband. Dermot worried about you from day one because there was no wind the day you were born. Dermot said it was a bad omen. He was so proud of your creativity, Caitlinn, and your ability to notice God's world and be in sync with it. You are so like him. I'm not certain it's a good thing, but you were born with your grandfather's gift of foresight."

"Your brother was a special spirit, too, and when Mark was born, your grandfather was over the moon, he was so happy. Burying our three sons was difficult for me, but their deaths hit your grandfather even harder. Dermot had a premonition about that hunting trip and tried his best to talk your father out of going. We were all so angry after Mark died because we adored your brother, and your father was such an arrogant fool. Your grandfather felt so guilty afterwards knowing he hadn't done enough to save his grandson. After losing Mark, when Dermot confronted how his rage had endangered you, it killed him. I could see the life forces draining out of him as he read your letter, and nothing I said to him eased his wounded heart. He was convinced that if he had forgiven his son-in-law's mistake or tried harder to stop the trip, you would have been spared a life frozen in hell in Canada. Montana is a harsh mistress. There are many ways to die in this land. Mark's death was an accident. Yes, your father shouldn't have taken Mark up into the Crazies that weekend, but your father wouldn't listen to reason. Your father had to watch his own flesh and blood die slowly and your father couldn't help him, couldn't hold him as Mark breathed his last breath on this earth. After Mark had tried to save both their lives, and we all blamed your father instead of supporting him in his horrible burden of loss and guilt. Your father suffered terribly, Caitlinn. He knew he should have listened to Dermot, but he was too stubborn. Nobody, including my daughter, would speak to him for months. It's so much easier to cast blame, to judge, than it is to follow Jesus; your grandfather believed that with every cell of his body. That his sin, his hatred, his failure to forgive as Jesus taught us, and his failure to be there for your father, contributed to your suffering, my darling girl. I've always felt foresight is not a gift, but a curse; however, God chooses his servants who are strong enough to carry the cross and gives them the shield of discernment to guide them in His work on this earth. But such discernment and His cross is a heavy, heavy burden to carry in this secular life, Caitlinn, and we don't always know how to wisely use the gift of His power or how to manage the weight of His cross. If I had any power in this life, my dearest, dearest girl, I would spare you from all of this and make sure you have a normal life, but God has spoken. He chose you for a reason, known only to Him. All I can do is to remind you to *never* give up on hope, Caitlinn, *never* give up on love and *never ever,* even in your darkest moments, forget how much your grandfather loved you. And how much I still do."

Grandma hugged me and would never say anything more on the subject of Grandpa's gift, the burden of His cross, or my grandfather's hatred of my father. Instead, she tried to steer me towards the creation of beauty with all the crafts she taught Jo and me in the warmth of her kitchen. "Song and laughter are the best defenses against the cruelty of this world, Cait," she would say if I tried to question her more about discernment or being a servant of God. "And stories. Always listen to your elders and the stories of your people and your land. Listen and remember. Your grandfather's Irish family understood why their oral traditions were so valuable in this life. There was a reason why Jesus told his disciples parables—stories inform in ways that direct speech cannot. People don't have defenses against a well-crafted story, but they don't like being preached at and they do have defenses against your sermons."

I always struggled to reconcile what my grandmother said about my father's pain with what he did to me in Canada and how my mother allowed him to abuse me. I tried, but I couldn't forgive my parents or find the way out of all of my emotional confusion. On some level, I understood that when Ralph beat me, I was spared dealing with his emotional pain. Dealing with my husband was so much simpler for me than dealing with my parents. Physical pain inflected upon me by Ralph was a piece of cake compared to the sexual abuse of my father. Time healed physical pain; time did not heal emotional pain. Ralph's anger and brutality were easier for me than the twisted love of my grieving parents and all of their guilt about our beloved Mark. I made Ralph mad, he beat me, end of story. Nothing complex about that. Ralph never loved me, my parents did. Ralph, I could explain, predict, and protect myself against most of the time. I could never protect myself against my parents, except by refusing to interact with them.

I refused to look when we drove past the remains of Maiden Rock. I focused straight ahead. I could anticipate every rock, every tree, every barn on the road to Kelly Canyon. In the weeks to follow, I spent hours strolling along the creek with Julia and Elizabeth who chattered at me like magpies. If I shut my eyes and listened to the mountain water bubbling over the rocks, I could almost hear my older brother's voice gently encouraging me to use the stones to cross the creek.

"Come on, Cait. You can do this. Put your feet where I put mine. Square on the rock, not on the edges." Mark taught me how to stay safe. After my brother died, I wasn't safe. Not in my parent's house, not in my husband's house.

Jo insisted that I remain with them until I got over my altitude sickness. I had been a flatlander too long; it took my blood several days to adjust. I was still weakened from my ectopic pregnancy. I did not argue. Jo and I had long conversations in her kitchen about the demise of my marriage. Jo's eyes filled with tears when I described the events leading up to leaving Ralph. Jo was hearing some of my history for the first time, but I wasn't being completely honest. I did not tell her about Ralph kicking me, causing my first miscarriage. I did not tell her about Ralph pushing me down the stairs after I used up his Q-tips trying to play a practical joke. I did not tell her how I found the courage to leave a violent relationship by watching a movie and internally reciting some of its dialogue.

Jo also knew what my ideal of family meant to me. She remembered how proud I had been of my mother's musical talent and how devoted I had been to my grandparents. The totality of my break with my parents worried Jo. Ralph worried her. I worried her. I could see the concern in her eyes, hear it in her voice. I understood, because my actions haunted me. I felt trapped in a contradiction. I had an ideal of family and I could intellectually determine how I should behave towards my parents, but they didn't behave like my ideal of parents. I had to survive and I couldn't be the daughter my heart longed to be. I couldn't be the wife I longed to be, either. I knew I couldn't keep living a lie. When I broke contact with my parents, was I healing my soul or destroying it? Where was my soul when I lashed out in anger, striking my husband whom I had vowed to honor and obey before God? I couldn't reconcile my ideal of family or my faith in God with the cold, hard reality of my relationships.

I couldn't survive on the world's Pollyanna view of niceness. There was nothing nice or kind about my life after my beloved brother died. Nothing. Where *was* the wisdom and practical advice on the *how* of following Jesus? I wanted to follow his teachings. I wanted to forgive, but I also wanted to live. I couldn't find *the how* guidance in the Protestant

Bible of my mother. I looked. It wasn't there. Since I couldn't find any answers to the questions I sought, all I could do was put one foot in front of the other and keep on going, keep on hoping. Maybe, I would find answers somewhere, from someone. My job now was to survive until I could find the grace I hungered for. Or grace found me. The grace which would heal me and free me from a life devoid of love. The grace which might show me how to make a difference in this secular life for other people and to make sense of all the pain I had endured. The grace which would set my soul free from eternal pain. *Was I waiting for a sign or a savior?* I didn't have a clue. All I knew was that I was at a crossroads waiting.

I could tell my lack of a job disturbed Jo, also. She frowned when I said I hadn't asked for a divorce yet. I didn't reassure her. We'd been friends too long. Cheerful platitudes would alarm her further, so I said nothing.

At the end of the week, Jo drove me out to the airport to rent a car. She wanted to come over to McAllister and help me clean out my grandfather's cabin. I wouldn't let her. Jo was responsible for taking care of four children and her husband and I knew my cabin would be full of mouse droppings. I wasn't willing to risk her health. We compromised. I would stay with the MacKinnons for another week until I had the cabin scrubbed down, and then I would move in for the summer.

The first day working at the cabin, I took the shutters off the side windows. I rigged up a platform. The shutters were big and heavy and I couldn't handle them from a ladder. I worried about losing control of them and breaking the window glass. When I took the first one down, it was too heavy for me to place on the ground. I dropped it and lost my balance. I managed a little better with the second shutter. I went into the cabin to call my nearest neighbor,

Frank O'Neill, who was in his sixties. Frank had lived with my grandparents and knew my parents before I was born. Frank had promised my mother to act as my godfather. Despite my grandmother's best efforts at matchmaking, Frank had never married. He lived alone across the road, far enough away that when he stood outside his house, he was about ¼ inch high.

Frank's warm Montana voice filled my ear. "Yup, I knew it was you. Saw you lose that shutter. Call me when you take the others down, Cait."

I had forgotten Frank had a telescope. He used it to watch the eagles that nested near the top of the mountain behind my cabin. He used it to watch his neighbors, too. I made a point to remember not to do anything embarrassing in his line of sight.

Frank came over later in the morning to help me with the remaining shutters and to give me a couple of fire extinguishers. He gave me a quick lesson on how to use them and which ones to use on specific types of fires. Afterwards, we stood in the warm sunshine chatting, and he offered to provide me with water since I had no well. I used six-gallon containers to store water and I could get by on less than three gallons a day. I was willing to go down to the neighboring town of Ennis to the gas station to fill up my containers for my weekly supply of water, but Frank was insulted by that idea. I promised to get my water from him. Frank offered me the use of his shower too, but I declined. I wanted to be as self-sufficient as possible. I was tired of living dependent upon men, even my godfather. Frank listened patiently while I made my independence speech and then he nodded, saying, "All well and good Cait, but I made a promise to your grandmother and your mother which I intend to keep."

The next task was to acquire a truck, so I could return

the rental SUV. I went down the road to one of the old timers and asked him if he had a truck for me. As a rancher,
he'd kept every car, truck, and piece of machinery he'd
ever owned back behind the barn. The Montana women
I grew up with used every scrap of fabric to make quilts
and crocheted rugs, nothing went to waste. Montana men
were no different. Old timber, old machinery was kept in
case it could be used in the future. In Montana, you could
always tell the old timers from the newcomers. The newcomers threw away the old and bought new. The old timer
grinned at me. "Well, Cait, I could fix up Uncle Jake's old
rig for you, as long as you don't mind the bear claw marks."
Jake's nephew proceeded to tell me the story of his distant
cousins from Indiana who left food in the truck during a
back country fishing trip despite his uncle's stern warning. Apparently, Jake was still fuming about the Hoosier
fools who thought walking bare foot in rattlesnake country was a good idea, wanted to throw watermelon rinds
behind the juniper bushes in bear country because rinds
are biodegradable, had no clue how to set up their own
tent because they hadn't practiced before coming to Montana, and were responsible for ruining the paint job on
Jake's favorite truck. Jake's nephew winked at me, "Uncle
Jake told those goddamn fools *they* were biodegradable in
grizzly country. I wouldn't bring it up if I was you, unless
you enjoy listening to Uncle Jake turn the air blue. Forty
years later, my uncle is still complaining about those pot
smoking commie hippies from Indiana."

I bought the light duty '58 Apache Chevy, complete with
her old bear claw scratches. In her prime she had been a
beautiful truck, now her bright red and white two-tone
paint job had faded under the intense Montana sun to an
almost pastel pink. The old '58 might not have looked like

much, but she drove smooth as silk and from her new tires to her engine, she was as steady as a good stock horse. I couldn't have bought a more reliable ride, if I'd bought a new truck over in Bozeman. Uncle Jake had been one of my grandfather's hunting buddies, so I felt blessed to drive Jake's faded red truck, and Jake's nephew knew who I was and he did right by me. Maybe my godfather, Frank, had something to do with this transaction as well, but if he did, I never heard about it.

I returned the rental. Jo and the girls gave me a ride back to my cabin. As youngsters, Jo and I had had some grand adventures together on the mountain. Jo had loved my grandparents' stories and songs as much as I did. Frank and Jo were the last people in my life who had known me when I was whole, before my world fell apart after my beloved brother died. While I could hide from Jo, Frank was too perceptive.

"Cait, I'm your godfather. Why did you leave your husband? What was he doing to you? Don't lie to me, Cait. I've seen badly used horses. I've worked with too many abused animals to miss what I'm seeing in you."

I said nothing.

"Tell me when you're ready. I never trusted that husband of yours. If he comes around here, you will tell me?

I nodded. Maybe Frank having a telescope wasn't such a bad thing after all.

At the close of long days of cleaning I watched the sunsets on my mountain from the vantage point of my grandfather's favorite rock. One evening, in a fanciful mood, I thought the twilight world was like an Irish band. The Tobacco Root Mountains as the bass provided the beat. The sky was the fiddler and across the valley, the Madison Mountains were the flutes and penny whistles. First, the Madisons would play, their snow-capped peaks illuminated soft pink, introducing the lilting, thin melody line. The sky with its soft shades of purple waited patiently in the background for its turn. Then, when the flutes and whistles were finished, the sky fiddled against the bass, layering notes, building up intensity, swirls of orange against shades of blue and green. Thick clouds, purple on the tops and bright orange on the bottoms, danced across the stage. The bass remained solid, the mountains always present with their comforting rhythms, their darkening slopes majestically topped with retreating white snow-caps. Then the song wound down, the last notes fading into the silence and the gentle darkness of a mountain spring evening.

These spectacular Montana sunsets kept me alive as a teenager. They played to me, reminding me there was grace and beauty in life. Grandpa had said Madison Valley sunsets were gifts from God. After Grandpa died, I comforted myself by imagining sunsets as Grandpa's prayers and hymns for me. Celestial mass performed for a lonely girl whose father was touching her in forbidden places and whose grandfather had left her when she needed him the most.

I hoped my beloved mountains would embrace me again this summer, that the winds would caress my hair and kiss my face. People had always hurt me. First my parents, then Ralph. Why was Montana more loving than the people in my life?

~ Chapter 4 ~

SCONE, NEW SOUTH WALES, AUSTRALIA, 1994

It was meant to be a joke, those DNA tests.

When her eldest brother wasn't calling her sprog, Ross was calling her a foundling because of her being the only redhead in the clan of Scots living in Hunter Valley. Ruthie wished she could roll back time. She missed the old Ross, the jokester, the strong one who always made her feel safe. Especially after that horrible phone call nine years back.

"Yo, sprog. You have to listen to me. I wanted a little sister. Mum said I could order one from the catalogue. The postie brought you. Mum said as long as I took good care of you, I could keep you. You have to listen to me sprog or I'll have to send you back."

Ruthie was only four when her oldest brother caught her in the stables again, disobeying her father's standing orders to stay away from the horses. When she sassed him, Ross said she was a foundling and that he was in charge of her. Tears running down her face, Ruthie flew into the kitchen wrapping her arms around her mother's legs.

"Ruthie, Ruthie, Ruthie. You must learn to tell when Ross is joking." Nora pulled her youngest child into her lap. "I will tell you a secret." Ruthie quit sobbing. "Watch Ross's eyes. When he is having a go at you, his eyes will crinkle right at the corners. If his eyes are dark, you are in big trouble. When you were a baby, I needed his help and I asked Ross to take care of you. Listen to your brother. And if you go anywhere near those stables again, you will have me to deal with and there will be no jokes, young lady."

When the results from her stupid DNA test joke had come in the post, Ross was staying with Ruthie and her husband, Steve, in Hunter Valley, as he always did in between projects. Ruthie watched as all the color drained from her brother's tanned face. He sat so still she knew he wasn't breathing. His jaw muscles clenched twice before his chair fell over backwards. The kitchen door slammed shut. Ross whistled for the dogs. Pounding hoofs faded into silence.

Coming home long after dark, Ross went straight into his room, leaving again before sunrise. Each day was the same. An early morning whistle for the dogs, the kitchen door slamming shut, the fading sound of horse hoofs, approaching darkness, the barking of dogs coming home, the thunder of a fast ridden horse, more doors slamming. Weeks went by. Efforts to engage Ross in conversation resulted in cold blank stares.

Ruthie took a chance. She waited up in the kitchen for her older brother and ambushed him when he hung up his hat.

"Guess the joke's on you, Ross. You're the foundling."

At first, Ruthie regretted her words, but the familiar

crinkles started around the corners of his green eyes, spreading into a smile lighting up his tired face.

"Come here, sprog." Embracing her, Ross rubbed his knuckles gently across the top of her head as he used to do when she was little and he caught her red-handed doing something she shouldn't. "If you weren't pregnant, I'd turn you over my knee and give you a proper one."

"I'm so sorry, Ross."

"You weren't to know, Ruthie. You don't have anything to be sorry about, nothing at all."

Long into the night, brother and sister drank tea together at the same kitchen table where Nora had told her mother that she was carrying a Yank's bub. Several months later, in the beginnings of a sunrise, Ruthie drove Ross to the airport.

"Call me when you have those bubs," Ross said to his sister.

"Call me when you land in Rapid City, Dakota."

"Only if you promise to name those bubs, foundling and sprog."

Ruthie hugged her brother tightly, grateful for any of his jokes, no matter how lame.

~ **Chapter 5** ~

SCONE, NEW SOUTH WALES, AUSTRALIA, 1994

"Ross, it's Steve. Ruthie had our twins—boy and a girl. She wants me to ask you to be their godfather."

"Why not Brian? He's closer."

"Nah, Ruthie wants you. You know all the stories."

Except the most important one, Ross thought.

"Okay, on one condition, Steve."

"Which is?"

"You have to name the twins sprog1 and sprog2."

Steve laughed. "Fuck that shit, Ross. We like Nora and Jacob. Are you okay with that?"

"Absofuckinlutely."

"Ruthie says she'll wash your mouth out with soap if you talk like that around her bubs."

"She probably will have to."

"Here's Ruthie, she has something to tell you. Bye, Ross."

"Ross, I found something. Remember Mum's glory box,

the one you shoved up in the attic after Mum and Dad died to make room for you and Shelley? A couple of weeks before the crash, Mum was going through her chest and I thought at the time she'd been crying, but when she saw me, she shoved everything back in real fast. She acted like everything was fine, but I know it wasn't. Something was troubling her. I think I know what she was looking at. It was a book about a cattle drive with an inscription in it. Here, I'll read it. 'For Nora's bub, all my love, Paddy. 1962.' There's an unopened letter addressed to Mum inside the book from a Paddy O'Neill with an American postmark. I guess you can open it if you want. I'll have Steve put them both in the post to you."

"Ta Ruthie. Hey, congratulations on the bubs. Gotta go, sprog. Love ya darlin'."

Ruthie was going to say something else to her brother, but the international call dropped.

~ Chapter 6 ~

MADISON COUNTY, MONTANA, 1999

I had come home to start a new life. No more teaching archaeology to reluctant university students—I was going to be a writer. JoAnn's cousin was an editor in a big publishing house in New York City. He offered to help me. My project for the summer was completing my novel set in the early copper mining days of Butte, Montana, at the turn of the century. Every Montanan knew the story of the epic battles between the three Copper Kings: Marcus Daly, William Clark, and Fritz Heinze. Their political machinations had influenced Montana's history for over a hundred years and had spilled outside the state borders, resulting in the passing of the 17th amendment to the Constitution of the United States that guaranteed direct election of senators. If I worked hard all summer, I thought my novel could be done by early August.

I relished being home. For some people, quality of life is

the theater, the opera, or a good restaurant. For me it was clear sweet-smelling air, beautiful textured skies, and people who spoke with poetry in their voices. I had dreamed for 24 years to be back among my own people, back under the familiar skies, back home. Home, where the roads are mostly gravel and dust. Home, where everyone gives you a casual wave when you pass them on the road. Not the full hand wave of the Midwest—the casual Montana wave—two fingers off the steering wheel. Home, where my neighbors had moved their house back from the road but left the front porch in its original location. When you turned the corner to go up into the foothills, there it was. A front porch with no house nestled amongst the cottonwoods along the creek was Montana to me. Montana history was full of odd puzzles such as porches with no houses, and behind each one was a fascinating story.

I had missed those stories. The stories in Montana were as endless as the wide expanses of big sky. According to Grandpa, the land where people were few and far between, the enormity of space, distance, and horizon grew story-tellers the way the Midwest grew corn. Grandma would scoff at Grandpa, teasing him by claiming that Montana grew ornery people the way Iowa grew soybeans. Grandma's favorite story about Meadow Creek was about Jake's ornery uncle who got his revenge on his brother after their father died. Apparently, one brother stayed in the Madison to ranch with his parents, while the other escaped off to Helena and a desk job. The will stated the city brother was to have 10 acres of the ranch and his brother, who was executor of the estate, gave him 10 acres all right. A ribbon of 10 acres running along the highway, too narrow to be of any practical use.

The nearest town and my post office box address was

McAllister, which had been a lively community during my grandmother's childhood. The first post office in Madison Valley had been here, and before the Madison River was dammed to form Ennis Lake, the easiest place to ford the river had been in the north part of the valley near McAllister. Now, if you blinked when you came down Highway 287 from the north, you'd miss what little was left of the town situated around the crossroads of Highway 287 and Meadow Creek Road. It had consisted of a grocery store with a single gas pump, the post office, a community center, a Methodist church built in 1887, small tourist cabins, and the tavern when I was growing up, but the year before I arrived from Illinois, the Crossroads Market closed and the tourist cabins were being torn down. The schoolhouse my grandmother had ridden her horse to every day was a private house, somebody bought the community center and moved it onto private property, and the church, through misbehavior by the Methodist bishop in the late 1920s, had become Presbyterian, as trespassers were forced to become debtors with no say in the matter. The first church constructed in the Madison Valley now sat abandoned, surrounded by cottonwoods with only cows for company. Sometimes, somebody down in Ennis would organize a work party and paint the church or put on a new roof, but the stories of a once vibrant congregation were distant memories only to be found in fading photo albums in attics and the typewritten manuscripts down at the county library. About all that remained of my grandmother's hometown was the Bear Claw Bar and Grill and the post office across the road. The Bear Claw was known throughout Southwestern Montana as one of the great rural steak places. The decor was rustic, with plenty of dead animal heads and stuffed fish, and a bar that ran the length of the front room. There was a large dining room with a fireplace in the back. My godfather Frank had owned the Bear Claw since his retirement from forest firefighting. Frank's sense of humor was evident in his labeling of the restrooms located in the hallway between the front bar and the dining room. A wooden plaque with an Irish Setter served as the identification for the ladies, since women set themselves on the toilet. A pointing hunting dog identified the men's room, since men pointed at the toilet, mostly. I gave Frank a hard time about his labeling, but he said his patrons were smart enough to figure it out, although I overheard two old cowboys arguing at the bar, saying sometimes they needed to set but they didn't know if they were supposed to use the ladies room for that or swap the signs to indicate how they were using the facilities. Frank laughed at them and said, "If you want to be helpful boys, leave the toilet seat the way you found it, just like you leave the ranch gate the way you found it." The local residents were loyal to any establishment with a sense of community and attention to personal service, and Frank's bar was the busiest eating establishment in the valley. You couldn't put a price tag on the luxury of walking into the Bear Claw and hearing Frank's cheerful salutation, "How ya goin'? Alright?"

Ennis, seven miles south of McAllister, was the closest town of any size. Ennis had 700 residents, two hardware stores, a lumberyard, two groceries, a pharmacy, a computer repair service, plus numerous gift boutiques, tackle shops, and restaurants. If you needed anything exotic like underwear, sneakers, or window glass, you had to drive 60 miles into Bozeman. When I was a teenager, the local banker decided to subsidize the rustication of the storefronts to mimic the worn false front gold camp look of neighboring Virginia City. The merchants agreed to the makeover as part of the community effort to increase revenue from the tourists who were traveling to or from Yellowstone Park. As a result, Ennis looked more like a Hollywood movie set than a Montana ranching town.

North of McAllister, over the mountain pass, was Norris, which in more prosperous days had been the end of the Northern Pacific railroad line. The isolation of Madison Valley itself had never been compromised by a railroad. When the railroad arrived in 1890 to the Alex Norris ranch, civilization shifted from the mining town of Red Bluff three miles to the east to the intersection of 84 and 287. The arrival of railroads had an uncanny ability to reshape the Montana landscape. With the abandonment of the railroad to Norris, another Montana town was fading away, leaving only tombstones and sagging buildings. The mountain pass between Norris and McAllister was known as the Norris Hill, which was a bit of an understatement. The locals judged the performance capabilities of their rigs by how fast they could get over the pass. If you could keep your speed over 65 and still make the hill, you had a noteworthy pickup. I didn't push my old truck. I didn't know what her limitations were.

The days of excitement in Norris were over. The railroad was gone, leaving no evidence of Madison County's iron link to the outside world. My great-grandparents would ride up to Norris, stable their horses, and take the train to the city of Butte for special purchases. The Norris train depot was moved to the outskirts of Ennis when the railroad spur was abandoned. Now, Norris was simply a cluster of small buildings at the intersection of two highways. It had a bar, a post office, a community hall, a used car lot, a tire repair shop, a Mexican restaurant in the old school, and a modern gas station. One day on my way into Bozeman, I noticed that the used car dealer in Norris had increased his inventory by 50 percent. He had added one car. Norris also featured a small dog that liked to sit right in the middle of the highway, daring the odd car to hit him. When that ceased to amuse him, he rolled in whatever road kill he could find. There wasn't much to do in Norris anymore, even for a dog.

An easterly turn on Meadow Creek Road out of McAllister took you to Ennis Lake, still labeled Meadow Lake on the old painted sign by the highway. The community had been known as Meadow Creek until the postmaster, on a whim, renamed the town after himself. The lake had acquired a new name as well. Everyone in Madison County called the manmade lake, Ennis Lake. Even the mapmakers recognized the change. However, no one thought it important to repaint the sign along Highway 287.

A westerly turn out of McAllister on Meadow Creek Road took you past the old community center, the stately cottonwoods, the faded white church with the steeple topped with a gold-painted dome, and the rough road to the cemetery atop the hill where my great-grandparents and my grandparents were buried, along with numerous other family members. A little further up, the pavement bifurcated into South and North Meadow Creek Roads. Then the pavement ended, the gravel began after the old Meadow Creek schoolhouse, and the road snaked up into the Tobacco Roots.

Grandpa built my cabin in the 1930s. The exterior was half-logs over a basic frame construction. The interior was plaster walls. The material used in my cabin for the foundation, chimney, and the porch columns came from the Washington Bar diggings up North Meadow Creek. The big round stones had been left in twisted piles by the dredge mining process. Stream beds all over Madison County had been transformed into alien landscapes by blasting water to separate the rocks from the earth in search of the veins of gold lying below the surface. Miles of stone scars remained across the county as a silent testament to the rape of the land for precious metal.

My cabin was small—30 feet by 20 feet with a partial loft. As a child I had slept in the loft on a mattress on the floor and now, as an adult, I planned to sleep downstairs in my grandparents' double bed. When I arrived that spring, I discovered that mice had been living in all the mattresses. Frank helped me take the mouse-infested bedding to the county disposal site and I bought new mattresses with the extra for the loft, just in case I ever had company. The old heater that Frank advised me not to use and a wide chest of drawers were against the back wall near the defunct fireplace. I had my grandparents' matching wooden rocking chairs. Two bookshelves ran along the south wall, where the 1930s porcelain-topped table sat with four matching maple chairs. The brass bed and the old freestanding wooden kitchen cupboard, the Hoosier, were on the north wall.

My propane stove sat on a small table next to the freestanding cupboard. Between the wall studs, Grandpa had built a narrow cupboard for food. I had wanted to purchase an old oak icebox to match the Hoosier, but they proved to be too expensive, so I made do with a modern red plastic cooler. The end of the south wall near the front door had a mirrored cabinet and shelves for the basin and pitcher set. Grandpa had decorated the cabin by framing portraits by Winold Reiss of Montana Blackfoot Indians from old Great Northern Railway calendars. Both the cabin floor and ceiling were tongue and groove pine. The privy was out back past the shed. Even though my cabin was primitive, I loved every square inch because of my happy childhood memories.

For better access during hunting season, Grandpa had situated his cabin and his shed near the road. His remaining 100 acres spanned half of the mountain that rapidly rose 600 feet above the cabin. The climate was too dry to support lots of trees and the topsoil too thin to facilitate dense growth. Except for the lush alpine meadow at the top of the mountain, I owned about 100 acres of rocks and sagebrush with widely spaced trees. At this altitude around 6,000 feet above sea level, the limber pines grew. They had supplied the Indians with nuts and were the principal type of vegetation, along with sagebrush and juniper. There were numerous interesting rock formations on the property including one outcropping Grandpa and I called Indian Rocks because of the six different Indian faces we could see in the rocks. We had found Indian artifacts around the formation, thus reinforcing the name.

For me, the top of my mountain, where I could see 90 miles in all directions, was a thin place, a natural chapel, a sacred place for healing. I spent long mornings hiking the mountain, taking photographs, sitting on rocks lost in thought, gathering flowers, picking up ancient Indian artifacts. One brilliant morning as I sat on my front porch steps drinking my coffee, I watched all the different colored butterflies alighting on the wildflowers throughout my unmowed yard. I noticed each type had their favorite flowers; they weren't random in which ones they visited. The rhythm of their beating wings and their delightful flight patterns stirred an old longing. After finishing my coffee, I drove into Bozeman and bought myself a new guitar, never imagining the role a simple purchase would play in altering my destiny. All summer I recalibrated my senses and united my breathing with the rhythmic breathing of the world. I could smell the lightning again, predict accurately the arrival of storms, hear the music of the wind coming down the mountain, tree by tree.

I was using the movie, *Cleaveth Unto the Dust*, as a guide for additional reading. In the prayer recited by Father Paddy, I found an approach I could use, one that spoke to both my intellect and my heart. The movie had used the ancient Irish prayer, "The Deer Cry." According to legend, this prayer was the one St. Patrick prayed that granted him the spell of concealment from his enemies during the time the saint was spreading Christianity throughout Ireland. "The Deer Cry" or "The Breastplate of St. Patrick" was considered a shield of divine protection because St. Patrick and his monks had been turned into deer, thus escaping detection from the pagan king. In the library, researching the history of St. Patrick and "The Deer Cry," I had discovered additional sources of comfort—Celtic blessings, which are neither poems or prayers. Blessings are a uniquely Irish communication form, combining both poetry and prayer. Reciting the appropriate blessings for rising in the morning, lighting the hearth fire, traveling into town, or going to bed provided me with a structure for the lonely days, a rhythm to mark the passage of time, a salve for my wounded soul.

During my research of Irish blessings, I ran across the description of the four Celtic seasons. Rather than start a season with the solstice, as the western world marked the beginning of summer or winter, the Celtics placed the spring and fall equinoxes as the midpoints of two main seasons defined by their festivals, Lughnasadh and Beltane. Lughnasadh was celebrated on August 1, marking the start of the autumn season, rather than September 22 or 23. Beltane, marking the beginning of summer, was the festival for the living—a time of great optimism. May 1 marked the beginning of that Celtic season. Samhain started October 31 at sunset, because the day started at sunset for the Celtics rather than at sunrise. For simplicity, November 1 was considered the beginning of winter, and due to the shorter days surrounding the solstice in December, Samhain was the beginning of what was termed the dead months. Imbolic or Celtic spring began on February first and marked the Festival of St. Bridgit. Imbolic in old Irish meant "in the belly," and lambing season occurred during Imbolic. The start of winter and summer were important Celtic thresholds between the living and the other world. These beginnings were referred to as thin times and they could be dangerous, especially for the unaware. The ancient idea of thin places, such as where the ocean meets the land, and thin times like October 31 or May 1 fascinated me. Sometimes when I thought about a famous painting or a haunting melody, I wondered if people could create thin places with paintings, music, and photography. Remembering how important the movie, *Cleaveth Unto the Dust,* had been in my life, I wondered if the director had created thin places at key points of that film with his creative addition of soulful music and his use of majestic landscapes. I certainly had felt there were times in the movie, especially under the Dakota skies during Father Paddy's recitation of "The Deer Cry," where something otherworldly had occurred, or maybe Ralph was right—I wasn't normal and I should keep my weird ideas to myself.

I was writing, most of the time. Maybe other writers might achieve thin places with their lyrical phrases, but I struggled with my sentences. Sometimes, my novel behaved like a toddler, refusing to listen, refusing to do my bidding. When the characters were being obstreperous, the dialogue singing off key, and the plot wandering off into the thickets of tangled underbrush, I literally tossed it under my bed.

"Time out for you," I would say and return to the short stories I had been writing for Jo's family. My stories were nostalgic how-to pieces; a series set in Montana. I didn't struggle when I composed my children's stories. They seemed to write themselves. I had sent several to my editor, but I didn't expect anything would happen with them.

After a trip into Bozeman to my childhood neighborhood, I wrote another grandma story about making a cherry pie. How do you know when cherries have worms? Grandma knew. Wormy cherries floated when you washed them in a bowl. Wormy cherries made a smacking sound when you pitted them. Jo's daughters were delighted with their new story.

The quiet summer on my mountain had been good for me. I felt the months of May, June, and July truly had been a time of celebrating hope and life, as the ancient Celts believed would happen during Beltane. Three months after arriving in Montana, I was finishing up my first draft of my novel for my editor. My life had a comforting rhythm. I was feeling more balanced, more in control. I looked forward to the Celtic fall season of Lughnasadh starting August 1—the time of maturity, harvest, music, and storytelling—hoping I could continue my healing process. I could feel my soul healing when I repeated my Celtic blessings during different times of the day, and I felt my heart reawakening to the wonders of living. No more putting one foot in front of the other across barren deserts of emotional wastelands. I was breathing again and enjoying life. I was day dreaming. All the time day dreaming. While I was dreaming too much, I was running out of money.

One evening at the end of July, when I was down at the Bear Claw Bar and Grill, Frank asked me to come work for him. "Cait, when you were born, I made a promise to your mother and to God to watch over you and be your extra parent. No arguing with me, now. You want to argue with someone, take it upstairs," Frank was pointing to the heavens, "I figure you need the money and I need good help. Win, win."

Starting in August at the beginning of Lughnasadh, I waitressed for the lunch crowd during the week and evenings on the weekends found me behind the bar with my godfather. I had no way of knowing that seeds planted that Lughnasadh season working at the Bear Claw Bar and Grill at the crossroads in McAllister would take a full year to germinate. Frank showed me how to mix drinks, how to laugh at the foibles of rich out-of-state rude folks, and how to ignore drunken propositions without making men angry with me. I enjoyed working with Frank and meeting new people. Then the bad news came in the mail from my editor:

Dear Cait:

You are a fine writer but I'm not convinced that you are a fiction writer. In fiction, historical details should be props, used to set the stage in a novel and thus used sparingly. Show don't tell. Rather than telegraph emotions of your characters, demonstrate through their actions how they are feeling. Describe their body language, for example.

Just because something actually happened to you, doesn't make it a story. Life is random; good fiction is not. Characters face problems, they solve problems or die trying. In real life, people muddle along rarely facing or solving much of anything. Characters have motivation and that's what the reader wants to understand, since real life is so darn incomprehensible.

Your novel as is can't be published. Your children's stories show more promise. My guess is that you aren't trying as hard with them and you completely understand your audience.

I had no intentions of giving up. Maybe, my editor's letter wasn't the bountiful harvest I had hoped for, but it wasn't a failure either. I simply had to work harder and mature my writing skills, much like beginning farmers have to master their craft as they learn about cultivars and methods for care of the soil. I was super grateful to Frank for his assistance, and knowing that I was useful at the Bear Claw kept me emotionally steady. I read the essays Douglas had suggested and dug into my rewriting.

As winter approached, staying at the cabin became impractical and I moved in with Frank, staying in his spare room, driving down to the Bear Claw with him whenever the bar was open through the slow season. When we were closed, I helped him repaint, clean, restock, and remodel.

"That you, Cait?" Frank called out from the stock room, one bitterly cold day in January.

"Yup."

"Haven't heard you sing since you were a youngster. You have your mother's voice. It's great to see you smiling again, too."

~ Chapter 7 ~

SCONE, NEW SOUTH WALES, AUSTRALIA, 1995

True to his word, Ross flew south to Hunter Valley for the twins' christening after wrapping the shoot in the Dakotas. Ruthie didn't recognize her brother when he got off the plane. He had shaved his head for the role and gained weight. When Ross didn't have much to say on the drive home, Ruthie first attributed his silence to jet lag. As the months passed, Ross's auburn curls returned and hours of hard manual labor on the farm slimmed his waistline and toned his arms, Ruthie could physically see her brother returning to her, but his unusual silence continued. When she mentioned her concerns to her husband Steve, he shrugged, "Be grateful Ross isn't slamming doors and being reckless on his horse. At least, he's not waking up the twins."

One morning, as the twins napped, Ross entered the

kitchen where Ruthie was sitting at the kitchen table. He set an airmail envelope down on the table as if it would break when it touched the hard surface. "Have a read and tell me what you reckon it means."

Ruthie recognized the writing on the envelope postmarked Emigrant, Montana USA as the unopened letter she had sent to Ross from their mother's glory box. She gently took out the tissue-paper-thin airmail stationary. As she unfolded the letter, a small black and white photograph emerged. Ruthie studied it, wishing the man's hat wasn't hiding his face and wondering what that strange rock formation was behind him. Ross didn't speak as Ruthie turned her attention to the letter, reading the flowing cursive script out loud:

"My dearest Nora,

Your father wrote me last month about your marriage to Jacob Sutherland and the news of your baby son. Jacob is a fine man. We worked together on the fire brigade. As I remember, his wife and their first baby died in childbirth, so I know you and the baby must be a blessing to him.

Give your son the book and tell him you knew a REAL cowboy once.

I do wish with all my heart I could have found the words to change your mind about marrying me.

Faithfully, yours
Paddy."

Ruthie started to make a joke, but checked herself. Ross looked too much like he had when he first read the DNA test results a year ago, except this time not even his jaw was moving.

"Well, Granddad must have liked Paddy pretty well. He

wouldn't have written to just anyone, certainly not to a man who got his daughter up the duff and fled the country." Ruthie paused, "Ross, I think Granddad knew Paddy wasn't told Mum was carrying his child. Mum apparently refused to marry Paddy. I wonder why? What's the postmark date?"

"1962." Ross's voice was almost a whisper.

"I did some more checking, Ross, after I found this letter and the book. Mum and Dad lied about when they were married. They always told us it was 1959. Their marriage license says 1960, four months before you were born. I think Dad knew you weren't his son from the beginning. You remember how proud Granddad was of his only child. He would have defended Mum's reputation with his life. Mum was a good girl, but she was young. I can't see her sleeping around. Mum adored you, you know that. I think Mum really loved this Paddy O'Neill. Maybe Granddad and Dad came to some arrangement. Dad was a wizard with horses and Granddad did need help around here. Did you know Mum and Dad got married up north at his uncle's sheep station? You know how many sticky beaks there are in small country towns. I think they went up there and stayed long enough to prevent the chinwagging. Remember, Brian was born up there at that sheep station, too. Maybe," Ruthie hesitated, "Maybe, Paddy O'Neill is your biological father."

"Why didn't they ever tell me?"

Ruthie wished she could say something to heal her brother. She got up from her chair and wrapped her arms around him, kissing the top of his auburn curls. "Dunno, Ross, I wish I knew."

Of the book, *The Greatest Cattle Drive*, with its distinctive red dust jacket, Ross said nothing to Ruthie. Unbeknownst to anyone, Ross had read the book Paddy sent him several times, and before returning to Australia had ridden his motorcycle west to Montana, to Paradise Valley, asking questions of old timers in the local bars. He was realistic about his chances of finding the man after all these years, anyone who might have known a Paddy O'Neill in Australia was dead, but if he couldn't know the man, Ross could know the land that had formed his father—a real American cowboy.

In Emigrant, Montana, nobody remembered a Paddy O'Neill from 1962. The old timers, when asked about a possible cowboy, were patient with Ross.

"That's a lot of water under the bridge, son. The biggest cattle operation in these parts is the Story Cattle Company. If your man was a good wrangler, he probably worked for them. Gotta understand son, these big ranches hire a lot of men who come and go with the wind. After 40 years, nobody is gonna remember much."

When Ross showed old timers the photograph, asking if anybody knew where the strange rock formation was, he didn't get any further. Again, people were helpful but not optimistic that he would find it.

"Do you know when this photograph was taken?"

"No."

"Well son, we had a huge earthquake in 1959 down in Yellowstone. Lot of damage. If it was near the park, it might not be standing anymore. Do you know that it was taken in these parts?'

"No, I just have the 1962 Emigrant postmark on a letter, this photograph, and a book about Nelson Story. I'm looking for my father."

"There's a lot of rock formations like this in Montana, could be anywhere, son. Around here, everybody knows the story of the greatest cattle drive. If you've got the time, you should go over to Virginia City. It still looks a lot like it did during Story's time."

Ross rode his motorcycle over into the Madison Valley where Nelson Story had driven the Texas Longhorns to the gold camp of Virginia City in 1866. In the small towns in Madison County, Ross pulled into local pubs, sat quietly in corners, listening to the voices and the stories of the place he thought his father might have come from.

In the summers that followed his first trip to Montana, Ross continued to visit the Madison Valley each August in rhythm with the beginning of the Celtic season of Lughnasadh. He concentrated his time there, the beginning and the ending of the greatest American cattle drive. For reasons, Ross didn't understand, when he was in the Madison Valley he wasn't interested in the carnal. The Madison Valley had a calming effect on him, much like being in a church back home or at one of the sacred spots in Ireland he had visited. He thought of the Valley as his safe place and he didn't want to create any drama with women there. After the results of the DNA test, Ross had rejected his father's teachings. If he wasn't a Sutherland, he didn't have to be a gentleman around women. If they willingly agreed to come into his bed, he used them, and left them with no regrets. He didn't owe them anything other than a good time. Random hook-ups were always a roll of the dice, but that was their attraction—the uncertainty, the danger, the thrill of the pursuit culminating in completely owning and controlling another human even for a brief few minutes, no responsibility, no commitments, no attachments. No woman could hurt him again if he was a rolling stone.

Ross couldn't comprehend why his parents hadn't trusted him with the truth. He would have forgiven them, if only they hadn't lied to him. Why had he sacrificed his darling boy to save a man's legacy who lied to him? Why had he sacrificed his marriage to a woman he loved to save his parents' life work? Why had he put his career on hold? Shelley had been right. He should have sold the farm and chosen her and their son. He'd been so angry with Shelley and her ultimatum. He'd made such a huge mistake. There was no going back now. Those bridges had been burned beyond repair. And for what? He'd made Shelley and David suffer, all because of that damn lie. Yes, the farm was his inheritance from his mother's side of the family—the Larkins—but the lie had started with the Larkins. It was the Larkins' part in the lie that wounded Ross the most. How could he trust women again after his mother's betrayal? His grandmother's betrayal? The lie didn't change his love for his siblings or the twins; his parents' lack of trust in his heart wasn't their fault. The land hadn't betrayed him, the Larkins had. Ross still felt a deep connection to the land in Scone, but it was difficult for him to be there for long. Everywhere he looked, he was reminded of the lie that was his life, the people who had doubted the strength of his heart, and the family that had betrayed him with their lack of trust in his understanding of Christian forgiveness. Brian and Ruthie both had been shocked and hurt too by the DNA results, but for them it was different because they knew their stories. The Larkins hadn't lied to them, only to him. Ross didn't know who he was anymore, where he belonged. He felt like his soul had been ripped out of his body along with his heart. Ross knew he was morally adrift, but he didn't care anymore. His whole life had been a lie; what difference did anything make anymore? Why not seize carnal pleasure wherever he could find it, since his life was a big cruel joke?

~ Chapter 8 ~

FLORENCE, ITALY, SPRING 1998

"My dearest Ross, I treasure what we have, this friendship with no strings. You bring me such delight and joy. You listen to me and you learn, and my life's work takes flight with the angels when I watch your face light up with understanding. *Ti amo cosi tanto.* But I am a swan. I mate for life. You, my dearest heart are … ."

She paused, trying to lessen the blow, "You, Ross, you are a hopeless romantic."

Ross looked up, meeting her eyes as she spoke, and dropped his head again. One hand grasped the thumb of his other hand, switching back and forth. I'm not a romantic, he thought. I'm a mongrel, a rat bastard. I've gone from one extreme to the other. From the chastity of Father Paddy to a global womanizer. How many women had he taken to his bed since he left Dakota? He didn't even remember.

It was all a blur. What had he become? What had he done with his soul? With his heart? With his dignity? Small wonder Isabella was setting him free. She was far too clever to let herself be another entry in a man's long list of sexual conquests.

Isabella knelt beside Ross resting her forearms across his thigh. She took his hands in hers, stilling his repetitive movement. "I am content in my life. My life is predictable like the tides and the phases of the moon. I don't want to change that. To risk the tears, the fighting, the breaking of hearts."

"You, Ross, you belong to Australia. I hear it in your voice when you speak of home. I hear it in your notes when you sing the songs of your bush. Australia owns you, my love. I cannot compete with her. You could not breathe trapped here in Florence, no matter how much you love her architecture, her history, her art, or me. And I am far too old to think I could be anywhere than here. In my beloved Florence."

Ross leaned forward in his chair, reaching for his wine goblet, took a long sip, and started to speak.

"Shh," she touched his lips with her forefinger. "You know here," as she laid her hand on his chest, "I am right. Let us not break each other's hearts with false hopes of what cannot be."

Ross returned his crystal wine goblet to her gilded marble-topped table. The firelight gleamed off his unfinished wine. In one fluid motion Ross arose from his brocaded chair leaving Isabella still kneeling on the floor.

At her door he hesitated, turned back, and she came into his arms. Bending down, in a succession of kisses, he brushed her lips, her forehead, and finally the top of her head, before drawing her tightly to his breast. I can always remember the smell of her hair, the taste of her skin, the sound of her breathing, Ross thought. Releasing the woman he loved, he slipped out her door without a word.

Isabella leaned heavily against her closed door as the fire crackled, and when the wood shifted in her marble fireplace its dancing light illuminated her tears.

~ Chapter 9 ~

MADISON COUNTY, MONTANA, 1999

Ross realized he wasn't likely to find his father or get any answers to the questions that haunted him, but he could tell the story of the book his father thought was so important he sent it around the world to a son he didn't know he had. With that end in mind, Ross began preparation for a film about Story's trek, intending to both direct and produce this movie because he wanted full control of the storytelling process. As he'd been clever in his investments and careful with his spending, Ross had plenty of money to finance his directorial debut. Unlike many of his celebrity friends, he had always been frugal, never wasting money on drugs or the material trappings of fame. After the divorce, he'd set up trust funds for his own son and his son's half siblings to ensure their schooling, including uni. Ross's half share from the Larkin Stud Farm paid for the odd motorcycle and his ordinary living expenses. His half share would only continue to generate solid income following the opening ceremonies for the 27th Olympics in Sydney. The planned ceremonies would open with 120 stockmen and women riding their Australian Stockhorse beauties into the arena while carrying the white flags with five interlocking rings to the theme of *The Man from Snowy River*. The Larkin Stud Farm of the Upper Hunter Valley in New South Wales was destined to become internationally famous for its contribution to the Sydney Olympics.

The initial budget for a sweeping Western filmed across multiple states had been 70 million. Costs were significantly reduced by Ross's meticulous approach to filming and choice in casting. He'd convinced his best friend to star in the movie for a reduced fee and a percentage of the gross. If the movie made a profit, Ross would get a major percentage after replenishing his investment. He'd decided to find financial backers for 20 percent of the film, partly to give his project more credibility and partly to ensure his ability to cover any potential cost overruns. Even if the film was a total box office flop, he'd be financially unaffected given his ascetic lifestyle. Other than buying his ex a modest house in which to raise their son, there hadn't been any major expenditures during his acting career until now. He had ample funds to finance a project of this magnitude. After winning his second Oscar for his lead role in *Unto the Dust*, Ross could ask and did receive between 10 to 20 million per film. The possibility of his failure in storytelling and in his debut directorial effort kept him awake at night, not the prospect of losing his own money. Westerns were no longer in vogue in Hollywood, but Ross didn't care. He was telling the story of his country. Ross was convinced that the real American cowboy, Paddy O'Neill, was his biological father and making the story of *The Greatest Cattle Drive* had always been his soul's destiny. If his mother had been more forthcoming, Ross wouldn't have spent so much of his life searching for the place of his geographic resurrection. Ross Larkin Sutherland had had no control over his own story, but he had control over the telling of Nelson Story's epic journey.

The fourth summer Ross visited the Madison Valley, he concentrated his free time at the Bear Claw Bar and Grill in McAllister. The owner of the bar intrigued him with his classic Aussie greeting, the food was excellent, and there were always lots of locals to swap stories with over a coldie. Many evenings, after researching in the Gallatin History Museum in Bozeman, or the Montana State University history archives, Ross would pull his motorcycle into the Bear Claw for some tucker before going down to his motel in Ennis. That summer something else caught his interest—the Bear Claw had a new waitress.

Being a student of human character and behavior, Ross liked to watch people in their natural surroundings and make guesses as to their stories. He couldn't get a good read on this woman, though. She seemed comfortable around the owner of the bar and some of the older cowboy regulars as if they were family, but oddly cold and distant around any of the other men who came into the bar. She wore no wedding ring, so that didn't explain her disinterest in men's advances. Nor did she interact with any of the women customers. She knew her job; she was the most efficient waitress he'd witnessed in his summers coming to small bars and restaurants in southwest Montana. Most Montana waitresses attended to one table at a time, instead of multi-tasking like servers in big cities. This waitress must not have spent her life in Montana, because she didn't work like a Montanan. When Ross tried to flirt with her, he got absolutely nowhere. She was polite and all business. He was sure, she had no clue who he was and he started watching her more intently, especially as the evening lengthened and people got more inebriated. She never lost her cool and wasn't rude. When a man at the bar tried to pick her up, she acted more like a young boy than a young girl. She wasn't batting for the other team; Ross had a good radar for avoiding those awkward situations; she just wasn't engaging. It was her hypervigilance that intrigued him the most. She knew where everyone was at all times, who came in, who left.

Her lack of interest in his advances didn't bother his male ego. During his wild years, he'd become quite masterful at seducing any woman he set his eye upon. Ross hadn't met a woman yet who could say no to him once he turned on the charm and started the pursuit, until the movie shoot in Florence. Since then, he'd repented. The new waitress was pretty enough to catch his eye and hold his interest, but his initial attraction to her wasn't carnal. The attraction was something else he didn't understand. He didn't want to fuck her; he wanted to get to know her. Sometimes when he watched her during that Montana visit, he felt like he did know her. Known her for a long time, but they'd never met before. Of that he was certain. He would have remembered. The long-legged blonde with the braid to her waist, who waitressed at the Bear Claw intrigued him; she had a story. Ross was determined to hear it, but he was running out of time. His next movie started filming soon in London, then he was home to Australia for the holidays.

Ross always looked forward to Christmas. It was the one time each year that he could count on seeing his son, because David had such a good time with his younger cousins and his aunt and uncle on the Larkin Stud Farm. Ross wasn't certain David looked forward to spending time with him, but David seemed content living in Sydney with his stepfather and Shelley. If David was thriving, that was enough for Ross. He didn't need to know how David felt about him or the divorce. Ross could only play the cards life dealt him and while he had deep regrets about losing his son to another man, he kept those feelings to himself. No reason to hurt those he loved more than he already had.

Australia was a harsh land and Ross had learned from a young age not to think in terms of fairness. Life wasn't fair and nothing good could come out of thinking for one second that it should be. What was fair about his father Jacob losing his first wife and child in childbirth? Nothing, but Jacob focused his energy and grief on raising another man's son, saving rescue horses, the odd abused dog, and breeding the best Australian stockhorses in New South Wales. Ross had nothing but good memories of growing up in a house full of love, good food, hard work, endless stories, song, and laughter. His mother's practical jokes were legends in the Hunter. Folks still told the story of his mother and a stockman and what they did while Granddad was having a pint at the pub in Scone. He was grateful to Steve for continuing his family's breeding business. Steve's house was always full of love and humor, just as Jacob's had been and Granddad's had been before. Steve didn't play practical jokes but Ruthie was keeping up the Larkin family tradition. Ruthie had the internal strength and the kind heart of her father Jacob. She never spoke of life being fair, she channeled her energies and grief about losing both her parents at a young age into helping domestic violence victims and building a home both for her own twins and for Ross's son. When Ross reflected about the man who raised him and his half siblings, he always felt humbled by their strength and grace.

While he was in Montana doing research for his movie, Isabella surprised him with an invitation to Florence following his London shoot, and Ross relished the thought of their reunion although it meant cutting back his time with his family in New South Wales. He hoped Isabella had changed her mind about starting a serious relationship with him. Even though she had sent him away that night, in the subsequent weeks and months, they had established a pattern of regular phone calls and, best of all, Isabella wrote him letters full of beautiful sketches and charming stories from her life. When he had the opportunity, he reciprocated with packages full of drawings he made on location and short handwritten humorous anecdotes of events on set. The urgency in her voice when she extended her invitation worried him, but he hoped his spiritual recentering following her initial rejection was the reason for her call. Ross hadn't spared any details in his letter containing his confession to Isabella. He missed her terribly, particularly the time they spent drawing and painting in the countryside of Tuscany the year before. As their emotional sharing through letter writing deepened their love for each other, Ross could hear the difference in her voice when they spoke on the phone. He sensed there was some past sorrow she hadn't spoken of that might explain why she maintained her distance despite the increasing strength of their connection. He hadn't asked her to give him a second chance, but he'd made it clear more than once how much he loved her. He hoped his months of celibacy would earn him another chance at her heart. Few things in his adult life had made him happier than playing in the sandbox of intellectual ideas with Isabella Rossi. He felt loved, seen, and supported by her in ways he'd never imagined possible. Yes, he loved her for her physical beauty, but her spirit and her intellect held him captive, not her body, which she had never shared with him. He'd enjoyed the bodies of too many beautiful women who meant absolutely nothing to him, but Shelley and Isabella haunted him in the darkest hours of night when he couldn't sleep and he wondered why he couldn't keep the women he actually loved in his bed.

Whatever happened in Florence with Isabella, Ross looked forward to spending the next season of Lughnasadh in Montana in the summer of 2000. He relished the chance to flex his storytelling muscles and direct *North to Montana*, the story of the greatest American cattle drive sent to him when he was a bub by the mysterious Paddy O'Neill who had loved his mother, Nora Larkin. He'd been working towards his goal of directing his entire adult career. Year next was shaping up to be a great one. If Isabella didn't want to give him a second chance, such was life. No matter what happened, he would be happy to see her again. After all he was still a rolling stone, albeit a celibate one. Ross always counted down the days until his annual time in his safe place of Madison County in America's Big Sky Country, and if the mystery woman with the gorgeous long blonde hair and magnificent legs was waiting for him in the bar at the crossroads, so be it. If she wasn't, then the cosmos had spoken. Ross had no doubt, he could soften her up if she was still working at the Bear Claw next Lughnasadh season. He lived for a good challenge almost as much as he lived for a good story.

Water

I was born in a drouth year. That summer
my mother waited in the house, enclosed
in the sun and the dry ceaseless wind,
for the men to come back in the evenings,
bringing water from a distant spring.
Veins of leaves ran dry, roots shrank.
And all my life I have dreaded the return
of that year, sure that it still is
somewhere, like a dead enemy's soul. Fear
of dust in my mouth is always with me,
and I am the faithful husband of the rain,
I love the water of wells and springs
and the taste of roofs in the water of cisterns.
I am a dry man whose thirst is praise
of clouds, and whose mind is something of a cup.
My sweetness is to wake in the night
after days of dry heat, hearing the rain.[4]

Wendell Berry

~ Chapter 10 ~

MCALLISTER, MONTANA, 2000

Late in the spring, I moved back into my grandfather's cabin and cut back my hours at the Bear Claw Bar and Grill. Frank understood my need to rewrite my novel. While I felt like a different person, renewed in body and spirit, my beloved Montana was heading into trouble.

June had been a more typical month with sunny days intermixed with some rain. But in mid-July, the temperatures soared, humidity plummeted, and the drying winds began to blow. Restless winds that sucked the lifeblood out of everything. People rubbed on extra lotion, gardeners watered continuously, ranchers irrigated, and forest rangers worried. July melted into August. Another Celtic season was beginning. Before my brother's accident, the final quarter of the Celtic year stretching from August 1 to October 31 had been my favorite season—a season known for its maturity and harvest. For Montana, during this Celtic season, the maturity belonged to the forests with their floors full of underbrush, and the harvest would depend upon the wind.

The old timers down at the Bear Claw started talking of the bad summer fires of 1949. The year the thirteen smoke jumpers died in Mann Gulch 20 miles from the Montana state capital of Helena. Before my family moved to Canada, my grandparents used to take me on a favorite summer trip—the boat ride down the Missouri through the Gates of the Mountains. As we rode through the beautiful canyon in the boat, Grandpa would point out Mann Gulch and tell the story of how his cousin lost his life on the steep arid slopes. Grandpa's cousin was one of the 13 who hadn't been able to outrace the flames that blew up on that hot late-summer afternoon in August.

Fire was a fact of life in the West. I had seen my godfather Frank return from days of fighting forest fires, black from head to toe. I had traveled the backcountry with an axe, a canvas bucket, and a shovel as part of the requisite gear in a four-wheel drive rig. When we had campfires on the mountain, we built them in holes dug deep in the ground, so the flames were never higher than the surrounding dirt. We kept a full bucket of water nearby just in case, and no fire was ever left unattended. I had cringed for 13 years every time a smoker in the Midwest threw their lit cigarette butt out of their car window. Fire was a constant fear in Montana. This year, the third of an extreme drought, the shadow of fear was lengthening rapidly.

As the winds continued to blow, bringing dry lightning and no rain, the old timers reached further back into their collective memories of bad years. Back to August 1910, when the forests of Idaho and Montana exploded and 3 million acres burned in 48 hours. For five days that year, the smoke from the holocaust consuming the Bitterroot Range darkened the continental United States north of the 42nd latitude. In places as far east as Minneapolis and Montreal, the smoke from the Bitterroot Forest fires created an eclipse of the sun, forcing people to carry lanterns at high noon. When the blessed snows and rains finally came in late August, 85 people had died—74 of them firefighters, entire towns had burned, and millions of acres of prime timber had been lost. After that particular Celtic season, attitudes towards fires changed. Flame became the enemy to be fought military style. All fires out by 10 a.m. was the new policy of the Forest Service. With the change in attitude came the change in the forests themselves. Mature forests of 25-75 trees per acre were replaced gradually by forests with 800 or more trees per acre. Old stands with fire-resistant thick bark surrounded by lush cool meadows were replaced by spindly sickly stands—perfect conditions for the fast-moving crown fires so feared by firefighters. Before the Big Blow Up, forests in the Northwest averaged about 10 tons of fire fuel per acre; 90 years later the same forests contained an estimated 35 tons per acre. As the winds continued to blow, talk around Meadow Creek said this year could be as bad as the Big Blow Up of 1910.

Frank didn't talk. He was a man of action. He was over at my place the middle of July with his chainsaw. Montana was starting to burn and Frank was starting to work. He cut down all the juniper trees within 200 feet of my cabin. When I protested, he glared at me, and reminded me that junipers were a firefighter's worst enemy. They spread fiery torches everywhere, creating spot fires that jumped defensible fire lines. When Frank was done with the chainsaw, he came back with his Pulaski. The Pulaski—part axe, part hoe—was a lasting legacy of the 1910 fires. A firefighter's tool, it had been designed by a veteran of the Big Blow Up, Ed Pulaski. Together, Frank and I built the five-foot wide fire line, encircling the cabin, the shed, and the privy. Inside that protective circle, there could be no juniper, no sagebrush, no long grasses, and no lower limbs on trees. "Keep the grass mowed down tight, Cait. Clear as much sage brush on the other side of this circle as you can and cut as much cheat grass as you can manage." We moved my woodpile outside the circle and recovered it with the tarp. Frank looked at my firepit. "Absolutely, no more outdoor fires. Too risky." He looked at my wooden roof with its cedar shake shingles. "Cait, our next project is re-roofing your cabin with fireproof shingling."

Down at the Bear Claw over beer, down in Ennis over coffee, and down along the county gravel roads—pickups pulled next to pickups—people continued to talk, continued to worry. The hot, dry winds continued to blow. July 31, the eve of the beginning of the Celtic season of Lughnasadh, dry lightning ignited 70 fires in the Bitterroot Mountains. What fate the winds would bring, what harvest they would make during Lughnasadh, no one knew. Montana was waiting for another fall of rain.

~ Chapter 11 ~

SCONE, NEW SOUTH WALES, AUSTRALIA, 2000

Ruthie slammed the kitchen door. What was she going to do with that son of hers? This was the second time in a week, the teacher had sent a letter home complaining about his language. The teacher's conversations with Jacob were not yielding results. Steve wasn't much help; his response was a simple shrug, and then he was back to training horses. Ross was coming home tomorrow for a long visit before he made his now annual visit to Madison County, Montana, in search of his father, maybe he would have some ideas. He was Jacob's godfather.

As they drove back from the airport, Ruthie explained the situation. Ross laughed at her dilemma, "I'll tell Jacob what our father told me when I got in trouble at school for saying 'Absofuckinglutely,' after the teacher asked me to clean the blackboard. Mum was about to wash my mouth out with soap and Dad stopped her."

"What did he say to you."

Ross winked at his sister, "Can't tell you. Secret men's business."

Ross took Jacob riding the next morning. On the hill, above the farmhouse, Ross dismounted near a rock and gestured to his six-year-old nephew. "Sit over here with me, sprog, we need to have a word."

Pouring a cup of tea out of the thermos from his saddlebag, Ross handed it to Jacob. Cupping the warmth in his little hands, Jacob sat down on the rock next to his uncle. "When I was your age, your Granddad brought me up here with a thermos of tea. We sat right here. It was bloody hot that day. Flies all around your face. The teacher wasn't going to let me come back to school if I didn't clean up my mouth."

"What did Granddad say to you, Uncle Ross?"

"My father told me Sutherland men are gentlemen. Gentlemen don't swear around the ladies. Ross, he said to me, you're a Sutherland. You figure it out."

Jacob sipped his tea in silence and then asked his uncle, "Did you figure it out?"

Ross hesitated looking at his nephew, "Not always. Your Granddad was a good man. You will be too."

If little Jacob used the f-word after that at school, Ruthie never heard about it, although she did hear him say softly under his breath some years later, "Fuck a duck, fuck a goddamn duck" when he hit his thumb with his hammer, just like her father used to mutter when he had mishaps with hammers. Ruthie knew exactly who had taught her son to say that curse.

~ Chapter 12 ~

MCALLISTER, MONTANA, AUGUST 2000

One evening in early August, I went down to the Bear Claw for supper. I'd had a hard day of rewriting—the section of my novel I was working on was misbehaving. I needed a break. The pickup trucks were parked up and down Highway 287 on both sides for the entire length of the town of McAllister. I pulled up near the bar, parking on the shoulder about eight o'clock, adding one more pickup truck to the lineup. I hadn't talked to a soul all day. Hopefully, one of the locals would be at the bar, or an interesting stranger. I enjoyed talking to people I would never meet again. The level of conversation changed and people were more forthcoming. I had learned that my first summer working at the Bear Claw.

I nursed a beer while waiting for my steak. I liked listening to the general background chatter and being able to watch people at the Bear Claw without having to remember their orders. The bar was becoming my living room, just as it was for most of the locals in this tiny town in Montana.

When my steak came, I asked Frank for some advice. I had been having some problems with a pack of dogs that came around my cabin. There were three of them, a mastiff, a blue heeler, and a Doberman Pinscher. The sheriff laughed at me when I called him. Madison County was too sparsely populated to have a dogcatcher. He said he couldn't do anything until after I got bit. I was asking Frank if he'd seen the pack around his place. He had his yard fenced in, so he could go from his house to his driveway late at night and not have any nasty surprises. Plus, he had a German Shepherd named Jack. I worried because I had to go from my cabin to the privy late at night and I didn't want any nasty surprises either. I considered the pack of dogs a nasty surprise, regardless of the hour.

"Use the Montana three S's solution," Frank gave me his advice with an accompanying wink.

Someone had sat down on the barstool to the right of me. I looked briefly, but I didn't know him.

"Shot, shovel, and shut-up, Cait," Frank explained.

I made a face at him. Frank knew I didn't like guns.

"Hey, mate, what about a coldie? Make it a Guinness," the newcomer interrupted.

"Just call me, Cait, next time you see them and I'll help you."

Frank nodded at the newcomer and turned to walk the length of the bar to get the Guinness. I noticed that down at the other end of the bar, Jake and Ike were at it again. Jake, the former owner of my Chevy, and Ike were both hunting companions of my late grandfather. Jake was 85 and had been born on a ranch across from the old Methodist church on Meadow Creek. As a bona fide Montanan, he was quick to correct anyone claiming to be a native who had a dubious genealogy. He didn't let them get away with misrepresenting themselves as Montanans if they hadn't been born within state borders. Jake was particularly firm with Ike.

Ike was 93 and extremely sensitive about the fact that he'd been born in Glasgow, Scotland. His family had moved to Ennis when he was nine months old. Ike liked to remind people that he'd lived in Montana longer than most people ever could, an argument that failed to impress Jake. Jake was uncompromising on the definition of a Montana native. If you weren't born in the state, you could never be a real Montanan. It didn't matter how many cousins or aunts and uncles were natives or how many generations of grandparents were Montanans. Ike's place of birth was his soul's heaviest burden and Jake wasn't about to lighten it for him. Jake was too stubborn and too ornery. Jake was a Montanan.

Frank stayed above the dispute. He was born in Wyoming and damn proud of it. If anyone asked for his opinion, he was apt to say that God spelled heaven, *Wyoming*. If pressed to be serious, his green eyes would sparkle and Frank might elaborate, "You don't have any control over where you're born. You have control over how you live. That's what really matters."

Jake and Ike were both widowers and they frequently ate out together. They took turns paying the bill, but rarely could remember whose turn it was to pay. Frank thought their quibbling over the tab was amusing and he was willing to wait patiently while they sorted out their debts. The waiter down in Ennis at the Western pharmacy was less patient. He hurried up the collection process. One lunch hour, I happened to overhear the waiter ask Jake and Ike to name a number between 52,000 and 51,000. The waiter gave the person who gave the first response the check. Jake, as the younger of the two, had the better hearing and he got the check that day.

I looked at the newcomer. He was dressed like a Montanan—jeans, blue shirt cut Western style, and a horsehair belt with a Navajo turquoise and silver buckle. The only unusual part of his clothing was the leather motorcycle jacket. I looked down at his feet. Sometimes, that was the key to distinguishing a local from a rich outsider. His feet were encased in the smooth tooled leather of expensive cowboy boots, not the boots of a working local, but I had a weakness for men in cowboy boots—the sensuous curves of the instep, the stance created by the heels, the elongation of the leg, and the music of a booted walk.

He was in his late-thirties or early-forties with gorgeous curly auburn hair. The curls were all different sizes with the tightest ones along his neckline and around his ears. The light from the bar was reflecting off the gold highlights of the looser ones across the top of his head. He sat tall, and I thought he had to be several inches over six feet. He also looked vaguely familiar, but I couldn't place where I might have met him. I also had the feeling that I should know an older version of him, oddly unsettling. He caught me looking at him and met my gaze. The newcomer broke eye contact with me to look down the bar at Frank who wasn't getting the requested beer. Frank was laughing at something Ike had said. The stranger growled to no one in particular in a deep, low voice something about how the Montana three S's don't stand for super speedy service. I realized he had an accent, but I couldn't decide yet if it was British or Australian.

I said, "This is Montana. You're lucky Frank's not

making you get your own. If you want good service you have to leave the state. Montanans are never in a hurry and they're awful at service."

He inquired, "You a local girl, luv? Well, you aren't bad at service."

I was having trouble concentrating in his presence and I wanted to understand why. In my job, I talked to strangers all the time, but this one was doing something different. I really wanted to escape, to retreat across the bar so I could sit in the corner and observe him without having to stay present and respond to him. What was he doing to create this effect upon me? When I talked, his face and body stilled, and when he spoke, he used his whole face. I had the distinct feeling we were the only two people in the room; how was he creating that illusion? I'd been working at the Bear Claw for over a year. I'd learned to deflect men's attention out of necessity. My confidence in maintaining control was wavering under his focused attention. *Move, Cait. Concentrate, Cait. Go do your job.*

"I'll be right back." I slid off my stool, escaping his force field circle of energy, and walked down to the end of the bar. "Hey, Frank, why don't you hand me that Guinness?"

Frank frowned. I smiled at him and tilted my head in the direction of the glowering stranger. Frank looked down the bar and handed me the bottle after popping the cap without comment. "I get the tip, Frank, if there is one," I winked at my godfather. Behind me, I could hear that Jake and Ike had moved on to the next stage of their arguing—whose turn it was to leave the tip.

"Here you go," I said, placing the bottle of beer in front of the stranger, "Montanans don't like to spread themselves too thin."

"Thank you. Too thin?" His right eyebrow was raised.

"Yeah, it's not that Montanans don't care. It's that they are used to doing one job at a time. They don't dual task at all. Service jobs require that you dual task. Plus, in Montana a business transaction is just an excuse to socialize." We both looked down the bar at Frank, Jake, and Ike. I smiled at the stranger, "Socializing, what can you do?"

"Do you live around here?"

"Sort of. I grew up over in Bozeman, but both my grandparents' families used to ranch in this valley. My grandmother grew up in the Meadow Creek area. I've been living in Illinois for the last 13 years, and I came out to my cabin to get away. I've been writing."

"What do you write?"

"Different things—children's stories for my friends and my current project is a novel."

"Would I have read anything you've written?"

The chances of any one person having read my words were infinitesimally small. Under his intense gaze I felt threatened and before I could stop myself, I said, "I don't know, do you read?"

In that moment, with the back light highlighting his curly hair and the stubble along his jawline, with his tense physicality focused solely on me, I thought the stranger looked like the mountain lion I saw stalking his prey late in the spring sunshine up the canyon.

Frank wandered by and asked me if everything was okay. No, I was not okay, but I couldn't tell Frank. I worked in this bar and Frank expected me to handle myself. Tonight, this stranger was coming through all my defenses. Nothing, Frank had taught me was working. I started to stand up. The stranger reached out lightly touching my arm. "What did you mean, 'Do I read?' Do I look like someone who can't?" His eyes had changed. The light was twinkling off his irises and the outer corners of his eyes were crinkling as if anticipating a future smile. His mouth had wicked curves, although he was not smiling yet. "Sorry. Forget it. Don't go. Let's start over. I'm just a cheeky bastard from Down Under who *can* read." A radiant smile lit up his face. I sat back down while Frank hovered nearby.

"May I buy you a drink?" the Aussie asked with his hand still resting on my forearm. His touch was making me feel warm and unfocused. I had not experienced that sensation in years. I nodded.

"Cait'll have another beer," he addressed Frank. I was trying to figure out how he knew my name. "And save her a trip, mate, bring me a second. That one didn't touch the sides."

The Aussie turned his attention back to me, "Maybe in Montana the three S's stand for shoot, shovel, and shut-up, but in Australia the three S's stand for slip, slop, and slap."

He ran his hand up and down my forearm, stopping at the wide-beaded bracelet I always wore on my right wrist. The sensuous movement across my bare skin was intensifying the unfocused warm feeling spreading through my body. "You'd need it with skin this fine. Slip on a shirt, slop on Factor 15 sunblock, slap on a hat. Ozone depletion Down Under is serious business."

I couldn't think about the ozone, I was remembering a time as a grieving teenager when my skin was not fine. Raw and peeling, some places so badly that they oozed clear fluid as if my father's abuse caused my whole body to cry. During my 16th summer spent with my grandmother in Montana, I began to heal and my skin peeled so much, Grandma joked she could have reconstructed another me as if I was a snake growing a new skin and slithering away

from the old one. The stranger would not be compliment-
ing me and touching me if I looked like I had when I was
a teenager. My heart was picking up speed, recalling the
spring and summer I didn't want to remember. Maybe if I
concentrated hard enough, the world would go sideways
and I could exit the Bear Claw through the worn floor
boards.

When Frank brought the two beers, he did not look too
happy, he had been watching me and I never could hide
anything from him. I smiled faintly at Frank, shaking my
head slightly to let him know I was fine, even though I
wasn't and my godfather knew it.

"Now, about this other matter. Why don't you think I
can read?" the Aussie's voice had dropped in tone and volume. His words were for my ears only. Whatever earlier
impression I had of the coiled energy of a predator about
to spring on its prey had vanished, leaving only intense
feelings of calm. His fingers tracing the beadwork on my
wrist lightly and slowly felt reassuring, not aggressive, not
sexual.

"I'm sorry, I was being bitchy," I said, looking at him
straightforwardly, testing him. I was hoping if I played nice
but unpredictable, he would go away. If I could make him
go away, I might head off having a panic attack in public.
My deliberately random reactions usually worked on men
at the Bear Claw by throwing them off balance, but my response seemed to have the opposite of my desired effect.
The stranger seemed even more intrigued and attentive.

He laughed. "You do have a bit of a bite." His hand moved
off my bracelet onto the bare skin of my forearm. His fingertips were making light, spiraling circles up to the rolled
sleeves at my elbow. His touch did not feel reassuring anymore, it felt overtly sexual.

I tried changing the subject. "What brings you to the Madison Valley? Fishing?"

"No. I'm not here to fornicate with arachnids. I'm on the job—filming a Western."

He straightened up on his stool, removing his hand from my arm. The tingling from his touch lingered. He looked at me for what felt like an eternity, saying nothing. I stared back at him wondering, what on earth fornicating with arachnids had to do with fly fishing? What did fucking spiders mean anyway? I didn't understand the stranger's silence. I hadn't said anything noteworthy, although the odd feeling of familiarity I had felt when I first saw him now made sense. I must have seen one of his movies? Which one? When? I had never paid any attention to Hollywood celebrities. That was Ralph's passion. He always remembered which actors had played in different movies and he even knew who all the famous directors were. Ralph made a point to make me feel stupid about my complete lack of interest in popular culture. I was sure Ralph would have recognized this stranger sitting next to me immediately, but I had no clue who this person talking to me was. No idea at all, nor did I care to know.

"Don't you know who I am?"

I shook my head.

"You don't know me?"

"No. Why should I?"

"Ross Larkin Sutherland."

"Caitlinn Burnett."

Ross laughed. "You still have no idea who I am, Cait, do you? It's all over your face. Oh, my sister is going to enjoy this story when I ring her next. She'll be teasing me for months. Saying it's what I deserve for being a tall poppy. My long overdue comeuppance." He was still chuckling.

"Well, I'm glad you're amused. All I know about you is that you apparently don't fuck spiders."

"Ouch, that's harsh. Ladies shouldn't swear, Caitlinn."

"Maybe, I'm not a lady, Mr. Sutherland."

Ross smiled slightly and shrugged, "Nah, you are." He looked down the bar, watching Frank interacting with Ike and Jake.

Because I was becoming curious about this good-looking man paying me attention when men never did, unless they were staggering drunk, I decided to confess something to Ross. "Although when you sat down at the bar, I did have the sensation I know an older version of you, but I couldn't figure it out. I'm really good with faces and names. I've never met you before, but you do seem oddly familiar. I don't pay any attention to pop culture or the whole celebrity nonsense, if that's where you're going with your song and dance. I'm a Montana girl. That stuff doesn't matter to Montanans. At all. Ever. The only thing that matters to us is if you are a reliable person who can be trusted when times get tough. Your money? Your fame? Your family's social status? None of it means jack shit out here. And it *really* doesn't matter to me."

"Good onya, Cait. Rather Australian of you." Ross tilted his head while biting his lower lip, watching me for a while. I didn't react; I gazed back at him, using the silence to admire the perfection of his nose, the beautiful strong line of his jaw and chin, his deep-set eyes, the sensual curves of his lips. He was attractive, but not in a well-manicured pretty-boy Hollywood sense. The stranger looked like he could do hard physical ranch labor alongside any native Montanan male and keep up. He did not look like the sort of man who would mind getting manure on his boots or dirt under his fingernails. A deep voice startled me out of my reverie, "Maybe you saw, *Cleaveth Unto the Dust*, the picture about the 1916 Easter Uprising in Ireland during the Great War? I played an older man in that film."

"No. No." I was shaking my head, "What part did you play?" I didn't remember anybody in the movie who had stunning curly auburn hair, resembled a mountain lion, and was quite handsome.

"The main character, Father Paddy O'Donnell."

I was beginning to feel queasy. "No. I ... I ... I don't believe you. Father Paddy is old. And bald. And fat. And *Irish*." I emphasized Irish.

"The power of good storytelling. Plus, extra weight, makeup, and a very good accent coach."

I was remembering the brilliant azure eyes of the priest, eyes the color of the Western skies, the last thing I'd seen before blacking out from loss of blood. Ross's eyes were not the priest's eyes. "I don't believe you," I repeated.

Ross recited from Father Paddy's prayer in a perfect Irish brogue,

"I arise today
with God's strength to pilot me:
God's might to uphold me
God's wisdom to guide me
God's eye to look ahead for me ..."[5]

The pain of that day gripped my chest again, I couldn't breathe, I was dizzy, memories merged, blended, and warped, from passing out on the floor to Ralph's mocking face as the red marks of my fingertips darkened across his cheek to ending with the stranger's quizzical facial expression. *Got. To. Leave. Now.* I got up so fast, my stool almost tipped over. I headed for the ladies' room. I was in the middle of a full-blown panic attack. I could not be driving. I would have to wait it out someplace safe. All alone. With the Irish Setter. Waiting until the panic attack subsided and I could retreat to the safety of my grandfather's quiet cabin.

Inside the solitude and safety of the bathroom, I sat on the closed toilet seat, trying to quiet my breathing. I could not use my usual technique of reciting Father Paddy's prayer against the real Father Paddy. *Breathe Cait. In and out. Slowly. You are okay. Breathe. Just breathe.* When my heart quit racing and my breathing slowed, I ventured out into the hallway and went back into the main part of the bar. I hesitated looking across the room at two empty stools where we had been sitting.

"Hey, Cait. Thought you'd gone wrong. I'd just convinced the waitress to have a look after you." Ross's warm, deep voice was right in my ear with his hand firmly resting on my shoulder. I twisted around. Ross towered over me. He was well over six feet. "Whoa, luv," Ross said gazing down at me and taking my elbow to steady me, he led me back to our spot at the bar.

When we were seated and Ross had ordered me another beer he asked, "What was that about?" His face was relaxed, but there was an edge to his voice.

"You don't have the right color eyes."

Ross laughed. "That's what the director said. He wanted blue all the time, azure blue to match the Western skies. The color of your eyes, Cait. My eyes change color. Bothers some people. I wore colored contacts. I can't get rid of most fans fast enough, but you," Ross paused, "You, I want to talk with and you disappear faster than a snowflake in the outback. Why?"

I took a big, deep breath launching into a partial

explanation. "I was watching *Unto the Dust* when I was sick and while I was recovering, I used it as inspiration. I should have recognized you. I'm such a fool." I was not about to tell him how many times I had prayed for an *anam cara* like Father Paddy to guide me. I was never going to tell Ross about using his prayer to give me the courage to slap my husband and leave a relationship that was literally killing me.

Ross's eyes narrowed. He finished his beer, gestured at Frank for a third, and said, "I wouldn't worry about that. My sister Ruthie met me at the airport after the shoot and she walked right by me."

I nodded, feeling a little safer.

Ross continued, "Sounds like *Unto the Dust* hit an emotional chord. That's all I ever hope for. What did you think of *The Last Man*?"

I shrugged.

"The one about the mob in Chicago during the '20s. I played the copper who falls for the mobster's moll. I won an Oscar for best supporting actor for that role."

"Haven't seen it."

Ross took a very long swig of his beer. Then, he asked, "So, Cait, what's your day job?"

"I used to teach archaeology at a university in Illinois. Last year, I decided it was time for a change. I'm trying to write full time now. I'm divorced from my husband. I'm enjoying the independence of not being dependent on men. I help Frank here at the bar until I sell my writing."

"I know you work here. You waited on me last summer. How long have you been divorced?"

"Ralph and I separated shortly after my illness."

"Which was?"

"Which was what?" I asked, trying to understand how

Ross could remember me from last summer. I had no memory of such a force of personality. Men did not flirt with me. They left me alone, and that was exactly how I liked it. I would have remembered anyone who flirted with me so aggressively.

"Illness?"

"Ectopic pregnancy. I thought I was having a miscarriage. If the neighbor hadn't stopped by when she did, I would have died. I was watching your movie and I fainted when I got up to answer the doorbell. She saw me on the floor through the window. I was starting to go into shock from loss of blood. She called 911 and they smashed in the front door." I was somewhere else again, remembering how angry Ralph had been because his front door had been damaged.

"Why did you need to watch a movie for inspiration?"

"Why do you need to ask such personal questions?" I didn't want to talk about Father Paddy and how lonely I had been or how fond I was of the character of the priest. I definitely didn't want to tell this stranger that I was convinced his recitation of "The Breastplate of St. Patrick" had shielded me from death long enough for my neighbor to find me, thus saving my life. I absolutely didn't want to discuss Ralph, or why I hadn't gone to a doctor when I first realized my fourth miscarriage was going so wrong.

"I don't have time to be superficial." He paused, glanced up at the ceiling and then back at me, "Rightyo, let's try something else. Do you miss teaching?"

"Yes, and no. I don't miss the whining about grades. There's nothing worse than grownups begging for grades they didn't earn … ."

Ross interrupted me, "Perfect opportunity to quote the 11th century mathematician, Cait."

"The moving finger writes; and having writ,
Moves on: nor all thy piety nor wit
Shall lure it back to cancel half a line,
Nor all thy tears wash out a word of it."[6]

Ross went on to answer my next unverbalized question, "Edward FitzGerald's ripper translation of "The Rubaiyat of Omar Khayyam." You haven't read it? Ah, Cait, you need more poetry in your life."

Ross flashed a big grin, followed by another rapid-fire question, "What do you miss about teaching?"

"I miss having a regular audience. I have to write all my stories down instead."

He was on to the next question, "Were you good at teaching?"

I felt like I was being interviewed. I shrugged. My first response was to say, not good enough. *Stay positive, Cait. Don't get too serious. Make a good impression. Try to be normal.* I made an attempt, "I won a teaching award. Good teaching is half explanation and half mob control. I didn't have trouble with either. I didn't have trouble with discipline, I ran a tight ship. I didn't tolerate any nonsense. No one talked or read the paper in my class. No one left class early, either."

Ross didn't offer any comment. He seemed uncomfortable, which I was accustomed to because I frequently had that effect on people. Apparently, my intensity levels disturbed them. Why did I think Ross would be any different? Time to go home. If one of us were going to end this conversation, I would rather be in control. I could leave first.

Ross polished off his third beer. "Hey, mate, give us another round." Frank scowled at Ross, but brought him his requested round.

I interjected, "Oh, no. I think I should go home."

"Ah no, luv, don't leave me all alone here in the wilds of Montana. You can't leave now. You haven't explained to me why you're here tonight. You're letting me crack onto you. You usually knock back all the blokes who have a go. Why is that?"

I didn't quite understand everything he was saying to me, but I understood the general gist. I was halfway off my barstool. "Who's keeping track?"

"I am. You've changed."

I blushed and the unfocused warm feeling was back. What on earth was he talking about?

Ross continued, "Why are you chinwagging with me tonight, instead of giving me your usual brush off?"

"I haven't seen anyone all day. I just came down tonight for someone else's cooking and a random conversation. Here I am talking to you—Father Paddy. Too weird."

"Oh, God," he groaned. "Here it comes."

I sat mute, half-perched on my barstool. Ross was glowering at me.

"Here's where you start asking me stupid questions. I like it better when you treat me like an ordinary fella, Cait. Forget Father Paddy."

"What's the stupidest question you've been asked?"

Ross made a face and said in a falsetto voice, while wiggling his head side to side in exaggeration, "What part of you is the character and what part of the character is you, the actor?"

"Writers get that too," I replied without sympathy, feeling on safer ground, repositioning myself solidly on my barstool.

"Oh?" He raised his right eyebrow.

I hesitated. Ross wasn't glaring at me anymore. I said,

"For example. Ten years ago, I wrote a story for a friend who was eight years old. I couldn't find the right book for her birthday gift, so I decided to write her one. Anyway, she really liked it, but the principal character in the story was based on my grandmother who had just recently died. People would ask me, 'Was your grandmother really like that? What a wonderful woman. You were really lucky to have someone like that in your life.' And I would feel awful, because I didn't know where my real grandmother stopped and started in that character. Some parts of the character were other women in my life. The question made me feel like a fraud, which is probably silly but it was my reaction. The character of Grandma was a creation. It was a fiction, and trying to explain and analyze took away from the beauty, from the unity. I don't know, I just hated it. Yet, on some level it seemed like a reasonable question. I just couldn't come up with a reasonable answer." I paused.

"Next time someone asks you that question, give them an answer. Tell them this: If you have to explain your art, whether it's film, music, photography, or writing, it's not successful. It's not working. Art should stand alone without analysis, without explanation, without apology. Ideally, art should just be. So, the question of what part of a character is reality and what part is fiction has no meaningful answer."

"I can't be that rude."

Ross began tapping syncopated rhythms with his fingers on the polished surface of the bar. I started talking fast again.

"I know when writers start out, they tend to be autobiographical in their writing. They always say to write about what you know and that you shouldn't stray too far from your own experiences. I'm so afraid of making mistakes. I base my characters on the people I've had experience with, so I can concentrate on the writing mechanics and the plot. The same is true with the setting. All my fictional writing takes place in Montana, because I love it so much. I can describe it in detail for any season. Writing about it is paying homage. It's as if I'm making love to a place. I hated where I was living in Illinois. I never felt connected to that physical spot. I refused to calibrate."

Ross interrupted me as his fingers stilled, "Calibrate?"

I realized I would have to explain. This was embarrassing. I never talked about my abilities. They were silly. Ross was listening, though, and his focused attention was seductive. "When I was little, my grandfather taught me to pay attention to the world. Grandpa used to call me his little druid. I learned to predict the weather by listening to the wind, watching the sky, feeling the change in the air. I could tell you within a degree what the temperature was. I could estimate humidity levels, too. I could tell how fast the wind was blowing. Estimate wind chill. I was calibrated. I never tried to do that in the Midwest."

"Why not?" Ross was completely motionless.

"Because if I understood the light, if I knew how the clouds moved, then I would be acknowledging the place and I just wanted to go home to Montana. This state is alive to me. I belong here in this place. Oh, I'm sorry. I'm talking too much."

"No worries, Cait. I don't mind. Believe me, you're the most interesting woman I've met in yonks." Ross smiled, shifting his position on his stool. Something I had said about Montana must have piqued his interest. "Go on. Please." His body was now square to mine, his feet tucked into the rungs on opposite sides, his long legs forming a right angle around me. His forearms were resting flat on his thighs, his hands loosely clasped together. He was leaning forward into my personal space. The earlier nervous diffuse energy was totally absent.

Father Paddy was sitting beside me. With his body, Ross was physically carving out a safe place for us in the midst of the crowded bar. I wanted to tell Ross exactly how I felt about writing and all the times Ralph hurt me, but I exercised control and focused solely on my feelings about writing. "When I first started writing, I worried constantly about putting myself out there on paper. I was horrified at the idea that other people would read my thoughts and feelings. But that's the whole point, right? Sharing? Great writers reveal themselves. It's hard to get the confidence to bare your soul. I hope as I mature as a writer that I become more confident and more willing to take chances. Did that happen to you in your career?"

Ross's brow wrinkled slightly, "Yes. I take more chances now. You're spot on about sharing." Ross's voice was richer in tone, warmer. "Exposure of the soul is the core of what I do; it's all about honest communication. That's why I try to understand both the characters and my fellow actors before the shoot starts, because that extra information allows for extra exposure of the soul, extra honesty of emotion, extra communication. Honesty is always the key. I learned something critical during my last movie, *The Florentine Conspiracy*. I learned to detect the difference between forgeries and real art."

"Why was that critical to your acting?"

Ross smiled broadly, sitting up straight again while keeping his legs in the same position, "Because I learned how to see. *Cleaveth Unto the Dust* taught me how to listen. That's the best part about my job, Cait, paying attention.

A lot of people think acting is about getting attention. Well, maybe it is for some fellas, but not for me. I could give a rat's arse about the celebrity part of my job. The magic of creativity for me is in the paying of attention. I learn so much along my creative journey of storytelling and acting. As soon as I hear picture's up, rolling, speed, marker, set, and the director calls action, I'm in the zone. I'm completely consumed in the moment doing what I love best. Performing is unbelievably exhilarating. It's more arousing than foreplay." Ross hesitated gauging my reaction.

"I wouldn't know anything about that," I replied straight faced, refusing to react to his sexual reference. "If *Unto the Dust* taught you to listen, which movie taught you to see?"

Ross cocked his head sideways, briefly caught the edge of his lower lip between his teeth and then sat motionless, studying me for the longest time before jerking his head upright and answering, "In *The Florentine Conspiracy*, I was a diviner."

"What's a diviner?"

Ross's eyes sparkled, accompanied by a laugh in the back of his throat when he spoke, "I played a Scotland Yard detective investigating an international art theft ring. My character was a diviner. Diviners detect forgeries by how they feel. They get a special vibe in the presence of genuine masterpieces. They're calibrated to quality. Ah, Cait, I had so much fun with that role. We filmed in London and Italy. I had a fabulous time in Florence, met lots of lovely people. I actually got pretty good at artistic style detection. I had a magnificent teacher."

"Did you really learn how to detect forgeries?"

"In principle. Isabella Rossi is an authentication expert and she served as the technical advisor on the film. She tried to teach me as much as she could. But it's an art. Make no mistake about that. Isabella's greatest gift to me was teaching me to see. We discussed my dream of directing. She encouraged me to be more painterly in shooting scenes. Composition matters to me, ya know, the precise placement of people and objects on a set, like a still life. The importance of filming at the right time of day or year to capture the moment. After months spent with Isabella, I think more like her now, more like a painter, to notice how the light plays on objects in the sunlight, in the moonlight, during cloudy days. By showing me how she approaches her own plein air painting, Isabella elevated my expectations for myself in regards to filmmaking.

"Excuse me, what's plein air painting?"

"Oh, sorry Cait. Plein air is French for painting outdoors." I wasn't particularly interested in the Aussie's recollections of the woman named Isabella or French outdoor painting, but he was amusing to watch while he talked about both. Besides, if the Aussie was doing all the talking, I could disconnect and admire his physical beauty rather than being uncomfortable and tongue tied when he asked me questions and I was required to speak.

He didn't miss a beat as he returned to his passionate recounting of his time in Europe painting outside, "We had some magical afternoons in the Italian countryside while Isabella painted. As a result of her encouragement, I started making extensive storyboards and thinking about each camera shot as a quick drawing on my current film. I've always been pretty decent at drawing, but Isabella gave me permission to take it to the next level. Isabella kept telling me that I only had to have the painter's eyes, not the painter's hands. She kept telling me I had the basic draftsman skills; that was good enough. Develop your painter's eye was her constant mantra to me. I can do a small sketch and the storyboard artist can work from that. Because of Isabella, I've been to all the major Western art museums in the U.S. studying how cattle drives and cowboys were painted and photographed by their contemporaries. Studying the framing of the Western landscapes. Your Charlie Russell is amazing, and his work has informed me greatly in how I want to visually present the story of my movie on film—Russell's attention to detail and the beauty of his paintings without all that Hollywood singing rhinestone cowboy nonsense. Because of her job and mine, Isabella had access to galleries in the off hours, so I could go with her and view the art without fans knowing where I was or what I was doing. Nobody wanting a piece of me. In those moments of stillness in the presence of past art, I could feel the power of the unknown, Cait. Beauty as a balm for the weary soul. I've always been involved with the narrative, and my childhood interest in music made me aware of the emotional importance of an authentic soundtrack, but Isabella provided me with the last bit for solving my whole directorial puzzle—conquering the visual. Now, in the past, I've worked with directors who make heavy use of storyboards, but I never really and truly understood their full artistic potential until my time with Isabella. Storyboards, because of all that thinking beforehand on paper, cut costs and that's critical for me as an independent filmmaker on this shoot. I don't have the luxury of a Hollywood-style massive budget. The storyboards are a great tool for me, instead of the antithesis of trial and error with multiple takes."

"I'm sorry, but what are storyboards?"

"Best way to think about it, Cait, is to imagine planning out an entire movie by drawing a comic book of it on paper in quick sketches. The storyboards reflect the script in terms of the narrative, but their real importance is in the visualization of the script. Alfred Hitchcock was a big user of storyboards, and he was extremely creative with the camera. I want to be like Hitchcock. I don't want to make another horse opera, I want to make a monumental film tribute to the American West and the strength of the people who built it, where scenes remind you of an Edward S. Curtis or a L. A. Huffman photograph with their majesty and wonderful historical detail. I'm hopeful that I have the experience and the confidence to make a great movie and do justice to a great story."

I wasn't sure if I was in the presence of a magnificent articulate artist or the most arrogant man I had ever met in my life. Exactly why should an Aussie care about a Montana story? It wasn't his story to tell. Montanans are perfectly capable of telling our own stories. We do not need some egotistical celebrity from Down Under to tell our stories. I was on the fence though, since the character of Father Paddy had been important to me in my own life, but the Aussie actor in the flesh certainly was a bit much. I resorted to my old playbook—when you don't know how to react emotionally in a situation, don't react at all. I did wonder who Edward S. Curtis and L. A. Huffman were, though. Ross clearly thought I should know who he was talking about and I did not want him to think I was a total ignoramus. I had already made a fool of myself over Father Paddy and my stupid panic attack. And Isabella, the magnificent teacher? Ross's voice changed when he spoke her name. Clearly, he and Isabella had more than a professional relationship. I couldn't inquire further. Grandma always said, "People will tell you what they want you to know—listen carefully, be respectful of their privacy, and don't pry."

"Isabella teaching me about art authentication also introduced me to the visual elements of art, so I can guide my developing appreciation of art in addition to having the vocabulary to talk about it. I'm always interested in improved communication. It's one thing to be appreciative of the creative process, but if you want to improve it, you have to be able to talk about it in a knowledgeable way with fellow creative minds. If you can't speak their language, it's hard to have a meaningful conversation. If you want to build an audience, you have to be able to communicate with them as well. In other words, you have to have the language of the expert and an understanding of the novice experience, so you can bring them along. Nobody likes to be talked down to in this life. I don't want my audience to think that I'm condescending ... ," Ross hesitated. His brow wrinkled as his eyes narrowed. "Is something wrong, Cait?"

"No. Why?"

"You're frowning at me."

"I am?"

"You are. Am I boring you?"

"No. I was just thinking that usually I'm the one in the room giving the lecture. That's all."

"I am rabbitin' on a bit."

I reached out to gently pat his forearm, "No, no, it's okay. You're fine." I needed to reassure Ross, because I was genuinely intrigued by his expository style of conversation. "You were saying something about art authentication. Do you mean like establishing context? I understand the importance of that. Artifacts are useless in my field unless we know precisely where they were found in three-dimensional space, complete with exact measurements. But how did Isabella help with your character? I understand your point about communication and translating complex information gracefully to make it accessible to a novice. That's what good teachers do."

"Exactly so, Cait. Establishing provenance is an important part of art authentication, but that wasn't Isabella's focus because I was playing a diviner, not an art historian. Isabella decided I had to learn all the visual elements and how to look for them in a piece of art in order to discern quality. She was correct. With her teaching, I could understand the diviner's gift in a more three-dimensional way. She taught me the old-school ways of detecting forgeries before the use of X-rays and chemical analyses of paint. Using old school techniques with representational art meant that the best way to tell a forgery stylistically is to turn it upside down and examine what you see. Look at both the details and the overall composition. Is the work spontaneous? Or is it forced? Does it have rhythm? Or is it static? Do all the components form a harmonious whole? Forgers just copy, they don't create. They often don't understand how the two-dimensional objects they're copying interact in a three-dimensional world. Forgers can't capture accurately the volume, the mass."

Now, I had no idea what Ross was talking about, he had lost me.

"Look Cait." Ross grabbed a napkin off the bar and a pen out of his jacket. He was sketching our two beer bottles on the napkin. "If I'm the original artist, I know how objects are shaped, I know how they're positioned in relation to each other. The work I'm creating is my idea, my conception. A forger doesn't have access to all that information. A forger is working off something that's already one step removed from reality." Ross stopped, regarding me steadily, evaluating my expression.

When I nodded, he continued as the enthusiasm in his voice was increasing, "If I have the bottles in front of me, I can see how the light reflects, I can see how far apart they are from each other. If I have a question, I can examine them and get my answer. But ... ," Ross swiftly moved the bottles off the bar and held them between his legs, "Imagine how hard it would be to recreate those two bottles from this drawing." He glanced over at me to see if I was still engaged. I smiled and nodded again. I understood.

The bottles came back onto the bar. "Acting is no different. I could just show up on the set and read my lines. That would be akin to being a forger trying to copy a masterpiece. If I can recreate the character in my head, then I can be three-dimensional instead of two-dimensional in my acting. It's like the difference between having these two bottles in front of me to work from versus this napkin drawing. This is really critical, Caitlinn." Ross's face was glowing with excitement. "If I focus all my intellectual, physical, and emotional energies into the character, I can achieve harmony and unity. And harmony and unity are the essence of quality."

I thought Ross looked like a Christmas tree, all lit up and beautiful.

"But at the same time, I can't get too consumed by details. That's the other way you can spot a forgery. Too much overworking of details. Always, look at the hands in a painting. Forgers have a terrible time with hands. Watch a great actor's hands in a movie. Even their hands will be involved in telling the story. Mediocre actors worry about stupid details like their boots or their leather belts or their beaded jackets, instead of recreating their character's emotions." Ross's voice had a trace of sarcasm. "Mediocre actors can never be better than forgers. They're frauds in a sense, because they just copy, they don't create. Here's a tip, next time you see a film, watch the actors' hands. If they're mediocre actors, their hands will be stiff, no spontaneity. If they're chain smoking on screen, you'll know something else about them, Cait. Actors try to defend their smoking as part of the character. Don't buy that bullshit. They're out of their league and they're hoping nobody will notice. They smoke on screen because they don't know what to do with their hands."

"I try to live the physical part of the role. Ya know why? I can get insights as to how the character talks and moves. Living the part frequently gives me a line on what the character is feeling and thinking. Let's me be more three-dimensional."

I was back to thinking about Father Paddy. Ross really could draw well, maybe he was more honest than arrogant. Before I could stop myself, I asked, "Did you live the part of the priest?"

Ross took time to take another long swallow of his beer. His face had become an expressionless mask. He took his time setting the bottle back down on the bar. His booted feet shifted from his stool rungs to mine as he leaned forward again, closing the space between us with his hands clasped together, elbows resting on his thighs just above his knees. Ross's outstretched forefingers moved up and down across the side of my thigh and his voice was barely audible over the bar chatter as he growled, "What exactly are you asking me, Cait?"

I could feel my face turning beet red. I could not meet his intense gaze. Ross reached over and brushed the side of my face with the coolness of the back of his hand. "Sorry, Cait. Didn't mean to embarrass you. The answer to your question is yes. I gave up sex." His matter-of-fact tone of voice, accompanied by his lack of facial expression, produced a calming effect on me, "First thing I noticed when I was studying for the part and staying at the monastery was the importance of chastity. The monks focus their sexual energy to other ends. Fascinating. Giving up sex is liberating. You learn to truly listen to people."

Father Paddy had responded to my embarrassment, but Ross Larkin Sutherland was not my beloved Father Paddy, or was he? I had to know if the man beside me understood what he was doing, "Can I ask you a question?"

"You can ask. Dunno, if I'll answer."

"How did you learn to listen with your whole body?"

Ross sat up straight again, tilting his head slightly while smiling faintly, "Very perceptive of you to notice that, Cait."

"Well, are you going to tell me?"

"I learned from the monks. Do you want to know why it's important?"

I nodded, but I was pretty sure, having experienced Ross listening with his whole body, that I already knew. I was wrong.

"Listening with your entire body does two things. One, it creates a safe place for people to share their opinions and feelings. In my line of work and level of fame, my life is people filthy. I have to be able to figure out really fast what people want from me and if I need to have anything more to do with them past being initially polite. There's too much at stake for me to associate with fuckwits or sycophants. I use whole body listening as a time saver. It's an existential machete to slice through bullshit. The second thing is more important. Priests use the same nonverbal technique as a spiritual gateway. Their job is to listen to confessions and extend guidance with the hope of repentance and redemption. They hear enormous amounts of evil and sorrow. The only way a human can carry that load is do one of two things: become hardened and cynical or let God carry the load. When a priest listens with his whole body, or when anyone in the field of providing social services or mental health listens with their whole body, they become the vessel through which God passes to the person who needs to be heard. In that way, the mere mortal isn't carrying the emotional burden of thou. God is. Yes, I can do the physical part of listening with my whole body for secular reasons, but I've had my battles with the spiritual part. Learning to listen with my whole body has hurt me deeply."

"How so?"

Ross looked away and then added, "Well, it didn't hurt my acting, I got another Oscar."

"What did it hurt?"

Ross switched position on his stool, no longer facing me, his entire body straight ahead with his feet returning to the rungs of his own stool. His elbows rested on the edge of the bar; hands loosely clasped over each other. He was focused on something directly in front of him, maybe visible through the window located behind the bar. He cleared his throat, still looking straight ahead, not at me, "My girlfriend at the time wasn't at all understanding. She left me. I'm not certain what bothered her more: all those visits to the Irish coastline to see the sacred sites or the fact I wouldn't touch her. Amber hated Ireland." After a lengthy silence, while continuing to look at something out in the darkening landscape as the last light of day faded into night, Ross added with firmness, "And me."

"Sounds like you lost yourself in your role."

Ross shifted again. He bent forward, elbows resting on

the bar, his forehead resting on his knuckles, and then he looked at me sideways, his eyes half hidden due to his head position, his voice deepening and lowering, but with an unmistakable forcefulness, even if only I could hear him, "Wrong. Caitlinn. In the end? I found myself again."

I was not going to be intimidated. I was not afraid. For some strange reason, I found the self-confidence to speak my mind, my truth to this odd stranger from Down Under, "Maybe you found yourself, but I lose myself when I write. It's pure escapism. I find the process intoxicating. A good session of writing just takes over my whole conscious reality. The everyday annoyances fade into the background. I get completely swept up in the characters and their lives. Sometimes, I have trouble paying attention to the people in my real life. Does that happen to you? Do you have a private life? Are you married? Do you have kids?"

"No. No. I'm not married anymore. I have a son. Anyhow, Cait, what are you doing later on tonight?" Ross had straightened up and returned to his previous position, giving me his full attention. He placed his hand on my beaded bracelet again, running his fingers over the design motifs. I moved his hand off my wrist. Ross did not seem at all chaste at the moment.

"Sleeping alone. Why are you so interested in a divorced middle-aged woman? I'm 36 years old, what could I possibly have to offer you?"

"Bloody hell, Cait, thirty-six isn't middle-aged. Don't sell yourself short. I prefer older women. They are more interesting stories. More depth to their emotions. In my experience, older women are superior lovers. More grateful."

"I don't need a charity fuck from you."

"Ah, Cait, I know you don't." Ross was about to say something else when a tall, narrow-hipped blonde man with an enormous handlebar mustache thumped him on the back.

"Ross, are you about ready to go? I need to get back to town. Kathy will be pissed off if I'm out late two nights in a row."

Ross made the introductions. "Cait, this is my mate, Charlie Douglas. Charlie owns the Rocking R down in Ennis. Charlie, this is Caitlinn Burnett. Caitlinn's a writer … ." Ross was interrupted by Charlie's boisterous reaction.

"Caitlinn? Is that really you? How have you been? My God, I haven't seen you since you kissed me at the Ennis Rodeo."

Ross was glowering at Charlie. Charlie was not paying Ross any attention. I was remembering kissing a young tall cowboy, who had just won the bucking bronco event on a warm dusty evening. I had a huge crush on Charlie Douglas back then.

"Caitlinn's grandfather, Dermot Gallagher, used to announce the Fourth of July rodeos. Cait gave out the prizes and the kisses. How old were you, Caitlinn? Twelve?" Charlie winked at me. "You must be the writer that my wife said was living up at the old Gallagher cabin this summer." Charlie hit his forehead with the palm of his hand. "I'm such an idiot. It never occurred to me it might be you, Caitlinn. You always were the cutest little thing and look at you now. My, my. I'll be damned. I'd have come up and paid you a visit if I'd known Dermot's beautiful granddaughter was back in town. Last I heard, you were married and living in Illinois. Figured you'd have a house full of kids by now."

I involuntarily reacted to Charlie's last remark as if I had been punched in the gut. Ross frowned and cleared his throat. "Later, Charlie." Ross, raising his eyebrows at Charlie, gestured in the direction of the Bear Claw front door with his head. His intent was abundantly clear, "Cait and I have some business to settle."

Charlie gave me a big smile. "I'm real sorry about your grandparents, Caitlinn. We all miss them. Good to see you, Caitlinn. If this Aussie son-of-a-gun doesn't pan out for you, give me a try. I'm always up for some fun." Charlie patted Ross on the back good-naturedly and said, "I'll be in the truck. Take your time, cowboy."

"Can I buy you dinner tomorrow, Cait?" Ross asked.

"I don't know." I was watching Charlie leave the bar. From the back, he was the same. Twenty-four years had not marred the graceful stride of his booted walk or altered the fit of his carefully starched and pressed jeans. Charlie had perfect, straight, crease lines running from the hem up to his attractive backside. *Up for some fun?* Had I had too much to drink or had a married man made a pass at me?

"Please." Ross had laid his hand on mine. The door was closing after Charlie. I noticed when I quit thinking about Charlie that Ross was sitting motionless in his distinctive open position.

I hesitated. "All right. Where do you want to go? This is as good a place as any around."

Ross nodded. "I'll pick you up at 8 p.m. Where do you live?"

"It would be easier to meet here."

"Where do you live?"

"Here, I'll draw you a map." I sketched him a map on the dinner napkin. Ross stood up quickly. He took the napkin in one hand and put his other hand on my shoulder. Ross bent closer to me. "Thanks, Cait. I hate to let you out of my sight, but Charlie and I are going riding first thing in the morning."

I nodded.

"Catch ya later, Cait." Ross flashed me one of his radiant smiles. Frank was watching. He caught my eye and raised an eyebrow. I paid my bill, saying nothing to my godfather except goodnight.

I went outside to stand on the porch, listening to the night sounds. I watched the lights of the cars coming down the Norris Hill wind around the darkened slope and then come back into view. There never was much traffic this time of night. It was hypnotic to watch the lights get brighter and bigger and then fade away again, as they went down the valley towards Ennis. What am I doing? The fun of talking to strangers at the bar was knowing that you would never see them again. I was breaking all my rules. I watched the lights twinkling across the valley—ranch houses nestled against the foothills. In the west, just above the peak of South Baldy, a shooting star arced across the sky. I made a wish. I shivered. The August evening Montana wind was hinting at the snows to come, as it blew down from the mountaintops. I climbed in the truck and drove home to a dark cabin.

Wet Evening in April

The birds sang in the wet trees
And I listened to them it was a hundred years from now
And I was dead and someone else was listening to them.
But I was glad I had recorded for him
The melancholy.[7]

Patrick Kavanagh

~ Chapter 13 ~

The next evening, Ross was prompt. Five minutes before 8 p.m. I could hear the sound of a motor approaching. Right below Frank's house, he came into view, but I had not anticipated what I was seeing. Since, I had abandoned the cowboy boots and jeans of the previous evening for a skirt and sandals, I wondered how Ross expected me to accompany him on a dinner date. I was about to find out. I watched skeptically from my front steps, as Ross rode his Harley up my drive.

After he turned off his bike, he stood silent for a moment, looking all around, "Beautiful up here. Wonderful smell. Goodness, you have a lot of birds. My father taught me to recognize birds by their calls. Here in Montana, I'm at a loss, Cait."

I pointed to the juniper down by the driveway, "Well, that one with the yellow breast and the sweet song is a meadowlark, which is Montana's state bird. Over there on that tree is a red winged blackbird. These little birds with long beaks that act like my cabin is their house are house wrens." I pointed to the spruce nearby my cabin. "They're bossy little things, they fly back and forth from the spruce to my cabin complaining about me being on my own front porch. If it helps, I can teach you the ones I know."

Ross watched the wrens for a bit and chuckled softly, "That'd be sweet as. Ta, Cait."

Earlier there had been light rains around six and the heavy clouds from the brief storm were still lingering, texturing the clouds overhead, purplish blue hues mixed with shades of gray and white. Wet Montana sage had a distinctive odor, and the pure mountain air after a rain was heavenly. Unfortunately, the storm had not lasted long enough to reduce the fire danger. At least there had not been much lightning. August storms in Montana were problematic. Dry lightning with no moisture was every Montanan's nightmare during fire season.

The combination of recent rains and late-evening sunshine produced the most vivid colors on the foothills and the mountains along both sides of the Madison Valley. Some parts of the valley, such as the geological terraces down along the Madison River, were in shadow; other parts were in full sunlight, depending on the position of the clouds. As far as I could see, all these ribbons of sunlight and dark shadows made an exquisite patchwork. For me, nothing matched the beauty of the changing evening landscape of my home country, especially after a storm. Grandpa always said he could never be bored watching the light and shadows change in Montana of an evening. "TV and theater are for city folks," Grandpa would say, "Give me the skies of Montana any day for entertainment."

"Would you like something to drink, before we go?" I asked Ross.

"That would be lovely."

"Locally brewed ale, okay?"

Ross nodded. I went into the cabin and came back out with two raspberry ales. I handed one to him. We sat on the front porch stairs where I perched on the top step with Ross sitting to my right, two steps below me. He was awfully close, so I pulled on the hem of my short skirt, regretting my choice of attire for the second time that evening. Ross took a good long swallow of his ale and leaned backwards towards me with his elbows braced on the step below me. After a few minutes he said, "Well, the view is spectacular, the company charming, but this beer is awful. What is this shit, Cait?"

"I like it," I said defensively.

Ross leaned over on his elbow and twisted to look up at me. The sun highlighted his curly hair and I heard his leather jacket rustle when he moved. The evening breeze brought a whiff of his cologne. With his stubbled cheek inches from my bare thigh, he replied, "I don't."

I stuck out my tongue at him.

Ross laughed. "Hey, Cait, you can't ride my motorcycle in this short skirt. Too dangerous." Ross ran his forefinger playfully along the side of my thigh, starting at the knee. His face was still only about an inch away from my bare thigh. I could feel the warmth of his breath on my bare skin in the cooler evening air. Ross's traveling finger was almost to the hem of my skirt when I put my hand on top of it, halting his upward advances.

"Okay. I guess I'll have to change," I said, firmly moving his finger off my leg at the same time. I was desperately trying to ignore my loins' involuntary reaction to Ross's physical proximity to my bare thigh and the suggestive movement of his finger. *Good grief. Why couldn't my mind control my body? How could my body betray me like this?*

"Don't do that. I like the skirt. We'll take your truck,

instead. Ready to go?" Ross stood up swiftly and offered me a hand up. I took his outstretched hand and he handed me back the bottle, three-quarters full. "Sorry, luv, I'll hold out for real beer."

"I don't care." I turned away abruptly and went inside to get the truck keys, clean myself up, change my underwear, and retrieve my jacket. I worked really fast. *Get control, Cait. Take control. You can do this. Everything will be fine. Evidence of body betrayal removed. You've got this. Believe. Breathe.* I locked up the cabin and walked down to the truck. Ross was walking around it, running his fingers over the rounded detailing along the truck bed that ended in the rear taillight. He looked up at me, "'58 Apache. Sweet as a bikkie."

"You know your trucks."

"I do. What are these scratches from?" Ross asked, while running his forefinger along the multiple scratches on the driver's side.

"A bear trying to get into Jake's truck about 40 years ago due to out-of-state idiots who left food in the truck in bear country, despite being told not to. My grandpa always said, 'Be careful who you ride with. Fools will get you killed.' Or in this case, damage your beautiful truck."

Ross chuckled, "Well, Cait, there's no shortage of fuckwits where I come from. Some folks are just several bubbles off of level and you have to stay clear of them. Your grandpa sounds like a wise fella."

I got in behind the wheel feeling somewhat mollified. At least Ross appreciated my truck and my grandpa's wisdom, even if he didn't like my taste in ales. I rolled the window down on the driver's side. Ross leaned in with his arms on the door. "Move over. I've always wanted to drive one of these."

I moved over and Ross slid in behind the wheel in a fluid movement. "Am I safe with you driving?" I asked.

"Nah, nobody's safe with me," he said grinning.

"Oh, great," I replied with a smile. "But, I trust you won't be throwing watermelon rinds behind my juniper trees."

"Nah, I'm not that stupid. I grew up in the bush." Ross winked at me. "Say, Cait, what's with the number plate?"

"2 Lazy 2? It's a family joke. When I was little, I thought all places out of town were ranches and Grandpa laughed at me, saying this land was only good for raising gophers. Grandpa used this as his base for hunting and fishing. He ranched over near Bozeman. I was so disappointed that this wasn't a real ranch, Grandpa humored me and told me to figure out a brand for our new gopher ranch. My brother Mark came up with 2 Lazy 2. Too lazy to fence in the property, too lazy to dig a well, too lazy to run stock, too lazy to whatever. I love vanity license plates. Montanans have taken them to a fine art. Vanity plates around here can be very creative, unlike the incredibly boring monograph plates in Illinois where people put their names or their initials on their cars. How lame can you get? You'll see a lot of vanity plates in Bozeman. Watch for them."

"We have personalized number plates in Australia."

Ross drove slowly so he could look around. In fact, he drove so slowly the dogs at the Alexander ranch below were confused. They made a game out of chasing the few cars and trucks that passed by the ranch house. The three of them would wait in the tall grass by the side of the road under the old wagon Mr. Alexander kept in his front yard. When a vehicle got within range, they would come racing out onto the road and put up a fine chase. The Chevy was going much slower than they anticipated and their rhythm was thrown off. Ross, laughing at them through the open window, did not help their dignity any. When I turned around to look back, they were sitting in the middle of the road looking befuddled. I told Ross he wasn't being sporting. He was supposed to drive faster. He grinned, tilting his head sideways, and in the natural light I could see the long thin scar under his jaw line. I reached over and traced it lightly with my forefinger, wondering why I had not noticed it before, when I realized Ross always sat on the right side of me. He had done it in the bar and again tonight on my porch.

"What's this scar from?" I asked.

Ross slowed the truck down and looked directly at me. "I'll tell you my scar story if you tell me yours." His expression and tone reminded me of a small boy daring another. Having thrown out the challenge, he then accelerated, returning his attention to the road as it got rougher.

I involuntarily covered my right wrist with my left hand, my mind racing. How could Ross know about the scar under my beaded bracelet? Had Frank told him? Frank would not betray a confidence. I hadn't ever said anything. Maybe, Ross really didn't mean anything by the remark. We all have scars. I had no intention of telling him about my wrist. *Come on Cait, get a grip. Any scar story will do.* I studied Ross's profile. He was concentrating on his driving because we were getting to the section of the road that was extremely rutted from the summer's lack of rain. The vibrations of vehicles traveling at constant speeds over the unpaved roads caused the evenly spaced ruts. Grandpa referred to these resulting road conditions as washboards. Driving was tricky. Drive too slow and the jarring rattled your innards. Drive too fast and you could lose control going around the corners. Ross was searching for the optimum speed. When we came down out of the foothills, along North Meadow Creek, Ross had to drive right next to the edge of the road because the county road grader had been at work that afternoon. There was a big pile of dirt containing sharp chunks of rocks running down the middle of the road.

I thought of a story I could tell Ross, guaranteed to distract him, just in case he had noticed me touch my wrist. "All right, you go first."

Ross started, "When I was five, I got too close to a horse's hindquarters and she kicked at me. She didn't make contact, but I lost my balance and fell onto the edge of my shovel. My father had warned me to stop mucking around, but I didn't listen. Probably the only reason, I'm still alive. Knocked some sense into me. Before that, I was a holy terror. Deep cut. Dad did bloody good first aid."

"I never noticed your scar in the movie."

"No, you wouldn't. They cover it up with makeup or shoot from the other side."

"Does it bother you?"

"No. Why should it? Best thing that ever happened to me. After that, when Dad told me to do something, I paid attention. Your turn, Cait."

I was nervous. I was not convinced I should be telling Ross this story, but it was preferable to the possibility of being asked about my reaction to his challenge. My delivery was rapid fire, "I was taking Intro Psych as a freshman and we had to do labs with white rats. I didn't like rats, at all. The lab instructors showed us how to handle them. You can't pick them up by the tip of their tails because their tails can break off. You can't just scoop them up either, because they're instinctually afraid of anything coming down on them from above. You have to pick them up by the base of the tail and flip them up on your arm. You have to keep your arm next to your body so the rats feel secure, and you use your other arm to block them from climbing. Rats are always looking for higher ground. And you can't lose your cool, because then the rats get scared and start pissing. Anyway, I forgot. The rat was on my arm, but I didn't block its climbing. I kept leaning backward, away from the rat, and the rat kept going up until he was on my shoulder. I was wearing a V-neck sweater. The rat went down my front. I lost it. I started screaming. The only part of the rat I could see was the tip of its tail sticking straight up out of my sweater. My lab partner freaked out and he wouldn't help me. The instructor had to come over, and reach down inside my sweater, and grab the rat firmly by the base of the tail and yank him out. The rat didn't want to come out. He left scratch marks on both my breasts. And they hurt."

"Do you still have scars?"

"Small ones." I thought maybe Ross would make some off-color remark or say something sympathetic. But he didn't. He didn't say anything. The silence grew. Damn. I never should have told Ross that story. It wasn't even my story, although I had witnessed it. Why did I lie? I was such an idiot. I looked out the side window, wishing I was somewhere else.

In the stillness, as Ross drove my truck, I noticed that he kept his hands on the steering wheel the way Grandpa said you should drive on rough gravel roads—thumbs close to your forefingers, sort of like a swimmer's hands, so if the wheel moves suddenly due to a rut or pothole in the road your thumbs will not get broken, which is particularly essential in a vehicle without power steering like my old Apache. As we reached pavement near Grandma's old elementary school, not far from where South Meadow Creek crossed the North Meadow Creek road, I couldn't help but notice how smoothly Ross shifted gears. If I had not seen his hand move the stick, I never would have known my truck had shifted into a higher gear, because his release of the clutch and his acceleration were so smoothly coordinated I couldn't feel anything. I found the artistry of his shifting warmly seductive, and in our silence I admired his tanned hands. Ross had large, beautifully shaped hands with long fingers which reminded me of other men I had known in my life who were carpenters, potters, or guitarists where male hands widened and strengthened from physical labor. While I found talking to Ross unsettling, being with him while he skillfully drove my truck down the roads of my childhood was oddly calming—a contradiction I couldn't reconcile.

When we reached the intersection to go down to the Bear Claw, Ross made a sharp left and then accelerated into his turn. *Cold darkness was everywhere. My shoulder hurt. My heart beat rapidly. A predator was stalking us. Ross was driving my Chevy rapidly, skidding into gravel.* The darkness of my premonition dissipated as my Chevy passed the sign for the Meadow Creek cemetery where my grandparents and their three infant sons were buried. I looked at Ross and he glanced my way while flashing one of his electric rapid smiles animating his entire face. I knew without a doubt in that moment, my grandparents would have approved of Ross because he knew how to drive Montana roads skillfully in Jake's old truck. I heard my grandpa's voice, *"He's a good man, Cait. He'll keep you safe."* The old Methodist white clapboard church with its gold dome atop the narrow steeple came into view between the cottonwoods lining the Meadow Creek road and I focused on keeping my breathing steady, trying not to think about my premonition of darkness, skidding 1958 Chevys, and an injured shoulder, or my grandfather's reassuring message.

Frank raised an eyebrow in greeting when Ross and I walked into the Bear Claw together, but he made no other reaction to my dinner companion. I asked for a table in the back because I wanted to eat without Frank circling around like a herding border collie. The silence between Ross and me in the pickup had been awkward enough. I was looking around the bar to see if I knew anyone. Where were Jake and Ike when you needed them? Maybe I could ease my discomfort if I could find someone familiar to talk with for a few minutes. I could excuse my behavior, because Montanans always take time to talk to their neighbors. When Montanans come into a restaurant, everyone looks up to see if they need to say hello. It wouldn't be acceptable to be rude to your neighbor, but outsiders find the practice odd. The only familiar face was Frank's, and talking to him would only make me feel worse. He clearly did not approve of my dating Ross. I could tell by his silence when we entered the bar. We went back into the dining room, and Ross did not sit across from me where the waitress put the menu, he sat next to me, to the right, with his facial scar away from me. Under the table, his knee was firmly touching mine. We both examined our menus, although I found it hard to concentrate because I kept reflecting on my premonition while coming around the corner onto the Meadow Creek road. Grandpa had never spoken to me from beyond the grave, why now? Ross broke into my reflection by asking me how I knew the bartender.

"Oh, Frank's my neighbor and my godfather. He was very close to my grandfather. Sort of the son Grandpa never had."

"He looks at me like I'm going kill his sheep."

"Frank's protective of me, that's true. He's the only

family I have left in Montana."

"What's his last name again?"

"O'Neill."

"Does he have any cousins or brothers around here?"

"Frank's from Wyoming. I don't think he has any family. That's why my grandparents took him in. My grandparents had buried three stillborn sons and they kind of adopted Frank."

"When was that?"

"Let's see, my mother was 12 and Frank was 14, so it must have been sometime around 1946, 1947. Grandpa needed help on the ranch. He hired Frank for the summer, and then Grandma and Grandpa asked if he would like to stay on through the winter. They couldn't pay him, but they offered room, board, and a chance to finish school. Grandma was insistent on that part. Frank rode the bus into school with my mother and when he graduated down in Bozeman, he enlisted to fight in the Korean War. I don't know when he came back to work with my grandfather again. You'd have to ask Frank. He never talks about those years."

"Was he in Australia in 1959?"

"I don't think he's ever been to Australia."

"He has."

"How do you know that?"

Ross's face was a complete blank. He shrugged, refusing to answer me, as if I had asked a stupid question not worthy of a response.

"Why the interest in Frank?"

"Doing research. Just getting to know Montanans."

I changed the subject, "When does your movie start filming?"

"After Labor Day." Ross smiled.

"Why are you here so early?"

"I came a month early to iron out some details, plus I like to learn accents. It's fun to absorb some local color. You're pretty absorbing."

I gave him a fake smile. That explains it. I had not taken the older women make superior lovers line seriously. Ross was doing research. Being the topic of his research meant I did not have to worry about his wanting anything else from me. Something I couldn't deliver.

"Well, in that case, you should meet Jake and Ike, the two ranchers that were distracting Frank last night when I got you your beer. Remember them?"

Ross nodded.

"Between the two of them, they have lots and lots of local stories, most of which are drop dead funny. I can introduce you to them, sometime."

"Ta, Cait. That'd be brilliant."

I relaxed, thinking about Frank's litmus test for outsiders. Frank maintained you could predict how long newcomers would last in the valley by how attentive they were in listening to Madison County stories. Frank was amazingly accurate in his predictions. I wondered how high Ross would score on Frank's test. I asked about his latest project, "What's your movie about?"

Ross brightened. "It's an old-fashioned Western entitled *North to Montana*. It's about the first commercial cattle drive to Montana from Texas in the 1860s. Nelson Story ... ."

"You're joking."

"No. Why would I do that?"

"My best friend's husband is descended from one of the cowboys who rode with Story. Luke knows all about that cattle drive. He dresses up as Nelson every time the

Pioneer Museum has its cemetery walk. Luke stands by the Story marker and tells all the good stories. His wife does Lady Blackmore. Would you like to meet them? They live up the canyon outside of Bozeman, next door to my grandparents' old place. Luke breeds cutting horses and Jo's an artist. She made my bracelet. I could take you over to Bozeman and show you all the Story landmarks."

"I'd be keen to meet your friends, Cait. That'd be sweet as. Ring me up. I'm staying at the Lone Mountain Motel in Ennis."

I smiled and agreed to call him. Ross continued talking about the movie, "When I was in Dakota, my sister sent me a book called *The Greatest Cattle Drive*. I loved the skies in Dakota, so this story gave me a reason to come back to the West. Two ranchers from Hamilton, Montana, wrote the script for me. I'm a little nervous, but I'm working with a great crew. Most of them were on the Ireland shoot, and Mike Turner is an old friend of mine. Plus, the script is in great shape. The job is so much easier if the script is in place at the beginning. I don't much like it when the script is being rewritten the night before the scenes are shot."

"This is an independent film. There's no big studio behind it, but I truly love classic Westerns. I don't give a damn about commercial viability or changing the characters to enhance the likelihood of getting critical acclaim. I don't make movies for the critics; I make them for the audience." Ross looked self-conscious at this point. "The other reason I'm double-stoked about doing this movie is that I get to work with Hollywood's newest star, Heather Adams." He smiled at me. "All my Christmases have come at once."

I was remembering Ross's physical transformation for Father Paddy. "Are you going to have to gain weight?"

Ross looked puzzled. "Why would I need to have an

awning over the toy shop to direct a movie, Cait?"

Then he grinned as his booted foot stroked my calf under the table. I could feel the silky smoothness of expensive leather on my bare skin. Ross winked at me and continued, "I think you missed something. I'm not playing the lead, Mike Turner is. I'm directing this picture. It's my first time. I'm what they call a virgin director."

For the second time that evening, I felt like a complete idiot. Awning over the toy shop? What did that mean? I was not going to ask. *First time? Virgin director?* How did I miss that Ross was directing not acting? I couldn't think straight with Ross's boot rubbing my calf. *Oh. No.* Now, I understood the meaning of the Aussie slang expression. I shifted position away from the suggestive movement of his foot. I hoped I wasn't blushing. Thank goodness, my loins were not staging their own rebellion again. I could concentrate as long as Ross wasn't touching me while making sexual innuendos.

I asked him, "How old is your son?"

"Fifteen."

"What's he like?" I was recalling Ross's account of his scar because he had failed to listen to his father.

"He's a good boy."

"Not a holy terror like his dad?" I asked playfully.

A mask came down across Ross's face, darkening it like the shadowed Montana landscape when a cloud passes across the sun. He became still. His eyes locked mine. When Ross released my gaze, he jerked his head slightly before answering, "No."

I didn't understand his reaction, but talking was preferable to another long silence. "Where does he live?"

"With my ex."

"Are your parents still living?"

"No. Where are your parents, Cait?"

"Canada." It was my turn to be defensive and reticent.

"Do you see them very often, Cait?"

"No." I needed to control this conversation. I asked, "Do you have any other family in Australia, Ross?"

"Yes."

"Do they have children?"

"Yes."

"Do you visit your family often?"

"Not often enough."

I tried a slightly different tact. "Do you get home very often?"

"Define home." His face was a total blank.

"Well, there's the philosophical answer and the mundane answer. Sometimes, they describe the same place, like for me when I was a child. I have always considered Montana my home in the philosophical sense, because it's the only place where my heart and soul are at rest. The mundane answer doesn't address the spiritual. It's more practical, it's where you keep your stuff. Right now, my home is Montana in both the mundane and the philosophical sense." I said the last statement firmly. I took a breath and looked Ross directly in the eye and asked with determination, "So. Ross. Where do you keep your stuff?"

"I carry it with me."

"All of it?"

"No. My family has my horses."

"Don't you have an apartment or a house somewhere?"

"No."

"Are you serious?"

"Yes. Why would I make jokes about something like that."

"And your heart and soul? Where are they at rest, Ross?"

I asked gently, thinking about his lonely lifestyle.

"On the four winds, Cait. I'm a *peregrinatio pro Christo*, a guest upon the world."

"A what?" I frowned. Ross shrugged and offered no explanation for the Latin phrase. I guessed it was Latin. "Okay, when was the last time you saw your family?"

"This past summer."

"When was the last time you were in Australia?"

"Are you deaf, Cait? I told you. This past summer." Ross started tapping his fingers on the table.

I was too stubborn to give up. I tried a different angle of questioning instead. "Have you seen him since your divorce?"

"Whom?"

"Your son." I tried, but I could not keep the exasperation out of my voice.

"Yes, I've seen him." Ross was reacting to my frustration. "What are you implying, Cait? That I'm a bad father?"

I decided not to react to the challenge about responsible parenting by changing the subject. "Last night, you said I've changed. What did you mean by that?"

Ross shifted in his chair so he could look directly at me. At least, he had stopped that dreadful tapping. I felt trapped in his gaze. I dropped my head. I waited, fiddling with my bracelet, discomfort growing in my stomach. When I looked up from my hands, Ross was still watching me.

"This isn't my first time in McAllister. I was here last summer for about two weeks spotting locations, doing research in Bozeman. I sat in the corner of the bar most evenings and watched you with O'Neill. One night, you waited tables and you served me. You've changed."

"How?"

Ross shrugged, "Well, you're talking to me for one thing. And you smile more."

I did not want to think about the fact Ross had watched me for two weeks last summer in the Bear Claw without my realizing it. Maybe it was safer to ask some more questions about his family. "What about your parents, Ross?"

"What about them?" Ross was back to tapping his fingers on the table top.

"When did they die?"

"Fifteen years ago."

"Both of them?"

"Yes."

This was hopeless. I hadn't really wanted to come to dinner in the first place. I had only come because I thought Ross needed company. I didn't have to put up with his awful tapping. I stood up out of my chair and said, "Look, Mr. Sutherland, this was your idea. I don't have to put up with your nonsense. Give me back my truck keys."

"Ah, Cait. I'm sorry I was rude. You're a writer. I have to remember not to treat you like one. Please don't leave."

I sat back down, perched halfway on my chair, ready to exit.

Ross explained, "When my wife was pregnant, I had to do a lot of publicity for *The Last Man*. I got so tired of answering the same questions over and over and over again." He did a good imitation of a female American reporter. He nailed the intonations and the accent. "'How do you feel about becoming a father?' What a stupid question. I thought I was going to jump out of a window I was so bored, so frustrated. But I wanted the movie to do well, so I started learning how to cope with the press. I learned to deflect questions I didn't like. I learned to answer only the part of the question I wanted to answer. I learned to interview the journos. It's amazing how many people are starved for a good audience, a fine pair of ears. People tell me all sorts of stuff. It's a helluva lot more interesting for me to interview journos rather than listening to myself say the same old thing over and over again. So, Cait, I'd rather listen to your stories. You can read mine in magazines. I *am* sorry for being such a bastard. Forgive me? Please?"

I nodded, repositioning myself and my chair under the table. Ross's knee found mine again. This time, I didn't move away, I pressed back, maintaining the contact. I made a mental note to read the next magazine story that I saw on Ross Larkin Sutherland. I wondered why Ross was so defensive about his family. I had secrets. Apparently, Ross did too.

The waitress brought our salads and we ate in silence. When Ross was done with his, he asked me, "Why did your marriage fail, Cait?"

Ross's question caught me off guard. Talking to Ross reminded me of Montana weather. Half the time, you couldn't predict what was going to blow in, so you always had to be ready for anything. I could remember days when I was a child when the temperature would plummet 50 degrees in a matter of a few hours if the wind started blowing out of the east. I wasn't ready for this, though. Why should I talk about my marriage? I had not asked Ross about his. But he'd just apologized and I didn't want to argue with him, anymore. I did not want to tell Ross about my hatred of my father, about the sexual abuse that had started when I was 12, or about my anger towards my mother. I had self-control. I exercised it. I told Ross another lie to distract him. Hopefully, this one would go better than the last one.

"Q-tips."

I had his full attention. "Q-tips?" he repeated. Wrinkles were deepening across his forehead.

"Yeah, you know Ross, those things you use to clean your ears, the sticks with cotton wrapped on the ends." I was starting to enjoy myself. I was getting exactly the reaction I wanted. Ross was not disappointing me.

"Oh, you mean cotton buds. I know what Q-tips are used for. What I don't know is what the bloody hell you're talking about." Ross was glowering at me for the second time that evening.

Ross might have intimidated me again, if he hadn't resembled Frank, who taught me to play ruthless cribbage. When I visited my grandparents as a child, Frank was often there too. He had spent many long, snowy winter evenings with me, playing cards and telling me endless stories. I was young and I loved the attention. I loved Frank. He was a gentleman. My fond memories of Frank and my grandfather served me well in my life, because they reminded me men could be decent. They could be kind. They could be loving.

When we played cards, Frank would tell me tall tales with a perfect poker face. He pulled my leg so often, I had to learn how to tell when he was kidding. I was a stubborn little kid, full of pride, and I hated not knowing when Frank was serious and when he was not. I started to watch his face intently, studying him, remembering every detail to match the expressions against the stories. I learned to watch for the telltale wrinkles around the corners of a man's eyes when he told a joke. I learned to watch for the twinkle of the light off the iris. Frank taught me to play a mean game of cribbage.

Frank liked to test your knowledge of the rules. He liked to test your concentration. He also liked to intimidate his opponents at cards. If you were winning, he would glower at you. With his size, he was scary, except it was all an act. Frank was a tease. As a hotshot firefighter, he had all the macho traits down to a fine art. When I was a toddler, Frank traveled across the country from region to region during fire season. Watching Ross sitting next to me in the soft light of the Bear Claw dining room, I was remembering Frank and our card games. I watched Ross carefully when I told him my Q-tip story. I watched his face, his body, his eyes. Testing him, to see if Ross could take it as well as he could dish it out.

"Ralph got mad at me because I went over the yearly allotment of Q-tips." I paused.

"Caitlinn." His voice was stern, but I was watching and his eyes were giving him away. They were twinkling and tiny laugh lines were gathering around the edges. He growled, "Finish the story."

I was having a hard time keeping a straight face. "Ralph had a huge box of Q-tips when we got married. I didn't think anything of it. I just used them. We had that box for years. One day, he got all upset because his Q-tip box was gone. Apparently, he thought he was set for life with that one box. He was genuinely upset. He wanted to know how we could have used up the entire box. I told him we used them on ears, on belly buttons, and stuff like that. He actually started adding up how many Q-tips I possibly could have used and the numbers weren't working. Ralph was mathematical; he graduated in engineering. I finally had to admit to the Q-tip experiment."

I paused again and waited. Ralph craved control and order in his life. Years of working as a manager of production operations had made him obsessive about sources of variability. If there was an assignable source of variability in product production, you dealt with it. You never ignored it. In quality control applications you eliminated identifiable variability. That's how you maintained high quality. The manager in Ralph wanted to get the process that was me back under statistical control. His engineered solution was brute force. Whenever I varied from Ralph's idea of proper behavior, I paid the consequences.

"Caitlinn, finish your story. What was the Q-tip experiment?" Ross's reaction brought me back to the present. His voice was low. His eyes had narrowed and darkened. He turned up the negative energy and gave me his best glowering performance.

I waited for exactly the right amount of time before explaining. "Vaseline and Q-tips. The old exploding Q-tips routine. You put Vaseline on the end of the Q-tip, work it around to flatten the cotton end and stick them on your body. It's a gag I learned from a late-night talk show. A comedian got bored at a party and came staggering out of the host's bathroom with Q-tips stuck on his face and backs of his hands, claiming there had been a horrific accident. The Q-tip box exploded. I just tested it out. It works. If you use enough Vaseline and break the Q-tips in half, they really will stick out on your body like porcupine quills." I stated my conclusions adamantly in my best instructional tone.

Ross started laughing. He slid down in his chair. His ears got red; he was laughing so hard. When he recovered, his eyes were soft. I was relieved.

"Caitlinn, you are absolutely mental. I don't believe you about the cotton buds. You'll have to show me." Ross had an obnoxious expression. "I don't believe they'll stick up all over your body like a porcupine." Just as rapidly, his expression changed as he thought of something else. "But why did Ralph spit the dummy? What was his problem?"

"Ralph claimed he needed a constant. He claimed it was important to be able to count on something in this life full of change. Ralph's box of Q-tips was his constant and I had violated it with my nonsense."

Ross was shaking his head. He started running his hand through his thick brown curls. He was bouncing his leg up and down under the table. I could feel the vibrations. "Well, I dunno, Cait, sounds to me like your ex was a couple of stubbies short of a six pack."

A different waitress, dressed in a tight short skirt, came by with our entrees. Frank had just hired her yesterday. I hadn't met her yet. Frank liked slender women with great legs, and most of his wait staff wore skirts when they served tables for dinner. Under cross examination, my godfather had confessed to me that he wanted a certain look on the dining room floor to keep the well-heeled customers coming back. He had blushed deep shades of red when I confronted him on his sexism, but based upon this new hire, my accusation had not altered his criteria for evening female servers. The new waitress didn't know who I was, but she recognized Ross. I could tell by the way she looked at him. She didn't say anything, though. I detached, content to observe Ross interacting with another woman. He looked directly at her whenever she asked questions, and I noticed he watched her longer than he needed to as she walked away. Apparently, Ross like Frank, noticed women who had shapely legs. Ralph never paid any attention to waitresses, regardless of their body type or attire. Ralph was a snob when it came to social class and considered wait staff unworthy of his attention, unless he wanted something, and then he became rude and demanding. I asked Ross about the hazards of being recognized in public.

"That's nothing, Cait. That's what I like about Montana. I can breathe here. I feel like an ordinary fella again. You have no idea how special that is. It's like a gift from the heavens, like rain on the outback. Other places, all hell can break loose if some fan is a fuckwit goin' troppo. I need that like I need a third armpit. That's the worst thing about being famous. People can act very odd. I learned to be boring and not stand out in a crowd."

I agreed, "Montanans figure you'll tell them what they need to know. That, unfortunately, is one of the reasons the crazy people come out here to hide. We don't ask enough questions of them. I think it's part of the Western experience. What matters here in Montana, is the measure of who the person is, not their reputation or their monetary worth. As the cowboys say, when a life or death situation comes up you want to ride with someone you can trust."

Ross nodded; he knew what I meant. "Aussies don't much like it if you ask too many questions, either." He winked at me, maybe to acknowledge that he had not appreciated my inquiries into his personal life.

"Tell me about your novel, Cait."

"I'm writing a historical romance set in Butte, Montana, about two Irish families. At the turn of the century Butte was one of the most ethnically diverse cities in the West and a Gibraltar of Unionism. The Irish dominated, though. My story is set against the backdrop of the War of the Copper Kings that altered Montana's future forever and that of the U.S. as well. Do you know why we have direct election of senators?"

"Nah, Cait, I'm an Aussie, remember. You yanks are so ethnocentric."

"Sorry, it's because William Clark, one of the three

Copper Kings, bought his way into the U.S. Senate. He reportedly spent ½ million dollars in 1899 to get elected by the legislature. The whole country was scandalized by the way mining interests were buying their way onto the national stage. Standard Oil bought out the Anaconda Copper Company which was owned by Marcus Daly, and that began the outside control of copper in the state. The copper company owned most of the newspapers in Montana until 1959. Other states talk of company towns. Montana was a company state. It's part of the reason Montanans don't care about what happens outside their borders; for years their news was controlled, and they only read what the company wanted them to know."

Ross interrupted, "Well, Cait, I can tell you're interested in this topic, but it sounds pretty boring to me. Your novel better have lots of good sex in it to hold my interest."

Dealing with college students, I had learned to be gentle with my feedback. Ross was not wasting any energy on being gentle. He looked at me steadily, reaching over to rest his hand lightly on my right wrist, "Have you seen all my movies, Cait?"

I shook my head.

"Well, luv, most of them are bloody awful. Can't score a goal with every kick."

Ross withdrew his hand and tilted his chair on its rear legs, watching me before speaking again, "Cait, what's the emotional core of your novel?"

"How the landscape affects people and alters their behavior, and how the people betray the landscape."

Ross released his chair back down to the floor with a thud and said, with enthusiasm, "Good onya, Cait. Very Australian. Just remember, we don't always get a second chance in this life to explain ourselves. Make the first chance count. Work on your synopsis. It should be a carrot that entices the questioner to ask for more details, to ask for the second carrot. You didn't offer me any carrots; you just did a mind-numbing detail dump. Gibraltar of Unionism? What the bloody hell is that? Ya know Cait, maybe the Aussie bunnies stole your carrots." Ross was imitating a bunny eating a carrot.

I laughed. Ross was being so ridiculous with his imitation of a bunny stealing my carrots that I could not stay peeved at him. He reminded me of my brother Mark, who also teased me when I was too serious.

Ross became quiet again and sat still, watching me for a while. He leaned over the table towards me braced on his elbows and in a low voice asked, "Why *do* you write, Cait?"

"To reduce the sense of isolation people feel. Modern society is compartmentalized—everyone living in their little boxes of space, not connecting to the land, not connecting to each other. Music has always helped me cope with personal loss. I would like to be able to connect to others the way my favorite songs connect to me in my pain, the way Father Paddy connected to me when I needed inspiration and motivation."

Ross nodded. "The power of a good narrative to stir the heart and feed the spirit. I don't work to entertain; I work to communicate. There's a big difference." He paused, tilted his head sideways, chewing on the edge of his lower lip. He took his hand away from his chin and pointed his forefinger briefly at me before continuing. "Ya, know," he leaned back in his chair looking at me intensely with his hands folded across his abdomen, "That was a great compliment, Cait. It means a lot to me."

It was close to midnight when we left. We were the last customers to leave the dining area. We walked through the front bar area, which was completely empty with all the chairs turned upside down on the tables for the nightly mopping of the floor. Frank must have been in the kitchen, because I could hear familiar voices. During the almost four hours Ross and I had spent talking, Frank had walked through the dining area several times, checking up on me. I ignored him. Frank never walked through the dining room area during business hours. He trusted his staff once he had them trained up. He always concentrated his time behind the bar keeping the regulars happy in the front room. I knew exactly what Frank was doing, walking through the dining room—being nosey. I was enjoying Ross's company. I found his outrageous flirtation exhilarating, but mostly I enjoyed his insights on religion, creativity, and storytelling. I had not had anybody to talk ideas with for such a long time. I hadn't realized how hungry my mind was for the delightful satisfaction of stimulating conversation. Frank wasn't much for talking. Jake and Ike were amusing, but they didn't talk ideas; they talked about fishing and hunting when they weren't telling stories about the old days. Jo and I mostly talked about children, cooking, crafts, and gardening. We certainly did not discuss art authentication, spiritual reasons for listening with your whole body, or the importance of the narrative. I did not need my godfather interfering with or judging my spending time with Ross, so I was relieved that Frank was nowhere to be seen when Ross and I left.

The moon was waxing, but still bright enough to illuminate the landscape on the way home. Ross kept the speed down as we headed up the Meadow Creek road past the old church. Before the split into the North and South forks, the paved part of the Meadow Creek road tended to have big potholes, and Ross was not taking any risks.

As we started up into the foothills after the Alexander ranch, a jackrabbit appeared in front of us. He crossed the road halfway and then started hopping right down the middle. Ross slowed down, waiting for the rabbit to do the sensible thing and get off the road. But the rabbit did not, he hopped faster, staying just in front of us. Ross commented, "I dunno Cait, I like Montana women, but you have the stupidest animals out here. Of course, maybe he reckons you'll toss him a carrot, one of those you left out of your novel description."

I groaned. "Oh, please, you're never going to let me forget that are you?"

Ross laughed. As if on cue, the jackrabbit had abandoned the road for the safety of the sagebrush.

I asked Ross to stop just before the bend in the road by Frank's place. "Turn off the headlights. Look, the moon is so bright you can see your moon shadow. My brother and I used to go for bike rides in the moonlight."

"Do you have any bikes up at the cabin?"

"I've got one."

"Is it a man's bike?"

"Yup."

"Brilliant." Ross started up the truck again before I could ask him what he had in mind. He drove the truck up to the cabin. "Where's the bike?"

"It's in the shed. Let me get you the key."

I opened up the front door, turned the lantern on, and tossed the key to the shed to Ross. He caught it with one hand, disappearing around the corner of the cabin. He returned with my late brother's bicycle, which I had recently fixed up. "Hop on," he said, patting the bar. "Ride sidesaddle."

"With this skirt? You're kidding, right?"

"Wrong. Hurry up, Cait, you're wasting precious riding time. Nobody can see up your skirt except the jackrabbit and he's too busy hunting the missing carrots you left out of your novel synopsis. Stop stressing. Put your hand on my shoulder. I'll hold the bike steady, you'll be right. Once we get going, keep one hand on me and the other on the center of the handlebars. All you are meant to do is keep your body centered over the bike frame, I'll do the hard yakka."

Ross helped me get balanced. I did what he asked of me, remembering my brother Mark teaching me how to place my feet on the stones to cross the creek safely when I was little. Ross knew what he was doing, so I quit worrying and started enjoying myself. The velvet night embraced us. Watching our moon shadow following along beside us was hypnotic. Back up on the far side of the mountain, a coyote howled and a dog from the ranch below answered back. I could hear the trucks going over the Norris Hill, shifting down working their way up the 7.5 percent grade five miles away.

At the end of the road, Ross slowed down. "Now, when I stop, Caitlinn, you have to jump off quick smart."

I did, and Ross laid the bike by the side of the road. I was standing looking south towards Ennis. The whole valley stretched before us. Here and there, lights twinkled back. I could hear Ross come up behind me, his boots crunching on the gravel. I stayed put. His moon shadow merged with mine. Ross put his arms around my waist, drawing me closer. "It's lovely up here. Have a listen, Caitlinn, I want you to know how much I enjoy your company. I like the way you make me feel."

"How do I make you feel, Ross?" I leaned back into his embrace.

"Relaxed and comfy, Cait."

"Oh, like old clothes?"

Ross turned me around to face him, in lieu of a response. He held my face in his hands and kissed me gently and slowly. Stroking my loose hair back from my face, he brushed my forehead with his lips, "Thank you for tonight, Caitlinn."

We rode back to the cabin in silence. Ross put Mark's bicycle back in the shed. We said goodnight in the moonlight. I stood on the front steps and watched his red tail-lights weave up around the bends in the road and disappear. I went straight to bed and fell asleep immediately.

Prelude

I have gathered these stories afar,
In the wind and the rain,
In the land where the cattle camps are,
On the edge of the plain.
On the overland routes of the west,
When the watches were long,
I have fashioned in earnest and jest
These fragments of song.

They are just the rude stories one hears,
In sadness and mirth,
The records of wandering years,
And scant is their worth
Though their merits indeed are but slight
I shall not repine,
If they give you one moment's delight,
Old comrades of mine.[8]

Banjo Patterson

~ Chapter 14 ~

I had trouble staying asleep. Each time I woke up, I listened carefully to the night noises, but there were only the usual sounds. Not like the long ago night when a pair of owls landed in the upstairs loft window, scratching their claws against the glass as they flew into their evening perch. I was staying with my grandparents my sixth summer. I had been afraid. I had lain in bed in the loft working up the nerve to look outside. When I did, I was eye to eye with some strange creature. Half of an owl's face was peering back at me, with his mate cuddled up beside him. I told my grandparents the next morning that I initially thought the clawing sound was a bear. Grandpa found the image of a bear scratching on a second story window quite funny and made jokes about bears on ladders at my expense the rest of the summer. I was not afraid now; I had been through too many lonely nights. I was curious, however. I got up and looked out the back window. There were no owls, no bears, only the familiar dark outlines of the shed and the trees. I went back to bed, but my sleep was fitful.

At dawn's first light, I gave up trying to sleep. I was dressed and headed for the privy when I opened the front door. There was Ross sitting on the front steps, with his leather jacket draped over his shoulders. I looked for his bike, but I didn't see it.

"G'day," he said simply, twisting around to greet me. He did not get up from the steps.

I stood in the doorway of the cabin frowning, "What happened Ross? Are you okay?"

He nodded, but I thought he seemed rather pale. His characteristic intensity demonstrated in the previous evenings was absent. "I had a flat front tire about a mile from here, near the ranch with the dogs. I can't ride on a flat too far but I got the bike back here, all right. Had to take it slow. I've been wondering all night how to admit to you that I am absolutely at your mercy." His tone was only half in jest and his face expressed no emotion.

"Where is your bike?" I walked out onto the porch looking for his Harley.

"Parked down on the road behind the tree. I didn't want to ride it up here."

I perched on the porch railing near the stairs where Ross was sitting. "You should have woken me up. I have an extra bed. Did you get any sleep at all?"

"No."

"I'm sorry."

Ross shrugged. He was looking down the valley at the changing light of the dawn. He said softly, "Don't worry about me, Cait. The cabin was dark when I got here. I reckoned you were asleep. No reason to wake you."

"What did you do all night?"

"Watched the stars. It's gorgeous out here. I can't

remember when I've seen so many shooting stars in one night. Like a parade of ancestral souls cascading across eternity. It was magical to sit under these skies and realize that no one in the world knew where I was or what I was doing."

I wasn't thinking about stars. I certainly wasn't thinking about cascading ancestral souls. I was problem solving. I addressed the first problem. "It's Sunday, Ross, so the bike will have to wait until tomorrow. I'll have to drive you into Bozeman first thing in the morning to get what we need to fix your tire."

"We?" He looked up at me with his brow furrowed.

"How else are you going to fix the bike? You don't have a spare."

"Or a patch kit. I can't believe I didn't put one in the saddlebags when I picked the bike up. I haven't been thinking too clearly, lately. Too much on my mind." Ross had his head in his hands and was running his fingers through his thick curls. He looked up at me again. "You don't have to take me into Bozeman, Cait. Isn't there something closer?"

I shook my head. "Nope, Bozeman is it. Don't be embarrassed. We get flats out here all the time. When the county grades the road, the exposed quartzite can be super sharp."

"I appreciate your help, Caitlinn. Are you certain you want to go to all that bother? There must be an easier solution."

There probably were other solutions. I liked the idea of having a chance to spend more time with Ross, so I wasn't considering any other alternatives. "No. I was planning to go into Bozeman tomorrow anyway to see my friend, JoAnn MacKinnon. Besides, you'll be a captive audience and I can bore you with my old Bozeman stories." I smiled at him, hoping to get some sort of reaction. I missed the radiance and energy Ross demonstrated the previous evenings at the Bear Claw.

"Ah, Cait, your stories aren't boring."

I started solving problem number two. "Can I make you breakfast before I drive you back into Ennis?"

"I wouldn't mind a feed. I would like to watch the sunrise, though, before we go back." Ross sounded wistful. He didn't seem in any big hurry to leave, either.

"In that case, we should take our food and hike up to the top of the mountain to watch." I paused, thinking about Ross's low levels of energy. I rephrased my offer to cover for his male ego, "We could see more of the sunrise if I drive us in the truck up to the top on the back road."

"Righto." He didn't offer to help, nor did he show any inclination towards movement of any sort.

I went back in the cabin and put some water on to boil for eggs and coffee. I got out the big thermos and filled up the coffee filter with grounds. It was not fancy coffee, but it was better than my traditional cowboy coffee with the grounds thrown in. I added some grapes from the cooler to the bag, along with two cans of oranges and the can opener. When the eggs were done, I let them cool off while I made the coffee. I closed the front door for a little privacy. With the extra hot water, I washed my face and whatever else was in easy reach without taking off my clothes. I double-checked my appearance in the mirror because I wasn't used to company for breakfast.

"Okay, I have to do one more thing and then we're all set to go," I said, shutting the door behind me. "Here, put this stuff in the truck. I'll be right with you." I went around the corner of the cabin to the privy. When I climbed into the pickup, Ross sat on the passenger side with the food at his feet. I backed down off the hill to the gravel road, past his parked bike, and started up the steep road to the summit. The mountain road wound around various rock formations, making a series of hairpin turns. As an undeveloped road, there were no safety railings and no margins for error. I had learned to drive on such roads and considered them a metaphor for life in the West. In Montana, there were few safety railings and never any margin for human error. "Montana," my grandfather used to say, "is a harsh mistress. Respect her and never forget how important it is to pay attention to her sky and her winds." Once on the top of the mountain, we drove across the flats for half a mile. At my gate, I stopped and Ross got out. I tossed him the key to unlock the gate and he waited until I had driven through to close it again. He didn't lock it. When he got back in the truck, I told Ross he could have left the gate open, since there was no livestock around to attempt a grand getaway.

"Nah, I'm a bushie, Cait. We always leave the farm gates the way we find them. Code of the bush. Stuff you learn as a youngster sticks with you."

I drove down a disappearing road across the top of the mountain. The road had never had a load of gravel and the plant life was taking over. Ruts could barely be seen and the sage was starting to grow taller. I needed to hire the grader out of Ennis to come up and regrade the road when I got a bit of money ahead, maybe next year. I could not afford the maintenance expense this season. My grandfather kept this property in good working order but I had neither his extensive local connections nor his skill set. I only had Frank, and I resisted asking for help as much as I could because I didn't want to abuse his kind nature nor use up my social capital. Driving us to the end of what remained of the road, I parked my truck. Ross carried the bag of food and I carried the blanket I kept in the truck. He followed me as we hiked out to my grandfather's favorite place to watch sunrises and sunsets—a rock outcropping. From the outcropping facing west, a person had a commanding view of the North Meadow Creek drainage and the Tobacco Roots. To the south, the entire Madison Valley was visible, 90 miles down to the faint distant mountains of Idaho.

I thought of my mountain as an ancient grocery store since almost all the major foodstuffs in the diet of the Indians could be found there except water, and that was readily available albeit 500 feet below. The gullies were filled with gooseberries and chokecherries. On the southern flanks, Montana's state flower bloomed. The bitterroot provided the Indians with a rare delicacy to flavor their pemmican. This time of year, if you looked carefully, you might find the tissue paper-thin remnants of the tubular flower lying on the surface of the ground. Across the slopes, limber pines and prickly pear cactus provided additional foodstuffs. Limber pine nuts provided much needed fat for winter diets since wild game tended to be lean. The ground was always sprinkled with deer and elk sign because Grandpa's mountain had been prime hunting ground for the Bannock and Piute tribes who traveled north every spring from their wintering grounds in Nevada before the arrival of white settlers.

I'd often imagined the natives standing at that rock outcropping over the centuries, watching the migrating herds of elk. Historically, there had never been big herds of buffalo in the Madison. The Bannock traded with other tribes for the cherished buffalo robes. Some of the artifacts Grandpa and I had found were over 1,000 years old, according to the archaeologist at the university in Bozeman. The elk still came through my property in the fall, although not as often now that ranches were being subdivided throughout the valley. Just below my favorite spot was the prominent rock outcropping with the six heads, the one my grandfather and I named Indian Rocks.

I climbed up on the big flat rock and Ross followed, seating himself beside me. Out of the protection of the trees, the wind was chilly. I had my winter jacket, so I handed Ross the blanket. He draped it over his shoulders and poured the coffee. We ate quietly and watched the world come alive. The sun came over the mountains slowly, casting light across the drainages of the Tobacco Roots. The colors played across the sky, illuminating the foothills, highlighting the ancient river terraces, and turning the snowcapped peaks fiery red. As the sun rose, the patterns shifted and the colors changed. I shivered. The rock was cold.

"Come here, Cait," Ross invited, holding the blanket open. It looked tempting. I was shaking.

"Thanks, but I'm okay, Ross." The old approach/avoidance issue was manifesting itself again.

Ross shrugged. He didn't ask me again. I realized, looking at him in the early morning light at close quarters, that I couldn't discern what color his eyes were. I remembered what he had said about his eyes changing color. In the bar in reduced light, they had seemed gray, now they seemed green. Except they weren't green, either. The area around his pupils was specked with gold. The rest of the iris seemed to take on different colors depending on the light. "What color are your eyes, Ross?" The question popped out before I could stifle it.

He hesitated, gazing at me thoughtfully, "What color do

you think they are?"

I looked carefully. They actually changed from green to blue while I was studying them. "I don't know. They're the most unusual eyes I've ever seen."

He smiled faintly, "That's what my Mum always said." Ross spoke softly. "She said the eyes were the windows to the soul and it wasn't clear what color my soul was."

"That's an odd thing to tell a child."

"Cait, I got into heaps of bother when I was an ankle biter. Mum always said it was a pity she couldn't put an old head on my young shoulders. She'd get so exasperated with me."

I shivered again, drawing my knees up to my chest. This time, Ross did not waste any words arguing with me. He stood up, resettling himself behind me while wrapping the blanket around both of us. He wrapped his long legs around mine, his arms wrapped around mine, as he held me in the position I had taken when I was cold. I relaxed into his warm, strong embrace enjoying the smell of his leather jacket mixed with his cologne. Ross was not radiating sexual energy and he was not taking advantage of our physical proximity. I didn't feel threatened or excited, so I let Ross hold me. I liked the way he felt and the way I felt. We sat without a word, watching the show of light and color, shadow, and shape.

"Do you believe in God?" His low, deep, sensuous voice by my ear startled me.

I hesitated, "How can you sit here with this view and not believe?"

"Exactly so."

"This is a special place for me, Ross. It's a thin place, where heaven and earth meet. The last few years have been difficult. I feel more centered here. I've watched a lot of sunsets and sunrises from this spot."

Ross hugged me gently in response. I knew he understood what I was telling him. He whispered in my ear, "I've been in thin places before." He shifted his position, moving away from me slightly. "I should clarify something, Cait."

I waited.

"I only gave up sex when I was working on *Unto the Dust*. I made up for lost time afterwards. I'm not proud of my behavior. I was a root rat. I had a come-to-Jesus moment sometime back and decided I didn't need to be having sex with women I didn't love and who didn't love me."

I wondered why Ross was telling me this. If he thought I would reciprocate by revealing my sexual experiences, he was sorely mistaken. The silence between us lengthened. I listened to the steadiness of his breathing, felt the morning sun getting stronger on my face, heard the wind coming down the mountain tree by tree, and I found the courage to respond. I reached up out of the blanket and stroked the side of his face, tracing his scar. If my relationship with Ross continued to progress, the evidence of my earlier lie would surface since I had no scars on my breasts. I took a big deep breath.

"Well," I began, "Since we're doing confessions, I have one."

Ross waited.

"The rat story did happen. I was there in that classroom, but it didn't happen to me."

"I know."

"How?"

"I'm a bushie, Cait." Ross moved his legs tighter around me and held me closer. "I know what rodents like in a tunnel. You don't have enough cleavage to form a tunnel a rodent would find attractive." Ross nuzzled my ear whispering, "And you're not a screamer. Don't worry, I'm a leg man and I don't need a screamer." He shifted his weight drawing back again.

I was grateful Ross wasn't angry with me for lying to him. I leaned back into him and he sighed into my ear, "Maybe someday, Cait, you'll trust me enough to tell me about your real scars."

A sparrow hawk circled above us, screeching a warning. We both looked up, watching him circling overhead before flying westward over the hollow containing Grandpa's cabin still nestled in the early morning shadow of the mountain.

Ross caught me off guard with his question, "What's your baptized name, Cait."

"I've never been baptized."

"Why not?"

"My father didn't answer to anyone. Certainly not to God, certainly not to a congregation. He said baptism was pagan, for savages. Modern man didn't need religion. Religion was for weaklings, an emotional crutch for those who couldn't face the truth."

"How do you feel?"

"He was wrong. I should have been baptized. It worried my grandmother. Mother should have insisted. Mother had already asked Frank to be my godfather, and Dad canceled the whole thing at Grandma's church at the last minute. My grandmother was furious. Some of the guests had already arrived, and Grandma had to make apologies. She had gone to a lot of trouble to arrange for the pastor to drive over from Bozeman, so I could be baptized in the Meadow Creek church where everyone in my mother's family had been baptized. The church isn't used on a regular basis anymore and Grandma had to call in a few favors for my baptism. Afterwards, when the yelling stopped and my father was out of earshot, my mother made Frank promise to look out for me anyway. He kept his promise. Frank always keeps his word."

Ross was hugging me a little tighter. "You're never too old to be baptized, Caitlinn. What's your middle name?"

"I don't have one."

"Really?"

"My parents fought so much over my first name they didn't have the energy to fight over a second. I have half a name." Fitting, I thought, for half a person.

"Do you believe in fate, Caitlinn?"

"You mean preordained fate?"

"Yes."

"I don't know. I'm too much of a control freak to accept that. I'd like to think I have choices, that I should take responsibility for my behavior. I had some nasty things done to me as a child under the rubric of no free will. I can't believe my life is preordained. That would let too many people in my life off the hook."

"Do you believe in déjà vu?"

"I don't know, Ross. Do you?"

"Yes." Ross's voice was barely audible. "I feel like I've been here before. Not seen these rocks, but felt them." He paused, "This place feels like Durham, England. I was at the cathedral to visit St. Cuthbert's grave. I had the one of the worst visceral … ."

I rubbed his thigh to reassure him. Ross responded to my gesture by altering his position. He bent around me, his stubbly cheek rasping against mine. "I had to leave the cathedral. The walls were crying."

"Do you know what happened at the Durham Cathedral?" I asked him.

"No."

"After the Battle of Dunbar, Oliver Cromwell imprisoned the healthy Scots in the Cathedral at Durham. He had no regard for the sanctity of the Catholic Church and there wasn't enough room in the castle for all the prisoners. So, he turned the cathedral into a great big prison. My ancestors spent time in that dreadful place. That's why none of the original wooden interior survived, the prisoners burned it for cooking and warmth. Except for the ornate Prior Castell's clock that the Scottish prisoners refused to burn because of the beautiful thistle carved on the clock's crown. The thistle is the symbol of Scotland and it reminded the prisoners of who they were and to stay faithful to their form of religion. They were fighting for the right to worship God as they saw fit. Not worship God by how the psychopath, Cromwell, insisted they worship. Their fight is the origins of the constitutional belief in separation of church and state. Some of those that survived their stay in the cathedral were sent over to the colonies in the spring as prisoners to work in the iron mills of New England."

Ross spoke low. "I didn't know. I just assumed they put the prisoners in the castle. That explains a lot."

The sunrise colors had left the sky its daytime blue and the pinks on the hills had faded into daylight shades of green and brown. The sunrise was over. Whatever security I had felt during the sunrise was gone. In the daylight, I was uncomfortable with the increasing intimacy with Ross. I was getting stiff. My movement caused the blanket to fall away, exposing us both to the chill of the early morning wind. Ross responded by getting up. He reached down to offer me a hand, pulling me up to my feet. Then he turned abruptly, jumped off the rock, and started walking down the slope.

I gathered up the breakfast remains, picked up the blanket, and followed him. Ross stood looking south down the Madison Valley towards Idaho. The mountains far to the south were a faint blue outline against the distant horizon.

"You can see the mountains in Yellowstone Park and behind them the mountains in Idaho. They're 90 miles away. In fact, you can see 90 miles in all directions from up there." I gestured first to the mountaintop behind us with the bag still in my hand. "And down there's the Bear Claw." I pointed to the cluster of trees down below to the east.

"I can see why it's important to you to come here. There's something spiritual about this place."

I wanted to focus on the practical and I didn't want to discuss spiritual issues anymore with Ross. I didn't know him well enough. I asked Ross a practical secular question, "What do you have to do today?"

"I'm off. We don't start shooting until next month. I'll have plenty to do in about 10 days. What are you required to do today?" Ross's motionless concentration was confusing me. Ordinarily, if a man acted in such a manner, I would have interpreted his intentions as sexual. Something else was happening. Ross wasn't undressing me with his eyes; he was peeling back my skin as well, exposing my soul.

I answered his straightforward question, fighting to remain calm under his piercing gaze. "Well, I always write in the afternoons no matter what. That's the only way you can get anything accomplished. Discipline. Discipline. Discipline. Someone once said that the hardest thing about writing is putting your butt on the chair and keeping it there. I need to go down to Ennis for a few things at the pharmacy. You want to go back to the motel? I'll buy you lunch at the Western Drug pharmacy cafe."

"No thanks on lunch, Cait. I'm knackered. I do like the

quiet of this place and I do like the peacefulness of being with you."

His last words created a warm feeling for me, replacing the previous fear of exposure. I wanted to reach out and touch him. I resisted, focusing instead on his state of exhaustion. *Ross gave you a problem, Cait. Solve it.* Breakfast had not restored his color. Ross needed sleep, badly. "Why, don't you stay at my place for the day, Ross? You can take a nap. It's nice and quiet out here. Afterwards, if you like, I'll make you supper." I was anticipating an argument, so I tried to preempt it. "It's no trouble at all. Besides, I haven't had anyone to make a fuss over all summer."

"Beauty." He said the word in two distinct parts, the first low, the second as a question with a lilt on the end.

"It is beautiful up here."

Ross looked startled and then he smiled. "Nah, Cait, bit of Aussie slang for you. Beauty means great." Something caught his attention and he started walking further down the slope towards the big rock formations shaped like Indian heads. "What's this?" He asked, gesturing to a small Celtic cross carved out of cedar half-hidden behind a sagebrush.

"A memorial to people I've lost."

I didn't know if I was looking at Ross Sutherland or Father Paddy O'Donnell. I turned away to regain my composure. When I looked back at him, Ross had squatted down low on his heels to trace the carved patterns of the Celtic knots of my cross with his finger. He got up slowly and walked around to the back of the cross, squatting down again, heels flat on the ground. I didn't know what he was doing until he made the sign of the cross. Standing up without acknowledging me, Ross walked further down the slope to Indian Rocks. He disappeared around the base of the formation and I waited for him. When he reappeared on the other side, I walked down to join him.

"Do you know the story of this rock formation, Cait?"

"No." I replied, frowning at Ross.

"There are at least six different faces in this rock. They're not all the same age or sex, either. One's definitely a child. Almost like a family. Waiting. Something happened here, I can feel it and it wasn't good."

I smiled, but Ross did not smile back. "Well, it would have been Indians against Indians because the Bannock Indians and the white settlers always got along in the Madison Valley, which is why the Madison is such a special place. The Bannock Indians prided themselves in never shedding white blood, according to the old timers, and the pioneers didn't shed Bannock blood either. But the Bannock did have trouble with the Blackfeet. In the early times, according to the stories told to my great-grandparents by visiting Bannock Indians, their people used to travel in small family units when they came north. After the Blackfeet obtained horses, they widened their territory and the Bannock Indians had to start traveling as a tribe for increased safety. If a small summer hunting party was attacked here, it would have been before 1730, when the Blackfeet acquired horses from the Shoshone."

The idea that a family had been massacred on my grandfather's mountain bothered me. I hadn't ever given the matter much thought, but Ross's previous story about his experience at the Durham cathedral gave me pause. Did he sense things I couldn't? *Focus on the secular, Cait.* "I don't really know, mind you, I'm just speculating. Maybe it's time to move along here. You need to get to bed," I said, looking at my watch. "And I have to get to town and back so I can write this afternoon on schedule."

We walked back to my truck, followed by a silent drive down the steep mountain road to my cabin. I took the breakfast things inside, leaving the blanket in the cab.

"Are you positive you don't want to come to town with me?" I asked him again once we were both inside my cabin.

"If it's all the same to you, Cait, I'd rather stay here and sleep." There were dark circles under his eyes, accompanied by a look of longing on his face, no mischief, and he didn't look at me, only at my grandparents' bed.

"Okay, but let me change the sheets." I started towards the bed, but Ross intercepted me, holding my arm.

"Nah, Cait, it's okay, don't stress."

I hesitated, "Well, at least let me change the pillow case." Ross released my arm and, moving out of my way, he sat down heavily on the old kitchen chair. I pulled a clean pillowcase out of the drawer and removed mine. I straightened up the bedclothes, smoothing the top quilt flat, and folding down the edges the way Grandma always did for company.

"Are you certain you don't mind me staying here without you?" Ross asked.

"No, I don't mind at all."

"I'm not very exciting company."

"Doesn't matter Ross, I don't need to be entertained. Don't apologize. I have stuff to do. I'll be fine. I have to write this afternoon, remember?"

He nodded.

"Do you need anything from town?"

"Could you go by my motel and pick up some things?" Ross was pulling an object out of his left front jeans pocket. He handed me his key. "It's cabin 10 at the Lone Mountain Motel."

"What do you need?"

"My kit from the bathroom and a change of clothes. Anything will do. Doesn't matter."

"Can I get you some better beer at the store? All I have is that fruity stuff."

Ross looked embarrassed at my reference to his dislike of my favorite ale. "I'm sorry, Cait, if I was rude the other night. Could you pick up some Guinness or Harp?"

"Yes, anything else?"

"Maybe, some tea. English tea."

I nodded. "Have a good rest." I turned to open the door. Ross already had his boots and socks off and was working on the buttons of his shirt. I hesitated and started to say something.

"What?" He looked up from his buttons. A single copper corkscrew curl was partially covering his right eye.

"This is really weird. I'm going into town, and there's a movie star undressing himself in my cabin. Too weird for words. Nobody will ever believe me. I don't believe it."

"Don't, Cait," he pleaded.

"Don't what?" I asked.

"Don't ruin this, Caitlinn, please. Just keep treating me like an ordinary fella. You have no idea how important that is to me. It's what I like about you. You don't patronize me. You don't want to own a part of me. I feel like a regular fella around you. Please don't stress. Don't ruin this."

"Ruin what exactly?"

"The lovely ordinariness of being with you, Caitlinn." At that moment Ross did not look like a movie star. I was struck by how he could change quickly like a chameleon. One day he could be flashy and charming and the next day he could be so quiet and withdrawn you wouldn't notice him except for his exuberant curly hair. I realized that if Ross had been like this when I waited on him last summer,

I would not have remembered him. He had become part of the background of my cabin, almost as if his spirit had left his body, leaving me nothing human with which to interact. Ross was like Christmas lights, drab when they are off and breathtakingly beautiful when they are turned on.

I was flustered, and the warm unfocused feeling was back, only stronger. "Ordinary. Okay. Got it. Take care. See you later."

I shut the door softly behind me and released a big sigh. I didn't think this situation was ordinary in the least. Less than 36 hours ago I had a simple existence with no complications, and now I had an international movie star sleeping in my bed. I should have put Ross upstairs in the loft. The sheets were clean up there. What was I thinking? On the way into town, I had trouble concentrating on my driving. The events of the last 36 hours kept playing in my mind like a hypnotic movie. I could feel Ross's hand on my forearm when he first asked me to stay at the bar. I could see our single moon shadow. I could taste his gentle kiss in the moonlight. I could feel his arms embracing me under the blanket in the brisk crystal-clear mountain air as dawn painted the skies and the mountains. And most of all I could see those soft bottomless eyes pleading for something he evidently needed and thought I could provide. I tried to put Ross out of my mind. But as hard as I tried, his plaintive request, 'Don't,' echoed in my ears all the way into town.

~ Chapter 15 ~

When I arrived back at the cabin, it was half-past twelve. I opened up the front door quietly and stepped inside, being careful not to slam the screen door. Ross was asleep. His clothes were in a folded pile on the floor. I did not look too closely because I didn't want to know if Ross had left any on when he crawled into my bed. I put his kit bag on the table and laid his fresh clothes on the chair.

Finding Ross's things in cabin 10 had not been difficult once I turned on the overhead lights. The curtains were drawn against the hot Montana sun and the windows were all closed. Immediately, I knew why Ross preferred to sleep at my cabin. My grandfather's cabin smelled of sage brush, fresh air, the faint scent of pine, accompanied with the sounds of birds chirping and flies buzzing around. My cabin was full of life. Ross's room smelled of cleaning fluids with a backdrop of dust with no sounds of the natural world. Yes, everything was tidy and spotless, but there was no life here, no presence of God's world. Two music cases leaned against the wall side by side, both appeared to be acoustic guitars. One was huge. I resisted the temptation to open them. I did take the time to read through the titles of books stacked neatly on the motel desk. There had been the usual airport reading fare—best-sellers and military thrillers. What I had not expected was the dog-eared copies of Dante's *Divine Comedy*, Thomas à Kempis' *The Imitation of Christ, The Confession of St. Patrick,* and a book of Thomas Merton's poems. *The Greatest Cattle Drive* with its distinct bright-red dust jacket was on the top of his pile of books. My grandfather had owned a copy of that book. I opened it, lost in memories of Frank reading me this story the long winter he lived with us while he was recovering from the accident that ended his firefighting career.

After the Civil War, when the gold camps in Madison County, Montana, exploded in population, meat was in short supply. Nelson Story recognized the potential to make some serious money. Leaving his young bride, Ellen, in Virginia City, he took all his cash, heading south to Texas where he invested in a thousand longhorns. With a party of 27 cowboys and the latest in Remington rifles, Story drove his herd north to Montana. When I opened the familiar book, I was so busy reading the inscription to a Nora from somebody named Paddy, I almost missed the escape of a small black and white photograph as it floated out settling gently at my feet. I picked the photograph up to look more closely at the cowboy standing by a familiar rock formation in Bridger Canyon. Why does Ross have a photograph of Frank in this book, I thought, turning the photograph over. "Paddy O'Neill, Montana, 1962" was written on the back. Maybe, I remembered wrong. Maybe Frank does have kin. I tried to identify the man, but the shadow of his hat brim was hiding a lot of his face. The cowboy looked like the photographs I had seen of Frank with my mother's family before I was born. I had never seen this photograph before, however. Odd. I reread the inscription inside the book cover. I didn't remember Ross ever telling me his parents' first names. Could Ross be the bub the book was intended for? An O'Neill from Montana photographed at the opening of Bridger Canyon? Grandpa never mentioned anybody with that name living up Bridger. Except for Frank. Maybe Ross bought this book in a second-hand store. No, wait. Ross said his sister from Australia sent him this book when he was in Dakota making a movie about a priest named Paddy. Why would his sister send him an American book about a cattle drive? I refrained from reading the letter firmly tucked into the book's center, although I did look at the return address—"Paddy O'Neill, Emigrant, Montana, USA". The airmail envelope was addressed to Mrs. Nora Sutherland, Larkin Stud Farm, Scone NSW Australia. Why would a cowboy from Emigrant send a book to a relative of Ross's in NSW along with his photograph taken in Bridger Canyon? This was too weird. There were a lot of Scots and Irish in Montana. O'Neill is not an uncommon name, but there were too many coincidences for this to all be random chance. No wonder Ross was asking questions about Frank. The inspiration for his new movie had come from a book sent to some close relative of Ross's around the time Ross was born. I was certain about that part, but mystified about Frank's relationship to a man named Paddy. There is a story waiting to be told. I laid the book back on the top of the pile as I had found it. I did not want Ross to know I had been snooping like a fool.

Ross also had several collections of Australian bush ballads, an assortment of Montana histories, and a history of Irish saints. A small CD player with a pile of CDs was on the nightstand. On the dresser was a small replica of a Celtic cross with a green serpentine base. Three white stones and a seashell, all four worn smooth from pounding waves, sat next to the cross. Also on the dresser stood a framed faded color photograph. The frame was rather battered and in the photograph were five people standing in front of a light-colored stone house with a wide veranda. It had to be Ross's family. The older man's face was partially hidden by an Australian bush hat. He stood with his arm firmly around the waist of the woman next to him. She was wearing a print dress with an apron and was quite beautiful with short curly hair. Off to one side were two younger men, one with a head of curls. At the feet of the curly-headed young man sat two Aussie sheep dogs. The two men looked almost like twins, except for their hair. Squeezed between her parents, her one arm wrapped around her mother's legs, a red headed girl was partially hiding behind her mother's skirt.

The only other photograph in the room was on the bedside table. The photograph was taken at a beach. Ross was standing between two women—a beautiful older woman with a stylish haircut and a younger girl with a riot of red curls framing her smiling face. Ross was holding a toddler in some sort of swimming costume, complete with a wide-brimmed floppy hat. I wondered if the blonde was his ex and if the toddler was his son. I assumed the young girl must be Ross's sister, but Ross had said so little about his family, I had no way of knowing.

I would not be able to ask Ross anything about the cowboy by the Bridger Canyon rock or the family photographs without admitting to prying. Feeling guilty, I tiptoed out, leaving behind all my unanswered questions in the darkness of a sterile motel room.

Upon returning to my cabin, I put Ross's requested beer

in my cooler. He stirred a little when the bottles clinked together as I laid them on top of the ice block. I put the tea in the stainless canister and I wrote Ross a note explaining that I would be down the road by the creek until 5 p.m. unless it started raining. Then I would be on the front porch. I detailed where everything he might need was located and explained he could boil water if he wanted to wash. I filled the big enameled kettle with fresh water and placed it on the propane-stove burner. I got out some extra towels and washcloths from the dresser and left them next to his kit bag on the table. I put the washbasin on the table, along with the pitcher and a spare bowl.

My briefcase full of my latest draft of writing was leaning next to the bed. I picked it up, lingering there, watching Ross sleeping. His wild curls fell across my white pillow. I wanted to touch a curl, extend it out and watch it bounce back into shape. I refrained. His long eyelashes formed half circles across his cheeks and I would have lingered longer but for the embarrassing possibility that Ross could wake up and catch me admiring him.

I always enjoyed the short hike down to my creek. I set up on my favorite rock near the water and got down to some serious writing. Down along the stream, in amongst the trees, there were few distractions unlike up on the summit where the surrounding mountains and the sky demanded my attention. I had been writing at the same time every day, long enough I could always concentrate when necessary. That was the value of a strict routine. As soon as 1 p.m. rolled along, no matter what the events of the day had been, I could always get into the zone, as I called it. Today was no exception.

By five o'clock, I was completing a chapter. A thunderstorm, typical for that time of day, was gathering force over the Tobacco Roots. Looking at the clouds and listening to the wind, I judged I could just make it back to my cabin before it hit. The clouds were dark and heavy as I walked up the gravel road and the wind was shifting as I approached the cabin. I wondered if Ross was awake. The rain began as big, fat, heavy drops as I stepped onto the porch. This type of rain left indentations in the soft dust, but little mud. It always amazed me how if you got caught in such a storm you would be soaked, but the earth would be pock marked. The ground was so porous, the water was absorbed immediately. The weather in the Madison Valley was the stuff of legends. Grandpa liked to tell the story of the frozen horse found in the branches of a tree up Wall Creek after a frightful winter where the temperature was recorded at 50 degrees below zero in Ennis. The snow had been so deep in places it buried entire trees, and a poor horse broke through the snow surface and froze to death only to be found high in the tree come spring. Frank described the Madison as the only place on earth where the winds could blow from every direction all at the same time and did.

The storm had further darkened the cabin as I lit a few of the candles in their wall sconces above the table. A loud thunderclap startled me, but Ross slept through it. I walked over to the bed and gently stroked his curls back from his forehead. I allowed myself to take a handful of his hair. I pulled the curls to their full length, released them, and watched them regain their curving form with determined energy. Another handful? *No, Cait. Behave yourself.* I touched his face instead, stroking the smooth contours of his upper cheekbones. "Ross, Ross, it's time to get up."

He opened his eyes and rolled over with a groan. I retreated. Restricting my attention to the next order of business, I turned on the stove burner for heating the wash water.

"Do you want to wash up?" I asked, looking over my shoulder at the bare-chested man yawning and nodding positively to my inquiry.

I poured some of the boiling water into the pitcher, mixing it together with the cold water from one of the six-gallon storage containers. I tested the temperature with my fingers. It was fine. I set the hot kettle down on the trivet near the table for future rinses. I had been washing my hair in this fashion for months now.

Ross got out of my bed. He was wearing black-knit boxers and nothing else. I desperately wanted to stare, but I didn't want to encourage him. Ross appeared oblivious to the effect he was having on me.

"Clearly there's a system here, but you'll have to explain it to me," he said, surveying the arrangement of pitchers and bowls.

"Well, you start at the top and work down," I said. "Wash your hair first and end with your feet."

"Just so. And how did you derive such a system, Cait?"

"Grandma taught me how to bathe this way. She called it a whore's bath. I spent a lot of time at this cabin as a child. Grandma was a big believer in staying clean. Grandpa used to kid her. He said she just came out here to boil water for washing. Every time he turned around, Grandma was boiling water for either coffee or cleaning. Grandpa said Grandma was ruining his fun. He wanted an opportunity to get very dirty and stay that way."

Ross grinned, "Well, this looks like a classic setup to me, where the women know how to do something and they yell at the men for being stupid and making a big mess."

"Do you want me to help you?"

"Please."

"Okay. Just step over here and we'll get started. After I do your hair, I'll go upstairs and you can do the rest by yourself."

He started to walk over to the table, and I started laughing nervously.

Ross stopped abruptly with a frown transforming his face, "What's so funny?" He was glowering at me. The nap had restored him and his familiar intensity was back full force.

"Oh, nothing," I replied, almost doubling over. I felt like a teenager with an attack of the giggles. I was clutching my abdomen.

"Out with it, Cait. What's so damn amusing?"

"I'm sorry. I've never even seen anyone famous before and now here you are. A famous man, half-dressed, in my cabin, asking me to wash his hair."

"Ah, Cait, I'm not asking, I'm begging," Ross responded with a grin.

I continued to double over in laughter. "Oh, that helps a ton. Begging, not asking. That's even worse. Famous and hardly dressed, begging to have his hair washed."

"Here, maybe this will help."

Ross slid both hands inside his waistband of his shorts, pushing them down. I could see the line of hair spreading down from his navel, the anterior curve of his pubis bones. I had had so much trouble in physical anthropology, mastering the art of sexing human pelvic bones. My professor had laughed at me when I got frustrated in osteology lab. "You must have a mental block, Cait. You're the only one in class who identified all the anatomical landmarks of the bones correctly on the last test. Put the evidence together. Concentrate. You're observant, you can sex skulls without any problems, sex the pelvic bones." Ross's implied intent had suffocated my mirth. My heart rate was increasing, breathing getting shallower, anatomical landmark names of pelvic bones were tumbling over each other in my head interfering with my thinking. *Cait. Get. Control. Now.*

"What do you think you're doing?" I demanded, using my best indignant teacher's tone.

Ross laughed. "Trying to help you, luv. I can't drop my fame but I can drop something else."

"No. No. Don't you dare. No. Don't you *dare.*"

His eyes were overflowing with merriment. "Ah, Cait, you should never have double-dared an Aussie." With a deliberate final push, Ross dropped his shorts to the floor and stepped out of them. He was still laughing.

I locked eyes with him and refused the temptation to look south. I also refused to allow myself any facial expression. I was not going to give him the satisfaction of a reaction. I focused on the one thing he had left on—the silver cross on a chain around his neck. I tried to remember what I had read about the origins of the circle around the classic Celtic cross. *Think, Cait. The circle design first appeared on the island of Iona and was thought to have served as a stabilizer for the wide arms of the stone cross. What was the name? St. John's cross? Or was it St. Martin's cross? Concentrate Cait. Don't panic. Stay calm.* Ross was advancing on me, his palms upraised in mock surrender. His deep voice interpreted me.

"You're so much fun to tease, Cait, I can't resist. Calm down, I don't want to fuck, just get my hair washed. Truly."

"Glad we're clear on that." I grabbed one of the towels off the table and shoved it into his middle, partially covering him. I could still see the graceful curve of his hip bones, the contrast of smooth white skin against the tanned, the spread of curly hair on his muscular inner thighs. "Put that on. You're impossible."

Ross chuckled as he wrapped the towel around his waist.

"Okay. Stand over here." I grabbed his arm and pulled him in front of the table. "Bend over." I was struggling for control. Ross had beautiful skin, smooth like polished marble, no imperfections. The hairs on his forearms glittered red-gold in the soft light of the candles. He was solid. Not the highly sculpted muscles of gym rats but the rounded big muscles earned from honest physical labor. I had an overwhelming urge to run my hands over his body, the same urge I have to stifle when I'm in an art museum in front of a great sculpture. When the body aches to feel what the eyes see.

But I also knew how to detach, especially if the physical stimulus was sexual. The sensory stimulus of Ross's body so close I could feel his heat no longer registered. Maybe Ross did want to have his hair washed and nothing more. I didn't care. There was a job to do and I did it. I pushed his head into the bowl. The water from the pitcher came next. Ross spluttered as the heavy flow of water ran into his face. As I poured the remaining half of the contents of the pitcher over his head, wetting the dry hair under the steady stream, I ran my fingers through his curls, making certain they were all wet. His cross was tolling a plaintive protest on the side of the metal washbasin. His spluttering got louder.

"Be brave," I admonished. "Hold still."

I was rough. Ross protested after a particularly vigorous rubbing of shampoo, "Ouch, you're pulling my hair."

"Nonsense, it's good for your scalp circulation."

"You're a tyrant, Cait."

"No. I'm not." More spluttering followed the rinse. I shoved another towel from the table under his face and dried off his eyes. I slapped Ross lightly on the back. "All done." I opened up the front door and threw the soapy water out into the yard.

"I'm going upstairs. Call me when you're decent." I resisted the urge to look at Ross clothed only in his towel, vigorously rubbing his curly head.

I climbed up the ladder to the loft and lay down on the mattress. What had that been about? Ross's intent when he dropped his shorts was not sexual. He had not been aroused. I had checked as I shoved the towel into his groin. Ross claimed he had been teasing me. His demeanor as he advanced on me totally nude was identical to my brother's when Mark wanted to get a reaction from me. Ross was amazingly comfortable in his own skin. I could never be that relaxed totally exposed to a stranger.

I listened to the water pouring into the metal bowl followed by the sound of splashing. Normal sounds of bathing were reassuring. I stopped wondering if I was safe in this cabin alone with Ross. My heartbeat slowed. The door opened and the wash water thudded on to the ground. I could hear Ross brushing his teeth, pulling on his clothes, and zipping his zipper. His head appeared over the edge of the loft as he tugged playfully on my foot. "Your turn," he said wiggling his eyebrows and winking at me.

"Forget it, Ross. I took a bath yesterday."

He laughed and backed down the ladder.

I came down and started making supper. Ross got his Guinness out of the cooler and sat on the edge of the bed. He didn't say anything as he drank his beer. When he was finished, he got up to walk across the room picking up my guitar case.

"Do you mind?"

"No, go ahead, please."

Ross tuned up my guitar and played a few chords. He stood up again, this time pulling my notebook full of handwritten lyrics and guitar chords down from the bookshelf. It occurred to me that while I had been checking out his reading material in his motel room, he had been checking out mine. He sat back down on the bed flipping through the pages, picking out the notes and chords to a few songs without singing. He was a good guitar player, much better than me.

Ross looked up at me and said, "Sing me something."

"Like what?"

"Anything. Your favorite."

"Let me think for a minute. Okay. I like this one. It was written by John Jacob Niles in the style of old Scottish border ballads."

I started out softly because I was nervous. "*Oh, she was a lass from the low country ... .*" Ross was motionless. I wasn't certain he was even breathing, his entire being was focused on my voice. His extreme stillness was reassuring. As my stage fright eased, I finished the last chorus without my voice wobbling:

"And she sleeps in the valley where the wild flowers nod
And no one knows she loves him save herself and God."

"Sing another. Another favorite."

"Well, this one is Scottish too in origin but it was recorded as a sea shanty. It's called "Lowlands." I began the first verse:

"I dreamed a dream the other night.
Lowlands, Lowlands away my John,
I saw my love all dressed in white,
My Lowlands away.

She came to me at my bedside,
Lowlands, Lowlands away my John,

Ross shifted his position on the bed. His face seemed paler than before. "Jeez, Cait don't you know any happy songs. These are enough to drive a fella to drink."

"Happy songs are trite, and these appeal to my Scotch/Irish angst. When I have my perky epiphany, you will be the first to know. In the meantime, I like sad, sad, *sad* songs."

"Perky epiphany? What the bloody hell is that?"

"Well, that's when I have a revelation and get in touch with my perky side."

"Oh no, please don't, I can't stand perky women. Caitlinn, don't you know any songs that aren't depressing?"

"One." Grandpa used to sing this song to my older brother if Grandma wasn't within hearing distance. Grandpa didn't realize I had been listening.

"Sing it."

Ross fell over backwards on the bed. "You are mental. That's the worst song I've ever heard. It's positively vile."

"Sorry, Ross. Serves you right."

He groaned and then he sat up again. "Now, Cait, you must

know some other song that's not so wretchedly sad. A bloke can only tolerate limited amounts of extreme tragedy."

I started singing, "*My sweetheart's … .*"

"The hell with that, Cait. Be serious. You have a great voice and I like to listen to you sing. But life is about rhythm and balance, light and dark." Ross paused, giving his words extra emphasis, "Sad songs and happy songs. You've got to know another song that's not so bloody depressing."

I almost laughed at him but he was too serious, "All right, all right, I hear you. Maybe this one will work." I sang "The Riddle Song." It really was the only truly happy song I knew.

"A cherry when it's bloomin' it has no stone,
A chicken when it's pippin', it has no bone,
The story that I love you it has no end,
And a baby when she's sleepin', there's no cryin'."

"That's more like it." Ross worked out the chords on the guitar and then asked me to sing it again with him. I had finished setting the table while we sang.

"Listen up, Cait, here's one for you that's neither trite nor sad." Ross launched into a song about a station head in Australia who hired a driver for his wife. The driver was given explicit instructions about swearing in front of the lady. There was only one problem:

"The poor bullock driver looked blue,
In fact, he was almost despairing,
He knew that fair words wouldn't do,
For bullocks won't move without swearing;
So, says he to the lady behind,
Alas his request was unholy
I say mum, will you be so kind

I laughed with appreciation. The image of the frustrated oxen driver asking permission to cuss was vividly drawn. "Well, that is pretty funny. Supper's ready."

We sat down to eat. Ross seemed lost in thought or merely hungry. We started and finished in silence. I boiled water to clean up the dishes. I carefully took off my beaded bracelet and set it aside where it wouldn't get wet. Ross did not speak until the water was bubbling loudly in the big enamel pitcher on the stove.

"I'll do the wash-up," he said, gesturing at the dirty dishes. "Have a sit down."

Ross washed, but I insisted on doing the drying. He said no, I should stay seated, since I'd done all the cooking but I could sing if I wanted to help.

"Even sad songs?"

Ross rolled his eyes and shrugged. He had soap bubbles up to his elbows.

I sang him my grandfather's favorite, "The Three Ravens," which dated back to the early 1600s and told the story of a knight who dies under a tree after being wounded in a battle. He is discovered and properly buried by his pregnant mistress who mysteriously comes to him in the form of a deer.

> *"She buried him before the prime,*
> *Down a down, hey down hey down.*
> *She was dead herself ere even-song time,*
> *With a down, derry, derry, derry down, down."*

"That's a haunting tune."

"It's written in Dorian mode," I replied elaborating. "One

of the lesser-used minor modes."

"How do you know that?"

"It ends in G."

"No, Cait, I mean how do you know about modes?"

"My mother." My mother had been classically trained in music and she had been frustrated by my father's refusal to leave Montana after they were married. They had met in school back east and she had hoped to have a career in opera. My father, from the East Coast, preferred the western lifestyle and reneged on his promise to her to take the engineering job in New York City. He took the job with the Montana Highway Department, instead. She never forgave him. Rather than share that information about my family with Ross, I started in on another song, "The Great Silkie." Silkies, according to Grandpa, were shape-changers who would remove their outer seal skins to assume manly form in order to make love to human women. In this case, the silkie lover is from Skule Skerry, a tiny island off the north coast of Scotland, and the shape changer portends his human lover's unhappy future before leaving her forever,

"And thou shalt marry a gunner proud
And a right fine gunner I'm sure he'll be
For the very first shot he e'er shall take
Will kill both my young son and me.

Alas, alas, the maiden cried,
This weary fate's been laid for me;
And then she wept and then she died
We buried her north in Skule Skerry."

"Ah, Cait." Ross did not seem to share my love for eerie shape-shifter songs. "You must know some other happy songs."

I was getting tired of Ross's constant criticism of my choice in music. My grandfather used to sing me the first verse of an old Southern lullaby when I was young. Later, I found the second verse in a book and added it to my repertoire. I sang Ross the pretty verse Grandpa had taught me:

"Hush you bye, don't you cry,
Go to sleep little baby,
When you wake, you shall have
All the pretty little horses."

"That's beautiful, Cait."

Ross was smiling. He seemed satisfied with the effect of the lullaby. I went in for the kill. I sang the second verse.

"Way down yonder in the meadow,
Lies a poor little lambie,
Birds and bees peckin' out its eyes
Poor little thing cries 'Mammy'."

As soon as I was finished, I regretted what I had done. Ross's eyes were luminous and the hurt was unmistakable. I said, "It's a slave song. The mother can't watch her child and work in the fields. She's worried about her baby."

"That was harsh, Cait. You set me up."

"Well, maybe I did. But I like that song. Not all lives can be pretty and safe."

"What does this song tell me about your life, Cait?"

Damn. I wished Ross wasn't so perceptive. The gentleness of the first verse, juxtaposed against the brutality of the second, resonated with the abandonment I felt because my mother let me come to harm when she left me all alone. I heard the rain start. It was a gentle pattering on the roof like toddler footsteps. The cabin was warm and the light from the candles was soft. The long shadows played across the wooden ceiling. This was no time to be arguing. I apologized. Ross shrugged. I tried to make amends, "I don't like it when songs lose their souls, their identity."

After my cruel set-up from the song, "All the Pretty Little Horses," Ross was wary. "For instance?"

"The old Scottish ballad, "Loch Lomond." Do you know that one?"

He nodded.

"Ever heard the missing verse?"

Ross shook his head. So, I sang it,

"Oh cold was the moor, where our brave laddies died
In the mists so thick on that morning,
And long were the nights that the bonnie lassies wept,
For Prince Charlie's dream had died a bornin'."

"That's the keystone of the song, it's about the '46, the defeat of Bonnie Prince Charlie. You remember what happened after—the Brits decimated Scotland. Millions of Americans blissfully sing that song and have no idea what it is really about. I hate it when songs get sanitized and pasteurized."

"Whoa, Cait. I agree with you about pasteurized songs and soul and such, but where did you get that extra verse?"

"Grandpa Gallagher. He always sang it that way. He'd learned it from his dad."

"Nah, Cait, the musicologists are going to argue with you. They don't consider "Loch Lomond" a Jacobite air. They claim that's all bloody nonsense."

I was getting annoyed again, "Why do you know so much about this song?"

"I've spent some time in Sydney with some serious music blokes when I was doing theater. They used to talk about that song being interpreted as a Jacobite tune." Ross's tone softened. "I like to read about the old song catchers like John Meredith and John Lomax."

I seized the olive branch Ross offered in his conversational segue, "Who's John Meredith?"

Ross had an apologetic expression. "Sorry, Cait. Meredith was an Aussie bloke who recorded old timers singing bush ballads in the fifties. Sort of like your John Lomax only 40 years later. Ya know, a ballad hunter."

"How do you know about John Lomax?"

"I was looking at his book on cowboy songs when I was researching night herding songs for *North to Montana*. The songs the scriptwriters were using weren't all that interesting. I wanted some distinctive ones. Aussie tunes won't work."

"No, I don't suppose they would … ." The building storm outside distracted me. The wind howled and the cabin moved slightly with the gusts. The intensity of the storm hit with such force that you could actually hear the wall of rain start at one end of the cabin and spread across the surface of the roof as the wind brought the storm down off the mountain. Ross got up and opened the front door of the cabin. "Massive fall of rain," was his only comment after stepping outside onto the porch. The thunderclaps were close. He closed the door promptly, which caused several of the candles to extinguish in the resulting strong draft. I shivered from the influx of outside air.

I asked, "Would you mind too much staying out here tonight? You could sleep in the loft. I really don't want to drive down to Ennis and back in this storm. That way we can take care of your bike tires in Bozeman in the morning."

Ross shrugged. "I don't mind, if you don't."

I relit the candles and we went back to our music. Ross returned to the topic of the soul of a song. "Ya know the biggest battles I have on the set are about the soul of the character or the soul of the movie. Maintaining the integrity, staying true. You won't believe what some of the Hollywood ratbags come up with. I swear, we could do a film on the Shackleton expedition in the Antarctic and they would try to work in sex scenes and car crashes. Anything to satisfy the market researchers' demographics. Story gets pushed to the rear unless you fight for it. I'm not interested in doing anything that doesn't have integrity or soul. My days of prostituting myself are over. Now, here's a song with soul:

"Or how shall I,
Who love, who bless thee,
Invoke thy breath for freedom's strains,
When e'en the wreaths in which I dress thee,
Are sadly mixed, half flowers, half chains?[10]

"Lovely. What is it? Sounds like "Danny Boy"."

Ross nodded. "Earlier," was his only reply and he was on to the next song. He sang me a couple of Australian folk songs about the transported convicts. I was having fun; it had been a long time since I had sat down with someone and spent an evening swapping songs. It had been my favorite pastime in college, but after I got married, I quit doing it. Ralph didn't like me to sing. He said I sounded like an old alley cat in heat. I came home one day from work to find Ralph had thrown out all my music and my guitars. I wondered how I could have let something that I once had loved so passionately be stripped away from me.

Ross interrupted my musing. "Have you ever read any of the Australian bush poets, Cait?" I shook my head. "Great stuff. Many seem akin to song lyrics in their structure and rhythm."

"You could set them to music, if you wanted to be able to sing them."

Ross had a quizzical expression. I continued. "Take Woody Guthrie for instance. He was a prolific poet. Sometimes he wrote his own tunes, sometimes he borrowed old standards, and most recently an Englishman has been writing music for Guthrie's love poems. You could either borrow existing melodies or write new ones."

Ross said, "I'm listening, Cait."

"Chances are a lot of the bush ballads were inspired from older folk songs. You could look for matches. I could help you. I can transcribe music. Most folk tunes aren't that complicated in structure. Do you have any favorites in mind?"

"I'd love to be able to sing Henry Lawson's "Ballad of the Drover.""

"Write down the verses."

I handed Ross a pencil and some paper, which he rapidly covered in neat handwriting. I read them out loud. The cadence was familiar.

"Up Queensland way with cattle
He's travelled regions vast,
And many months have vanished
Since home-folks saw him last.
He hums a song of someone
He hopes to marry soon;
And hobble-chains and camp-ware

Keep jingling to the tune ...

The thunder growls a warning,
The blue forked lightnings gleam;
The drover turns his horses
To swim the fatal stream.
But, oh! the flood runs stronger
Than e'er it ran before;
The saddle-horse is failing,
And only half-way o'er!"[11]

I had an idea. I retrieved Lomax's *Folk Songs of North America.* "This tune might work. Give me the guitar." I picked out the notes to refresh my memory. Taking Ross's verses, I wrote down the first Lawson stanza above the notes for the "Little Old Sod Shanty on the Plain." The match was tolerable; it would take some fiddling to make it fit precisely. I could make it work, though. "Here's a first pass," I said and proceeded to sing the first two stanzas. I thought Lawson's second stanza made a good chorus. I said so.

"Let's go through the whole song, Cait. That way I can remember the tune."

I gave Ross back my guitar since he played better than I did. I held the music for him sitting close beside him on my bed. We sang all eight verses intermixed with the refrain. Ross smiled broadly at me when we finally finished. One of his radiant smiles. "That was really magnificent! Thank you, Caitlinn."

For a minute, I thought Ross was going to kiss me, but my guitar came between us. He was glowing with excitement. He asked, "Do you sing with other people very often?"

"No, I used to and I'd forgotten how much I missed it. I've really enjoyed this singing with you."

He nodded twice. "Yeah, me too. We'll have to do it again sometime. I like playing and singing songs. It reminds me of my childhood."

I did not feel comfortable sitting close to Ross on my bed, now that we were done singing the "Ballad of the Drover." I moved to the relative safety of my grandmother's rocking chair, opposite my bed. Ross tilted his head to one side and looked at me, chewing on the inside of his lip. After a long pause, he said, "Here's one for your Scotch/Irish angst, Caitlinn."

"She goes out every night to a ball or a party.
And leaves me here rockin' the cradle alone.
And it's by the Lord Harry if ever you marry,
Be sure don't be rockin' the cradle alone.

Heigh-ho, heigh-ho, my dearly, heigh-ho.
Perhaps your own daddy will never be known."

The tune was extremely difficult, and Ross never faltered. He clearly had sung it many times before. It seemed like an odd choice, given the unusualness of the melody and the loneliness expressed in the words. The pathos of the song was having an effect on my own emotions. Sitting there in the golden candlelight, with the storm raging outside, watching Ross sing, I thought about how much I wanted to rock my own baby. How much I wanted to feel a tiny body up against my chest. How much I wanted to smell baby hair against my face. I must have gotten a little misty-eyed because Ross stopped playing. "Are you crying, Cait?"

I shrugged, but I was crying.

"Why?" Ross set my guitar down in its case on the floor and stood up. He walked over to me. He ran his hands lightly down my braided hair, undoing the rubber band at the end of the braid.

"It's okay. It's nothing." I didn't want to talk about my failures to have my own babies. Ross unbraided my hair, freeing one strand then another. He had finished undoing the plaits and was now spreading my hair slowly out across my back, caressing the long strands with his fingers. When he did speak, his voice was low and gentle, his head down next to mine, "You could talk to me, Caitlinn."

"I know." But I didn't want to talk.

Ross gathered my hair together in one hand and draped it forward over my shoulder, kissing the nape of my exposed neck. He was humming the tune to "All the Pretty Little Horses" as he hugged me. His embrace was light and tender.

I did like the feel of Ross's hands through my hair and his kisses, but the old flight response was building. It won over. I got up and reached for my coat and started pulling on my boots. "Do you want to go to bed soon? I need to. I'm exhausted."

I went out into the storm down to the privy, the only really bad part of having no amenities. I had mixed feelings about the weather, because unless there was substantial rain the extreme fire danger would worsen with the lightning. I could only pray it would rain enough.

Ross went out as soon as I returned. I used the time alone in the cabin to quickly get undressed for bed. The spare mattress upstairs was already made up, so Ross was all set. I was sitting up in bed under the covers when he came back into the cabin. Ross took off his wet boots and hung up his leather coat. His hair was soaking wet, plastered to his head. As he dried his hair off with one of the towels used earlier in the evening, he shook his head like Frank's dog Jack after a swim, leaving a tousled mass of reddish-brown curls. He ran his fingers through his thick hair for good measure. As he picked up my guitar, Ross flashed me one of his radiant smiles saying, "Tuck in, Cait, I'll sing you to sleep."

Sitting on one of my kitchen chairs, opposite my bed, Ross sang our new version of the poor drover who drowned with his saddle horse in the flood-swollen river during the storm. I fell asleep thinking about my brother whose horse came home without him, so like Ross's favorite song. Only, my brother hadn't drowned with our dog in a storm filled creek. My father had killed him. My brother didn't leave a grieving sweetheart like the Aussie drover; he left a little sister to bear the brunt of the aftermath of his death.

The next morning, I awoke to fresh coffee and a warm cabin. Apparently, Ross had figured out how to get the propane heater going while I slept. I could get spoiled with this kind of treatment. Ross came stomping up the front steps while I was drinking my coffee. He smiled broadly when he came through the door, with his pants legs wet up to his knees—he looked adorable with his dimples showing and those wet pants, so much like Teddy when he got all dirty and happy. "Gorgeous out there, been hiking around. Marvelous. Wonderful patterns where the raindrops catch in the spider webs across the grasses. The eagle is up. He was giving me a hard time. Beautiful country you have here. Brilliant, you found your coffee."

"Thanks. It was heavenly to wake up to a warm cabin and fresh coffee."

Ross beamed. "My ex would kill for a coffee in the morning. Funny enough, that's one of the things I still miss, making her coffee. Strange how life's simple rhythms can matter so much."

I nodded. "Did you find your tea?"

"Too right, Cait. Thanks for thinking of me. I think I'll have another cuppa."

I got up, boiled some more hot water for Ross, and made some breakfast for both of us. Ross was silent for most of the time I was cooking and then he asked out of the blue, "Cait, could you read me some of your novel?"

I hesitated. "Tell you what, I'll read it to you when it's all finished. But if you want to hear something and don't mind the subject matter, I could read you one of my children's stories I wrote for the MacKinnon girls."

"Please do."

I got out "Afternoons with Grandma, Darning a Sock," which I had written for JoAnn's oldest daughter. The story was about a little girl from a big family who spent Saturdays with her grandmother. I prefaced reading with the comment, "This is the story I wrote for Elizabeth for her birthday 10 years ago, when she turned eight."

"When her boys were young, Grandma used to threaten to teach them how to bake pies, darn socks, and iron shirts. She said any self-respecting son of hers should be able to do those things before they left home. She herself had learned how to do those things, and many others, from her Grandma Kilgore and she still cherished those memories of long afternoons with her dear grandmother. When she wanted to pass on these life skills to her boys, she just wanted to honor her own grandmother's memory. It didn't seem to bother Grandma that her prospective audience was male. Her tall Montana sons thought otherwise. They compromised on pie. Her three boys made the best pies in the county, but had yet to pick up a needle or an iron. It was an ongoing family joke. She would tell them they were not too old to learn new tricks like darning socks or ironing. They would reply,

"Yeah, Mom, when you get Dad to teach you to change the oil in your car." Grandma would laugh and warn them that she was going to hold them to that bargain. "You just wait. I'll become a grease monkey and I will live long enough to see you with a needle in hand." But she hadn't been seen anywhere near the machine shed where Grandpa fixed his machinery. Instead, she had settled on her granddaughters as a potential audience."

When I was all done reading, Ross commented, "Beautiful story, Cait. You have a gift. I almost want to learn how to darn a sock myself."

I smiled. "You know what was one of the best days of my entire life?"

Ross was motionless in his whole body listening stance.

"That morning last spring when I was staying with Jo and Luke. Elizabeth and I darned socks from the book I wrote her 10 years ago. She did such a beautiful job and she was so happy. I could feel Grandma with us in that room, in that place. I had finally passed on my grandmother's legacy. I could breathe again."

"You must have really loved your nana."

I was getting a little misty-eyed again. "Grandma always stuck up for me and watched out for me. No one else loved me like my grandmother did. As long as she was alive, I felt safe, and when she died I felt so deserted, so lost, so vulnerable. I wrote this story right before she died. The day after I finished it, I got the news of her death."

"What about your parents?"

I did not want to talk about my parents. "What about them?" I asked tersely.

Ross's eyes narrowed and he tilted his head frowning slightly. "It's a lovely story, Cait. You wrote it just for Elizabeth?"

"Yup."

"Fabulous gift. My nephew Jacob had a book about a dragon and a little boy named Jacob. He thought he was the boy in the story. He used to go to bed with that book. Having a story written for you, well that's pretty special, Cait. Very kind of you."

I was embarrassed by his compliment, so I started working on cleaning up the breakfast dishes. Ross dried without my asking, and in the silence I thought about our morning conversation. I appreciated Ross's comment about writing a story for Elizabeth and how he recognized my gift to her and her gift to me in learning my grandmother's craft. I appreciated the way Ross didn't push me about my parents when I couldn't talk about them. I also noticed that if I didn't push him, he would tell me about his family. Not a dump of encyclopedic life details, but rather little small snapshots of the people he clearly loved.

Ross watched while I poured the extra hot water that hadn't been used for washing dishes into a large thermos, and asked me what I was doing. I explained it was nice to have warm water on hand for washing and Ross responded with a comment about my interesting lifestyle. I tried to explain my interest in low levels of technology. "There's a rhythm and grace to the simplicity of this life style that soothes my soul."

Chewing on his lower lip, Ross paused, then asked me, "Why do you need to live a monk's life in this monastic cell, Cait?"

I hesitated. The temptation to tell Ross what troubled my soul was strong, and his expression was compassionate, but he was a man who could be quite flippant and dismissive. I could not be certain how Ross would react to my story, and therefore, I broke his gaze, shrugging a response rather than answering him honestly. Changing the subject, I started addressing the details of the day. "We better leave for Bozeman around 11:30, I'll call my friend JoAnn and see if she can meet us downtown for late lunch. But before then, I really need to do some editing, since I'll be gone this afternoon. You don't mind, do you?"

"No, I'll just grab a couple books off your shelf here that looked interesting and go upstairs. I must be relaxing because I'm really tired."

Ross went up into the loft, leaving me to work, and the quiet morning went by quickly. We were getting ready to leave when I remembered something I needed from the cabin. I had my camera in hand when I walked down to the truck, as Ross's mask descended across his face. "What's that for?"

"I always carry my camera when I travel. Since I've been writing my grandma stories, I frequently see things I'd like to use as illustrations or maybe I want a photographic record for later detailed descriptions. I see more of life's details now that I travel with a camera."

Ross smiled. "Roger that. Do you want me to take some snaps of you?" he asked.

I nodded. He took several of me by my truck, and then he asked me if I would like to take one of him by the cabin. Photographing him by the cabin sparked an inspiration for me, a possible creative solution to a problem I had been wrestling with all summer. Ross noticed my expression and asked me what I was thinking about. I was not paying too much attention to him, and I said something vague about an idea for a story. Ross asked to see my camera again. He fiddled with it, set it on the hood of the truck, pushed a button, and stood next to me. He put his arm around me and drew me close saying, "Smile, Cait." The camera clicked, and the two of us were recorded for posterity. I liked that thought. I hugged Ross back, and when he bent down, I hoped he would kiss me which he did.

"Thanks," I said, and walked back to the truck.

Even with the photography, we got started right on schedule. I drove, and on the muddy roads I was grateful for my mudflaps. Without them, the earth of Montana would have plated my truck inches thick with mud. The worst section after a storm was the first mile out to the county road, due to the two tricky hilly curves right below Frank's place. The road did not have much of a gravel base, and several vehicles traveling through the mud would compact the molecules creating slippery conditions. As it turned out, several vehicles had been through already this morning, deepening the ruts. I could feel the Chevy's rear wheels trying to budge in line and get in front. In retrospect, I should have put something in the rear of the truck for better traction. I was relieved to get through the tough sections without incident. Successful driving in bad conditions was a matter of pride, and as a Montana native, I did not want to get stuck with Ross as a passenger in my truck. As a Montanan, I needed to know my ride. But more importantly to me, I needed to be a trustworthy partner with whom to ride.

As we approached the Alexander ranch, I asked Ross if he knew where the Story trail came through. No, he didn't. I stopped the truck.

"If you look up this slope along the fence line, that faint discoloration in the grass is the old trail. It's more visible at certain times of the year. When we cross the Norris Hill, I'll pull over and show you the trail as it crosses the pass. Charlie should be able to arrange a ride with you along this part of the trail. Remember to ask him."

"I'm familiar with the Norris Hill section of the old trek and Charlie and I have ridden the part between Ennis and Virginia City. But I had no idea you and Frank lived so close to this section of it. Thanks for pointing it out to me. I appreciate knowing."

Once on the county gravel road below the Alexander's ranch along the North Meadow Creek, the surface of the road switched from slippery to spine-jarring. This section of washboard reminded me of a piece of dark brown corduroy with its deep wales filled with water. The sun was reflecting off each wet rut. We reached the half-grated section of the road and I slowed down to a crawl. Wet newly graded road was extremely slick. I was glad to finally reach the safety of dry pavement. We turned north on Highway 287 and rode in silence, but a comfortable one. We got passed a lot on the Norris Hill. I didn't push my old Chevy especially up a steep grade.

At the top of the Norris Hill, I pulled in next to the historical marker. "Come look," I said to Ross. He joined me, looking out across to the faint ruts below the banked highway. "There's the old trail, and if you look along the edge of these foothills, you can see the area of my cabin. The stage coach route or the Story trail explains why Meadow Creek was the first area settled in the Valley. Where Ennis Lake is was the easiest way to ford the Madison River if you were coming from Bozeman."

"Interesting." Ross fell silent and we stood there for about 10 minutes, looking at the old ruts and then at the vista of the Madison Valley spreading all the way down to Idaho. After the heavy rains, all the mountain ranges were clearly highlighted against a cloudless azure sky. I was pleased with Ross's intense interest in my home country.

As we drove down the pass towards the town of Norris, I

broke the quiet with stories about my childhood. Grandpa Gallagher had grown up in this country and ridden all of it on horseback as a child. I repeated the stories I had heard. Grandpa describing driving livestock over the pass to the rail station in Norris and making all the cars wait for his flock of sheep. The Northern Pacific's spur line, constructed in 1890, ended at the old Alex Norris ranch and the town of Norris grew because of the spur line, which was used by the residents of Madison Valley for transporting passengers, goods, and animals to the outside world. All along the highway, deep into the Madison River canyon, I was telling Ross every story I knew about the land, its people, and my grandpa.

Ross listened intently. I could tell he was interested in everything I said, because he kept his body still. "I'd love to ride this country on horseback. Do you ride, Cait?"

I shook my head. "Nope."

"A Montana girl and you don't ride horses?"

"Urban Montana girl, and my father won't let me. He was overprotective. He didn't want me near them."

"Did you want to learn to ride?"

"Yes." It was only one of the many things my grandfather and my father used to fight about.

I asked Ross a question for a change, "Have you been riding long?"

"Since before I could walk. My father and I were joined at the hip. Mum used to joke she was glad when she had my little brother Brian, because my father stole me away from her as a wee bub. Mum claimed after I was weaned, she never saw me again. I was with my father all the time. He lost his first wife and baby in childbirth, so when I came along, I was his consolation prize. Or something. Dad ran one of the oldest stud farms in Upper Hunter Valley. My sister Ruthie and her husband Steve have the family business now. I like to help train horses, but the last few years I've been gone too much on location. You should learn to ride, Cait. Embrace life."

"Right. In between pouring beers and putting commas in my novel."

Ross ignored my comment and I remembered other times in the past few days when he didn't respond to something I had said. He asked, "Tell me, what would you do with your granddad if you didn't ride?"

"Everything: fishing, hiking, four-wheel driving, lots of exploring. Grandpa knew this country like the back of his hand. He loved it so much. Grandpa's the reason I studied archaeology. He said the landscape should be a major character in our lives and we should listen and learn the stories because the land holds all the memories of past lives. When I'm on a dig, I always feel like the land is gifting me memories so I can reconstruct the lost stories. My best childhood memories are times spent with my grandparents." I was remembering how my parents interacted. The angry fights, the long silences. Life with Ralph had been even worse. Before I could stop myself, the question was out, "How can people who should love each other be so cruel?"

I had tears in my eyes, remembering my family. Even though the road was winding and we were coming into the river canyon, I stole a glance at Ross. He was looking out his window at the sunlight sparkling off the white caps of the Madison River. The wind left over from last night's storm was creating turbulence across the water. He said softly, without looking at me, "Only people who love you have the power to really hurt you."

"Your family?"

"Yes."

I didn't want to ask another question. I read once where if someone is in great pain, you shouldn't probe around in their wounds like a surgeon. You should wait, shine a soft healing light on the sores, like gentle sunlight early in the morning. I waited for Ross to say something. A slow-moving truck with a big boat was in front of me. He went over the centerline each time he went around a corner. The Madison River road had a lot of blind, sharp corners, and the imprecise driving made me nervous. I slowed down to create more room between us and the out-of- state driver who didn't know how to drive the canyon safely.

Ross began again softly. I could barely hear him. "I had just finished the shoot for *The Last Man* in L.A. when my sister Ruthie called. My parents were up in Queensland on business when their landing gear didn't lock on the plane Dad was flying. My little sister had to tell me our parents were dead, Cait, she was only 15. I had to go home. I had no choice. I sent for my wife, Shelley, and our son, David, after I decided to run Granddad's stud farm. My brother, Brian, needed my help, too. He's good with the books, but Dad didn't teach him to train horses. Dad taught me. The first few years after my folks died, Shelley agreed I had to take care of Ruthie and the farm, but after Ruthie graduated, Shelley decided I should sell the farm and move back to Sydney, since Ruthie was going there for uni. That's where Shelley and I had met—Sydney—doing theater together. I started doing movies, because that was my medium. Theater was hers. I wanted to do movies in the States, the big time. I got an offer to do a movie in L.A., about three years after our marriage. I took it. *The Last Man*. Fabulous script. Great director. I couldn't turn it down. Shelley loved being in Los Angeles. She loved the parties and the ceremonies.

Going back to Australia to work on a stud farm with a bub, after the glamor of Hollywood, was Shelley's idea of a living hell. She hated the farm so much that she was making my life a living hell. I made a tough choice. Brian and the farm needed me. Shelley didn't. It was that simple. Shelley asked for a divorce, and I gave her whatever she wanted. My lawyer said I could have asked for joint custody, but I'm gone so much overseas, it didn't seem fair to David. I let her take my son and go to live in Sydney near her parents. I bought her the house she wanted. Shortly after that, Shelley got married again. I put my career on hold and saved the family business, but I couldn't save my marriage and I can't raise my own son."

I wanted to ask more questions, but the road was demanding my full attention. Ross was still. I thought his stillness was not from inner peace, it was the paralysis of pain. I could feel it without looking at him. I wanted to reach out and touch him to reassure him, but I was in the worst part of the canyon. I needed to keep my eyes focused on the road, both hands on the wheel, because the old Chevy did not have power steering. The truck was still in front of me and it was still crossing the centerline on each curve. If anyone came in the opposite direction around the blind curves, we could all be in trouble. I slowed down. I could not get a straight shot to pass the truck and trailer in front of me. I never pushed my old Chevy, and I would need a lot of room for passing. I stayed behind the truck with the boat, trying to be patient.

Bonny Portmore

Oh, Bonny Portmore, you shine where you stand
And the more I think on you, the more I think long
If I had you now as I had once before
All the Lords in Old England would not purchase Portmore

Oh, Bonny Portmore, I am sorry to see
Such a woeful destruction of your ornament tree
For it stood on your shore for many's the long day
'Til the long boats from Antrim came to float it away

All the birds in the forest they bitterly weep
Saying, "Where shall we shelter, where shall we sleep?
For the oak and the ash, they are all cutten down
And the walls of Bonny Portmore are all down to the ground.[12]

Traditional Irish folksong

~ Chapter 16 ~

We stopped at the repair shop in Bozeman to drop off Ross's front wheel and then we joined JoAnn at the pizza place on Main Street for lunch. Jo was waiting for us on the bench outside of the front of the restaurant. Jo sat as often as she could with this pregnancy. She was due in mid-October, and her fifth child was promising to be active and strong.

I introduced her to Ross and we walked into the restaurant. I noticed Ross had a wary expression on his face, as if expecting trouble. His body language was tense as well. Nothing happened. People looked up as they always do in Montana and went right back to their business. Ross asked to sit in the back booth, away from curious eyes. The waitress looked him over carefully, but she did not make any comments. Ross slid into the booth, so his scar would be away from me and away from Jo. I sat down beside him, keeping a respectable distance. JoAnn started to tell me her children's latest antics. Ross started to relax and to expand into my personal space. He was leaning back—his long leg sprawling into my side of the booth, his arm casually on the seat back behind me. Under the table, his knee was finding mine. I didn't know if he was paying attention to our conversation or not, since he was looking off across the restaurant at the fishing mural on the far wall. Ross was not tapping, but he began playing with my braid absentmindedly. Out of the blue, he asked me what I planned to do for the winter.

"I'm hoping to go back to Illinois for the spring semester."

"Say, what? You said you were giving up on teaching, because the uni changed their policy on instructors, Cait."

"I know, but one of the professors is taking a sabbatical spring semester, and there's a chance they'll hire me to cover his class."

"Then, what?"

"I don't know." I was getting testy. Jo was frowning at me. She knew how much I wanted to change careers, and here I was talking about returning to teaching. Nobody knew I had lost all my course materials and my extensive library when I left Ralph. I did not want to alarm anyone and I did not want any interference. I actually had no firm plans past October, but I did not want to admit that to Ross or to Jo. I needed to pretend to be a strong woman in complete control.

"Why would you go back for one semester?"

"One semester of pay is better than nothing," I said with forced conviction. I'd never been good at deception of any degree.

"But they don't appreciate you, Cait. Why waste your time with a system that doesn't care? Explore the possibilities. Going back to Illinois is not exploring possibilities. It's not a solution. It's just retreating to something familiar." Ross had stopped playing with my hair and had taken his arm down from behind me. He was leaning forward over the table on his elbows, gazing intensely at me sideways.

"That's easy for you to say. Your career is going well." I was feeling guilty for lying to Ross about wanting to return to Illinois, and his assertiveness wasn't improving my mood.

Ross's voice dropped in frequency and volume. "Wasn't always that way, Cait. I had to do the Lazarus act after my parents died. I told you what happened. Please don't prostitute yourself. You've got a job at the Bear Claw, why do you want to go back to nothing? I think you have promise as a writer. You're a great storyteller, but you'll need to commit totally to writing—mind, body, and soul—to make writing work for you as a new profession. Complete dedication and belief in yourself. You, Cait, have a gift. Don't run from that God-given gift. Embrace it and fight for it. Accept your destiny. Unless, you're going back to Ralph and you don't have the courage to tell me."

Ross's eyes darkened. I was on drifting polar ice again. I was not going back to Ralph, but I was not going to tell Ross why. I would rather die first than tell Ross how I had lived with so much violence resulting in the death of two of my babies. Maybe I could justify the first murder of our child, but by staying with Ralph, I had condemned my third child to the same fate. Fortunately, JoAnn intervened in my unfolding nightmare.

"Ross, tell me about your movie. When Luke first mentioned a movie being made about his great-great-grandfather and Nelson Story, I didn't realize an outsider, an Aussie at that, would be telling a Montana story."

With Ross distracted, I had a chance to think about what

he had said about committing myself to writing rather than returning to teaching. I wondered if Ross knew I had been less than honest with him. He was not Father Paddy. I did not have to confess to him. I had no intention of returning to the Midwest. Twice before in my life I had almost died away from Montana. After watching *Cleaveth Unto the Dust*, I knew with certainty where my place of spiritual resurrection was. Ultimately, my body belonged in the soil of my thin place. I was home now and I was not leaving. When Ross opened up to me in the canyon about his marriage and divorce, I had mixed emotions. As long as Ross kept his secrets from me, I could keep mine from him. How much longer was that going to last? Ross was too perceptive, too much like Frank. I could not even confide in my godfather. How could I confide in a man I hardly knew, even if I might be developing feelings for him? How could I possibly tell Ross how damaged I was and still have him like me?

Jo invited us both to come out for dinner, so Ross could meet her husband, Luke, and see the horses. We accepted her invitation. Jo had afternoon appointments for marketing her jewelry with several art galleries, leaving Ross and me free to stroll around Bozeman. We were walking the downtown and I was pointing out the various historical landmarks, when we passed by one of the local schools. I explained how Nelson Story's mansion had been torn down to build the school Jo and I attended. I pointed out the metal statue of Nelson's grandson, Malcolm, which graced the front lawn. Malcolm was clad in his ubiquitous red wool, plaid jacket and wide brimmed Stetson with his enormous handlebar mustache.

"I know who Malcolm is, Cait. I've been researching the Story family in the MSU library and the Gallatin History

Museum. I've read all the professional accounts and I've read through all the Story personal papers and studied the family photos."

Okay then, since you know more than I do about Malcolm and his famous grandfather, I won't share my own Bozeman experience with you. The college students used to get extremely frustrated with Malcolm's driving style. He drove through town at the speed of a horse's canter in his old car with the big fins. The more cars he had piled up behind him, the slower he drove. Malcolm was ornery. Malcolm was a classic Montanan. Since Ross knew all about Malcolm and Story family, I would tell him a different story about two native Montanans who left their fellow native stranded on the school playground.

"What were you little girls doing?" Ross asked.

"Measuring how skinny our knees were."

"Not too skinny now."

"Hush." I admonished. "It was a wooden bike rack. We took turns putting our knees in. One slot was smaller than the others, and Diana Hamilton put her knee in and it wouldn't come out. Then the recess bell rang and we all ran inside, leaving poor Diana out on the playground."

"Ah, Cait, you were a cruel woman, even then."

I ignored him and waited. I was making him pay for that remark. I knew how much he hated it when stories weren't finished promptly.

"All right. All right, Cait, I'm sorry. What happened?" Ross was laughing. "I don't see any skeletons."

"The janitor came and sawed her out. The principal made us all promise not to play that game anymore. It was my first lesson in manufacturing and statistical control."

Ross raised an eyebrow.

"Sorry, it's important in manufacturing to make certain

that all the pieces are all the same size and meeting specifications. Quality control was Ralph's career. He was always talking shop." I hesitated and then I asked, "Do you want to hear another Diana Hamilton story?"

"Go, ahead."

"Maybe what I did to Diana at the bike rack was partial payback for when Diana and I were in second grade and we were playing school in my backyard. I always played the teacher because I was a bossy little kid. Diana didn't believe me when I told her four times two was eight, and I was adamant. I knew I was right. Diana got up from the picnic table and stomped her foot with her arms akimbo and yelled at me, 'My mother says I don't have to listen to you, if I don't want to.' That was the last time we ever played school together."

"And."

"My whole teaching career, I kept waiting for the other shoe to drop. Waiting for some college student to stand up and stomp their feet with arms akimbo and say, 'my mother says I don't have to listen to you, if I don't want to.'"

"And."

"Well, on my final class day of teaching maybe forever, because the university had changed their policies about adjunct professors, I had a student who had to leave early for a dentist appointment. He was a really sweet kid and very apologetic. I realized this was my last chance to drop the other shoe, so I took it. I acknowledged his apology and asked him for a favor. I told him my Diana Hamilton story, and since it was the end of my teaching career, I needed him to do me a favor." I hesitated, waiting.

"Caitlinn, finish the damn story."

"I asked him to stand up and repeat Diana's words, stomp his feet with arms akimbo, and storm out of the classroom."

"Did he?"

"Of course, he did." I waited for emphasis and for Ross's anticipated reaction.

"Caitlinn … ."

"You should have seen the look on my students' faces. It was priceless. I kept a straight face for a few minutes and then fessed up to my big practical joke. Good thing it was the last day of class, because my class was not happy with me. I had betrayed their trust. They were not amused. At all. The next class was, though. I told them what had happened and, since it didn't happen to them, they thought it was hysterically funny." I expected Ross to laugh like he had after the bike rack story, but he didn't.

Ross stopped dead in his tracks and looked at me, expressionless, before speaking, "You were lying at lunch about going back to teaching, weren't you?" His eyebrow went up a little as he finished his accusation.

I refused to answer him. I stared down at the sidewalk.

Ross put his arms around me, holding me close to him while kissing the top of my head. "Caitlinn, you are easily the most intriguing woman, I've ever met in my life, but you are a rubbish liar."

I apologized.

With both hands on my upper arms, Ross pushed me away from him, "Maybe, rather than repeatedly apologizing to me for being a rubbish liar, you could try being honest with me instead. It would save both of us a lot of time. I have a well-calibrated bullshit meter, ya know."

"I know."

"Caitlinn, why don't you try the truth for a change? If you don't want to share something with me, you don't have to. I'm not your interrogator, your counselor, or your priest, I'm just asking you to stop throwing shit at me, expecting me to be dumb enough to believe you. It's condescending and quite frankly downright insulting. I might be a famous actor, but I'm not stupid. Your class didn't appreciate you throwing shit at them, neither do I. I get why you pulled the prank because it *was* funny, but you might want to consider the aftermath of betraying the trust of people who respect you. Like me, for instance."

"Okay." I started to apologize again, but Ross put his forefinger across my lips, shaking his head.

"Nah, Cait. I don't need any more apologies from you. All I require is the truth as best you can manage it in the moment. Nothing more. And nothing less. Can you do that for me?"

I couldn't do or say anything. Ross was not angry with me, he was establishing boundaries. Nobody had ever done that before with me. The story of my life had always been that I could either maneuver my way through a situation through force of personality or men would exert their physical power over me and I had to submit to them in order to survive. I was lost in thought considering this new dynamic in my life as we walked back to my truck. At the intersection, we had to wait for the light to change and I looked up at Ross. The corners of his mouth were almost curving up into a smile, "Ya know I'm right, Cait. When you open your mouth, stories pop out like prairie dogs. You're a born storyteller, not a teacher." Ross pulled me into him again, holding me close until the light changed.

I hugged him back, because Ross was right. I had one last story to tell him before we went to Jo's for supper. We walked back to the truck and drove out to the edge of town to my old neighborhood. The street was a dead end with alfalfa fields stretching down the hill from the edges of abandoned yards. Construction vehicles lined the curb, but no one seemed to be around.

"When I was small, we lived out here." All that remained were the crumbling sidewalks leading nowhere in the overgrown grass. The university had purchased the houses and demolished them years ago. We got out of the truck and walked down one of the narrow concrete paths. "This is where we lived. This was the living room, my bedroom." I walked out the floor plan.

"And this, this is why we came out here. This is the tree my grandmother helped me plant. It's one of the first things I can remember doing with Grandma. I was in kindergarten and it was spring. I picked up a willow branch on the way back from school and carried it home. Grandma was visiting Mom that afternoon and she said we could grow a tree from it. I didn't believe her. She showed me how we could root it by putting the branch in water. 'Be patient,' she told me. 'It'll grow roots.' It did. Grandma helped me plant it a couple weeks later. I come here to visit this tree whenever I come home. I always meant to take a branch back to Illinois to keep the tree with me, but I never did. Just as well, I guess, since Ralph got the house." I sighed. "Now that Grandma is dead, the tree is dying too." I stroked the tree's trunk affectionately, adding wistfully, "I wish I could save it. Could you take a picture of me with Grandma's tree?"

I handed Ross my camera. He took several pictures from different angles. I took several of him with the tree as well. Ross asked me if I wanted to stay here for a while. He said something I did not quite follow about spending some serious spiritual time under a tree. Before I could ask him to repeat himself, he had walked back to the truck. He returned with my blanket, which he spread on the ground. He laid down, stretching out sideways with his long legs extended with his head on his elbow looking up at me. "Okay now, Cait, tell me why this tree is so important to you. I remember the part about how you and your grandmother planted it together. Don't repeat that. What else is there to this story?"

I looked down at Ross, and I looked across the valley at the familiar outlines of the surrounding mountain ranges of my childhood. Part of me wanted to tell Ross my family's troubles from A to Z, and the other part didn't fully trust him yet. Where to start? What to leave out? I was in a dilemma. This spot at the end of a dead-end street was not a safe place for me. All my memories from this spot were too close to my parents and too close to my childhood pain.

I considered telling Ross the real reason Grandma had been visiting when I came home with the willow branch. The elementary school had called about my language. Mother was hysterical. She was forced to deal with a problem she had been ignoring.

Grandma had been relieved to see me with my willow branch. Planting her favorite kind of tree provided a convenient distraction until my mother recovered from the embarrassment of a daughter who didn't speak English, at least not Standard English. As a toddler I had rearranged words in sentences, playing with grammatical structure. Mark and Grandpa thought I was funny and always laughed. I kept doing it. I played with words, too, making up new ones and recombining existing ones. Jo and Grandma understood me and so did Frank. Whenever my parents didn't comprehend my altered speech, my brother translated for me. I had no motivation to talk correctly until I went to school. When my mother was forced to spend time with me re-teaching me English, I was willing to give up my special language. For my mother. I got what I craved—her attention.

I could see the Bridgers from where I stood, and if I turned around, I would see the Spanish Peaks off in the direction of my cabin and the Gallatin Range closer to town. Mount Blackmore with its distinctive pyramidal outline reminded me of my mother's favorite story of the doomed Lady Blackmore. Jo played Lady Blackmore every year at the cemetery walk. How could my mother be so sentimental about a British tourist who died 100 years ago while on vacation and so blasé about her husband's behavior with his own daughter? Mother's eyes would glisten when she explained Lord Blackmore's purchase of the hill overlooking the town. He ensured that his wife would have a proper eternal resting place by planning Bozeman's first cemetery. No man in my adult life had ever concerned himself with my eternal needs.

I started pacing around the tree and clenching my hands. I decided to take control. I needed to sit down with Ross. I could do that. Ross had given me permission not to talk. I didn't have to talk. I could always distract Ross, the way men liked to be distracted. I could handle that.

I walked over to the blanket, and stretched out beside him. I pressed my lips hard against his. I wrapped my leg over his thigh and reached for his hand. I was moving against him while placing his hand on my breast. Ross kissed me back, but not for long. He disentangled our limbs and rolled over on his abdomen, rising up onto his elbows, looking at me sideways, "Caitlinn, what don't you want to talk about? Your grandmother, your childhood, or your parents? Here, I'll make it easy for you. I'll ask you one at a time. You nod or shake your head. That'll define the boundaries. I can deal with that. Will you talk to me about your parents?"

I shook my head no.

"Will you talk to me about your grandmother?"

I shook my head no.

"Will you talk to me about your childhood?"

I shook my head no.

"Okay, that was easy. Now where were we?" Ross was content to go back to kissing. He had called my bluff. How was I going to control interactions with him? Ross was always one step ahead of me, or more often he was at an oblique angle. I appreciated the way he defined boundaries and then respected them. I loved the way he kissed. Ross's kisses were gentle, not aggressive like mine. The way his lips caressed my face was the way I touched art— exploratory, to remember all the contours, all the details. When I moved in pleasure from the initial contact around my ears, Ross concentrated his attentions there. He was searching for and finding my most sensitive spots. Intervals of time passed when Ross just held me and stroked my hair. When he pulled me on top of him, I could feel him through his jeans and I half expected him to progress beyond kissing. He didn't.

When the sky started to cloud over, Ross said we best get going. We walked back to the Chevy. The almost daily summer mid-afternoon Bozeman shower was threatening. We got in the truck cab to the accompaniment of soft raindrops coming down in the sunshine. Summer in Montana was like that—mini weather systems could catch you unawares. My grandmother used to tell me about the baseball game when she was a child that went so horribly wrong. It was early summer in 1910 and baseball was

America's game, even in the small ranching communities like McAllister. During a local baseball game, a rogue cloud drifted overhead and no one noticed until too late. Seventy-five people were involved—four people seriously injured, nine severely shocked, and many others knocked to the ground by the lightning strike. The wife of the Madison River Power company had been holding a parasol to shield herself from the sun and the lightning bolt struck the steel rod and traveled through the metal stays of her corset before hitting the ground. Nearly all Mrs. Buck's clothes were torn from her body, even the hat pins in her hat melted. She was taken to the medic in critical condition with massive burns. When my grandfather would tell me to pay attention to Montana skies, my grandmother was apt to punctuate his admonition with the horrific story she witnessed at a tender age.

By the time we had driven across town to the repair shop, the brief showers were over, leaving a complete double rainbow arching over the valley. Ross paid for his new tire and a patch kit. We drove out to JoAnn's ranch at the intersection of Bridger and Kelly Canyons. As we walked into Jo's kitchen, our noses were bombarded by the exquisite smell of freshly baked huckleberry pie. When Ross was introduced to Ben, he squatted down on his heels, his boot heels flat on the floor to shake Ben's hand, and then talked to him for quite a while in that position. His voice dropped, so only Ben could hear their conversation. When Ross was introduced to Teddy, he did exactly the same thing. I had never seen a man do that with small boys before—get down to their level and talk to them mate to mate as if they were equals. Ross was more stand-offish with Jo's daughters. He said pleased to meet you, when introduced, but after that he more or less ignored them unless they spoke directly to him. Ross was equally formal with Jo. After meeting Ross, the boys were clamoring around, asking me to read to them. Jo hushed them and said I should shower first.

"I'll keep Ross entertained," Jo said to me, as she pushed towels into my arms. I didn't argue, and when I was done, I sat on the couch with little Teddy on my lap. Jo's family had a tradition of reading out loud together at night, regardless of how old the girls were. Elizabeth, the oldest, sat on one side of me and Julia sat on the other side. Ben climbed onto the back of the couch and draped himself lengthwise like a panther on a tree limb, so he could see the illustrations in the book we were reading. I was halfway through chapter one in Kipling's *Jungle Book,* and deeply engrossed in doing all the different voices, when I felt Ross's presence in the room. I looked up to see Ross watching us, his body at an angle—shoulder leaning against the doorjamb, hands thrust deeply into his pockets, ankles crossed. He shook his head slightly when I met his gaze. I understood he didn't want to interrupt us. When I looked up later from my reading, Ross was gone as quietly as he had arrived. I could hear Ross laughing in the kitchen, however. No doubt Jo was sharing one of her funny stories.

Halfway through the second chapter, Jo came and excused me from reading duty. "You should spend some time with Ross, Cait. Show him your grandmother's place. The owners moved back to San Diego and I'm looking after things for them. Here's the key. Take Ross through the house, they won't care. It's going on the market first of next month." She tossed me the key to my grandmother's old house.

Ross and I walked across the MacKinnon's barnyard and down the path along the creek to my grandmother's. The wind was shaking the leaves of the quaking aspens lining the creek. Here and there, because of the drought a few gold leaves were interspersed with the green. The leaves looked like thousands of flags twisting in the breeze. I loved to watch aspen leaves move against the deep blue of the late afternoon skies and listen to the leaves caressing each other. Of all the Montana sounds I lived without while I was away in Illinois, it was the whisper of aspens along Bridger Creek I missed the most.

Halfway to Grandma's place, Ross asked, "Cait, why didn't you and Ralph have any children? You're so beautiful with Jo's."

I stopped in the path and regarded him carefully. "I tried. I had three miscarriages. The first pregnancy was the reason Ralph and I got married. The ectopic pregnancy made four failures." I was rather cold in my delivery.

"Ah, Cait, I'm sorry." Then, Ross asked simply, "The dates on the back of the cross?"

I nodded. Frank had crafted the cross out of cedar for me the first week I arrived in Montana. I had spent part of the next six weeks, carving the knotwork and the dates of my four miscarriages. Putting up the cross on the mountain with Frank's assistance had helped ease the pain of my losses and had brought some closure for me. The cross was a tangible reminder to the world that four souls had been created by Ralph and me. It was proof of life. The fact that Ralph' actions had ended two of them was another matter.

Ross quietly embraced me. He did not ask any more probing questions, which I deeply appreciated.

I showed Ross the spot on the creek where Grandpa had first taught me to fish. We used worms for bait. A lot of people equated bait fishing with the seven deadly sins but Grandpa wasn't a purist. He didn't think of fishing as a Zen experience; it was simply part of his Montana life.

Sometimes, he fished with flies he tied himself and sometimes he fished with bait. He had the same laid-back attitude about what he did with the fish after he caught them. Sometimes he kept his limit and ate them, sometimes he released all of them regardless of size or limit. The fishing issue that Grandpa was passionate about was maintaining the integrity of the Montana streams and rivers, filling them with only native fish. The reservoirs and lakes in Montana were often restocked with hatchery varieties. Grandpa always had plenty of criticism for the Montana Department of Fish and Game stocking the Madison River with rainbow trout so the out-of-state tourists would have plenty to catch. Grandpa hoped the streams and rivers could stay pure and wild and never be artificially stocked. He didn't see why a Montana governmental agency should be concerned about catering to outsiders at the expense of native Montanans. Grandpa could get a bit radical once he got a bee up his bonnet, as Grandma would say. She made a point to ignore him whenever he mounted his fishing soapbox and began preaching.

I showed Ross where Jo and I first went sledding. I told him how Grandpa had laughed at us because we refused to ride our sleds down the hill. We were both three years old and we walked down the hill pulling our little sleds behind us. It was on the same hill that we first tried out our new downhill skis several years later. Grandpa ignored us that day. He did not have any patience with skiing or skiers. Although the popularity of skiing had increased after World War II, Grandpa was from the old generation of Montanans who thought careening down a mountainside on the equivalent of barrel staves was for lunatics. The fact that he had to pull skiers' cars out of the ditch all winter, when they drove too fast on the canyon road to and from the local ski hill, did not change his mind about the sport.

I showed Ross the barns where Grandpa taught me to milk. I described how safe I felt nestled in Grandpa's embrace, sharing the milking stool, his hands over mine coaxing the milk out of the cow's teats. Ross's eyes sparkled when I told him how proud I was when the first stream of milk tinkled into the metal pail. We walked through the chicken coups and I related the tearful morning when the double-yolked egg I had found broke in my jacket pocket before I could show it to Grandma.

Grandma's hollyhocks were still blooming tall along the south fence. I pulled off a few flowers and, remembering Grandma's instructions, I made Ross a hollyhock doll. Grandma's roses, dainty pink and white, were still winding up the trellises by the back kitchen door where we entered the empty brick house. Nobody ever came through the front door that I could recall. Grandma's visitors were back-door folks.

My grandfather had bought the two-story brick ranch house in the late-thirties. A master carver named Rodgers had built the brick house in the canyon around the turn of the century. He had arranged to have hard woods shipped in from the Midwest. As a result, it was one of the few houses in the canyon that had solid walnut doors and oak floors. Rodgers had died before he could finish the interior. The next owner trimmed out the house with simple pine moldings, not the ornately carved hardwood that Rodgers had intended. The milled planks of cherry and walnut were still in the barn loft when Grandpa bought the place. When Grandpa found all of Rodgers' carving patterns in a drawer in the shed, he had a new mission. He spent many a subsequent long winter evening with his woodworking tools, blissfully completing Rodgers' dream.

When I was a small child, I had delighted in the flowered patterns carved into the lintel moldings over each interior doorway and window.

My grandparents gave up the old homestead on the Madison, where rattlesnakes were a constant fact of life. Grandma used to tell me stories about her mother-in-law who, when she was first married and living on the original Gallagher homestead, would take a shovel every morning and kill the rattlesnakes that nested under the house in order to protect her young children. When Grandpa sold his family place, he also changed his occupation. He accepted a job doing construction work on the Bozeman schools funded by the WPA while still doing a bit of ranching on the side. Grandma loved the new place. She said heaven couldn't be more beautiful than the tree-covered slopes of the lush Bridgers. Grandma did not miss her old home in the southern Madison Valley, but my mother did. Mother felt smothered and choked by Bridger Canyon. The long shadows cast in the morning and evening by the mountains, blocking the sunlight in the canyon, depressed her. The trips out to the Gallagher cabin were some comfort to my mother. Especially when she could sit on Grandpa's favorite rock and see the faint purple snow-capped peaks of the Rocky Mountains of Idaho, 90 miles away.

Little had been changed in the house. The late afternoon sunshine danced across the scratched dark oak floors, sparkling over the boards with quarter-sawn patterns. Mark and I used to crawl across the floor looking for the boards with the best designs in the grain. I could still find his favorite one in the dining room—the one patterned with the golden ribbons shimmering across the surface of the narrow plank, the third one from the wall under the window framing the Bridger Mountain range.

"Cait, why did your grandfather move his family from the Madison Valley?"

"A mean snake stuck his tongue out at my mother and she was upset by it."

"Excuse me?"

I kept a straight face. "There were a lot of rattlesnakes around the original Gallagher place, and my mother was an only child. One day when she was a toddler, she came into the kitchen crying. Apparently, a mean snake had stuck his tongue out at her and she was quite upset by that rude snake. My grandfather went out the next day and bought this place. All he would say to my grandmother was at least there weren't any damn rattlesnakes here in Bridger Canyon."

"Now that's a great story, Cait. A rude snake." Ross chuckled before continuing, "I'll have fun telling Jacob that one."

"Who's Jacob again? You might have told me but I forgot."

"My godson. I'm godfather to both of my sister's kids—Jacob and Nora. Ruthie named her twins after our dead parents. Jacob loves stories just like my mother did. What about the 2 Lazy 2, Cait? Any rattlers around there."

"Grandpa's cabin is too high and dry for rattlesnakes. We were taught to be careful just in case, but no one has spotted any so far. Rattlesnakes like the lower altitudes along the river and some of the bigger irrigation ditches. Grandpa was big on concrete solutions to problems. He didn't mess around, especially not with the health of his only child. He and Grandma buried three sons. They were all stillborn. My mother was the only one who survived. Grandma told me that she was O negative and baby girls were stronger than baby boys. I don't know if she was right though, because I'm O negative which means my mother must have been too, so maybe it didn't have anything to do with gender."

Ross frowned briefly, but made no comment.

As we climbed the back stairs from the kitchen, I remembered sitting in the gloom, listening to my grandfather worrying that snowy dark morning in October, the morning after I heard the wolf. I sat down on the stairs, exactly as I had that morning 24 years ago. Memories were echoing through the empty house. I closed my eyes and listened to the old voices.

My grandfather had called the sheriff over in Sweet Grass County to get the weather conditions up in the Crazies where his son-in-law and his grandson had gone hunting two days before. My grandfather and my father had a huge argument before Dad and Mark left. I heard all the angry words.

Grandpa had firmly advised against going into the mountains with the forecast calling for snow in the upper elevations. The Crazies were notorious for dangerous weather that changed rapidly, trapping the unwary. When my father wouldn't listen, Grandpa lost his patience, "You're a damn fool, Burnett. There are other people involved here. One mistake and Mark could die. Or you. In life or death situations a man's judgment can make all the difference."

"What are you implying, Gallagher?"

"I'm not implying anything. The measure of who you ride with matters when you're in the wilderness. We all care about you and Mark. You need to be more careful. You take unnecessary chances."

My father responded with bitterness, "You goddamned Montanans. You think you're the only ones who know how to do anything. All I've heard since I moved here is how outsiders can't be trusted to do anything right. Fuck you and fuck Montana. I'll go hunting where I please. What I do with my son is none of your goddamn business. No one is going to tell me what to do. Especially not you, Gallagher."

Grandpa stewed and fretted when he hung up the receiver. The Park County sheriff had reported heavy snowfall in the mountains. I had sat all alone at the top of the stairs with the fear rising in my throat while my grandfather called the neighbors to arrange a search party. He called the MacKinnons, the Taylors, and then his hunting buddies, Frank, Jake, and Ike, from McAllister. Grandpa called the sheriff back to let him know how many people would be going out and where they intended to search. As he made the calls, my fear paralyzed my body.

I knew what was at stake. I listened to the stories told round the big oak table. When I was young, I had a favorite spot in the wood box by the back door of the kitchen. If I crawled into the box early in the evening and was very quiet, Grandma would not make me go to bed. I heard stories, hidden from the view of the adults. Mark was old enough to sit with the other men circled in Grandma's kitchen. The air would fill with wisps of smoke raising blue up to the ceiling lamp while Grandma kept their coffee cups full. My imagination was filled with stories of forest fires, bears, fish that got away, big snows, and hard times. Even at 12, I would sometimes sit on the floor behind the wood box and just listen to the adults. I had heard all the horror recounted over the past few years about the rogue bear killing livestock on the ranches abutting the Crazies. This one was different and more dangerous because he was a predator, a big black bear who killed for pleasure.

My father did not participate in the circled gatherings. He didn't like cigarette smoke. It burned his eyes and his throat. He also did not like being reminded that he was not from Montana. The fact that Frank and Ike weren't either did not placate my father.

That awful morning, I was still waiting like a sentinel, silent as stone in the upstairs hallway, when Ike and Jake arrived from McAllister with Frank to join in the search for my missing father and my brother Mark. The combined parties from Kelly Canyon and McAllister packed up their gear and their horses, prepared for several days or however long it took to find the missing hunters. It had not taken several days. Grandpa and Frank had found Mark and Dad in the twilight. The MacKinnon boys had found our horses the next morning.

The sound of Ross's boots echoing in the empty bedrooms reminded me of where I was. I stood looking at the flowers on the wallpapered walls. Whenever I was upset as a child, I would retreat to this bedroom and run my finger around the wallpaper flowers, one after another, until I felt better. I had been tracing the patterns when Grandpa and the others came home late that night with the news that Mark was dead and my father was in the hospital, near death with a severely broken leg and hypothermia. I reached out and traced the designs I had not touched in 24 years. The sharpness of the old pain subsided.

I heard Ross approaching.

"Where are you, Cait?"

"In here."

He came up behind me, embracing me.

"This is what I was doing when the news came from the search parties that my brother Mark was dead."

In the silence of that old house full of memories of my childhood, I told Ross the story of my brother's death. "My brother Mark and Dad had been hunting in the mountains.

It was late October. The snow had started the day before. They were riding down a steep trail. Coming around a blind corner, there was a bear. Mark was ready. It was like he sensed there was something wrong and he had his rifle out of the scabbard. Dad's horse slipped in the snow, throwing him. Dad broke his leg in the fall. Mark shot the bear, but it didn't die right away. The bear charged Mark, mauling him before it died. Mark bled out. There wasn't anything my father could do."

"Bloody hell."

I was not crying. I'd never cried for my brother. After Mark died, my old life vanished and it was easier to believe the accident had never happened. My last view of my beloved brother was not my Mark. The rigid, white-faced, black-suited corpse in the casket was a gruesome caricature of my tanned joyous brother. Mark was not dead. He was just gone.

"What did your parents do? How did your mother handle it?"

"Dad couldn't stay in Montana. Everybody blamed him for Mark's death. It didn't help that Frank and my grandfather saved my father's life. He hated being in debt to them and the fact that Grandpa had been correct about the risk of hunting in the Crazies really irked my Dad. He moved us up to Edmonton, Alberta. He took a job in a construction firm. Horrible place. So cold up there just south of the tree line. Ten months of winter and two months of mosquitoes. My mother never talked about Mark again. It was as if she had never had a son. She blamed Dad for going hunting when there was a heavy snow advisory and for going into bear country when Grandpa told them not to go. She quit talking, especially to my father."

"What did you do, Cait?"

"Nothing. There was nothing I could do. I never cried for my brother. He was just gone and no one would talk about it. I was all alone in my grief, so I didn't cry." I shuddered, recalling the icy silences of the emotional winter following my brother's death. Ross's face was next to mine. His hand found my wrist, the one with the wide beaded bracelet. He traced the pattern of the beads with his forefinger, "Cait, how did you get this scar?"

"After we moved north, I didn't see my grandfather ever again. My father wouldn't let me go visit. I was 14 when my grandfather died. I kept thinking about him dying alone on the mountain in the dark. I broke his heart with the letter I wrote to him. My pain killed him. I was so depressed and lonely, I cut my wrist. It hurt more than I expected and I didn't cut the other one. My mother came home early that afternoon and found me in the bathtub, because I didn't want to make a mess. Grandma came to get me for the summer a few days later. JoAnn was next door and she designed me this bracelet so people wouldn't ask questions. She makes me a new one when the old one gets too worn. How did you know I had a scar?"

"I saw it the night at your cabin when you washed my hair. You took the bracelet off to wash dishes, but I washed for you, remember? I guess you forgot to put it back on." Ross straightened up, kissing me on the top of my head. "Thank you for telling me your story. Trusting me enough."

Ross and I walked back along the road in silence, and I was content to hold his hand while listening to the gravel crunching under our boots as the shadows lengthened in the canyon. Now that my grandparents' home was up for sale again, I wished I could buy it back. Grandma had moved into town after the bitterly cold Christmas of

1982. Her last eight years were spent in a brick apartment building near the post office, a few blocks off Main Street. When she died all that remained of her husband's ranch in Kelly Canyon was this house and 120 acres. In the 12 years following my grandfather's death, Grandma had sold off the rest of the land piecemeal in 20-acre parcels. My mother wasted no time in selling the Kelly Canyon place to a young couple from California. I had inherited the cabin and 100 acres in the Madison Valley, because Grandpa had left it in trust for me. With the escalating land prices in Montana, there was no reasonable chance that I could ever afford to reclaim my family's Kelly Canyon property. As we walked back to the MacKinnons, it occurred to me I could look forward instead of backwards and be content in this moment walking with a man who had listened to my story with compassion. What was it Grandma always told me? *Never give up on hope and love.* Was there hope and love in my future with this man?

At dinner, I sat next to Julia with Elizabeth on the other side of me. Ross was across the big oak table, sitting between Luke and Ben. Little Teddy was in his high chair between Ben and his mother, Jo. Ross was entertaining the MacKinnons with his jokes. I offered to clear the dishes and get dessert. Sometimes, in social settings, I preferred to be on the periphery. I liked to detach from the specifics of conversation and lose focus. Midway through the job of loading the dishwasher, I did that. Behind me at the table I could hear all the sounds of laughter and lively conversation. I stopped working, letting the warmth of good friends in a safe place flow over me. Standing in Jo's kitchen was almost as good as being in Grandma's wood box while the people I loved told stories. Elizabeth interrupted my recollections by nudging my arm. "Can I help you, Aunty Cait?" I smiled and handed her the dessert plates and forks. She carried them across the kitchen.

Back around the table, Luke was describing to Ross the fishing trips he used to take with my grandfather into the Tobacco Roots. "Dermot Gallagher, Cait's grandpa, liked to load up the horses and go in for a week. He'd take anybody who wanted to come. Usually that meant Jo's dad and her brothers, along with my dad and my younger brother. Cait's godfather, Frank, frequently came along, sometimes Jake and Ike. We'd pack in our coffee, sugar, flour, and maybe some dried fruit. If you couldn't catch it, you didn't eat. Times are changing. Now everyone fishes for sport. Catch and release. Barbless hooks. Cait's grandpa would have a thing or two to say about that. Dermot was a big believer in conservation. He used to say there wasn't enough trout for everyone to keep their limit, but he liked to eat what he caught once in a while. These days if you go fishing up by Potosi, the streams are all C and R. Guys stand there with their high-dollar fishing gear and I swear they catch the same damn fish over and over again."

Luke was not in a good mood. He was not adjusting well to the rapid changes occurring in the Gallatin Valley. He frequently could be heard complaining bitterly about the Californication of Montana. Especially after someone had left Luke's gates open, letting his stock out, or locked up another one of Luke's favorite fishing spots. "It's getting harder and harder to get good access to the rivers. Last weekend, I took Ben over to the East Gallatin. You know what? Some jerk from California had bought the old Varney place. You know the first thing he did? He gated off the river access. I've been fishing that damn hole since I was six. One of the last good reg spots near here. You can't block river access. It's against the law." Luke's face was reddening, his voice rising.

Jo interceded by asking Ross if he had an opinion about catch and release versus regulation limits. Ross shrugged, smiling, "No, luv. I'm not much for fishing. But," Ross paused for effect, "I'm a big believer in shoot and resuscitate hunting."

Jo caught my eye across the room, her face contorted with worry. She was watching my reaction. Luke frowned and said in a rather annoyed voice, "What?"

Ross elaborated, "The logical equivalent to catch and release for big game—shoot and resuscitate hunting." Ross's face was perfectly serious.

Jo joined me at the sink. She put her arm around me. "Ross doesn't know about Mark, does he?"

I was scraping the food into Jo's compost container, thankful to have an excuse to be away from the table. "Yes, he does. I told him at Grandma's. Jo, I need a favor. Could you ask Luke to ignore Ross? I'm sorry he's being so obnoxious. I want tonight to go well. Ross has been nice to me and I like him. Please say something to Luke."

Jo hesitated, then she nodded and gave me a reassuring squeeze, "Okay, Cait, I'll do my best."

Behind me I could hear little five-year-old Ben's voice, "What's resuscitate?"

Ross proceeded to explain. "It's like kissing, mate. Ya know why mouth-to-mouth resuscitation with elk is so horrible?"

I turned around, to see Jo whispering in Luke's ear. Luke was nodding while she patted him on the shoulder. Ben's eyes were as big as platters. He shook his head in response to Ross's question. Ross broke the suspense with his answer, "They never brush their teeth, mate. Disgusting."

Jo's daughters reminded me of their mother. When we

were kids, if Jo thought something was funny, she would end up on the floor, curled up in spasms of laughter, and I couldn't count the number of times Jo got root beer up her nose, because I said had something funny when she was drinking. Both Julia and Elizabeth were now in danger of falling off their chairs. I carried the huckleberry pie over to the table. Luke looked concerned, but I smiled faintly at him. Ross flashed me one of his radiant smiles.

Luke redirected the conversation from the sensitive topic of hunting. He and Ross began discussing Nelson Story's successful cattle drive from Texas in the fall of 1866. One of the reasons Story had completed the trip was because he had invested in the latest technology—30 Remington split breech large frame carbines that used .56-50 Spencer rimfire ammunition. These newly developed guns could be fired five to seven times a minute making them a vast improvement over the much slower to load muzzleloading rifles. Story, himself, carried two Navy Revolvers rather than his newly acquired rifles and was a superb horseman who always rode superior mounts, which is why the usually fierce Sioux warriors were wary of Story. The Sioux recognized Story as a formidable adversary worthy of respect and caution. With a party of about 27 cowboys—Story hired a few along the northern trail—Story drove his herd along the Bozeman Trial, traveling mostly at night. Not only could they fire faster, the Remingtons had a longer range and superior accuracy compared to the Indians' weapons. Story's herd passed through the Indian controlled territory without major incident.

Jo excused herself from the table and Ross took charge of the final cleanup. He asked Julia and Elizabeth if they were okay with certain tasks, and when they had to ask him to repeat himself either because they didn't understand his strong Aussie accent or because of the rowdy noise created by their younger brothers, Ross calmly repeated himself. Ben was tugging on Ross's flannel shirt sleeve loudly, asking about mouth-to-mouth with bears and Teddy was yelling at the top of his lungs because his father had attacked his face with a wet washcloth. I found the increasing noise levels unnerving, but Ross appeared to be deaf and blind to the commotion. He was telling the girls funny stories and they were giggling, but they didn't stop working. In no time, Jo's kitchen was spotless and tidy. While the kitchen was under control, Teddy was not and Luke was beginning to lose his temper. I'd known Luke my whole life, I knew he was at his wit's end with Teddy's yelling and squirming around.

Luke muttered under his breath something about how it was time for the men to go out to the horse barns and step in some real manure, a backhanded reference to Ross's shoot and resuscitate nonsense. Luke lifted a scrubbed Teddy up on his shoulders and headed out the door. Ben grabbed Ross firmly by the hand, following his dad. A delicious tranquility embraced me. Since the kitchen was in order, I sat and talked leisurely with Jo and her daughters. I realized, sitting in the comfortable kitchen drinking coffee, that I should have spent more time this past summer with the MacKinnons. I had been far too absorbed in my novel. It was not just my novel that had kept me away. Jo's pregnancy reminded me of my own failures, and I didn't want to remember.

When the men came back, it was time to leave. I hated to go, but despite the coffee I was getting drowsy. The events and emotions of the last few days were catching up with me. I asked Ross to do the driving home. Ben was sorry to see Ross leave, so Ross placated him by telling one last joke, "What do you do with a crying baby astronaut, Ben?"

Ben grinned anticipating the punchline.

Ross winked at him and said, "Rock it." Ross kept his face completely blank while Luke groaned, but Ben and the girls all giggled.

As we left Bridger Canyon, I pointed out where the landmark, Maiden Rock, used to stand. "You asked me if my rock had a story. Well, Maiden Rock had a story. The Crow Indians said that a young maiden, Evening Star, promised her lover she would wait for him when he left her one afternoon. But he never came back and she refused to leave this spot. She kept her promise. She waited. They say she turned to stone when she learned he'd been killed. She was still waiting here grieving for her lover when the highway engineer blew her up to widen the road. The Needle remained intact but Maidan Rock exists only in memories now. It happened right after we moved north. I miss her."

Ross slowed down to look, but there was not much to see. The rock formation near the opening of the canyon, the solid symbol of true love from my childhood, was completely gone, only rubble remained. I didn't tell Ross my father's role in the demise of Evening Star, nor did I mention the photograph I had found in Ross's room of the Needle and a Paddy O'Neill.

As we drove across Gallatin Valley towards home, Ross was expansive. Since I was tired, I was listening to the cadences of his voice more than to the content. I noticed when he was happy; he made a sound in the back of his throat when he talked. It was almost a laugh. I thought it sounded like a smiling voice. There were a lot of smiles in his sentences during that half of the drive home, especially as he retold Jo's stories about her Bozeman encounters with famous Hollywood celebrities. I had heard most of Jo's stories, but not the one about Robert Redford that had occurred 10 years prior. For the filming of *A River Runs Through It*, Redford used the lounge of the Student Union building as a stand in for the press library in Helena because of the Leigh Lounge's preserved historic character—stenciled beams decorating the high ceilings, original 1920s light fixtures, and a gorgeous painted mural of Plains Indians on horseback above the huge fireplace in the center of the south wall of the beautifully wood paneled room. Ross enthusiastically recounted Jo's embarrassment, imitating Jo's voice exactly and doing a passable imitation of Redford's.

"Jo was late for her interview in the KGLT radio studio in the basement of the Strand Student Union. She was recording a promo for an upcoming art show downtown, in addition to the interview about her jewelry. It was summer and there weren't many students about, and certainly no camera equipment, so Jo was completely unprepared for what happened. Apparently, Jo moves quickly, much like you Cait, and she smacked into a man coming through the doorway of the Leigh Lounge in the Union. Jo looks up into the face of the man to apologize and instead blurts out, *'Oh, shit.'* Robert Redford smiles down at her, and says with a completely straight face, 'Hello, to you, too.' Years later, Jo is still embarrassed. I'm not sure who's funnier, Cait, you or Jo. You two are well and truly a deep bore of funny stories," Ross concluded with his signature smiling voice.

I knew Ross didn't consider Jo and I boring, maybe a bore meant something else in Australia. I was too sleepy to inquire and went back to thinking about how Ross's Australian accent faded in and out. In the bar, it had been quite noticeable with his speech full of Aussie slang and idioms. No doubt, he sounded like everyone else down at the local Aussie pub back home. But if he had something serious to discuss, where communication mattered to him, the slang dropped out, his accent moderated. He had been quite articulate in his lengthy explanations about art and forgeries. He was starting to use a Montana accent in his everyday conversations with me. I could hear it as our time together increased, which was particularly disconcerting when he pronounced his native Australian idioms and slang in my native voice. There was a musical quality to his voice, deep and sensual, which I really enjoyed. When we reached the Madison River canyon, he didn't talk much, he focused on driving. In the silence, I lost focus. The deer were down by the road at this time of night, on their way to an evening swallow of water, and in response Ross was driving carefully, because, as he said, the animals in Montana did not have enough experience with vehicles. He had no interest in giving them private lessons.

Once the canyon was behind us and we got away from the river, Ross asked if I had ever heard the song, "Another Fall of Rain." By this time, I could hardly stay awake. I said no. He stole a glance at me and saw how sleepy I was.

"Hey, Cait, use me as a pillow." Ross patted his thigh. "Lie down and go to sleep, I'll get you home. Just relax."

Grandpa's words cut through my foggy thoughts. *He's a good man. He'll keep you safe.* I trusted Ross. He was an excellent driver. The prospect of sleep and the afternoon memories of Ross's caresses by Grandma's tree were too tempting to resist. I spread the truck blanket over me and put my head in his lap. As Ross stroked my hair, he returned to talking about the Australian bush ballad. "I like how you can pack a lot of emotion in three minutes of a song. Last few years have been stressful for me. Bit parched on the emotional side, but these last few days I feel better, almost as if it's going to rain. Soft drops of renewing rain on the outback. Sorry, Cait, Aussies get sentimental about rain. I love this song.

The weather has been warm for a fortnight now or more,
And the shearers have been driving might and main,
For some have got the century who ne'er got it before;
But now all hands are waiting for the rain.
For the boss is getting rusty, and the ringer's caving in
His bandaged wrist is aching with the pain,
And the second man, I fear, will make it hot for him
Unless we have another fall of rain."[13]

Ross's gentle voice and touch were the last straws for my tired body. I drifted in and out trying to listen, but my feet were getting warm and feeling further away by the second. The visions of the parched Australian outback and the shearers waiting for the rain mingled with my own images of drought-affected ears waiting for poetry, or images of parched souls waiting for grace, or images of broken hearts waiting for love? My brain was free-associating in the last minutes of consciousness. The mixed images blurred into the final verse of the song, *"Some may meet next season, but perhaps not even then, For soon we all vanish like the rain."* I could not distinguish the warmth in my feet and body from the warmth of Ross's thigh on my face or his hand on my hair.

In the morning, when I woke up, the cabin was cold and there was no sweet fragrance of freshly brewed coffee, only the morning smells of dew-covered sage and juniper. I tripped over my jeans and boots when I got up and realized I was still in my clothes from the night before, or at least half of them. All I could remember was Ross singing in the truck. He must have put me to bed. I was surprised to find I didn't mind. I didn't feel threatened. I wasn't worried about the loss of control. I wasn't even embarrassed about Ross seeing my utilitarian, boring white underwear.

When I opened up the door for my morning visit to the privy, I wanted to find Ross on the front porch, but only a bare step gleamed back at me, shiny in the bright sunlight. Only the magpie greeted me with his hoarse cry from the top of the fir tree. Only my faded truck stood parked on the grassy slope. No big motorcycle. No Ross.

The morning dragged. The grasses were still too wet from the heavy dew for decent hiking. Besides, I wasn't in the mood for hiking. I spent my time aimlessly changing commas and semicolons in my novel. When the phone rang at noon, nothing had ever sounded as good in my ear as the deep Aussie voice of Ross Sutherland.

"G'day, Cait. We're having a sausage sizzle in the park by the motel tomorrow night around six. The whole mob will be there. I'd like you to come and meet everyone. Say yes?"

"Yes."

"Beauty." There was that lovely expression again ending in a lilt. "I'll come pick you up at five. No skirts, luv, you'll need to cover up those lovely legs. Wear your boots, too. See ya soon."

The cabin was silent. Ross's voice was gone. I was back to changing commas. I finally gave up on my novel. I got out my story about building a cabin and thought about the photographs I had taken of Ross the day before. I thought about how Jo's children had felt, their small bodies cuddled up around me—surrounding me with their interest and affection. I thought about the special places of my childhood—the roughness of the bark of Grandma's dying willow tree, the delicate vision of the shimmering aspen leaves along Bridger Creek, the smell of freshly baked huckleberry pie in the MacKinnon's kitchen, and the solid sound of Ross's boots echoing mine all through the sun filled rooms of the empty old brick house up the canyon. I started writing, and when I finished, I called JoAnn in Bozeman.

~ Chapter 17 ~

"How ya goin', Ruthie? Alright?"

"It's so good to hear your voice, Ross. How is it Up Over?"

"Sweet as. Is Jacob staying out of trouble?"

"I don't know what you said to him, but his teacher says he's been a little man at school."

"What about Nora? How is she going?"

"Oh, Ross, Nora's been playing one practical joke after another on her brother. Poor Jacob. Last night, she short sheeted her brother's bed. Who did she learn that from, I wonder?"

Ross laughed. "Guilty as charged."

"And your movie?"

"She'll be right. Guess what? I met a bloke last night who is descended from one of the drovers on the Story trek to Montana. Can you post me a hamper of good Aussie treats plus some of Mum's favorite Yorkshire tea and a jar of Vegemite, Ruthie?"

"Of course, Ross. Do you want the same stuff I usually

send you for the Turners?”

"Yeah, that'd be brilliant, but double it. Ta, Ruthie.”

"Any leads on Paddy O'Neill?”

"I did meet an O'Neill. He's a publican in McAllister just north of where I'm staying. He's been to Australia and was a hotshot firie. He knows his way around a station, but his name is Frank and he's from Wyoming. His goddaughter tells me he doesn't have any kin. But, guess what, Ruthie?”

"Yes, Ross?”

"I found the rock. The one in Paddy's photo. It's at the mouth of Bridger Canyon outside of Bozeman.”

"That's wonderful, Ross. How did you find it?”

"O'Neill's goddaughter showed it to me last night.”

"And … .”

"And what?”

"What's her name, Ross?”

"Who?”

"The goddaughter.”

"Caitlinn.”

"And … .”

"And what?”

Ruthie started laughing. "I'll send your hamper for Caitlinn with two of everything except Vegemite first thing tomorrow. You're gonna do the Tim Tam slam on her aren't you? Seriously, Ross? Be careful. You're only in Montana for a short time. Don't crack onto anyone and don't make any bubs.”

The problem with rellies is they know you too well, Ross thought. "Roger that. Love ya, Ruthie. Good night.”

~ Chapter 18 ~

Ross arrived at 5 p.m. sharp. I met him at the bottom of the driveway, by the edge of the gravel road. "I'd rather hoped you'd be wearing the skirt." The motorcycle was still running and he didn't get off.

I frowned slightly, wondering if I had misheard him.

Ross laughed and winked at me. "Then I could watch you change." He handed me a leather jacket out of his saddle bags and a helmet. "Here Cait, kit up. Put your foot there. Hang on to me. Mirror your body movements with mine when we're on the road, especially around corners. Always watch out for that—it's hot. You all right? Ready to go?"

"Yup."

"Brilliant." He revved the motor and we were off. I was a little apprehensive about being on a Harley and meeting his friends, but we had done all right on Mark's bicycle in the moonlight. I relaxed into the moment, amazed at how much more I could see and how free I felt on the bike as opposed to riding in my truck.

We drove through Ennis carefully. Most of the buildings along the main street had false fronts and upper balconies. There were plenty of big sculptures around town of wildlife and sportsmen. Ennis had been a hunting and fishing mecca for years. The wealthy sportsmen supported a higher caliber store and restaurant than what you would find in a comparable ranching town of its size elsewhere in Montana. But Ennis was far enough off the beaten track for tourists that it hadn't been robbed of its unique identity, unlike the tourist towns of Aspen, Steamboat Springs, Taos, Santa Fe, and now Bozeman.

People in Ennis were like the wildlife up at my cabin, since they did not pay much attention to moving vehicles, leaving safety to the drivers trying to navigate through the main part of town. The added hazard was the old Western pull-in parking instead of curbside parallel parking style. As a consequence of the pull in parking, people backed out and could not see oncoming traffic. I loved the old-time Western feel of Ennis, except for actually walking downtown. I had to remember that pickups, pulled in with brush guards, stuck out far into the sidewalk. One day, when I was daydreaming about the next part of my novel, I strolled into the solid metal of a brush guard hanging over the curb into the sidewalk space. Today, looking at all the parked dusty four-wheel drive rigs, I wondered what style of parking they used in Australia, and if I would ever get the opportunity to run into a bull guard.

We cruised through Ennis without incident, arriving on the outskirts of town. Our destination was a community park nestled in the curve of the road between Highway 287 and the Madison River. A small pond formed the centerpiece of the park, with a fenced-in playground for toddlers on the east side near the baseball field. Various pieces of climbing equipment were scattered on the west side. Benches were placed along the pond at even intervals.

"C'mon then, let's do the intros." Ross took my hand firmly in his. We walked over to the tables where his friends were picnicking. Charlie Douglas was under the roofed pavilion, busy at the barbecue. He waved a spatula at me, but didn't leave his post. Ross introduced me to Charlie's wife, Kathy. I recognized her from the library. She liked mysteries and she worked the morning shift at the Western Drug as a waitress. I remembered Charlie's suggestive comment and wondered what Kathy thought of her husband's behavior around women. Maybe I misinterpreted Charlie and it was all a bit of fun, the way men flirted with women at the Bear Claw. I'd always been hopeless when it came to discerning men's levels of interest in me as a woman. Grandma installed strict girl code in me. She always said, "No man who is taken is worth your time, no matter how much you like him. If any man with another woman is willing to cheat on his current woman, he'll cheat on you, too. Women need to stick together in this life. Men can be gentlemen, but they can also be predators." I started wondering which one my childhood crush was—a predator or a gentleman? Which one was Ross? Grandpa's assessment of Ross swirled around in my mind. How would I know? How could I test Ross and know for sure which he was? A gentleman or a predator?

While I was second guessing myself, Ross was attempting to introduce me to his other friends. I needed to focus. I resurfaced to reality in time to catch their first names— Mike and Sarah. They had come up from L.A. the day before. Ross was going up to Glacier with them the latter part of the week. Mike went back to playing catch with his two sons with a strangely shaped red and black football. Ross excused himself, saying something about helping Charlie with the cooking duties. I was left to make conversation with the women. I asked Sarah how she knew Ross. Mike's wife frowned at me and said impatiently, "Mike is in Ross's movie, dear." The 'dear' was not used as a term of endearment, it felt condescending. Sarah turned her attentions to Kathy.

I was turning red. Now I recalled Ross saying Mike Turner was starring in his movie. Why couldn't I remember things? Why hadn't I recognized Mike Turner? I was going to have to do something about my cultural naivete. Ralph would have recognized Mike Turner.

I grabbed a beer out of the cooler by the table and retreated away from the women. I headed for the pavilion and Ross. He had some odd round metal thing with a long handle and he was holding it over the barbecue where Charlie was cooking the hamburgers and the sausages. I asked Ross what he was doing.

"Making the Turner lads their toasties, kind of like your grilled cheese sandwiches, but heaps better because this jaffle iron seals the bread all around the edges. I promised the lads I would make them like my Mum's."

When Ross finished making the first one, the result was a perfectly round toasted creation with spiral marks pressed into the toasted bread. The cheese was nowhere to be seen, as it was sealed into the toastie. I watched him make the next one from the slices of white bread and grated cheeses. Two pieces of bread fit into the top and bottom of the contraption when it was opened fully, the cheese was placed in the middle of the slices and then the jaffle iron was closed up tightly. Ross tore away the corners of the bread on the outside of the closed iron. I watched him make a few more as he went back to arguing with Charlie over the proper way to grill steaks. Charlie liked his steaks cooked slowly and evenly. He said he didn't want the meat getting up and leaving while he cut it. Ross was trying to convince Charlie to sear the outside rapidly to seal in the juices and keep the steaks rare. Then they started arguing over buns versus a single slice of bread as the best way to eat a sausage. I was not paying enough attention to determine who was winning that argument. I went back to the picnic table and watched the Turner males kicking and passing the red and black ball.

When Ross sat down next to me at the picnic table and handed me my burger, I was trying to figure out what he had put on it. His was identical to mine.

"Here Cait, classic burger Aussie style."

I looked at it sidewise and Ross answered my unstated question, "Burger, bacon, cheese, lettuce, grilled onions, grilled pineapple, tomato sauce, and beetroot. Burger with the lot, minus the fried egg. Try it. You might like it. Nothing like a taste of Australia when a bloke is far from home. I wish I could get the local pubs to make me these, but as soon as I mention beetroot, they quit listening. They act like I'm pulling their leg, but I'm not."

I took a bite, not wanting to appear rude. It was different. I chewed slowly. I wasn't sure about the beet part. I ate it all, wondering why anyone would think putting beets on a burger was a good idea, never mind staining your clothing and surroundings like the red stuff from *Cat in the Hat*, with the runaway beetroot escaping from the bun. Maybe Aussies were less clumsy with their food than me.

Over dinner at the picnic table, Charlie started playing tour guide with Sarah and the Turner boys. He asked them if they'd been over to Virginia City. They shook their heads in unison, their mouths full of grilled cheese toasties.

"Well, you'll have to go. It would be on your way to Glacier. It's a restored gold mining town. Very unique. Ross and Mike will be filming *North to Montana* there, but that's not the real reason you need to go. There's this quirky old museum in a two-story stone building as you come into town. The main attractions are the petrified cat from 1868, the 100-year-old birthday cake, and Club Foot George's foot."

"Foot?" Sarah looked puzzled.

Charlie was enjoying the attention. His dimples were showing. "George's clubfoot is in a glass dome complete with portions of his rotted sock. You can buy a postcard and send it to your friends in L.A."

Sarah turned pale, "Oh, how awful."

"My nephew loved it." Ross was laughing at Sarah.

Sarah frowned at Ross. "You didn't really send such a horrible thing to Jacob, did you?"

Ross winked at me and answered Sarah, "Absofuckinlutely."

Sarah sighed.

Charlie patiently finished the story, "You have to understand the times, Sarah. In the winter of 1864, the townspeople of Virginia City were trapped. Anyone who tried to leave with their gold ended up dead. There was a gang of road agents operating in the area. The town was isolated, so the townspeople banded together and formed the Vigilantes. They tracked down the road agents and lynched them. In three months, they hung 22 men including the town drunk. According to legend, Sheriff Henry Plummer was the leader of the road agents. He was caught and hung pretty early on. Club Foot George was one of Plummer's gang. The story goes that the townspeople wanted to know which unmarked graves in the cemetery were the road agents' so they dug them up, knowing they could identify George from his foot. Then they took a souvenir."

I stole a glance at Mike. He was listening with no comment. He didn't seem at all bothered by Charlie and Ross teasing his wife and pushing her buttons. Sarah was taking their bait at every turn, though. Maybe Ross did that a lot, stirred the pot to get reactions from people. I had been the recipient of plenty of Ross's outrageous antics the last few days. I suppose if my brother, Mark, and my grandfather hadn't teased me so much I would not have tolerated Ross's nonsense. For the most part, I enjoyed it because Ross reminded me of the men from my childhood I adored before my life changed and the only males in my life were sadistic and humorless. Before his accident, Frank had been like Grandpa, but he'd changed since he nearly died under the tree. The new Frank was more serious and quieter. He still had a sense of humor, but he was not the larger than life alpha male I remembered. As a small child, I could remember Frank riling up my father and pulling my grandmother's leg constantly. My father would get quite angry in response to Frank, my grandmother would believe Frank's nonsense initially and then laugh with him at herself. My grandmother loved Frank as her own. Frank did not rile up my grandfather, though. Frank deferred to my grandfather and was always quite respectful to him. Frank didn't ever rile up Jake and Ike, either; Jake and Ike riled each other up enough, but Frank did find those two quite funny. Frank definitely did not stir anybody up at the bar; alcohol and male egos created enough trouble without deliberately giving people a hard time. Frank was all business with his employees; he was polite and fair, and if they did not return the respect and loyalty, they were shown the door immediately. Once in a blue moon, Frank would pull my leg, but mostly he was strong, protective, dependable, and present like my beloved Tobacco Roots.

"I like the birthday cake," Kathy interjected. "It's so sad to think that all the people who were at that birthday party have been dead for years, but the cake is still here."

Charlie explained, "The Chinese cook for a local ranching family made this beautiful cake for their little girl. It was so fancy no one could bear to eat it. They saved it and it's still intact. At the museum. 100-year-old cake." Charlie paused and then delivered his punch line, "Hey, just goes to show you can't have your cake and eat it too."

Everyone groaned. Ross asked me, "What about you, Cait? What's your favorite thing at the museum?"

I hesitated. "I don't have a favorite thing at the museum. I like the whole town. I love walking along the sidewalks, listening to the sound of my boot heels on the wood. I love looking at the old window glass in the storefronts, the way it ripples down at the bottom. I love the patina of the weathered boards with their edges curled up, straining against the confinement of the nails. I love looking through the shop windows. Looking at the old fancy boxes with the original clothes still in them. Time stands still in Virginia City. I like that. It's as if the last 24 years of my life never happened."

Ross was listening intently. Lines across his brow were forming. Beside me, Sarah sniffed. Charlie chuckled softly, "Caitlinn, you sound just like your grandpa."

Ross inquired of Charlie, "Did you know him well?"

"In these parts, we all knew Dermot. I used to go fishing with him. He was quite a story teller."

Ross was leaning forward with his elbows resting on the table, "What was your favorite story, Charlie?"

Charlie hesitated, thinking, then said, "Probably the one about dancing with his wife, Gwen, on the old highway in the moonlight."

"Go on."

"It was during the war. There weren't too many dances with the boys away, and Gwen missed dancing. Dermot would park the car on a flat stretch of paved road. Wasn't much traffic due to gas rationing. They'd dance in the moonlight to the Big Band music on the car radio."

Ross smiled at me, "Do you dance in the moonlight on the highway, Cait?"

"I don't dance on or off the highway."

"We'll have to change that. Get in touch with your romantic side, Cait." Ross was rubbing my leg with his boot under the table. I didn't want to acknowledge him in front of the others.

Charlie added, "Dermot was a romantic all right. Wasn't anything romantic about the way he died, though. All alone on the mountain."

Ross stopped playing with my leg. He was focusing on Charlie, waiting for the rest of the story. "I was the one who found him."

I froze. I had never heard Charlie's part in this story before. How to make Charlie stop? I did not want to hear intimate details about my grandfather's death in front of strangers.

Charlie was continuing, "I was down at the Bear Claw having lunch at the bar one Friday in the spring. Dermot came in to see Frank about something. He had a letter in his hand; he was upset, real pale. Said he was going up to the mountain to do some thinking. After he left, Frank said he was worried. Said Dermot was slipping away. Not eating. Lost interest in everything. Wouldn't go fishing. I asked Frank what was wrong. He said Dermot was worried about Cait here. Cait's family had moved north to Canada. What was it, Cait? Fifteen months, two years, you'd been gone?" Charlie gestured at me.

All eyes were on me. I shrugged. I focused on my wrist, fingering my beaded bracelet, trying to avoid Ross's perceptive eyes. I was not going to cry. I knew the end of this story. I was not going to cry. I was not. Not in front of Sarah.

"Next day, I stopped by the Bear Claw. Frank had just gotten a call from Bozeman. He wanted me to do him a favor. Go up to the Gallagher's and see if I could find Dermot for Cait's grandma. Gwen was worried. Frank had to work, so I said sure I would be happy to go. Took me a while to find him, though. He was up on top of the mountain on a rock. Cold as ice. Been there all night. Coroner said he died of natural causes. Unnatural causes, more like. Frank said he died of a broken heart."

The silence around the table was deafening. Sarah finally broke it by saying, "What a lovely evening. Why there's the moon rising over the mountain."

I hated her. I hated Charlie for telling my story in front of strangers who never knew my grandfather, never heard him tell a funny joke, never saw him smile, never felt his love and compassion. It was my story. He was my grandfather. Damn Charlie and his big mouth. I got up and started clearing the dishes off the table. Anything to be busy and away from judgmental eyes.

Ross was asking Charlie more questions about my grandfather's death. I couldn't listen. I had most of the mess from supper cleaned up before Ross made me stop. The others had left the table. Ross put his arms around my waist and kissed the back of my neck, "That's enough, Cait. You don't have to do this. You're my guest, not our servant." His hand reached out, covering my beaded bracelet, as I reached for the last of the used plates. "Please stop, Caitlinn. Come back with me and have a sit down. Please."

We walked to the campfire area where everyone had gathered. Another year, we might have had a fire at this time of night, but this year the fire danger was too extreme. There was talk around town that the governor of Montana was going to take the unprecedented step of closing public lands, affecting over 19 million acres of the state. Fires were continuing to threaten the towns of Hamilton and Darby in the Bitterroots. Where Ross and I had enjoyed a quiet Sunday at my cabin, the day hadn't been quiet for Montanans to the northwest of us. Their Sunday become known as Black Sunday, the day 70 separate dry lightning fires merged into what would become the biggest national fire complex of the 2000 season. Earlier in the day, Ross had been on the phone with the scriptwriters for his movie. They were under evacuation orders, along with over 900 fellow residents of Southwestern Montana. Originally, they had planned to come down to Ennis to meet with Ross and Mike, but those plans were now contingent on the fires burning around their homes. Ross's first shoot was getting complicated. Little did we know that the worst was yet to come.

We all sat in a circle without a fire. When I shivered, Ross got up and retrieved the extra leather jacket from his bike. He draped it over my shoulders, sat back down next to me, and put his arm around me, drawing me closer to him. Talk shifted to the planned trip the next day to Glacier Park. Ross and the Turners were coming back late on Friday and Sarah and her boys were flying home to L.A. on Saturday. I was surprised to find that the prospect of not seeing Ross for several days bothered me.

The conversation moved on to what Ross had planned to do in Yellowstone Park. He hoped to leave Ennis on his motorcycle around 8 Monday morning. He had his room booked at Old Faithful Inn for Monday and Tuesday evenings, and he planned to return through the Gallatin River canyon so he could take a rafting trip on Wednesday. I was envious. I had wanted to go back to the Inn since returning to Montana, but could not justify the expense on my Bear Claw salary. Ross interrupted my reverie about the historic lodge at Old Faithful, "Come with me Cait, it'll be fun."

I hesitated, "I don't know if I should. I need to finish up my book."

"How much more do you have to do?"

"Couple of days' work."

"Well, do it while I'm gone, and treat yourself with a bit of a holiday. Show me around. I would love your company and you could be my native guide. Take me where the locals go."

Charlie interjected with a grin, "Oh, you mean like hot-potting in the Gardner?"

"What's that about?"

"Well, there's this place called the Boiling River, outside of Gardiner, where the water's warm from thermal activity. Years ago, the big thing to do on weekends for college students was drive over there from Bozeman with a few beers. People would go in the winter when the snow was on the ground and spend the evening skinny-dipping."

"Whoa, Cait, I had no idea!"

I frowned, refusing to look up at him. "I've never been." I said shortly.

Charlie interrupted, "Cait's too young to have gone.

You could take her, Ross. It's too civilized for me. Now you have to go during the daylight and wear a suit. Can't drink, either. Park Service took all the fun out of it. This time of year, you wouldn't need a hat."

I looked up at Ross to catch his reaction. He raised an eyebrow and Charlie explained, "Kathy got cold ears when we went hot-potting in the winter. Just when things would get interesting, we'd have to leave. I solved that problem."

"How?" Ross looked amused.

"Bought Kathy a nice warm hat."

Ross laughed and pulled me closer to him in response to Charlie's account.

"There we were in the river under the bright stars, bare naked with our wool hats on. Didn't leave early that night."

Kathy kicked Charlie and told him to behave. Sarah sighed.

"I need a guide. Otherwise, I'm never going to hear all the good stories." Ross asked, "What else do the locals do?"

"Play practical jokes on tourists. When we were in high school, we used to take a stuffed mountain lion from my mother's antique shop and we'd drive down to Yellowstone on the weekends. We'd find some spot along the road in the park. Set the lion down and watch to see how many tourists would stop. When we got a pretty good crowd, I'd stroll over real calm and pick the lion up under my arm and walk off into the trees or get back in the car with it still in my arms."

Everyone, except Sarah, had a good laugh.

Charlie continued, "You'll see what I mean, Ross, when you get into the park. You'd swear some people have never seen a damn animal before. They line up in their cars and block traffic in all directions. You'll have a great time."

Ross jumped up and abruptly pulled me up off the log

at the same time in one smooth movement. "Let's go, Cait. Bye, everyone. Thanks again, Charlie, for organizing this. See you later, Kathy, Mike, Sarah." Ross touched his forehead with his forefinger and gestured goodbye to his friends. With my hand encased in his, I had no choice but to follow. I wondered what fire had been lit under Ross, although it was a relief to leave before Charlie thought of any other stories to tell about my grandfather.

Going up to McAllister from Ennis on Highway 287 was under a nine minute ride, depending upon the traffic. Ross drove fast. The trip took less time than it usually did when I drove my old truck. I leaned up closer to him. On a motorcycle, you do not have to talk. You can concentrate on the other senses—how someone feels in your embrace, how they smell, how the rhythm of their breathing matches yours. Ross slowed down when we reached the Bear Claw and the turn-off for Meadow Creek. He was watching for the potholes, and later for the jackrabbit. The jackrabbit appeared on cue and did exactly the same thing again— tried to outrace a motorized vehicle. Ross slowed down for him. The rabbit finally gave up and hopped into the safety of the sagebrush.

When we arrived at my cabin, I dismounted, handing Ross his extra leather coat and helmet. "Thanks for a great evening, Ross." I turned to walk up to my cabin.

"Cait, please come here."

I turned and walked back to Ross. He reached out, taking my hand while still sitting on his running bike, "Cait, please accept my apology. I'm sorry about Charlie and his story about your grandfather. Please forgive me."

"It wasn't your fault. Why do you care?"

"Because I give a toss, and Charlie made you uncomfortable. That's not okay. I enjoy your company and I'd be gutted if what happened tonight came between us. We've been having a good time together before tonight, haven't we? Tell me the truth, Cait. Please."

I hesitated. Even in the waning moonlight, I could see well enough to know that Ross was genuine in his concern for me. I felt I owed him the truth. "Yes, I've been having a good time with you, most of the time, but not tonight."

"I'm well and truly sorry, Cait." He gave my hand a gentle squeeze before releasing it.

"Do you want to come in? Have a cup of tea? A beer?"

He nodded, "Ta, Cait."

Inside my cabin, with the candles lit, Ross took a seat at my table. He ran his hands through his thick auburn curls and bounced his leg up and down, creating an annoying vibration in the cabin floor. I watched him, trying to interpret his nonverbal behavior and his lack of response to my earlier question. Still no answer to my question regarding beverage choice. I repeated myself, thinking maybe he hadn't heard me over the noise of his motorcycle.

"Can I get you anything? Tea? A beer?"

Again, no verbal response, although his leg and hands had stilled. Ross kept looking down at the floor, leaning forward in his chair, elbows resting on his thighs. I was sure he had heard me the second time in the quiet of my cabin, but for some unknown reason was choosing not to respond. I leaned against my cupboard, watching him, trying to figure out what was going on between us. Since I had no control over the situation, I waited quietly, my body mirroring his immobile one, remembering Grandpa teaching me how to see wildlife in the mountains. Whereas in the bar, Ross had reminded me of a predator stalking its prey, tonight in my candlelight he looked more like the white-tailed fawn Grandpa and I found early one spring day up in the Tobacco Roots. *"Notice, how the fawn is playing dead, Cait, to fool predators. Their heart rates actually decrease under threat. In one heart beat they can go from 155 beats to 38, and their bodies change position as well to mimic the dead. Predators prefer live prey to dead ones."* How did Ross create this effect? Sitting on my chair, he literally seemed like a tiny baby, not a six-foot-three muscular man. The prey, not the predator.

"Have you ever been to Yellowstone Park, Cait?" Ross broke the long silence while shifting position. He had removed his hands from his hair and was looking up at me, head slightly tilted, still leaning forward, his body compact, taking up as little space as possible in my cabin.

"Of course, I've been to Yellowstone Park. My grandparents used to take Mark and me every year in September." I still had no idea if he wanted tea or a beer. I chose not to ask him a third time.

"Would you consider coming with me, please? To Yellowstone?"

"Probably."

"It's a yes or no question, Cait. It requires a simple yes or no answer."

"Okay, okay, Ross. I'll consider it, but I really should be writing."

"You said earlier this evening you were almost done with your initial draft. You said you only had a few more days of work left. Can't you finish up while I'm in Glacier Park?"

"I suppose so."

"Please."

"Okay, okay. I'll try."

"Fair enough." Ross got up and headed for my door.

Pausing in the doorway, with most of his body blocking my view of the night, he said, looking back at me, "Thank you, Caitlinn."

I nodded and he continued, "I want you to know how much it means to me that you're willing to consider coming to Yellowstone. It's the last few days I have free before I have to start working. I need to make sure we're straight on something. I don't want you having second thoughts on me and backing out. I really want you to come, I really enjoy your company, Caitlinn." His facial expression was identical to the vulnerable one I had witnessed when he wanted me to keep treating him like an ordinary fella, "I have one room at Old Faithful, with one queen sized bed. I reserved that months ago. I can't get another for you. We've slept together in the same space before, right here. It was okay. Nothing will happen that you don't want to happen, I give you my word. We have lots of time. We're not teenagers. We don't have to rush anything. Will that work for you? Will you still come?"

"For a bloke who only wanted conversation when we first met, you are one smooth operator."

"Answer the question, Caitlinn."

I could hear Grandpa in my ear. *"He's a good man, Cait. He'll keep you safe."* I took a big deep breath and I heard myself saying, "Yes."

"Roger that. I'll ring you with the details when I get back from Glacier. G'night, Caitlinn."

I stood in my doorway as Ross walked down to his bike, started it up, and left with a wave. I was alone in the chilly Montana evening, watching his red taillights disappear and reappear along the road past Frank's place. After Ross left, I sat on my porch steps, looking at the lights across the valley. In the sky overhead, the first stars of night twinkled as if winking at me. I idly wondered if the stars could know something I didn't. I thought about the yearly trips Mark and I used to take with our grandparents to Yellowstone at the end of the season, close to the date of their wedding anniversary. How much those trips meant to all of us. How many stories Mark and I heard. How much history Grandpa shared with us about the park. How many new memories we made together, all of us having so much fun in John Coulter's Hell—Grandpa taking Mark fishing Saturday mornings on the Fishing Bridge at Yellowstone Lake, while Grandma and I stayed back at the inn keeping vigil for each Old Faithful eruption. Grandma liked to watch as many eruptions as she could during her stay, and since once was enough for my grandfather, Grandma loved having me as attentive company for the hourly show as much as Grandpa enjoyed his fishing time with his grandson. I thought about our cribbage games in the lobby of the old inn, the Saturday dinners in the inn's fancy restaurant—Mark and me in our Sunday best—Grandpa showing us Obsidian Cliff, coupled with endless details about flint knapping arrowheads, served to inspire my career in archaeology. My choice in career was critical to me, because the secrets buried in the land could lead to recreating forgotten stories in order to honor the people who came before us, as we did with the Franklin Expedition in the Canadian Arctic. I smiled to myself, remembering Grandma carefully writing postcards to all the people who attended her wedding because she and Grandpa honeymooned in Yellowstone. We had such fun together searching in the Hamilton gift shop for the perfect postcard for each cherished wedding guest. Grandma would tell me about a particular guest, and then I would try to match the postcard to the described personality. If the person was ornery, then they always got the mud pots postcards. If another person was of regal demeanor, they got the stunning vista cards like the ones of Electric Peak. Sometimes, Grandma and I got pretty silly and I'm sure the store clerks wondered why postcards could cause the level of mirth that ensued. So many good family memories in America's first national park. I hadn't been to Yellowstone since my brother died. Yes, it will be lovely to honor my grandparents, to revisit their favorite spots, to share their stories with Ross.

I thought about the story I had rewritten for Ross's nephew, Jacob. It was titled, "Afternoons with Grandpa: Building a Cabin." I had retrieved my earlier story out from under the bed. It was my usual mix of how-to instruction with the small details that typified Montana. I had written Ross in as one of the three sons and Jacob as the grandson. The photo I had taken Monday of Ross next to the cabin was on the cover. JoAnn had helped me do the computer work. We did a self-publishing job at the local copy shop. Afterwards, JoAnn and I had a leisurely break before I drove back to the cabin.

"That's a good story, Cait. I think Jacob will like it. Great picture of Ross on the cover. He sure is handsome. Are you two getting serious?"

I shrugged. JoAnn poked me in the ribs. "You've got him on the hook. I wouldn't throw Ross back in the stream. I'd keep him. He's a good listener and he has a great sense of humor. Ross is so intense and so passionate about stuff. Ross is *alive*, unlike that cold fish you married. C'mon, girl, you know Luke and I just want what's best for you." Jo was acting like a cat that had just swallowed the family goldfish. I remembered Ross had been quite pleased with himself when we left JoAnn's ranch. I wondered what these friends of mine were doing behind my back. I had no clue.

I worked hard all week, remembering my promise to Ross. My assessment of the amount of editorial work my manuscript required had been correct. The trip with Ross would be a good conclusion to a fruitful summer of writing. Saturday morning, my wash day, rolled around and I was gathering up my dirty laundry when Ross called. I agreed to stop by his motel enroute to the laundromat. Ross was driving the Turners to Gallatin Field Airport in a big rental van. The flight was not until the late afternoon, and the Turner boys wanted to see the Madison Buffalo Jump where the Indians used to run the buffalo off the cliff. Ross was making a side trip to Three Forks for them. They were taking 287 north out of Norris, up to the Headwaters of the Missouri. It was lonely, desolate country. Ross asked me if I wanted to go with them, because of my professional knowledge of the site. I begged off, not wanting to interact with Sarah again. I handed Ross a copy of my story, interrupting his persuasive appeal for my company. He looked surprised when I said it was my first attempt at a boy's story in the series *Afternoons with Grandpa.* "It's for Jacob. You can read it later and mail it to him." I gave him a quick hug.

Ross's brow furrowed and his eyes narrowed, "Are you getting your novel done, Cait? Are you going to the Park with me?"

I nodded. Sarah was coming out of her cabin. I backed away, increasing my distance from Sarah, watching as she hugged Ross in greeting. I overheard her say, "If you really care that much Ross, do whatever you have to. Make it work. You know what your sister, Ruthie, would say, 'Half flowers and half chains.'" Ross noticed me listening and gave me a big wink. Where had I heard that expression? It clearly meant something to them, but nothing to me. How did Sarah know Ross's sister? Sarah was pleasant to me in her goodbyes. Why had she changed her attitude towards me?

I finished up my laundry and spent the afternoon doing chores around the cabin. Although it had been a dreary day, the clouds cleared out after supper. I was both surprised and pleased to hear Ross's motorcycle come up the road about 8:30 p.m. I was on the grass near the front porch when Ross pulled up the drive. "Come for a ride with me?" he asked.

I got on behind him and we drove up to the top of the summit to watch the sunset. Ross didn't want to sit on my favorite rock. He wanted to hike up to the top of the mountain. From there you could see 90 miles in all directions, not just 90 miles down to Yellowstone. We stood close together and I named all the mountain ranges for him. When there was a pause in my geography lesson, Ross put his arms around me and buried his face in my neck. He said softly, "That story you wrote for Ruthie's boy, that gift you gave Jacob, is the sweetest thing. I don't think you know how much power your words have, Cait. I don't think you understand the power of your gift. Promise me, that no matter what happens between us, you'll keep writing. Promise me." He turned me around and lifted my chin with his finger. "Look me in the eyes, Caitlinn, and promise me you'll keep writing."

I did promise him. Ross's intensity was overpowering. I had never seen anyone care so much about creative expression, about art, about what I did.

He held my shoulders firmly. "Are you listening to me? Sometimes, I don't think you hear me."

Well, I heard him, but I wasn't listening. I was disconnecting, my mind was wandering, I was thinking of another story. But Ross brought me back to the moment by hugging me. While holding me close against his chest, he whispered in my ear:

"Twice or thrice had I loved thee,
Before I knew thy face or name;
So in a voice, so in a shapeless flame
Angels affect us oft, and worshipp'd be,
Still when, to where thou wert, I came,
Some lovely glorious nothing I did see.
But since my soul, whose child love is,
Takes limbs of flesh, and else could nothing do,
More subtle than the parent is,
Love must not be, but take a body too,
And therefore what thou wert, and who,
I bid Love ask, and now
That it assume thy body, I allow,
And fix itself in thy lip, eye, and brow.[14]"*

"That's quite beautiful."

"John Donne. Thank you again for that wonderful story you wrote for my godson, Caitlinn. You should send Jacob's story to your editor."

"You wouldn't mind?"

"No, why should I mind?"

"It has your picture on the cover. I don't want to take advantage of your fame to sell my stories."

"Nah, I don't mind." He was rather aggressive in his assertion. "Don't be so modest. False humility is sinful, ya know."

~ Chapter 19 ~

Sunday, I drove into Bozeman. I stopped by the library to send both my novel and my story for Jacob to my editor electronically. I took a big deep breath and started thinking about the trip to Yellowstone. I was having second thoughts. I had a tendency to cancel out on things at the last minute, a habit I had learned from Ralph. He would plan a trip, get you all excited, and then cancel the whole thing. He always claimed to be too tired, but it was the ultimate control game. I also had a tendency to second-guess new experiences. Taking a motorcycle trip with a man I had known less than two weeks was a new experience. I was trying to keep myself in line. I also had not learned yet how to cope with the anxiety produced by relinquishing control of my writing. Waiting for feedback from my editor about my novel was adding to my nervousness. The sense of limbo and lack of control brought out the worst in me.

The night before our planned trip to Yellowstone Park, I

could not sleep. At dawn, I gave up on sleeping and got up. I packed and repacked my clothes for the trip about five times. I got so exasperated with myself that I went into Ennis an hour early, trying to maintain some equilibrium. I was supposed to meet Ross at 7 o'clock for breakfast at the Western Drug.

The Western Drug was a relatively new addition on Main Street, with an eating section modeled after an old-style ice cream fountain. Like many places in Montana, the locals had their own name for the Western Drug—the pharmacy. Dual names for places served as another way to discern newcomers from native Montanans. Native Montanans knew the true stories of the state and its history and they had their own terms for those places. I used the terms I had grown up with not considering that Ross wouldn't know them. His reaction to me calling Butte, the Gibraltar of Unionism, had schooled me on the need to translate for him. If you were a native of Montana, you knew Butte, in its heyday, had been a union town and that it been the richest hill on earth. The magnificent story of Butte and its prominent role in American history had been the reasons behind my choice of topics to write about in my novel.

The pharmacy or the Western Drug had a great cook working for them and, shortly after opening, the locals discovered the food and started hanging out there—especially early in the morning, and especially after the old hangout for the locals had been sold. The old hangout had been turned into an upscale coffee shop. One thing you could count on in Montana, cowboys do not like flavored coffee. The Western Drug's coffee, in contrast, was straight up regular, and there was lots of it. Of course, like many places in the Madison Valley, if you wanted a refill, sometimes you had to help yourself. When the waitresses got behind in their service, one of the locals would volunteer for coffee detail without being asked. Seeing cowboys pouring coffee, but declining to take orders, always baffled the tourists.

My stomach was growling and I decided not to wait for Ross. Charlie's wife, Kathy, took my order of two eggs and fry bread. Since I was eating by myself, I needed some reading material. I left the table and wandered back to the magazine rack against the back wall. I did a double take. A two-dimensional Ross was sitting on the middle shelf as the cover story of a popular magazine. I couldn't resist. I bought it and a paper. The news in the paper increased my anxiety, because a lightning strike Saturday night had started a fire in the remote backcountry of Beaver Creek, which was in the area Ross and I would have to travel through enroute to West Yellowstone. Strong winds from the cold front had fanned the fire from a small 80 acres to 2,000 the day before. Montana was burning on the borders of my safe place of Madison Valley. If I needed a reason not to go to Yellowstone, forest fires would suffice, but what I found in the magazine about Ross fanned a different sort of fire.

I read the five-page article on Australia's movie star. I wondered which stories were the truth—Ross's or theirs? I wondered anew about his unwillingness to answer questions about his son. I looked at my watch; it was now 7:30. Ross was late, which was unusual for him. I had made up my mind to go back to my cabin and abandon this foolishness when Ross walked in the door. He looked tired, but he smiled when he saw me. Nobody paid any attention to him with his dark sunglasses, jeans, heavy boots, and a tee shirt under his motorcycle jacket. His billed cap, bearing the red and black fighter jet logo of an Aussie footy team, was pulled down, partially shielding his face. When Ross got to the table, he removed his hat and glasses, giving me a kiss on the cheek. "Sorry, I'm late."

He slid into the booth seat opposite me. He moved the partially finished breakfast dishes and asked me, "Going somewhere? You looked like you were getting ready to leave."

"I was."

"Why?"

"Ross, I'm sorry. I think maybe I should pass on this trip to Yellowstone. I really should be writing." I was having trouble meeting his eyes. I reached over to pick up the magazine and the paper off the table. The magazine was face down on the top of the paper. His eyes followed my reach. He beat me to it, flipping the magazine over with one easy movement. Ross's face on the cover of the movie magazine looked back up at us.

Ross leaned across the table, leaning on his forearms, shortening the distance between us. "What changed your mind, Cait?" Ross's voice was low and even.

I leaned back hard against the wooden bench seat trying to increase the space between us. I hesitated, wondering if there was any way to easily exit out of this increasingly uncomfortable situation. "I'm worried about the forest fires."

"What. Changed. Your. Mind. Cait?" His voice was even lower, and he enunciated each word carefully and slowly, his whole body frozen, not even his eyes were blinking.

The negative energy bounced around the room. It was palpable; you could almost smell it like you can smell lightning when the late afternoon thunderstorms cross the Madison Plateau between the Madison River Canyon and Four Corners. It was apparent to others in the Western Drug, as well, because the other customers were giving us sideways glances. The light from the window behind him was highlighting his curly auburn hair. He had not shaved since the first night at the Bear Claw, and his beard, a lengthening reddish outline on his jaw, was glowing from the backlight.

I wasn't any good at lying or being evasive. I felt like Ross knew what had changed my mind, he was waiting for me to tell him. I looked down at my hands folded in my lap. I was starting to clench them. I tried to compose myself. I couldn't lie to Ross. I could feel the paralysis setting in. Whenever Ralph and I would fight, I would experience this panic. I was a deer caught in the headlights of an oncoming truck. Frozen. Trapped within myself. Helpless. Hands and feet becoming numb. Time slowing down. Blood pounding through my head, blocking out any other sound. I closed my eyes, bracing myself against the blow that was predestined to hit before the world went dark.

Ross got up and came around to my side of the table and slid in beside me. Kathy picked that moment to come by for Ross's order. Ross said to her softly, with his voice full of compassion, "Give us a minute, luv." He put his arm around me and covered both my hands with his remaining hand. "Cait, open your eyes." His voice, gentle in my ear was for me only. I opened my eyes. Underneath Ross's large hand, mine were still folded together, fingers so tightly squeezed my fingertips were red with white splotches. Ross's embrace was comforting in its encompassing warmth and security.

He spoke softly again into my ear, "Cait, talk to me. Breathe in Cait, and talk to me. This isn't about forest fires, they're in the backcountry. They're not a problem yet. This is about something else. C'mon, Cait, breathe."

I took a deep breath, the warmth of his hand over mine was encouraging me to loosen my grip.

"Take your time, there's no hurry. Breathe deeply."

The smoothness of Ross's breathing was calming. The gentle movement of his hand on my upper arm was quieting my heartbeat. The feeling started coming back in my feet and hands. No one had ever dealt with one of my episodes before. If I had a panic attack in front of Ralph, sometimes he would leave the room, slamming a door behind him, but more often, Ralph would slap me hard across the face and tell me to stop being stupid. I unfolded my hands and wrapped them around Ross's hand. I wanted to tell Ross how much his compassionate response meant to me. I couldn't find the words. I held his hand between mine, instead.

Kathy returned, and I avoided making eye contact. Ross asked for the Number Two Special without looking at the menu, along with a cup of tea and a cup of coffee for me. Kathy asked, "The usual two pots of hot water, Ross?" He grunted an affirmative. Ross kept his arm around me, but when the food came, I let go of his hand. He ate with one hand, keeping his arm around my shoulder, his embrace safe and reassuring. When Ross was finished with his breakfast, and was working on his second cup of tea, he reached over for the magazine. He put it in front of me. "What did you read in here that upset you so, Cait? Tell me. Please."

"You never told me about your twins."

"I don't have any. My little sister, Ruthie, has the twins."

"This said you are the father of that actress's twins." I pointed to the magazine.

"It's not true. Some fuckwit journo made that mistake years ago and they keep repeating it instead of checking the facts." Ross paused, "Do you believe me?"

I shrugged, "I don't know what to believe."

Ross released my shoulder and leaned on his forearms braced on the table, looking at me sideways, sighing, "Well, Cait, I can't tell you who to trust. You either believe me, or you believe someone who makes a living writing half-truths for a superficial magazine. I'm a meal ticket for a lot of people. To them, I'm just meat, I'm not a person, I'm someone without feelings. They always look for dirt, because that provides them with a hook to capture the public's attention. Truth doesn't matter. Once something is in print, people read it, and because it's ink on paper, they believe it—the sanctity of the written word. Worst of all is how the lies never go away. They're just repeated over and over and over."

"I can't defend myself against the press. I don't try. I can only make sure that what they say doesn't change my life, doesn't change how I perceive myself, doesn't change my relationships, doesn't hurt my family. So, this is massively important to me. If you choose to believe this, and not me, then I need to know that now. I have to know if you will trust me." Ross emphasized the last word, 'me.'

I cradled the coffee cup between my hands. Ross leaned back against the bench, shifting his body closer to me while putting his arm around me again. Our thighs were touching from the hip to the knee.

I took a deep breath, "What about the car crashes?" The article had mentioned two incidents where Ross had totaled cars. One had been in L.A. and the other on the Pacific Highway north of Sydney.

He laughed nervously, "Well, I have had some nasty smash ups."

"Were you driving drunk?"

He shook his head, "No. In L.A. I was driving too fast after a heavy rain. I was bloody lucky to walk away. The accident in Australia was different. I came around a blind curve and there was a five-car smashup. I drove off the road. Figured everybody's chances were improved if I didn't plow into them." Ross hesitated, "I've done other stupid shit that's not in this article, though. I'm not making excuses, Cait, but while I was making *Unto the Dust*, I was angry. Angry at the world, angry at my parents, angry at myself. I wasn't pleasant to be around. *Unto the Dust* came at a bad time in my life. I wasn't kidding when I said I found myself again because of what I learned making that movie."

"I'm sorry, Ross." What else could I say? Nothing seemed adequate. I reached up to stroke his face. My fingertips found the scar under his jaw. I was recalling Ross's comment about listening to his father after the horse kicked at him as a child. Why was Ross angry with his parents?

"I can't undo my past." Ross continued, "The reality is, I was out of control for a while and the press doesn't ever forget." He shrugged, tapping the magazine with his middle finger. "This is part of the job. I stopped worrying about what people think of me a long time ago, when I realized that most of them were full of shit anyway. I'd be lying if I said I like what's said about me in the popular press. For these journos, it's flip, flop, flap, and loose with the truth. But don't feel sorry for me, Cait. I'm doing what I've always wanted to do. And I'm good at it. Not too many people can say that about their lives. I don't hate the press. The day that I do, I'm going to quit the business. But, if you are around me, you'll have to learn to deal with them. I'll be doing heaps and heaps of publicity for *Florentine Conspiracy*. It's got a chance of being massive. I'm doing all I can to promote it. There will be more articles like this one in the next few months. I have to sell my movies, I have to sell my image, I don't have to sell my soul. So, Cait, in the end, you have to tell me. What made you change your mind about the road trip to the park?"

I appreciated that Ross had not been defensive or evasive in his answers to my questions. He was not cajoling me or pressuring me to go. I appreciated that he wanted me to tell him what I was feeling. He wanted to hear from me why I was not going with him to Yellowstone, rather than making his own assumptions.

I paused and then said softly, "I'm not as strong as I look. I sent off my novel and I'm worried about it. Everything's at stake. I just finalized my divorce a few months ago. I don't know if I want to get involved with anyone right now. I like the independence. It's new to me. It's exciting. For the first time in my life, a man isn't telling me what to do and making my decisions for me."

"How valuable is your independence to you? Is it worth more than love?"

"I don't know."

"If you met the right person, would you walk away just because of the calendar?"

"I don't know."

"Thank you for your honesty, Cait."

Kathy interrupted us with the check, before I could respond. Ross got up without a word and I followed him. Outside the Western Drug, standing under the porch on the sidewalk by the wooden bench with carved bears on both ends, Ross turned to me and said, simply, "Do you want to come with me to Yellowstone, Cait? Yes? Or no?"

The space between us was increasing as he stepped backward in the direction of his motorcycle.

"Can I say probably?" I replied, while wiggling my eyebrows up and down at him, imitating the facial expression Ross used when he joked with me in the past.

Ross snorted, shaking his head while stepping backwards. With no expression in his voice, he replied, "Caitlinn, you're lucky I find you amusing. Do you want to come? Yes or no."

"Yes please, if you'll have me."

Ross nodded. I expected him to smile at me, but he didn't show any emotion at all. He simply reversed direction and extended me his hand, "Then let's give it a fair go, Caitlinn." I took his hand and he gave mine a gentle squeeze in response.

~ Chapter 20 ~

The road construction on 287 began right outside the southern outskirts of Ennis where the highway was completely torn up and slow going for motorcycles. Montana at its worst was nine months of winter and three months of road construction. I didn't mind. I liked the slowness of the trip because I could regroup after the meltdown of the morning and be physically close to Ross without interacting with him. I was extremely conscious of where our bodies touched and found the contact with his body reassuring, which was not how I usually felt about physical contact with other people. I usually preferred not to be touched.

Ross, on the other hand, was getting impatient with the slowness of the trip. When we had to wait for 20 minutes for the go ahead from the flagman, I tried to distract him. Watching Ross fidget and become agitated was like watching a caged animal. I was reminded of a previous summer when one of the richest men in America got a ticket for failing to yield to a flag man when 287 was being rebuilt on the north side of Ennis. The whole town talked of nothing else for weeks. Ross and I did not need that kind of notoriety.

I started to tell him stories. "When we get going again, watch for the big gate on your left. That ranch used to be owned by a movie star who moved here from California. He was having some construction done on his ranch house. One of the crew on the job had grown up in Ennis and offered to show the actor the teepee rings that were up along the ridges above the house. Most people are pretty thrilled to find old Indian artifacts. When they hiked up there, all the movie star could say was 'What the hell are Indians doing on my land?' The teepee rings were over 1,000 years old."

Ross laughed and relaxed, "Well, Cait," he said leaning back into me, "Not all of us movie stars are smart and good looking."

He straightened up when I poked him in the ribs. "You're awful. Didn't your mother ever teach you the meaning of humility?"

"Sorry, Cait, she gave up and taught me how to apologize instead." He rested both of his hands on my thighs, rubbing them slowly with his thumbs. I started to tell Ross about John Colter, who had been with the Lewis and Clark Expedition, and why Yellowstone was known originally as Colter's Hell, but the flagman gave the signal to start, and Ross had to pay attention to the road. When the construction ended, Ross pushed the speed of the motorcycle up to the speed limit. He was focused. I was unfocused, my thoughts in a muddle and my thighs tingling where Ross had touched them.

The southern half of the Madison Valley had always been one of my favorite areas of Montana. The colors were particularly beautiful on this range. The snow lasts on the peaks almost all year. On the whole, Madison Valley is sunnier than the Gallatin Valley. Best of all, the Madison Valley was my safe place, the place of my best childhood memories, the location of my grandfather's cabin.

As we traveled south and the valley narrowed, the landscape changed from dry sheep country to forested foothills. We passed the juncture of 287 and 87. Highway 87 headed south to Idaho. The entrance to Raynolds Pass was ahead and used to be isolated empty ranching country. No more. Houses, sprouting like invasive musk thistles against the slopes of the mountains, scarred the natural beauty. This area near Yellowstone Park was one of the fastest growing regions in the West. We headed up into the canyon where the quake of 1959 had claimed 28 lives the night of August 17. We pulled off at the earthquake visitor's center. The quake had registered 7.8 on the Richter scale, making it one of the strongest of the century. The mountain above the Rock Creek campground had split in two, cascading across the Madison River and halfway up the opposite slope. At that campsite, 19 men, women, and children were buried under half of the mountain. Others had died in different locations. The slide dammed the Madison River, flooding the canyon and putting enormous pressure on Hebgen Dam upstream. The remote physical location made communication with the outside world almost impossible. After the quake, both exits out of the canyon were blocked by the damage.

The visitor's center was built in the middle of the massive slide. Ross stood beside me, surveying the vast sea of boulders. "Imagine going to sleep with your family around you, safe and happy, and waking up to this. Gives a bloke pause. What really matters is family and nothing else." He paused, "What matters most to you, Cait?"

"Being independent and being able to write."

"That's harsh."

I was remembering other times when people had asked me similar questions about what really mattered to me, and I had been too literal, too analytical. I needed to say something to temper the severity of my remark. I talked fast.

"I'm sorry. I always take questions too literally and I never say the right thing. It's happened before. When I was in new member class for church with Ralph, years ago, we had to make these family crests and write into them what we valued most. It was one of those group ice-breaking activities." I glanced at Ross to see if he was following my attempted explanation.

He nodded, he apparently understood what I meant.

"Well, it was a disaster from my point of view. I put in truth, justice, and knowledge, and everyone else put in family, love, friendship, stuff like that. I felt like a freak, because none of that even occurred to me."

"Well, I don't think your answer makes you a freak, but it is revealing."

"Oh?" I wasn't sure I felt comfortable with the direction this was going.

"Sounds to me like you think, when you should be feeling, Cait." Ross's eyes narrowed, his head was cocked slightly to one side and he was chewing on his lower lip. "What I don't understand, is how you can be so passionate about some things and so dispassionate about your own emotions. It's almost as if you're afraid of something."

I started to give him a smart answer to deflect the seriousness of this conversation. Ross anticipated my response and placed his forefinger gently on my lips, shaking his head slightly. "No, Cait. Answer me, truthfully. Are you afraid of expressing your own feelings?"

I searched Ross's face, looking for any signs of taunting, scorn, sarcasm, or malice. There was none. He was motionless, waiting. I wanted to give Ross an honest answer. I hesitated, and the confusion must have shown on my face.

Ross sighed, "That's all right, Cait, we have plenty of time." He took my hand in his, warm and comforting. "Let's go."

The road climbed from the visitor's center. Ross was driving slowly, surveying the lake created by the giant slide. Along the right side of the highway, the stark white trunks of the drowned trees stood lonely in the green waters of Quake Lake. The lushness of the mountain forest on the other side of the road increased the contrast—lodge pole pines and quaking aspens versus the skeletons of the canyon's prequake vegetation. The trees standing isolated like toothpicks in the middle of the lake always made me shiver. We continued to climb up to the ridge known as Refuge Point, where 250 people trapped in the canyon that fateful night after the quake hit at midnight had gathered to escape the floodwaters of the blocked Madison River. There was no way out of the canyon for the refugees, and no way to communicate with the outside world.

Ham radio operators in West Yellowstone broadcast the first reports of the quake and the widespread damage throughout the area. Reports of damage trickled in, and by early morning it was apparent that the only way in and out of the canyon would have to be by air. All available aircraft in the tri-state area was mobilized to aid in the rescue efforts. Eight smokejumpers with first aid training were dropped to the ridge to help the stranded campers and fishermen. It took 18 hours to rescue the survivors. The wounded were airlifted out first by helicopter, while a makeshift road was cut through the slide to get the rest of the people to safety.

Flooding threatened the towns downstream of the slide. The blocked waters from the Madison River were wearing at the slide. If the waters broke loose, the mass of water would have devastated Ennis. Earthmovers were brought from the open copper mines of Butte to dig a channel to relieve the pressure of the blocked Madison River. The impressive channel cut through the massive slide was 250 feet wide and 14 feet deep. Hebgen Dam held. The danger of flooding passed, but not the physical and emotional damage. I had no way of knowing that the fault lines along the tectonic plates of my past were beginning to shift and their movement would leave a swath of destruction, scarring all of us forever. Ross and I would be no different than the 28 people trapped who had been under the collapsed mountain in 1959, before either of us were born. There would be no escaping destruction and death.

We traveled further past the Hebgen Dam and rode along the azure waters of one of the largest high-altitude reservoirs in the world. We turned south at 191, traveling down the tree-lined highway into West Yellowstone. I suggested a cafe near the entrance to the park. Sitting at the table, Ross was subdued, and I surveyed his face. He looked awful. I asked if the altitude was bothering him, since we were at a higher elevation than in Ennis.

He smiled faintly. "Well, I suppose the altitude might be part of the problem, Cait, but the biggest reason I'm knackered is that I didn't sleep last night at all. I could not get my thoughts to settle."

I didn't mind Ross's silence through lunch. I was lost in thought looking at the Winold Reiss Great Northern calendars decorating the walls of the café. My grandparents brought Mark and me here for supper before heading back home after our annual weekend in the park. They always ordered two banana splits for themselves and Mark and I usually had chocolate sundaes. Grandma always kidded Grandpa about his banana split dessert. She wanted him to share it, because it was a split and it was invented as the perfect date dessert, to which he would say no, it was called that because the banana was split and if he had to start sharing they would have to split up. Grandpa had proposed over banana splits in this very cafe under the gaze of the Blackfeet Indian elders. He had refused to share that night and he wasn't going to start sharing after all these years. Mark and I never could figure out why those two laughed so hard when they would launch into their banana split routine. As an adult, I suspected they were censoring their story for young ears. I asked Ross if he wanted one for dessert and he declined. He said he didn't like bananas with ice cream. He ordered one scoop of vanilla without any syrup instead. When he was finished, he asked me if I knew why the cafe was decorated like my cabin.

"Other way around. Grandpa decorated the cabin with Winold Reiss prints and calendars because he proposed to Grandma right here. They brought my brother and me to Yellowstone for the weekend every year to celebrate their anniversary. They had honeymooned in the park and stayed at the Old Faithful Inn."

Ross nodded, but didn't comment. Before we left, he walked around the cafe and studied each portrait carefully before paying our check.

After lunch, we walked around West Yellowstone. Ross and I walked close together; he never let go of my hand. If the sidewalks got crowded and we had to walk single file, he maintained physical contact by putting his hand lightly on my back or on the nape of my neck. His behavior reminded me of how protective JoAnn was with her toddlers. She never let them out of her physical range in public, in case she had to rescue them from danger. I wondered if Ross was doing the same thing. No one noticed us. We fit right in with all the other tourists on vacation. Ross wanted to do some Christmas shopping for his family back in Australia. I suggested that he buy gifts made in Montana. He asked if I had any ideas.

"Sure, let's go down to Eagles. They have a good selection. Eagles is one of the oldest stores here in town."

After making his purchases, Ross lost interest in shopping. He wanted some tea, so we sat at the soda fountain in Eagles, admiring the big wooden mirrors along the back wall and exquisite green and yellow tiled counter with its antique stools. Other than his comments about the historical beauty of the soda fountain, Ross had nothing to say. I was content to sit alongside him in a comfortable silence, reminiscing about my childhood trips with my grandparents. He was finished with his second cup of tea before he spoke. "I was late this morning because I got a call from the Madison County Sheriff."

"What about?"

"You want to hear a long story?"

"Yes."

"Well, when I took Mike's family back to the airport Saturday morning, I passed this hitchhiker on Highway 287 near the cemetery just north of Harrison. Ya know that country, Cait, there's nothing up there from Harrison to Interstate 90 except 20 miles of bleak countryside. I wondered why this old fella was hitchin' and where he'd come from. But we were going in the opposite direction. On my way back from the airport, Mike and I saw the same bloke standing alongside the road by the turnoff for Pony. In eight hours, he had walked maybe four miles, tops. Plus, it's really raining hard and it's about four. Nasty arvo. I've done a lot of hitchin' in Australia and I felt sorry for him. I stopped and picked him up."

"Turns out he's been hitchin' from Billings, trying to get down to Idaho for a reunion of his army buddies and he doesn't have any money. He'd walked out of the nursing home without his daughter's knowledge. He got a ride with a truckie who let him off in the middle of nowhere. I told him he should have stayed with the truckie until the other side of Butte and then hitched down route 15 to Idaho. That's a busier road. It was getting late and I didn't want to leave him in Norris. I took him down to Ennis, and Mike and I bought him a feed at the Western. I reckoned he could catch a ride from there. The old man's real grateful because the only people he'd seen for hours on 287 were my van and some kids who threw beer bottles at him."

"After supper, I thought he looked well and truly knackered. I told him I'd shout him a cabin at the Lone Mountain Motel overnight. Superior chance of getting a ride in the morning. The old fella kept thanking me and telling me he'd send me the money when he got to Idaho. I said I was just paying back kindness people had shown me."

"I checked him in at the Lone Mountain Motel and rode out to see you, feeling rather pleased with myself. I should have known better. Sunday, Mike, Charlie, and I went out horseback riding along the old Story track and I spent the evening in Mike's motel room discussing the movie until pretty late. I didn't get the message from the sheriff until this morning when I was supposed to be meeting you. Turns out the day clerk at the motel Sunday morning didn't understand the arrangement. When she saw the old man and my name and credit card number on the bill, she assumed the worst and called the coppers. The staff at the motel knows me, this fella clearly isn't me. He'd had been in jail half of the weekend. He had to call his daughter, and she drove over from Billings to get him. I guess she was as mad as a cut snake. I try to play Good Samaritan, and the shit starts to fly. I hope my next bit of charity gets a better reception."

"Maybe, you shouldn't pick up hitchhikers."

"Why, not?"

"It's dangerous, you could get killed or robbed."

Ross frowned. After a moment's pause, he jerked his head slightly and regarded me intently before speaking, "Do you always assume the worst, Cait? Don't you think it's important to be compassionate when people need you?"

"Not if it could get you hurt."

Ross's eyes narrowed, but he didn't respond. Instead, he looked at his watch and got up to pay the tab. I followed him out the door to the street. Again, I was relieved to be back on the motorcycle. I thought about my conversations with Ross since we had left Ennis. I had said one stupid thing after another. Ross seemed disappointed or perplexed by my responses to his questions. Why had I come on this trip? I knew the answer to that question, but I did not want to face it. I had agreed to come, initially, because Ross was charming and I enjoyed his company, plus I wanted to see the places my grandparents loved so much, but the argument at the Western Drug had provided a good opportunity to cut off the relationship before it got any more complicated. I knew why I wanted to say yes when he asked me again to come with him. I had come, because he had stayed present for me through my panic attack with no criticism afterwards. Ross listened. I didn't feel judged. No one had ever done that for me before. I liked the way Ross made me feel—excited, alive, challenged, and threatened. Ross also made me feel safe. Safe and threatened, sometimes I could not sort out how I felt. There were some emotions I could not verbalize. But I was sure of one thing—I did not want to let go of this new lifeline. Ross did not let me use the old excuses or the old defenses, he came through them trying to understand who I was and why I reacted the way I did. A younger me would have refused to come, after the Western Drug confrontation. A younger me would have chosen to hide. I had no desire to hide from Ross. I wanted Ross to find me.

I thought about how my therapist encouraged me to discuss not my intellectual rationalized opinions, but my feelings. "Talk to people, Cait," she would say. "Communicate. Tell people what you're feeling. You're good at telling people what you think. Work on telling them how you feel."

Ross stopped first at the Lower Geyser Basin where we walked around the boardwalks. I asked Ross point blank, "How do I make you feel, Ross?"

"I like the way you make me feel, Cait. You make me feel calm." Ross smiled slightly, the right corner of his mouth curving. He paused and qualified his assessment, "Calm, most of the time, and always useful, needed, protective, strong. How do I make you feel?"

"Alive, excited, challenged, and a little threatened. Sometimes very safe."

"Threatened and safe?" His right eyebrow raised.

"Hmm," I groaned. I had done it again. Put my foot in my mouth. "You have this way of looking at me. I feel like you can see into my soul, see through all my defenses."

"What do you need defenses against, Cait?" Ross was doing it again with his intense gaze—the peeling back of my protective skin. I looked down at my feet. I remained mute. He reached out and took me gently by the shoulders. He raised my chin with his forefinger. He sighed, "Truth is, Cait, I can't see into your soul, I can't figure you out at all. You're a puzzle. An intriguing, beautiful puzzle." He removed the forefinger from my chin and rubbed it down the bridge of my nose affectionately. He bent over and lightly kissed me on the mouth, took my hand, and continued walking around the geysers. I decided to keep my mouth shut for a while. I did not want to ruin the positive energy of his kiss with any more talking.

We arrived at Old Faithful in time for an early dinner. Ross and I walked around the boardwalk surrounding Yellowstone's most famous attraction. After supper, I asked Ross what he wanted to do. He shrugged, "I'm well and truly knackered. I'd be happy sitting on a bench like an old man watching Old Faithful. We can have a chat. We have a lot to talk about."

We sat down on one of the benches, watching the evening light change and listening to the commotion of the tourists around us. I told Ross how my grandmother liked to catch every eruption she could while staying at the inn and how we would watch them together. Old Faithful was due to make an appearance. The geyser started, spluttering at first and then roaring up into its full glory. We sat in silence afterwards, all the other travelers had left.

Ross put his arm around my shoulder and pulled me closer to him. "I'd like to have an old faithful."

"Oh, you mean a woman in a flannel nightgown?"

He leaned back away from me with one eyebrow raised, "Come again?"

"Women in flannel nightgowns. They're a constant like Q-tips. When you're married you like constants and old faithfuls."

Ross laughed. "Exactly so, Cait. Marriage as a safe haven from the chaos of the outside world—predictable. I'd like that. Do you have one?"

"One what?"

"Flannel nightgown?"

"No, I don't like nightgowns. They always end up all twisted around your waist and then they don't cover up anything."

His face lit up mischievously and his eyebrows were wiggling up and down, "Sounds like fun."

I made a face and shook my head. The air was getting cooler rapidly, now that the sun was dipping towards the horizon. I shivered. Ross stood up and offered me his hand. "Let's go in, Cait. I'm knackered and cold."

I did not want to go inside. The sleeping arrangements worried me. Despite all his flirting by Old Faithful, once inside his room Ross was all business. He asked what side of the bed I wanted and then disappeared into the bathroom. When he came out and started undressing, I grabbed his saddlebags with my stuff and ducked into the safety of the bathroom. I took a long time. When I opened the door, the bedside lamps were off. Only the night-light by the door provided any guidance. Ross was sound asleep. I slid in beside him and stayed near the edge of the bed, listening to his measured breathing.

I woke up stiff from having slept in the same position all night. Ross was beside me, crouched down flat on his heels. "Hey, Cait, wake up. Time to go. Breakfast in 10. See you down in the cafe, yeah?" He patted my thigh, which was still under the blankets. He rose smoothly and was out of the room before I could say anything or even sit up.

~ Chapter 21 ~

We continued our trip around the Grand Loop, stopping around noon at a campsite for a picnic lunch, which Ross had asked the lodge staff to prepare. Afterwards, we started some serious hiking. Ross and I had been walking for about an hour when we finally got to the edge of a beautiful small lake. No one else was around. Ross was standing quietly by the water staring off into space. I don't know what possessed me, but when I saw the pile of old dried out moose turds, I could not resist. Mark used to pelt me with them. I bent down and grabbed a handful. I tossed one at Ross. It bounced off his arm. "What are you doing?" he asked, frowning. His peaceful reverie had been disturbed.

"Nothing." I did it again.

"Nothing, hell. What is that shit?"

"Shit." I replied with a straight face. No wonder Mark had always teased me. This was fun.

"Caitlinn, what are you throwing at me?"

"Moose turds."

"Great, I've had the press pile shit *on* me, and now a woman is throwing shit *at* me. Caitlinn, didn't I lecture you in Bozeman about throwing shit at me?"

"Yeah, yeah, but that was about throwing condescending metaphorical bullshit at you. This is completely different. I'm not being condescending; this is moose shit, and it's not metaphorical. It's the real deal." I stuck my tongue out at him. "Sorry mate, bonding Montana style. Deal with it, in the moment, as best you can." I answered in my best imitation of an Aussie accent.

"I'll show you bonding Aussie style. In the moment, as best I can." Ross said, laughing.

I was getting ready to run, but he was too fast for me. He charged and, before I could breathe again, I was over his shoulder and he was moving down the trail.

"Put me down, *put me down*." I pounded his back playfully with slightly clenched fists. I couldn't move my legs at all, his grip was too tight.

"Okay, boss." Ross agreed, too quickly. I should have known better. He put me down all right, but as soon as my feet touched the ground, he picked me up again like a small toddler. He backed me up against a nearby tree, and there was no escaping. Ross kept his hands cupped under my thighs and kissed me firmly on the mouth. I kissed him back and wrapped my legs around his waist and my arms around his shoulders. What could happen outside in the open sunny spaces? The smell of the pine needles and the clear fresh air was familiar and comforting. With the tip of his tongue, Ross traced the outline of my upper lip. All his movements were slow and delicate. He was concentrating on the corners of my mouth, one side then the other. I relaxed and opened my mouth slightly to let in his tongue. My tongue met his, tips lingering, a circling dance round and round. Exploration was getting deeper, more intimate. The ridges on the roof of my mouth were being traveled. I melted into Ross. I didn't notice when his hands got under my shirt, I was too focused on the traveling of his tongue. His fingertips across the small of my back were creating ripples of warmth across the surface of my bare skin. I lost track of time. The warm ripples of sensation had moved around to my nipples as his thumbs massaged them. All that warmth and tantalizing tingling was interrupted when a hiker came around the bend in the trail.

"Oops, sorry," he said when he saw us.

Ross put me down, and smoothed my hair back from my face. I tucked my shirt back into my jeans. The hiker discreetly walked on down the trial. Ross looked at me and winked. I blushed. He had the most suggestive wink. "We'll have to finish this later." With that, he grabbed my hand, and we hiked back to his bike. We completed the loop, returning to Old Faithful around 8 p.m.

Following a late supper, we sat around the big fireplace in the lobby and told stories until Ross said he wanted to return to our room. Standing outside on the balcony, looking down to the lounge area below, I talked too much about how it was the largest log structure in the world and who made the furniture, trying to delay the moment when I would have to be alone with him again. There had been too much passion that afternoon. I didn't think Ross was going to simply fall asleep tonight. I was feeling conflicted about the situation. The warm memories of the afternoon were juxtaposed against cold recollections of sex with Ralph. How would it be with Ross? The choices were narrowing. Time was running out. Reality was closing in. I could hope that sex would be different with a different man, but what if it wasn't? I stalled for time, telling one story hard on the heels of another.

Ross listened patiently for a time, but then yawned. Taking my hand he said, "C'mon Cait, off to bed. History will wait until tomorrow."

Once inside his room, Ross dropped the keys on the desk and turned towards me. The afternoon spontaneity of dreamy playfulness under the canopy of sweet-smelling towering Ponderosa pines had disappeared. His expression was purposeful, all movements deliberate. Here in his hotel room, there was no question of what would happen next, no reassuring familiarity of the western landscape braking runaway passions. Sexual intent radiated out of him like heat from a wood-burning stove driving up the escalating temperatures in a confined tiny space.

Engulfing me in his arms, he bent down and kissed my ear aggressively. His teeth nibbling on my ear lobe alternated with his tongue's explosive wet licking. His embrace was tightening, and I was overwhelmed by the confirmation of how strong he was. I couldn't move. When he smothered my mouth with his, I tried to kiss him back, but his lips were crushing mine hard against my teeth. He seemed to grow taller. His lungs were sucking the air out of mine. I could feel his heartbeat. His rhythms were dictating mine. My heart couldn't keep up. I was hot, even though my jacket was sliding off my shoulders. I heard it drop to the floor. My shirt was slipping down. I was naked from the waist up and I was still burning from his body heat. He had my braid unbound. The pain from my pulled hair sparked my surging uncertainty. His tongue forcing open my mouth wasn't exploratory and tender. It was big, strong, and demanding. His palms were coals against the exposed skin of my back. When he pressed his muscular leg up between my thighs, forcing them apart, and I felt his masculine hardness against the inside of my leg, and his fingers undoing the zipper of my jeans, I wrenched my mouth free. All I could manage to say was a strangled, "No."

Immediately, he relaxed his hold on me and I slid free out of his embrace. Clutching my arms over my exposed breasts, I stuttered, "I'm sorry, I'm sorry, I'm sorry, I can't do this." I backed up from him increasing the distance between us.

He took a step forward. He loomed over me. He was consuming the oxygen in the room. The normally friendly curves of his mouth thinned and sharpened. His pupils expanded, darkening his eyes as the color receded to the edges. His auburn curls glowed from the light behind him. His eyes narrowed, wrinkles spreading across his forehead. The deep reverberations of his voice echoed as the room shrank, "Cait, I care about you, but talk only goes so far. I'd rather show you how I feel."

The claustrophobic fear of entrapment choked me. I needed the sunny wide-open spaces. I couldn't breathe. My heart thundered in my ears. I took another step backward, and when Ross stepped closer, I retreated again. The fear rose, wave upon wave. My whole body shook. Tears welled up in my eyes. I couldn't look at him. I could only beg for mercy. "I'm so sorry, Ross, I'm so sorry."

His challenging voice deepened. "What is the matter, Cait? What are you sorry about?"

Tears ran down my cheeks. I had run out of room to retreat. My back was against the wall. I was trapped in the corner of the hotel room with walls on two sides, the bedside table on the third, Ross blocking my way out. I slid down the hard surface of the wall to my knees with my head buried in my hands. I barely fit between the wall and the bedside table. I was rocking back and forth on my heels, rhythmically. If I try harder, I can fall backwards into the oblivion of my empty heart and leave all this confusing pain and fear behind. The room spun out of control.

Ross's hands clutched my shoulders, drawing me back upright. Cupping my cheeks in his hands, his thumbs gently caressed my cheekbones. Ross's urgent voice was bringing me back from the welcoming darkness of oblivion into the light, "Caitlinn, Caitlinn, what are you so afraid of? Me?"

The torment in his voice stabbed me. I looked up into Ross's face. All the sexual intensity was gone. He was motionless and I recognized his expression. It was the expression of Father O'Donnell when he listened to his parishioners tell him their heartaches and losses. Only, the luminous eyes urging me to trust him with my fear weren't the familiar blue of the compassionate priest. They were Ross's eyes and they were emerald green. Ross repeated the question, still holding my face in his hands, preventing me from turning away. "Are you afraid of me, Cait?"

"No ... yes ... ." I paused and Ross waited patiently, his head slightly tilted to the side. He focused all of his attention on me. I finally got the words out, "Not you ... sex."

"Why are you afraid of sex, Cait?"

"I'm not any good at it." For an instant, as emotions played across his face, I thought Ross would laugh at me. His eyes were crinkling up on the edges. But when he spoke, his mouth's curves stayed serious with his voice free of any humor.

"No, Cait, there's something else bothering you. I can see it in your eyes. Talk to me."

"Sex is complicated for me."

Ross countered, "It's complicated for everyone."

I straightened up and quit shaking. "How can it be for you? You know the most beautiful women in the world. Who am I?" I was trying to avoid telling him what was really bothering me.

"You, Caitlinn, are a very scared woman who is not answering my question." His voice was calm. "I think it will help if you talk to me." Ross released my face and was picking up the loose strands of hair around my temples, smoothing them back. The lightness of his touch was reassuring. There was nothing sexual or hungry about his movements.

I was still being evasive, "What if I don't measure up?"

"That's a bunch of nonsense, Cait, and you know it." Ross waited for the real reason, and I knew I would have to tell him. I couldn't out wait him. He wasn't going anywhere.

"My father ... ." My voice broke and I couldn't continue. I was sobbing again.

Ross waited. I couldn't stop shaking. I couldn't stop crying. He lifted me up and sat down on the edge of the bed. I was in his lap, cradled in his arms. I buried my face in his chest. I couldn't tell him. I could not form the words. I felt so ashamed and so dirty. He wouldn't want me after I told him. He wouldn't look at me the same way. I couldn't bear to cross over that divide and tell him my secrets.

Ross didn't try to calm me down. He didn't tell me to stop feeling sorry for myself, as Ralph used to do. He held me close. The harder I sobbed, the closer he held me. Finally, there were no more tears. He stroked my hair and kissed the top of my head. "I don't want to hurt you, Caitlinn. I can guess what your father did, but I would rather you tell me."

I began to find the words. They were the hardest to speak in my life, "I'm all messed up. I have holes in my soul."

"From what, Caitlinn?"

The words all tumbled out at once, one on top of each other. "My father used to touch me. I thought he loved me. He didn't. I wasn't a person to him. Just another pair of breasts. Just another pair of breasts to have whenever he wanted … ." The anger was making my voice sharper.

Ross sighed and pressed me tighter to him. The palms of his hands flowing over the surface of my bare back were as cooling as the winds blowing across sweaty skin. The pain in his voice was obvious. "Caitlinn, someone else's sin doesn't have to deprive you of happiness. What your father did to you doesn't make you unlovable. What happened wasn't your fault." Ross bent his head down and his lips briefly brushed my eyelids, my forehead, my mouth. His kisses were cool, affectionate, and short. Ross hugged me again, resting his head on mine, rocking slightly. We stayed quiet, frozen in that spot for a long time like lost explorers in an endless barren tundra of pain.

Ross shifted. "My legs are going to sleep." He helped me up. Standing by the bed, he put his arms around me and hugged me again, burying his fingers in amongst the bunches of my loose hair. "Caitlinn, you don't have to do anything, you're not ready for. All I ask of you is that you trust me. Please." His voice was low, gentle, and pleading.

I looked up into his face; his eyes were still emerald green in their wet, startling color. I nodded. Ross hugged me again and turned to go into the bathroom. When he came out, I went into the bathroom, closing the door behind me. I got ready for bed and turned the light out before opening the door. The bedroom was dark except for the nightlight. I slipped into bed. Ross moved and pulled me towards him. In the silence, he caressed my hair as I lay in his arms. When I was almost asleep, I moved away from him, performing an old habit. There were some circumstances where I didn't like to be touched. This was one of them.

I woke up to the sound of the shower. I looked at the clock, it was only 6 a.m. I didn't feel good. My eyes were all puffy, and I felt emotionally drained, but one thing was crystal clear to me. I didn't want to lose Ross. I was smart enough and practical enough to know that there are certain expectations in a relationship. I had heard of child abuse victims who refused to have sex. In my married life, I viewed sex like changing dirty diapers, something that had to be done. Whenever Ralph wanted sex, I had to yield. I had learned the hard way not to argue with him or to say no early in our marriage. After that, I didn't argue when Ralph demanded sex. I disconnected from my body and waited for him to be done, so I could get up and wash him off of me.

I looked at the clock again. It was getting late. I needed to wash my hair and get it dried. Ross was taking far too long in the shower. I was getting impatient. So, I did what was practical and necessary. I got in with him.

"I need to wash my hair." I had my back to Ross when I slipped in besides him.

"Really?" My heartbeat was deafening in my ears and the conflicting emotions were waging warfare in my nervous system. When Ross laid his hands on my bare shoulders, I jumped involuntarily.

Ross turned me around to face him. The spray of water not blocked by his body splashed my face, giving me an excuse to squeeze my eyes tightly shut. He shifted position and the excuse not to look at him vanished. "Caitlinn, open up your eyes and look at me."

I had to open my eyes, but I could not meet his. "Caitlinn, why did you get in the shower with me? What do you really want?"

The question was the companion to the one Ross had asked me under Grandma's tree, the other time I had offered myself to him with alternative motives. I needed to be honest with him, but the words were too revealing, too humiliating. When I tried to speak my brain froze and I felt trapped inside myself—an insect locked in Amber. I could hear with increased clarity the water hitting his back and dripping off him onto the tile floor. I could see the rivulets winding down his body, following the curves of his pectoral muscles, separating to flow around his erect nipples. On his right bicep, where the water wasn't a steady stream, I watched one drop run down the length of his tanned arm like a single tear running down the slope of a cheekbone. I couldn't answer him. I ducked my head, closing my eyes, retreating.

Ross inhaled deeply and exhaled slowly. I felt the brush of a kiss on my forehead and the solid contact of his wet skin all along the length of my body as he embraced me tightly. "Ah, Caitlinn, what am I meant to do with you?" His voice was husky and barely audible in my ear over the sound of the water. My hair, underneath his hands on the small of my back and the nape of my neck, gave Ross his answer where my tongue had failed me. His wet lips met mine briefly before he turned me away from him in order to wash my hair.

I could hear the shampoo sigh out of the bottle when Ross squeezed it into his hand. I could hear the water, the comforting sound as it rushed from the pipes, hitting his back. The bathroom air was warm and steamy. When he rubbed the shampoo on the sides of my head, he moved his hands in slow even strokes starting from the temples moving down to the nape of my neck. Each application of shampoo was the same—the soft sigh of the bottle, the strokes starting at my hairline and smoothly following the curve of my head. Ross stepped backwards in the shower so he could stretch my long hair out towards him. His hands ran the length of my hair, from the nape of my neck down to the ends. Each stroke more relaxing than the last. He moved aside out of the water stream and the water hit the back of my head, cascading down my back. I kept my eyes closed to keep out the soap and tilted back my head. Ross rinsed out the shampoo with the same silky smooth delicate movements. As he pulled the handfuls of hair apart to let the water wash out the soap, Ross lingered, holding each section of hair a little longer than the last.

When the last of the soap was twirling down the drain, Ross stepped back into the stream of water. His body sheltered mine from the water flow. His arms slid around my middle, drawing me back until our bodies met. Ross kissed the top of my head. His voice was startling after such a long silence. "Don't take too much longer, Cait, I'm really hungry." He slipped out of the shower before I could respond.

I was left exposed to the pounding water stream, trying to sort out my feelings. Relief and rejection mixed together were swirling round and round like the soapsuds carried by the water. When I dried myself off with the towel, I realized to my chagrin I had another problem. I hadn't brought my clothes into the bathroom with me. I stood in the bathroom with the towel wrapped around me, working up the courage to go into the bedroom. I must have stood there longer than I realized.

Ross's impatient voice interrupted my trance. "Hey,

Cait, what are you doing in there?"

I lied, "Trying to comb out my hair. It's a mess."

"Bring your comb out here, I'll do it."

I brought the comb out, along with the brush. I self-consciously had the towel wrapped around me, desperately wishing the towel was bigger. I shivered, partly out of nervousness. Ross reached into the saddlebags sitting on the bed and pulled out a red and black plaid flannel shirt. "Here, put this on." He helped me put it on, since I was holding the towel. Avoiding my eyes, Ross buttoned up his shirt over my towel for me. When he turned around to pull up a chair next to the bed, I dropped the towel onto the floor.

"Sit here."

I sat down with my back to him and asked him, "Don't pull, okay? I hate it when my hair gets pulled."

"Don't worry, Cait, I know what I'm doing." He took his time and gently worked through all the tangles with no pulling.

I asked, "Where did you learn to be so gentle?"

"Grooming horses. My father taught me. If horses don't like what you're doing you know it in a hurry. Where's your band? I'll braid your hair for you."

I was holding it. I passed it back to him over my shoulder. I avoided meeting his eyes. Ross didn't do a simple braid. I could feel him doing a French braid.

"Where'd you learn to braid like that?"

"My little sister Ruthie. She was always braiding when she was little, she'd braid my hair if I sat still. I learned fast to keep moving." His voice was affectionate and low.

"You and your sister were close?"

"Correction, Cait. Ruthie and I *are* close. It's us against the world." I waited, but Ross remained silent. He had finished braiding and was fastening on the band. He set the brush and comb on the floor by the bed. I stood up. Ross took my hand and pulled me back into his lap. My bare bottom met his clothed thighs. His arms encircled me as I relaxed my body against his.

"I need a friend, Cait. I don't need a quick fuck. I can talk to you. I don't want to lose that. Quite frankly, I'm worried about this shoot. I'd like to know that there's someone outside of the production that I can confide in, that I can trust. I can trust you not to gos. I'm 40 years old, Cait, my dick doesn't run my life anymore. Please. Don't let what happened last night ruin our friendship. I'm sorry I frightened you. Don't fuck me because you think you have to. I don't need charity fucks from any woman. We don't have to rush anything, ok? We can go slow, get to know each other better?" Ross was increasing his hold on me.

I nodded, uncomfortable with both his bluntness and the strength of his embrace.

"I don't know about you, Cait, but I need some brekkie … ."

Clancy of the Overflow

I had written him a letter which I had, for want of better
Knowledge, sent to where I met him down the Lachlan, years ago,
He was shearing when I knew him, so I sent the letter to him,
Just 'on spec', addressed as follows, 'Clancy, of The Overflow'.

And an answer came directed in a writing unexpected,
(And I think the same was written with a thumb-nail dipped in tar)
'Twas his shearing mate who wrote it, and verbatim I will quote it:
'Clancy's gone to Queensland droving, and we don't know where he are.'

In my wild erratic fancy visions come to me of Clancy
Gone a-droving 'down the Cooper' where the Western drovers go;
As the stock are slowly stringing, Clancy rides behind them singing,
For the drover's life has pleasures that the townsfolk never know.

And the bush hath friends to meet him, and their kindly voices greet him
In the murmur of the breezes and the river on its bars,
And he sees the vision splendid of the sunlit plains extended,
And at night the wond'rous glory of the everlasting stars.[15]

Banjo Patterson

~ **Chapter 22** ~

Pure sugar. Length at the water line, 45 feet. I shook my sugar packet, forcing the contents to the bottom. Tearing the paper carefully and pouring the sugar into my coffee, I avoided looking at Ross. One sip of coffee and I was back to reading the details about the America's Cup racer. I flipped the empty packet over, staring at the fuzzy brown image of a boat in full sail. One triangular fold and the boat disappeared, but I could see what amount of the packet to tear off to produce a perfect square. Two folds, creased with my nail, would convince the two layers of packet paper to tear. I heard the waitress come up to our table. I knew what I wanted. I waited for Ross to order first.

The tear left ragged edges. Corners laid together, reversed and folded again gave me the base I needed. I had folded hundreds of these cranes when I was sick. Folding cranes while watching *Unto the Dust*. Waiting for my body to heal from my ectopic pregnancy, I made cranes. Hundreds, but not the thousand I needed to reach grace. I had acquired a skill for when I was bored or uncomfortable. I could fold cranes. Make them nests. Fold and wait.

"Do you do a proper poached egg?"

"Poached?"

I looked up from my folding. Ross was glowering at a young waitress whose dark ponytail bounced back and forth accenting her confusion.

"No, sir. We only have what's on the menu." Her long fingers pointed to the list of possibilities in Ross's hands.

Perfect origami fingers, I thought, watching her graceful gestures. Not like mine. Pulling the fold out while easing the edges into place, I heard Ross settle for fried eggs over hard. Four more folds and the wings would be set. Grandma liked her eggs poached. She had a frying pan with an insert for four small pouching cups. Mark and Frank liked Grandma's poached eggs. I did not. The crane's tail and head emerged from the folded sugar packet. I pulled the wings down. One was pure white.

"Got any decent bread?"

"We have sourdough, whole grain ... ."

The other wing, speckled brown from the specifications of the 12-meter racer, curved downwards after I bent it gently towards the body. I could guess what Ross would say next to the waitress. He had previously informed me of his dislike for American bread. Suitable only for fairy bread, he claimed. Put enough butter and candied hundreds and thousands on it, Aussie children might eat it, Ross had said. Maybe. As I spread the crane's wings, the paper flexed upwards like a rounded bicep. Ross's edgy voice filtered back.

"And I need two pots of water with that tea."

"I'll have to charge you extra."

I stole a glance at the waitress. Red patches were deepening across her cheeks.

"Why? It's just hot water. To make proper tea, I need two pots."

I laid the folded sugar packet down next to my empty coffee cup, hoping to distract the waitress. Or Ross.

The young waitress noticed first. "Oh. That's so beautiful."

"Thank you." Picking up the crane, I laid the bird on her order tablet. "I'll make you a nest to go with it. And I just want a cinnamon roll with butter. Please."

The red patches were fading. She nodded and left, ponytail bouncing.

I reached for a second sugar packet for the crane's nest. Ross intercepted my hand with his. His eyebrow arched.

"I folded cranes while I watched your movie. I was going to make a thousand."

"And?"

"My elbows got tired. I press too hard when I fold. So, I made 567 cranes, not the thousand I needed."

"A thousand?"

"The legend is that if you make a thousand you will get your wish, achieve health, find peace."

"Make me one, Cait? Please?"

Riding up from the park, north into the mouth of the Gallatin Canyon, the next event on Ross's plan approached with each passing mile marker. I didn't want to think about getting into a rubber raft and going down the rock-strewn Gallatin River. I concentrated on the road beneath my feet. I concentrated on the heaviness of my helmet when I turned my head sideways against the draft. Something would come up and I could quietly escape rafting. Maybe I could just tell Ross no and save him some money.

Ross pulled off at the Taylor Creek trailhead.

"Need to stretch my legs."

Not wanting to stay behind with the motorcycle, I

followed after him. When he stopped alongside the creek and sat on a log facing me, I tried to fill up the silence.

"This is one of the old Indian trails into the Madison Valley. The other one is near the mouth of the canyon along Spanish Creek. The Bannock Indians ... ."

Ross interrupted, "Cait, how long have you been having panic attacks?"

I shrugged.

"Are you seeing someone about them? Taking anything?"

I frowned at him. "I'm okay."

"No. Cait. You're not. Caitlinn, have a sit-down." Ross patted the log beside him. "I need to have a chat to you. You owe me an explanation. Is it just me?"

I couldn't move, except to shake my head staring at the pine needles around the toes of my hiking boots. "No, it's happened before. It's not you."

"You're not going to tell me anything, are you?"

I couldn't respond.

"Are you going to go rafting with me?"

I didn't want to. The thought terrified me. Being stuck in a boat. Unable to leave. Could I go rafting? I found myself nodding yes.

"All right, then." Ross rose, heading back down the trail, leaving me with my ears full of magpie scoldings from the branch overhead.

I went rafting. When we were riding back up the canyon to the rafting company on the bus with wet bottoms and sand-caked toes, I wondered what I had been afraid of. All those years since Mark died, I had denied myself chances for happiness, for adventure. Not one minute of the raft trip had frightened me. I simply executed the commands of the guide. Left back, right forward, dig deep, hold. Ross sat in front of me in the raft as right paddle captain, and his body shielded mine from the biggest waves. I paddled when he did, concentrating on paralleling his strokes to keep our paddles from crossing. The passages through the whitewater flashed by in a blur of hard paddling. When the raft drifted downstream, the guide rattled off the landmarks one by one, told stories, and made conversation with the paddlers. After he discovered Ross was from Australia, the rest of the trip's conversations consisted of a lively interchange of whitewater challenges Down Under. Listening to them put my own trip into context. How could I be afraid on a river low from a five-year drought, tamed by the late season, with as much buck left as a retired rodeo bronc?

I had almost said no at the beginning of the trip. Standing in the hot sun, girdled firmly by a strapped plastic helmet and a zippered life vest, I felt like a toddler bundled up for a snow storm. The rafting guide demonstrated the importance of having our life jackets tightly buckled, so he could flip us back into the raft if we bounced out. Ross's anecdote about a previous trip where he bounced out of a raft and then bounced right back in again didn't help my confidence. Even worse was all that business about standing up too soon and getting your feet caught in hidden snags, waiting for your butt to hit bottom before attempting to stand up, and keeping your feet in front of you to better bounce off rocks. In the end, the eight-year-old boy from Ohio convinced me I would have to stay for the trip. With his brown curls spilling out of his helmet and thin brown arms, he was anxious to go down the river for his second time. "Last year we taco'd at House Rock and the guide fell on me. Think that'll happen this year, Dad? Remember, I wasn't scared at all. It was cool!" If a child could do this, then I would have to try as well.

Afterwards, we drove home and ate at the Bear Claw, sitting in our usual spot at the bar. I wanted to tell Frank all about my adventure, but tonight was poker night and he was with Ike and Jake, arguing over nickel bets and the truthfulness of Ike's fishing stories.

Sitting on my stool, I could remember the movement of the water, feel the warmth of the sun on my tanned arms, taste the river from the big splashes. All the river rafter's commands echoed with the names of the landmarks—Greek Creek, Seven Sisters, Screaming Left, Storm Castle, Mad Mile, House Rock, Turtle Rock. Ross brought me back. The constant movement of his leg bouncing up and down on the rung of my stool got my attention. Placing my hand firmly on his knee, I asked, "What's on your mind."

"Let's stay up all night and watch the Perseids from the top of your mountain. It'll be a barrel of fun."

My grandfather used to take me up to the top of the mountain as a child to watch the August meteor showers. The best night to watch them was behind us, but the show would go on for another week. "We don't have to stay up all night to see them, Ross. There will be plenty of shooting stars before midnight."

Ross had already made up his mind. "We can throw a mattress in the back of your truck with some blankets and watch in style. 3:00 a.m. is when the show really starts. C'mon, Cait, I'll make you brekkie up on the mountain in the morning. If you get too tired, you can go to sleep. We'll be up there for the sunrise. It'll be fanfuckintastic. Say yes, Cait. Please."

I shrugged and Ross was standing up, ready for the next adventure. We rode out to my cabin, and within the hour we were heading up to the summit in my truck. Ross parked so our feet would be pointing south, which is the optimum way to view the Perseids.

As the cold air crept in around us wherever the blankets weren't tucked in tight, the world stilled. The winds disappeared, taking with them the sounds of the cows down at the Alexander ranch, the trucks shifting gears on the Norris Hill, the whisper of the tree limbs. The silence of the landscape stilled our tongues. The quiet amplified Ross's breathing, and I could hear my own blood in my ears as my brain searched for auditory stimulation. Side by side on a single mattress, surrounded by the warmth of thick blankets, Ross and I co-existed under the canopy of stars. Two souls lost in individual thoughts, isolated under the immensity of the heavens, waiting for the display of specks of cosmic dust no larger than grains of sand. The sky above us, layered in stars, was thick with twinkling lights, and the Milky Way was truly white against the inky blackness. The shooting stars began to dance across the wide expanse of sky. Sometimes, I could see an entire path of the meteor arcing its way through eternity, sometimes only a glimpse of rapid movement in the corner of my eye. Most falling stars were white with bluish tones, but once in a while a special one would launch itself across our corner of the universe. Time slipped by and the wind sighed in the junipers near the truck.

Ross found my hand under the blankets. He sighed, echoing the juniper, "The skies are weeping."

I squeezed his hand, not sure what to say.

Ross continued, "Did you know the Perseids are also known as the Tears of St. Lawrence?"

"Why?"

"For St. Lawrence. Lawrence was a Roman deacon in the

third century. The Prefect of Rome ordered Lawrence to turn over the Church's fortune. So, Lawrence gathered up all the sick and the poor and claimed they were the Church's treasure. The Prefect, not being a bloke with a sense of humor, had Lawrence roasted on an iron grill. During his torture, Lawrence, being a bloke with a sense of humor, claimed he was done on one side and needed to be turned over. It's bloody important to be roasted evenly, ya know. Lawrence let them know when he was cooked enough, then he died."

"Lovely, story," I said.

Ross laughed. "Yeah, the red martyr stories usually are pretty grim. The point the monks made to me was that one shouldn't focus on the brutality of the martyrdom, but rather on the fact that the love of God and fellow men was so strong in the early Christian martyrs that their life flame burned longer than their bodies. This kept them alive longer than made sense, as an example of Christ's love for us. So, the takeaway should never be about the brutality of their martyrdom. The takeaway should be about their love and sacrifice in their service to our Lord and a remembrance of Jesus's sacrifice for us. The deaths of the red martyrs should always be an inspiration to us to be better, to do better. And ya know, somethin', Cait? St. Lawrence and the shooting stars this time of year always remind me to find the humor in this life. Lots of shit happens and if you don't have a sense of humor, you won't survive. Even in his last breath, St. Lawrence kept his sense of humor and his devotion to God's people."

"The skies do look like they're crying for us."

"Cryin' with us, Cait, not for us. There's a difference. I first understood the metaphor when I was in the outback at Cooper Creek. The winter night sky was huge, and I felt so empty."

"Cooper Creek?"

"I was in the middle of working on *Unto the Dust*. We had filmed all the scenes in Ireland and they wanted me to gain weight to play the priest as an older man in Dakota. Winter was coming on and we had to wait six months until spring. I had six months to kill, so I went home to see my family and work with my horses and get fat. Ruthie had convinced me and Brian to take a DNA test; she's always going on about genealogy and dead rellies. I gave in, mostly, so she would stop naggin' me about it. When the results came, I was staying with her and her partner. My whole world fell apart. Ruthie and Brian were full siblings. They were Sutherlands. I wasn't. My whole life was a lie. I made Ruthie's life hell for about a month, but I was thinking about what I had learned in Ireland and the places I had visited. The results of the DNA test were not Ruthie's fault, but it was hard for me to forgive her. Ruthie apologized to me and we had a long chat, as you do."

"Why Cooper Creek?" I interrupted, curious about the outback.

Ross continued his story ignoring my hints about talking less about himself and more about the landscape. I was better with stories about rocks and sand than with the emotionally explosive story Ross seemed to want to tell me. I started to move my ankles side to side and stopped, recalling how I felt when Ross listened to me. Verified as a person. Heard. Respected. I stilled my body. Ashamed of myself.

"I was adrift, Cait. The man I thought was my father had taught me everything he knew about horses and caring for the land. He was kind, patient, loving. Whenever I got into trouble, which was often, Dad would say to me, 'Ross, you're a Sutherland. Sutherlands are gentlemen.' It would have been easier if he had paddled me or yelled at me. I didn't like to be a disappointment to him, but it was all a lie. I wasn't his son. After Isabella rejected me, I realized that I had made a huge mistake. I had to get recentered, so I called my mate, Dan."

"To go to Cooper Creek?" I asked. "Why there?"

Ross refused to be hurried in his account, so I gave up trying. I owed him that, even if it was making me uncomfortable. I had not known him long, and he was telling me a lot of deeply personal stuff. Maybe, he had been truthful the night before when he said he needed a confidante. I realized I was witnessing a confession and I had no right to ask questions if I was truly listening with my whole body, as Ross had listened to me.

"I was in Melbourne for the International Film Festival, and in between my sessions I took a long walk. Frankly, the whole thing was boring me. People asking me the same bloody questions over and over again. I had to clear my head before I lost my temper or walked out. I wandered over to Parliament Square. It's in the Hoddle Grid. I stood for the longest time in front of Adam Lindsey Gordon's statue, thinking about his words carved into the base, *Two things stand in stone, Kindness in another's trouble, Courage in your own.* I hadn't been kind to people the last few years. I'd been a coward. In the end, Gordon committed suicide. Standing in front of the statue, I knew I'd let my parents down. I had to do better. St. Patrick's Church is close by. I went in. Into the cool darkened space. I lit prayer candles for my father and my mother. That's when I decided to make a movie about my father's country."

"I'd been coming up to Montana every August for a few years, anyway. Now, I had a professional reason. Making that decision after lighting the prayer candles, best decision

I've made in years. I felt lighter. I'd been walking around in a dark cloud. Fucking any woman who would have me out of anger. I felt like a hypocrite telling my nephew to behave himself at school because he was a Sutherland and Sutherlands are gentlemen. I hadn't been. Using the DNA test as an excuse was bullshit. I knew better. I could be better. I was destroying myself. For what? Why? Pride?

"When I was in Ireland, the monks warned me that drawing closer to God would unleash the demons. That I needed to be vigilant and not fall asleep. But I hadn't kept up my prayer life. The devil had won, but he wasn't going to win twice. I was not going down the rabbit hole of depression and suicide."

"On the way back to the film festival, I walked past the statue of Burke and Wills. It was as if the universe was telling me not to give up hope, despite the hard journey. Burke was my childhood hero. That night I called my mate, Dan, and we went walkabout. To Cooper Creek. Sometimes, if I can stare into the abyss, match the landscape with my thoughts and fears, I can see more clearly what needs doing. The land tells me, if I listen. I saw you for the first time after that trip. The one to Cooper Creek." Ross leaned up on his elbow and stroked my face.

When he laid back down without kissing me, I was disappointed. What should I do? What should I say? I was trapped again in a confusing muddle of uncertainty.

"You asked me about Cooper Creek, Cait. That's where Burke breathed his last. After his men deserted his supply depot. After he thought there was no hope, only death. It's bloody awful there at Cooper Creek. I could feel all this pain, Cait. It radiated from that spot. Just like the walls at Durham." I found Ross's hand under the blankets to reassure him. He continued.

"When I was in Ireland doing research for the role of Father Paddy, I ran across this passage from an elder in the Orthodox Church that said '*Stand on the edge of the abyss of despair and when you feel that it is beyond your strength, break off and have a cup of tea.*' That's what I was trying to do, Cait, find a place that looked like how I felt so I could stare into the abyss and choose to back away and go on living. Or not."

"I sat under the Dig Tree thinking this is what my life is going to be like if I don't make some changes. One long walk on the darkening plains of Erebus. One long fucked up, emotional wasteland. Watching the shooting stars falling like tears, I felt like the universe was cryin' with me."

I mustered up the courage to ask, "Who were Burke and Wills?"

"Burke and Wills were the first men to cross the interior of Australia in the 1860s, sort of like your Lewis and Clark, but they never made it back to Melbourne. Robert Burke was my childhood hero."

"What happened exactly?"

"Burke and Wills were late returning from the north, so everyone at the relief post at the Creek assumed they were dead. Supplies were running short, and the relief party decided to leave. They left Burke a note. The relief party cached supplies by the tree—the Dig Tree. Burke missed them by seven hours. Seven hours after months on the trek. Can you imagine? Burke and Wills gave up, Cait. They gave up on hope and trust. They stopped hoping and trusting. King made it out alive. Sitting under the Dig Tree, I could understand their sense of betrayal, but I couldn't understand why they gave up hope. Somehow, the desolation of the place gave me the space to decide to deal with myself. I didn't want to hurt my son or my sister by losing hope. I couldn't do that to them. Yes, I didn't know who my real father was. Yes, I had been lied to. Yes, I had a right to be angry. But I didn't have the right to keep hurting my loved ones with my selfish behavior. Under the Dig Tree, I realized that it didn't really matter, because my father told me I was a Sutherland and he raised me as his own. He used to sing "Rocking the Cradle" all the time. Jacob married my mother knowing she was pregnant with another man's child. He wasn't deceived. If Jacob Sunderland could accept me as his son and love me so much, then I could do no less than accept him as my father. Jacob Sunderland did his best by me, and all I was doing in my anger and my hurt was dishonoring his love for me and for my mum. Yeah, I had a right to be upset, but my father was playing the hand dealt him as best he could, and so was my mum. Rural Australia is a tough place for women. A young woman from a respected family, knocked up in those years, would never have been accepted again in polite society if people found out. My grandparents were trying to protect their only child from a lifetime of shame. My life was fine until Ruthie and I got the DNA test. A test shouldn't change what I knew in my heart and soul. My parents loved me and never let me down. It was time for me to grow up and stop whinging."

I wanted to ask more questions and tell Ross I knew about Paddy O'Neill. I wondered if Frank was Paddy, after all, and if Frank was the father Ross was looking for. Making a movie about his father's country could only mean Ross believed his father came from Nelson Story country. Now things made sense. Ross coming from Down Under to make a movie about Nelson Story. Ross asking so many questions about Frank O'Neill. Ross was researching his biological father's country, in addition to doing research for his job. No wonder Ross was so interested in everything I said about Montana. All my stories. I was not so naive or vain as to think a famous man was interested in me. Ross wasn't interested in me, he was interested in what I knew. I didn't care. I was enjoying his attention. I was not going to make a fuss or accuse him of anything to stroke my ego. I liked having an audience for my stories, and Ross was a great audience. Besides, I couldn't bear the thought of ruining this precious moment under the canopy of stars. Years of Ralph's unpredictable rages taught me to tiptoe around any topic I could predict might be volatile. Grandma taught me not to pry. I had to wait for people to tell me their stories. I would have to stifle my own curiosity and wait for Ross to tell me more about his search for his father. Or not. As for Ross's forgiveness of his parents, I had no response. How could I comment on something I could not do myself?

I was recalling Ross's earlier description of meteors as ancestral souls cascading across eternity. A red shooting star with a long streak skipped across the sky like a flat rock across the dark waters of a placid lake. The special shooting star stirred memories long buried. I thought about my brother. The darkness was providing welcome cover for both Ross and me to bare our souls. "Maybe there's something to the idea of shooting stars being the souls of dead ancestors," I ventured, tentatively breaking the silence. "The red one reminded me of my brother, Mark."

"Why did that star remind you of him?"

"Because it was special, just like Mark. He taught me to skip rocks. That day is so clearly etched in my mind. I'd been finding the smooth, flat, thin, round stones for Mark in the jumble along the shoreline of Hyalite Reservoir in the mountains above Bozeman. I was five, and my pockets were full of these stones. Mark laughed at me with my bulging pockets, 'Time for you to learn, Cait. We've got to lighten your load.' Mark held my hand and taught me how to release. It's all in the twist of the wrist. If you have the right shaped rock. When we had skipped all the rocks in my pockets, Mark scouted rocks until I could do seven bounces across the lake."

For the first time in 24 years, I was crying for my beloved brother in Montana, while the Tears of St. Lawrence streaked the black velvet skies, warm under blankets, with someone who listened to me, who heard me. Ross raised up on his elbow again, and this time he kissed me lightly on my forehead, along my hairline, and ever so gently on the lips. Ross kissed away my tears, all of them. I put my head on his shoulder as he pulled me closer to him.

I don't remember when I fell asleep. The sunrise was in full swing when the smell of coffee tickled my nose and stirred me awake. Ross's smiling face greeting me when I sat up was as radiant as the backdrop of the Tobacco Roots with all the shades of red and pink shimmering off the snow-covered tops. He handed me the steaming cup of coffee and hopped up into the pickup truck beside me.

"Isn't this grand, Cait? The stars were fabulous after you feel asleep. I lost count of the shooting stars, there were so many. But I made wishes on every star."

Ross put his arm around me, drawing me close. "When you get done watching the sunrise, I've got a surprise for you. Then I'll have to go back to town. I've got a meeting with Mike at 10."

After we drove back to the cabin, Ross said we needed to go for a ride. As I was putting things away from the night before, he kept looking at his watch. He said we didn't have much time, but he couldn't stand the suspense anymore, so we would have to hurry. Ross and I rode his motorcycle down the road towards the creek. Ross stopped the bike before he got to the creek, and pulled out a bandana out of his pocket and folded it into a triangle. "This is a surprise, Cait. Put this over your eyes." He revved up the motorcycle and drove a short distance. He stopped again patting my thigh. "Take off the blindfold, Caitlinn."

I got off the bike, while Ross stayed put with his motor running. I was looking at Grandma's tree. It looked terrible. It had been severely pruned. It looked naked. I was speechless, tears flowed down my cheeks. Ross laughed. "I guess I don't have much of a career as a Good Samaritan. One good deed lands an old man in jail, the other makes the lady cry. Better not give up my day job. Sorry, Cait, I've got to go. Meet me at the Bear Claw for dinner tonight? 6:30?"

I nodded and he roared off. When I got back to the cabin, I called JoAnn. She explained, "The Bozeman nursery delivered the tree out there Monday morning, while you two were in Yellowstone. Ross must have promised them movie premier tickets or something to get them to move that fast. He wanted them to plant it at your cabin, but they talked him out of it. They said the poor old thing only had a 50-50 chance of surviving the move and the spot by the creek was ideal for a golden willow. Ross was really adamant about moving the tree. He started telling me about some prime minister's goal to plant a billion trees in Australia, but they only planted 700 million. He's really into trees. I don't know, Cait, I've heard of guys giving girls flowers after a first date, but a tree? That man's a keeper."

I was thinking about all the planning that went into moving Grandma's tree. I was remembering Ross's expression when we had left that night at JoAnn's. I was remembering his expansiveness in the truck singing "Another Fall of Rain." Rain to heal the barren outback. Rain to heal a broken soul. I was stunned at how fast Ross had made the decision to have it moved. I couldn't think of a thing to say.

Jo could, though. "When Ross talked to me while you were in the shower, and asked for my help, I couldn't believe he was going to all that trouble for a tree that's half dead. He said the tree needed to be saved, because you loved it. He said something else about totems and spiritual journeys in the Dreamtime. I didn't have any idea what he was talking about. Jeez, Cait, if Ross cares this much about a tree, what's he like in bed?"

Blessing

The guarding of the God of life be on you,
The guarding of the loving Christ be on you,
The guarding of the Holy Spirit be on you,
Every night of your life,
To aid you and enfold you
Each day and night of your life.[16]

Unknown, Ancient Celtic blessing

~ Chapter 23 ~

When I walked into the Bear Claw that evening, Ross was not there. I was early. I sat at the bar and talked with Frank. He immediately started asking me questions, "What was goin' on down at the creek? Why did you move in that ratty old tree?" Frank had been looking through his telescope again.

"Ross had my grandmother's tree moved over from Bozeman. He wanted to plant it at my cabin, but the nursery said it would do better down by the creek."

Frank frowned. "Sutherland moved your tree? The one you planted with Gwen? From Bozeman?" I nodded. Frank shook his head, "I'll be damned. Who would have thought? He's an odd one."

"How so, Frank?"

"Sutherland started showing up here about four, five years ago. Always comes first part of August. He's around for a few weeks and then he's gone. When he first came in with Charlie Douglas, I noticed him because of his boots and his expensive motorcycle jacket. You know that cost a boatload of money, with all the cowhide and hand-stitched suede. The two of them got crazy drunk, but after that Sutherland came alone and behaved himself. He had this way of disappearing into the background. He reminded me of the Special Forces who were in charge of security when I was stationed in Korea. You can't distract them. They're always watching and listening. They don't draw any attention to themselves. No loud talking, no laughing, just yes sir, no sir, thank you sir, and maybe a random please. That's all you can ever get out of them. Sutherland was like that. He would not engage in small talk. Women would try to talk to him and get absolutely nowhere. He didn't talk to anybody. Just listened. I'd see him down at the pharmacy some mornings. Same thing. Just sitting like a guard in the corner with his back to the wall, listening and watching. One night last summer, Sutherland came in with Charlie again. They didn't drink to excess, thank God. After that, Sutherland started sitting at the bar, talking to locals, instead of sitting at his usual table in the shadows. He'd talk to men, but ignored women. Except for you, this summer. I wasn't too happy when he was making advances on you at the bar the other night. He sure wasn't taking no for an answer from you, Caitlinn. Sutherland moves too fast for my liking. You two didn't waste any time."

Frank hesitated, waiting for me to say something. The only time Frank called me Caitlinn was when he trying to make a point or was concerned. Just because Frank had a telescope didn't mean I had to tell my godfather anything about what Ross and I were or were not doing. I was not about to admit to another man that I was a failure in bed. I was not going to lie to Frank, either, and claim something that wasn't happening. I did not need protection. I did not need interference. I did not need judgment. I kept my face a complete blank, remembering Frank's cribbage lessons and his instructions on how to keep men at a distance here at the bar.

"Is Sutherland treating you right, Caitlinn? Are you ok?"

"We're okay, Frank."

"Well, you let me know the minute you're not, Caitlinn. Sutherland is too cheeky by my book."

"Cheeky?"

"Yeah, disrespectful, irreverent, sassy."

"Is that Aussie slang?"

"Yup."

"Have you been to Australia?"

"Yup."

"When?"

"After the Korean War. I met some Aussies when I was stationed in Korea. When one of them invited me to come visit his family in Hunter Valley, I went."

"Hunter Valley? Really?"

"Yeah, in New South Wales. Beautiful place. Looks a lot like Montana without the high mountains. Loved the people. I got a job on a local farm, joined the fire brigade, and stayed on for a few years."

"Ross grew up in Hunter Valley. His father, Jacob, had a stud farm outside of Scone."

"That Sutherland family? I knew a Jacob Sutherland. We worked on the fire brigade together. He married my boss's daughter after I left Australia. Sutherland is Jacob's boy?"

I hesitated, wondering how to answer Frank's question, remembering how upset I was when Charlie told my story to strangers. If Ross wants to tell Frank he's looking for his biological dad, Ross will tell Frank. This is not my story to tell, so I nodded.

"Well, I'll be damned. Jacob was a decent man. Sutherland isn't anything like Jacob. Sutherland is an arrogant son of a bitch. Jacob wasn't."

"Ross doesn't try to make a good first impression."

"So, I've noticed."

"Look at things from Ross's perspective, Frank. There are

too many people in his life. He takes new ones out for a test drive to winnow out the fools. You do the same thing, Frank. With SUVs and people. Remember what you called the damage on Ralph's Ford Explorer? On my father's jeep? Montana character, you said. You were adding Montana character. You said you were testing out the rigs. No. You weren't. You were testing my father and Ralph, and using their rigs as an excuse. Ross does the same thing. He just doesn't damage SUVs."

Frank chewed on the inside of his cheek and cocked his head, listening to me intently.

I winked at my godfather, "Ross is adding Aussie character to your soul, Frank."

"Touché, Cait." Frank grinned weakly at me. He looked relieved to see my grandfather's old hunting buddies bellying up to his bar. Jake and Ike had turned up at precisely the right time.

Ross slid in beside me, announcing his presence with a slight pat on my back and a quick peck above my ear. Frank approached, carrying a Guinness. He set it down in front of Ross and said, "On the house, Ross." Frank looked at me, and said with an accompanying wink, "The hitchhiker gets the other five bottles of the six-pack if he ever shows up in here."

Ross had a good laugh at his own expense. Frank continued, "Didn't your father ever tell you when you are dating a woman, you give her flowers? And in case Jacob never told you, Ross, flowers are a damn sight cheaper than a goddamn tree." Frank walked off. He was quite pleased with himself.

"What did O'Neill just say, Cait?"

"He said the hitchhiker gets the other five bottles of the six-pack if he ever shows up in here."

"Nah, nah, got that bit. How does he know my father's name was Jacob?"

"I told him, because Frank was working in Scone after the

war and he said he knew a Jacob Sunderland from the fire brigade. I had to tell him. He asked me, specifically, if you were Jacob's son. I didn't say anything about what you told me last night. That's your story to tell, I can't tell your story."

Ross leaned over and kissed my hair, saying nothing. He put his forearms down on the bar, interlocking his fingers together, resting his forehead on top of them. After a few minutes, absolutely still, Ross began to massage his forehead with his knuckles. His jaw muscles were flexing and relaxing in sync with the slow movement of his head against his fingers.

I was afraid to say anything or to touch Ross. I drank my beer in the silence, wondering what would happen next. I had just put my empty glass down on the bar, when Ross got up so suddenly his bar stool fell over. He was out the door. I debated what to do, and finally thought, what the hell. Go outside, Cait and see if Ross is still here. He's not Ralph, he's not going to hit you.

Ross was standing on the edge of the porch, looking up at South Baldy, rocking back and forth on the heels of his boots, up on the toes. He smiled faintly when I came through the door. I hugged him around his waist. I was too short to hug him heart to heart. Ross responded by putting his arm around me.

"Remember, Cait, when I sat all night on your front porch wishing on the shooting stars?"

"Yup."

"What if my wishes are coming true? What if I've found my father? What if he knows some of the answers to the questions I've had all these years? What if he doesn't want to have anything to do with me? How do I know Paddy O'Neill is actually Frank?"

"Ross, that photo in your copy of *The Greatest Cattle Drive* is Frank by the Needle up Bridger Canyon. Frank doesn't have any family. Frank lived with my grandparents up the canyon before the war. Frank loves rock formations. Especially the story of Evening Star turning to stone waiting for an eternity for a love she lost. Frank loved Maiden Rock and the Needle."

"My Paddy is Frank?" Ross asked me.

"I'm sure of it."

"Damn. O'Neill doesn't like me. I don't want to tell him he might be my dad if he thinks I'm a right tosser. What should I do? What would you have me do, Cait?"

I wanted to kiss Ross on his cheek, but he was too tall, so I hugged him tightly. "Whatever you do, I'll support you."

I went back in the bar. Shortly afterwards, Ross came back in and took his seat next to me. Frank wandered by and pointedly asked me if everything was okay. He was focused on me, completely ignoring Ross.

"It will be, Frank. It will be."

Ross spoke softly, "Frank, did you know my mother, Nora Larkin?"

I thought Frank seemed rattled by the question, but he replied in a matter-of-fact voice, "Yes, I worked for her father, Ross, your namesake, for several years."

"Did you ask my mum to marry you?"

Frank looked at Ross for a long time without expression and then nodded, "Yes, Nora turned me down. I couldn't keep working for her father after that. I left my heart on the Aussie tarmac the day I flew home. I've only ever loved your mother, Ross. That's the honest to God truth." Frank turned on the heel of his cowboy boot, abruptly walking away.

"I should go, Cait. I will see you tomorrow night. Usual time? Here?" Ross kissed the top of my head and was out the door before I could say a word.

Frank was in no mood for small talk. Ross had left. I went home to an empty cabin.

~ Chapter 24 ~

"G'day, Ruthie."

"How you goin', Ross. Alright?"

"I found him."

"Paddy?"

"Nah, yeah, ah Ruthie, he's been under my nose, the whole time."

"The publican? Cait's godfather?"

"Yup."

"Are you certain?"

"Yup."

"Why?"

"Cait recognized the rock in the photograph as being the one at the mouth of Bridger Canyon, outside of Bozeman. Frank lived with Cait's grandparents before the Korean War up that canyon. Cait made the connection. She recognized the cowboy as Frank. She asked Frank if he'd been to Australia, and he said he worked in Hunter Valley for our granddad, Ross Larkin, after the War."

"Did you tell Frank?"

"No. He still thinks I'm Jacob's son. He knew our father, Ruthie. Frank liked our dad a good bit, but he doesn't like me."

"Are you going to tell him?"

"Dunno. It's early days. Say, Ruthie. Are you still working with the CWA and the ally organization, White Ribbon, to reduce domestic violence?"

"Yes."

"I need your advice, Ruthie. No jokes. Please."

"Okay, Ross. No jokes."

"How do I help a victim of sexual abuse? What should I do?"

"Is it current?"

"No. In her past."

"Well, in my experience the best thing you can do is to stay present. Don't judge. Don't ask too many questions. Above all, don't criticize her past behavior by asking why she stayed in the relationship. Just listen. Be supportive. If she needs counseling, don't try to do it yourself. Encourage her to seek professional help."

"Can you send me some material?"

"Ross, what have you gotten yourself into? Is this about Caitlinn?"

"Yes."

"Oh, Ross. You don't need this right now. You've got millions of your own money invested in this film. You can't afford any distractions."

"Caitlinn is *not* a distraction. Is that what you tell Steve when he works with rescue horses? That the horses are a distraction from his breeding business?"

"I didn't say that, Ross. I'm worried about you."

"If abused horses and dogs are worth the time of your man, surely the woman I love is worth my time. I need your help, Ruthie, not your scolding.”

“I’m sorry, Ross. We worry about you.”

“I don’t need your fretting either, Ruthie, I’m not a child. I need you to send me some information from White Ribbon. Statistics, stories, strategies, recommendations, guidelines. Will you do that for me?”

“Yes.”

“Ta. G’night, Ruthie.”

The Old Australian Ways

Our fathers came of roving stock
That could not fixed abide:
And we have followed field and flock
Since e're we learnt to ride;
By miner's camp and shearing shed,
In land of heat and drought,
We followed where our fortunes led,
With fortune always on ahead
And always further out. . .

So throw the weary pen aside
And let the papers rest,
For we must saddle up and ride
Towards the blue hill's breast;
And we must travel far and fast
Across their rugged maze,
To find the Spring of Youth at last,
And call back from the buried past
The old Australian ways.[17]

Banjo Patterson

~ Chapter 25 ~

In the days that followed our motorcycle trip through the park, Ross and I spent as much time together as we could. Ross planned to use in his production what he termed "French hours"—nobody stopped working for lunch. He said he had worked with a director in the past who said giving the entire crew an hour for lunch broke continuity and concentration, wasting too much valuable time. If people needed to eat something, they grabbed it when they could and then they all went home at a reasonable hour until the next work day. The exceptions were filming night scenes, but Ross would adjust the following day hours accordingly. He wanted to give everyone two days a week off while they were in Montana, so they could go fly fishing or whatever else they found fun to do around the Madison, with the understanding that if production ran into problems later in the shoot they would all agree to work whenever necessary to finish the film on schedule. I got the distinct impression that Ross had convinced some people to work on his film with the promise of catered, expert-guided fishing trips that he had set up at his expense for his crew. Ross insisted on keeping a work/life balance on his set because he said everyone worked better if you treated them decently.

We hiked up on my mountain most evenings, except on weekends when I worked the night shift at the Bear Claw. Ross liked to watch the sunset from the summit, although I preferred the rock where we had watched the first sunrise together, but Ross always had an excuse to go up on top. We talked extensively about our childhoods, trying to catch up on years of past personal history. I came to appreciate how much Ross missed the rhythm of life in Australia. During the day, I was looking for my rhythm because I was at loose ends, since I had mailed off my writing to my editor. For the first time in almost three months, I had nothing specific to do. I worked on a few of my Grandma stories, but between daydreaming about Ross and worrying about the fires, I didn't make much progress.

One evening, Ross gave me a call and asked if he could come by. He sounded quite excited about something, but he wasn't forthcoming. I waited for him on my front porch steps. When he pulled into my driveway on his Harley he yelled above the motor, "Put the kettle on, Cait. Quick smart. I've got bikkies and lollies from Australia for tea. Arrived today in the post from my sister."

I boiled some water in my enameled kettle with the orange longhorn steer stenciled on it, while wondering what on earth Ross was talking about. Lollies? Bikkies? I knew from past experience, I was about to get an education. On what, I had no clue. I never would have guessed I had worms in my immediate future.

Ross brought his saddlebags into the cabin with him and, while I got out the tea things, he filled up my kitchen table with all sorts of packages, small boxes, and bags. Each one that emerged got another of his exuberant exclamations, ranging from beauty to brilliant intermixed with the occasional bloody brilliant. I turned around, wondering where I was supposed to put the tea cups, but Ross cleared me a spot. I poured the boiling water into a smaller blue-enameled coffeepot and placed it with the tea cups in the cleared-out area. I sat down for my lesson.

"Okay, Cait. Listen up. We're gonna have a proper tea. First, we've got the best English tea, courtesy of Ruthie." From one of two identical boxes, out came two tea bags, landing into my blue pot. Ross glanced at his watch, I guess for the proper steeping time since I'd seen him do that before. Then he opened up one of the packages with a tiny vivid multi-colored parrot on the rich brown wrapper. "These are the bee's knees, Cait. Arnott's Tim Tam bikkies made with real Queensland cane sugar and golden syrup, not that disgusting corn syrup you Yanks put in everything." A narrow, rectangular, candy bar shape coated in chocolate emerged from the packaging, as he continued, "There is no substitute for quality. What more could you wish for?" He ended with the most suggestive wink I'd ever seen him make.

I could feel myself reacting. *No, no. Focus on the cookie coming towards your mouth, Cait.* Stop thinking about Ross's lips and his caresses. I opened my mouth to receive his cookie, and he released it. I bit into it. Ross was correct. It was wonderfully flavored—the crisp wafer with the chocolate coating and the interior chocolate layer. Not too sweet. Very nice. I nodded my approval.

Ross looked at his watch again and retrieved the tea bags out of the coffeepot. I didn't have a proper teapot because the Gallaghers and the Burnetts only drank coffee. He poured me the first cup and I took a sip. It was much better than any other tea I had ever tried. I thought I might learn to drink tea if this type would be available. Ross was waiting for my reaction. "This tea is lovely, Ross. Thank you."

He visibly relaxed and took his first sip, "Now, that's a proper cuppa. Beauty." After he finished his first cup, he opened one of the bags filled with individually wrapped candies. "These are the best lollies in Australia, Cait. Minties. Been around since 1922." He unwrapped one. "Open up, Cait." As he popped the white toffee candy in my mouth, he continued, "It's moments like these you need *Minties*." He finished with an exaggerated flourish of gestures while passing me the wrapper, "Have a read."

The wrapper had two silly cartoons on it. The first was a whistling gas station assistant filling up the car with the gas nozzle inside the open window, rather than in the gas tank. Fill her up became literal. The second showed two anglers in a boat whose fishing lines had become tangled under the boat and they both thought they had a fish on the line. The outlandish situations explained the advertising jingle Ross had quoted, *It's moments like these you need* ... . If Minties' wrappers were indicative of Aussie humor, I had a new insight into the origins of Ross's outrageous wit.

"Okay, now we have to do the Tim Tam slam. We need more tea." Ross filled my tea cup again and handed me a second Tim Tam. "Bite off this little corner, go down to the opposite diagonal corner and bite off another tiny bit. Like this." He demonstrated. I held mine up for his approval after completing his instructions. He smiled, "Just, so, Cait. Now, watch me first, then you try it. Suck briefly from this end while the other end is in the hot tea. Not too long and not too hard. When you feel the tea coming up into your mouth, you have to flip it around quick smart, tea end into your mouth, and slam the whole thing in at once. Like this."

I watched him, and then it was my turn.

"Now, Cait, *now*. Slam it."

I did, nodding my approval with my mouth stuffed full of melting chocolate. The taste sensation was even more amazing than the dry cookie had been.

"Life will never be the same again. Tim Tam slam, Cait. Fair dinkum. Now you've been slammed up proper by a bloke from Down Under. You'll never be able to settle for anything else but Australia's finest, Caitlinn."

I sorted through the sexual innuendos implied by the whole Tim Tam experience, hoping I wasn't blushing. Or did I just have a filthy mind? *Good heavens.*

Ross was too busy creating my next taste sensation by unwrapping a purple candy bar to notice if my complexion had changed color. "Now try a bit of this." He held it out towards me, with his hand under the bar as I took a bite, and he caught the crumbling fragments before they hit the table. "Pretty good, yeah?" he asked.

I nodded, my mouth full of chocolate-covered, honey-combed freshness. The candied interior bits stuck to my teeth like my grandmother's airy peanut brittle as I tried to chew it. "Violet Crumble," Ross announced. "It's the way it shatters that matters. The big honeycomb bite. You've cracked a crumble, Cait. Now you've had the great Australian bite, have another." His smile lit up his face as he extended the bar to me for another bite. He finished off the rest of the bar in short order.

"What else have you got here, Ross?"

He was dividing his loot into two piles. "Those are for you, and these are for Jo's ankle biters next time you get to Bozeman. You must give these bikkies to Teddy—his own little bears with six different faces. There's a box here for Ben, too. They'll have heaps of fun with these."

Ross handed me the box of what looked like Teddy Grahams, but instead of having one smiley face on all the teddy bears, there were different faces. I turned the box over and got an instruction on discerning facial expressions: Cheeky, happy, sleepy, grumpy, silly and hungry. I wasn't in my cabin any more, I was in my counselor's office back in Illinois, talking about childhood sexual abuse and the damage it does to the victim/survivor's ability, even as adults, to interpret nonverbal behavior correctly. "Extremes you understand Cait," she is saying to me, "because that's where you exist, but intermediate emotions, you have to learn because they've not been present in either your childhood or in your adult life." She made me look at facial expression flash cards, trying to improve my ability to read nonverbal behavior the way normal children and adults do. My counselor never used that term, *normal*, but I understood what was implied. I was damaged. Didn't matter what word anyone used attempting to be kind, I accepted my reality. No reason to sugar coat it and pretend the damage was not there with polite phrases and vocabulary. I was not normal. Pure and simple. I vastly preferred honesty over pussyfooting around.

"Sorry, Cait. Hand it over. It's meant for Jo's rug rats. Tiny Teddies are for children."

I hoped Ross hadn't noticed my lapse. He was so damn perceptive most of the time, and I did not want to spoil his moment of sheer joy over sharing food from his home country with me. I concentrated on the remaining items on the table. The ones not in my pile or Jo's. There was the second box of English tea for example. Fortunately for me, Ross was too preoccupied with his sister's care package of Aussie treats, to notice my reactions. I asked about the other things, "What's that stuff for?" I pointed at a small, dark, glass jar with a bright yellow lid and a matching plain yellow label with a red diamond on it that said *Vegemite, yeast extract.*

"The best for last, Cait. These are for me, but you might like it. Dunno." Ross opened up the Arnott's yellow package of crackers labeled *Vita Weat* and then the dark glass jar. "Got any butter and a knife, Cait?"

I rose, retrieving the butter dish from the counter, and passed him a butter knife. Ross took two crackers, spread butter thickly on one and a thin layer of the deep brown paste from the jar on the other. Then he squeezed them together as the butter and vegemite escaped from the crackers through their many holes. "Here you go, veggie worms, the delight of every Aussie ankle biter."

I took a bite and frowned at him. Good grief. Vegemite was akin to eating a tablespoon of smoky salt. The crackers were tolerable, but that dreadful salty stuff? No, thank you.

Ross laughed at my facial expression and then loaded up his crackers, with his eyebrows wiggling up and down as he squeezed the worms out, licked them off top and bottom, and devoured his crackers. I was still frowning at him when he launched into a little ditty:

"We're happy little Vegemites
As bright as bright can be.
We all enjoy our Vegemite
For breakfast, lunch, and tea.
Our mummies say we're growing stronger
Every single week.
Because we love our Vegemite,
We all adore our Vegemite.
It puts a rose in every cheek."

I covered up my mouth, trying not to burst out laughing, "I'm sorry, that stuff is vile, even if your ditty is perky and convincing."

"Indeed. My apologies. But more for me, Cait. I quite like it. Actually, I'm stoked I don't have to share with you. Can't tell you how many times I wished I had a decent piece of toast and some Vegemite for brekkie with some good English tea, since I've been in the U.S. Now I can. Better than orgasms, mate." Ross was back to suggestively wiggling his eyebrows up and down, waiting for my reaction.

"If you say so."

He was still chuckling. I asked, "That worm stuff with the Vita Weats? Did you do that a lot back home?"

Ross sobered up instantly. "Bloody hell, *no*. Mum wouldn't let us. She said it was bad manners. She used to say growing up bush was no excuse for us being feral children. Mum was super strict about table manners, and she was always making sure we knew which fork to use and so on, because she said if we were ever someplace in high society, she was making sure we could handle ourselves and not be an embarrassment to the family. The Larkins are not rubbish, she would say, and my children will know how to behave in public as the ladies and gentlemen they are. Nah, Cait, Brian and I did the worm thing at home once, and only once."

"What happened?"

"Well, Mum was away for the evening at a Country Woman's Association meeting and Dad was in charge of tea and us. Ruthie must have been around three, since she wasn't using her feeding chair any more. Dad was in the lounge room with his cuppa and his pipe, listening to the footy on the wireless, so Brian and I, since we were on our own with Ruthie in the kitchen, decided to do the Vegemite worms as you do when you're teenage boys. Mind you, everybody did it at school, including us. Of course, Mum was in the dark. Our mistake was telling Ruthie we were eating worms, because then she started crying. Howling, more like. Dad came out of the lounge room, wanting to know why Ruthie was upset. In between sobs, she says, 'Make them stop, Daddy, they're eating worms. Ross and Brian are gonna get sick and die. Don't shoot them Daddy. Please.' Ruthie, even at three, understood the hard reality of the farm when horses have to be put down. Dad and the head stockman had been deworming the horses the day before, and little Ruthie must have been listening more than we knew."

"Then what happened, Ross?"

"Dad asked us if we would be making veggie worms at the table if our Mum was home, and we both shook our heads. He said, 'Why are you doing it now? You know your mum is boss." Then he looked straight at me saying, 'Ross, I expect better from you.' And that was all Dad had to say. He knew darn well, the worms were my idea. Brian was always too much of a happy little Vegemite to get into strife. Since I stirred Ruthie up, Dad left it to me to settle her. She was bloody hysterical, and I felt like shit because it was my fault. Brian and I never did veggie worms in front of Ruthie again or anywhere else Mum and Dad could catch us. Ever."

"Are you going to show Jo's boys that cracker worm trick?"

"Hell *no*." Ross looked quite offended I would ask him such a question. "I don't want to be haunted by my mum's ghost or my dad's. I might have scared my little sister before I knew better, but I'm not in the business of terrorizing ankle biters anymore. Teaching Jacob and Nora the odd practical joke in good fun as their uncle, oh hell yeah. Scaring them on purpose, absofuckinlutely *not*. Teddy and Ben are still children, you can't be certain what they actually understand about jokes versus the real world, and parasites in livestock aren't ever funny. You're from Montana, Cait, you should know that."

Trying to regain some advantage, I countered with, "Did you get Brian into trouble very often?"

"Not after the veggie worm bit, but it was my idea to swing on the Hill's Hoist with Nanna's laundry when Mum was bedridden. We were six and five. Problem was, it had rained during the night and some of the wash landed in the mud. I didn't notice until too late."

This was more solid ground for me than the prospect of terrorizing Jo's boys with veggie worms, "What's a Hill's Hoist?"

"Great Aussie invention for hanging out your clothes and bedding. It's made of galvanized steel and aluminum and it's got a crank so you can lower it or raise it. The lines are metal wire and they don't sag under heavy, wet bedding like the clothesline rope you Yanks use. The best bit is the Hill's Hoist rotates with the wind and, therefore, the winds can't blow the wash off the line. Ya know, like tacking into the wind if you're sailing. They're incredibly sturdy and they last forever. Every ankle biter has taken a spin on a back garden Hill's Hoist. When there was laundry, Mum always raised the thing up high so we couldn't reach it to play on, but Nanna forgot, because she usually did the cooking for the household and Mum did all the laundry and the cleaning. The Hill's Hoist was within our reach, we played on it and all hell broke loose."

"What happened?"

"Nanna was mad as a cut snake. First, she gave us the

cane and then she sent us to bed without tea. She was well and truly worked up, and the cane hurt like bloody hell. I didn't cry, but Brian did, he was still crying when Dad got home, hours later. In all fairness to my Nanna, she *was* worried about Mum and she *was* getting older. Mum was a late-in-life baby for Granddad and Nanna. Keeping up with all the cooking and cleaning plus my shenanigans wasn't easy for her. Granddad had died a few months before and then Mum had a miscarriage. Not a good time for any of us. Dad got us out of bed, checked us out to see if we needed first aid due to Nanna's caning, and then he hustled us into the kitchen. He made us cheese toasties. Brian loved cheese toasties and he finally quit crying. Dad didn't say anything until we had both finished our tea. Then he told me to go into the lounge room and apologize to Nanna. He told Brian to get ready for bed and said he'd read to us. If I remember right that night was the only time he read our bedtime story and tucked us in. Mum and Nanna usually took turns. After I apologized to Nanna, Dad had a word with only me."

"What did your father say?"

"I was to stay home from school in the morning and redo the wash under Nanna's supervision. All of it, even the stuff that didn't get muddy. Dad said I needed to respect the hard yakka women do and help out, instead of adding to their burden. Best way for me to learn was through experience and, no, he wasn't going to give me an excuse for being absent from school either. That would be on me to explain to my teacher why I wagged school. From then on, Brian and I were to clear the table after tea, wash the dishes, dry them, put them away, tidy up, and sweep the kitchen floor before going out to play, every bloody evening as long as we lived at home. Then he explained to me that everyone needed me to be a strong little man instead of behaving like a feral rug rat. 'You're the oldest, Ross. You're the strongest. Brian looks up to you. You set the example. Brian will learn from you how to be a little man. I need you to help me and your Mum needs you to help Nanna. You can do it, Ross, I believe in you.' I heard later that Dad told Nanna to never lay a hand on either of us again or send us to bed without eating. 'Sutherlands don't treat their horses badly; my sons won't be treated badly either. End of discussion. They misbehave, send them to their room and I'll deal with them when I get home.'"

"Did you really have to do all the laundry? You were only six, right?"

"Nah, yeah, well, Nanna had calmed down by the next morning and told Dad we would only do the muddy stuff and some of the smaller things, otherwise it would be too much work for her. After the washing, I helped Nanna with chores until she got tired of having me underfoot and told me to go play outside. She said I'd learned my lesson, which I had. After that I stayed out of trouble with Dad for the most part."

"What did your Mom say about all this?"

"What she usually said to me—I wish I could put an old head on your young shoulders. When I got older, she would look at me, shake her head and scold me with, 'sh' Ross not 'c'."

"What did that mean?"

Ross laughed. "Short for her admonishment, 'the word is should, Ross, not could. The question isn't if you could do it, but rather *should* you do it.' Mum had a sixth sense about me and she would redirect me with humor without getting Dad involved. But if Mum wasn't around, I could go off the rails, quick smart, like the time Nanna asked me to do something and I riffed on Mum's phrase, 'I would if I could and I could if I would.' I got sent to my room until Dad got home. Mum would have laughed at my cheekiness and I would have done what she asked of me, but Nanna didn't think I was funny and Dad supported Nanna. Dad was a stickler for being respectful to your elders and held a united front with the women against the tyranny of us ankle biters. At least that's what he always said if I complained. One disappointed look from Dad and I'd feel like a worm. I wanted to make Dad proud of me, Cait, but I had an acute knack for getting into strife. Dad always reminded me of my heritage, and then he would tell me to figure it out. He gave me room to correct my behavior and he never brought up my past mistakes. Dad said Brian was his thoroughbred and I was his silver brumby. When I was little, I took it as a compliment because *The Silver Brumby* was one of my favorite books."

"What's a brumby?"

"Feral horses in the bush, kind of like your Western mustangs. Good strong breeding stock for arid areas in Australia, if you can get the mares away from their stallion. Meant a lot to me to learn that your Frank and my Dad were good mates. Your Frank's a gentleman. Maybe, Dad saying that gentlemen stuff to me all the time was his way of honoring the man he knew my real father was. Sometimes I wonder if Dad called me his brumby because I was a bastard or because I had a proclivity to go feral. I dunno, Cait. Can't have been easy for Dad raising another man's son, especially one as strong-willed and cheeky as me. Lot of questions for which I'll never have the answers. Some things in this life are a complete mystery to be sure."

Sometimes, Ross was a complete mystery to me. One minute he could be overtly sexual and provocative and the next minute he'd be a perfect gentleman and almost old fashioned. The Tim Tam slam was fair game with me, but creating veggie worms with Jo's boys was off limits? The one thing I could count on was that interactions with Ross would be as unpredictable as Montana weather in the high country and equally as majestically beautiful. The other thing I knew from my time with Ross was I could trust him not to take advantage of me physically or sexually and, most importantly, he heard me when I said *no* in Yellowstone Park. Ross was Frank's and Jacob's son—a feral gentleman—respectful and loving, but with formidable internal strength.

Ross finished his tea and announced he was off back to town to meet up with Mike Turner. I tucked one pile of lollies and bikkies into a bag for Jo and her children and stowed my share in my bread bin for special occasions. I showed Ross where I put his special tea, and he gave me an acknowledging quick peck on the cheek. With his precious jar of Vegemite, his box of cherished Yorkshire Tea, and his Vita Weats carefully stowed in his saddle bags, Ross was off on his Harley in time for the sun's descent and its resulting brilliant colors brightening up his way down to Ennis and his awaiting sterile motel room. As I watched his tail lights disappear around the bend and then reappear further down the road, I thought there's never a dull moment when the man from Down Under is around. *Veggie Worms? Tim Tam slams? Hill's Hoists? Silver Brumbies?* I had a lot to share with Jo when I called her later tonight.

† † †

Mike and Ross were working closely together on *North to Montana.* Mike had agreed to do this shoot with Ross for less pay than usual, since they were old friends, and I could tell by watching them interact at the Bear Claw that Ross had a lot of respect for Mike's opinions. They were scouting additional locations and Ross happened to mention those outings to Frank who enthusiastically gave plenty of advice. Frank had become less wary of Ross since finding out Nora Larkin was Ross's mum. Ross's demeanor changed as well. He quit baiting Frank and pulling his leg. I suspected Ross was test-driving Frank in a father role, which meant that Ross had to be deferential. When Frank offered his help in finding backup locations for *North to Montana*, Ross accepted without hesitation. The day Ross showed up at the Bear Claw with a new model rented SUV, so Mike, Frank, and Ross could travel together, Frank wanted to drive the new rig. I happened to be behind the bar when Frank asked Ross if he could drive the next day.

I had to put a stop to that right away, "*Absofuckinglutely not.* Don't you *dare* let this man drive your rental SUV, Ross. You have no idea what Frank is capable of when he gets behind the wheel of the latest four-wheel drive. Don't you *dare* let him drive that new SUV."

Ross raised his eyebrows and winked at me. I was still fuming. "Is that a double dare, Cait?"

"This isn't funny, Ross. You have no idea what Frank does. *No idea.*" Turning to my godfather, I continued, "Confession time, buster. You tell Ross what you did to my father's new Jeep and what you did to Ralph's new Explorer. It's better it comes out of your mouth, Frank. You tell him. And don't sugar coat anything."

Ross looked at Frank, "Okay, then. Do you need another beer before confession?"

Frank grinned, "We need stronger stuff. Cait, two

scotches. Get out the Oban. Quick smart. Bring us the whole damn bottle."

Frank had done what every red-blooded Western male does with a new four-wheel drive rig. He took it off road and put it through its paces. Extreme off-road paces. Frank took vehicles places that no one else could drive with two full-size axles. The only reason the National Forest wasn't littered with wrecked vehicles is because Frank knew what he was doing. He got the vehicles back home intact, but not before Frank had added a little character. At least that's what Frank called the damage.

My father purchased the first Jeep Wagoneer in Bozeman. The light green Jeep had the controls inside the vehicle, whereas the older Jeeps required the driver to turn the hubs on the wheels. If you needed four-wheel drive, your hubs were either cold and snowy or wet with mud. The Wagoneer had a longer wheel base than the old Willys, which added another dimension to their off-road performance. Frank was itching to give my father's new fancy rig a Montana baptism. My grandfather was egging Frank on. My father finally gave in, and the three men drove over to the Tobacco Roots from Bozeman. When my father came home afterwards to yell at my mother, he turned the air blue. "Your damn father and O'Neill put a dent in the rain guard of my brand new Jeep. Afterwards, they tell me nobody has ever driven a vehicle over the pass. O'Neill and Gallagher took the route on horseback. They said the Wagoneer was worth every damn penny I paid for it, and then some. O'Neill is never coming anywhere near another one of my vehicles. That man is a maniac and your damn father is no better."

I glanced down the bar. I could tell by Ross's laughter that Frank must have concluded part of his ordered confession. The two of them poured more Scotch and Frank kept talking. Ross kept laughing.

I only heard about the Jeep's baptism secondhand but I was there when Frank took Ralph's new Explorer up the North Meadow Creek logging road, dropping down into the South Willow Creek drainage above Potosi Hot Springs. The problem had been the hairpin turns between the two creek drainages. The locals referred to that bit of road as Carmichael Hill, and it was widely considered impassable. Years of erosion and neglect had reduced the road to a good route for horses but not motorized vehicles. Didn't slow Frank down. We were fine until we started coming down the other side on a steep one-lane hill. At the bottom was a severely eroded hairpin curve with two exposed giant boulders. Frank stopped the Explorer and got out to assess the route. There was no good place to turn around, and backing up the slippery wet slope was not an option. Besides, what male ever wants to backtrack? Frank took one look at the eroded hairpin curve and said, brightly, "Not a problem, but I need both of you to get out to increase clearance. I'm going to need every inch I can get. Then we'll see what this new rig is made of."

Ralph and I watched in utter disbelief at the bottom of the hill as Frank drove our new SUV up onto the boulders. The front left tire of the Ford rested on one boulder and the rear right tire rested on the second. The downhill side of both boulders was washed out. The opposite wheels of the Ford were suspended in the air. Frank accelerated and spun the steering wheel at the same time, taking the Ford down off the boulders and cleanly around the curve. Sort of. The right passenger side, down by the bottom of the door, did not quite clear the rock and had a deep scratch as evidence of our passage over the famed Carmichael Hill.

Ralph's SUV was not the only thing that got damaged that day. After we dropped Frank off at the Bear Claw, we drove back to Bozeman to our motel. Ralph's anger about his beautiful new Ford Explorer came out of his fists and landed on me. Ralph was careful and methodical in his beating, and the resulting bruising remained hidden under my clothes. I could never tell Frank what his antics had cost me, but I could make sure that Ross had a head's up about how his rental SUV would fare if Frank was allowed to drive it. Besides, Ross needed to know the measure of the man he was riding with and the measure of the vehicle they would be traveling in together.

I never did know exactly where those three went to test drive the rental SUV, but Frank coached Ross through the driving and there wasn't a mark on the rental when they pulled into the Bear Claw. I know, because I went outside and looked carefully.

~ Chapter 26 ~

Ross could sit still if he had a good book to read, especially if he could talk about what he was reading. He shared some of Thomas Merton's poetry with me. Ross was especially fond of the poem written after Merton's brother was killed in World War II. The opening lines would always cause a quick catch in his voice, "*Sweet brother, if I do not sleep, my eyes are flowers for your tomb.*"[18] Ross felt Merton was like the ancient Irish bards who were both prophets and master wordsmiths. The bards had supernatural powers and could travel between this world and the next. The words themselves had power. Poetry was seen as medicine; it could cure ailments of the body and the soul. Ross reckoned Merton created passages into the other world with his words, the poems created thin places between heaven and earth, particularly when read aloud.

We had lengthy discussions about how the bards would learn their craft. The thought of memorizing 350 epic poems by reciting them in total darkness was fascinating.

I teased Ross. He always had the lights on when he read Merton to me.

One Merton poem echoed for days afterwards:

"We are exiles in the far end of solitude, living as listeners
With hearts attending to the skies we cannot understand:
Waiting upon the first far drums of Christ the Conqueror,
Planted like sentinels upon the world's frontier."[19]

I wondered if Merton had been writing about the white martyrs. *"Sentinels upon the world's frontier"* reminded me of St. Columba's description of Christian monks as guests upon the world. I asked Ross. He launched into an enthusiastic account of Merton's fascination with the ancient Celtic church. According to Ross, Merton had his own *anam cara* in the form of an elderly Cambridge scholar, Nora Chadwick. They never met. Their relationship was entirely by correspondence. I thought a person had to know their *anam cara* to which Ross responded, "St. Bridget never knew St. Patrick. She was six when he died, but she claimed she talked with him."

"How could that be?"

Ross shrugged. The incongruity didn't seem to bother him. "The old Irish were like the Aborigines, Cait. They were flexible about boundaries between time and space. Soul friends are always connected, even death can't separate them." I loved the notion of a soul friend, but the violation of natural laws conflicted with my rational view of the world. I needed a companion in this world, in this time.

Ross frequently played guitar while I cooked a late supper. Working on rock 'n' roll riffs, learning folk songs from me, teaching me Aussie bush ballads. I played an old Leadbelly recording for him on my battery-powered CD player, which inspired him to spend hours messing around with his 12-string guitar, reproducing Leadbelly's distinctive blues sound. I told Ross Leadbelly's amazing and tragic story. John Lomax had met Leadbelly when he was collecting folk songs in Southern prisons and had a part in Leadbelly's reprieve. Through his connections with Lomax, Leadbelly became part of the New York folk scene, recording with Woody Guthrie, Cisco Houston, and Pete Seeger. Leadbelly's famous song, "Goodnight Irene," was a commercial success the year after Leadbelly passed away of Lou Gehrig's disease. I'd finally met someone who shared my enthusiasm for Leadbelly's raw style. Most people didn't like him. Ross's reaction was classic, "What's not to like, Cait? A real man singing real songs. No pretense. No artifice. Art doesn't come any more honest than Leadbelly." Then Ross winked at me, "You just haven't been spending enough time with the right man."

One evening, late in August, I asked Ross if he had talked with Frank yet about his mum and his parentage. I was not going to take no for an answer. "You have to tell Frank that you're his son. He has a right to know the truth."

I could tell Ross didn't want to have this conversation. He was tapping syncopated rhythms on the kitchen table and he wasn't making eye contact. I used my best professorial voice, "Listen to me, Ross. The longer you wait, the harder it will be, and Frank will wonder why you didn't trust him. You two are getting along now. Frank respects you. Do you know how I know that? I'm a Montanan. If Frank didn't respect you, he would have found a way to mess up your rented SUV, just to teach you a lesson. Like he did with my father. Like he did with my ex-husband. He didn't, did he? There wasn't a mark on your SUV. I went out and looked. Not because I give a shit about your rental. I don't. I needed to know if Frank respected you as a man. Frank's my godfather. I care what he thinks about you and about us, but he doesn't show emotion and he doesn't talk. The way *you* can tell how Frank feels is to watch him and see what he does. The SUV told *me* everything I needed to know about you two. Frank does respect you. He doesn't think you're a bloody tosser, Ross. He doesn't. He likes you. He respects you." I paused, judging Ross's reaction, wondering if I was going too far into territory that wasn't my territory. Or was it?

Ross met my gaze. He'd stopped tapping somewhere in the middle of my big speech. When I paused, Ross nodded, "I'm listening, Cait. Finish your lecture."

In that moment, I made a split decision to ignore Ross's last remark. I took a big breath and went in for the kill shot—my final argumentative point. "Don't be afraid, Ross. Talk to Frank. He has a big heart. He'll listen. It'll be okay. You can't keep putting this off, Ross. It's important to you. It's important to me."

I looked Ross right in the eye. I was uncertain if I should continue, but he wasn't making any smart remarks about lecturing, he wasn't being defensive, he wasn't radiating any energy to fill the room to overwhelm me, he wasn't doing anything. He was just listening.

I recentered myself and finished a story I didn't have the right to tell, "Frank deserves to know he has family in this world. Frank's had a hard hard life. He deserves the truth. You *have* to tell him. Frank's father died when he was young, his mother committed suicide from grief. Frank was an only child. He was all alone. That's why he was moving from ranch to ranch, lying about his age so he could work. My grandma recognized a bummer—an orphan lamb—when she saw one. That's why my grandparents took him in and made him family. Frank is all alone in this world, except you and I know, he's *not* alone in this world. I can't tell Frank. It's not my story to tell. If you don't do it for yourself, Ross, please do it for me. I love Frank. Don't deny him his truth. He's suffered enough, but the truth has to come from you, Ross. Think about it. Frank only ever loved your mother, no other woman. You are the product of his one true love. You love stories so much, tell this beautiful one. Will you talk to Frank? Please. For me, for you, for Frank? Please?"

I stopped, waiting for Ross's reaction. I was afraid he would be angry with me for telling him what to do. He wasn't. Ross shifted in his chair and said to me in a calm, quiet voice, "What do you suggest we do, Cait?"

I hesitated and found the strength to answer his question, "Well, tomorrow is his day off from the bar. I can call and arrange for you to go over to his house. That's a safe place to talk. I'll come with you, if you like."

Ross nodded and said, "Okay. Please come with me, Cait. And could you make the call for me? Please?"

I made the call. "I need you to be kind, Frank. Ross has something to tell you. I need you to listen."

"Ross is going to make an honest woman out of you?"

"No, Frank, it's not about us. No jokes. Behave, Frank. Please, don't tease me or Ross."

"Okay, Cait. Bring him by about 7 p.m. I'll have fresh pie."

"I'll bring the Oban."

"That serious?"

"Yes, Frank. Please, behave yourself tomorrow night. Just listen to what Ross has to tell you. For my sake, if not for his. Okay?"

Ross and I walked over to Frank's and were greeted

with the smells of freshly baked harvest pie. Frank's pies were the stuff of legend around the county and harvest was my favorite. The combination of plums, peaches, apples, sour cherries, and blueberries resulted in a pie where each forkful tasted different and the colors were gorgeous. Frank had taught me to make his grandmother's crust over the winter, but I had no way to bake at the cabin with my portable camp stove. Ross was equally appreciative of Frank's baking skills. After pie and coffee, we all retired to the living room with our Oban bottle and glasses. The evening was unusually cool and Frank had lit a fire in his stone fireplace.

After Frank's accident, my grandfather had given him 40 acres of his hunting cabin's land and helped build him a house. Grandpa said Frank was family and family took care of their own, ignoring Frank's insistence that he would be fine. "Save your money to build a new career, Frank. Your days of being a horse wrangler and a hotshot firefighter are over." Grandpa understood the severity of Frank's injuries, even if Frank himself was still in denial. Because Grandpa built Frank his house and gifted him the land to use as collateral, Frank was able to buy the Bear Claw.

I poured everyone a shot of Oban and settled into the rocking chair in Frank's living room, leaving the men to sit close to the fireplace in Frank's matching dark leather wingback chairs.

Ross started by asking Frank why he was called Paddy.

Frank chuckled. "When I first went round to your Granddad's place looking for work, he hired me with a two-week test period. He showed me all around his farm, and the next morning when I arrived, he asked me to bring the horses down from the back paddock. I was confused, thinking I had heard wrong. Mr. Larkin repeated himself, saying field, the one by the old gum tree. Your mother overheard us and thought my ignorance of Aussie slang was quite funny. Nora was the prettiest girl I'd ever seen. She was only 15, but she was high-spirited and forward. She started calling me Paddy. She liked to watch me get flustered and blush. Nobody called me Frank after that."

"Mum saved the book you sent her, but she never opened the letter with the photograph. She kept them in her glory box and Ruthie, my sister, found them after Mum and Dad were killed."

"What happened?"

"Plane crash. Fifteen years ago."

Ross waited for the news to sink in. Frank sat still. The fire crackled. Ross got up and added more wood.

"That must have been very hard for you and your family."

Ross nodded. Frank's dog got up from his bed in the corner next to me and went over to Ross, resting his chin on Ross's knee. Ross petted Jack absentmindedly until Jack settled at Ross's feet.

"Why did Mum turn you down?"

"She didn't want to come to America. She really didn't want to come to Montana. I tried to tell her that the stories she had heard from the Aussie vets about the Korean winters didn't represent winter in Montana, but she wasn't hearing me. She said she was too young to get married."

"When did you leave her?"

"August 1, 1959. Worst day of my life. Mr. Larkin told me he would welcome me into the family if Nora said yes, but I would have to leave if she said no. That was our agreement when I asked him for Nora's hand. He said the decision was up to Nora, because it was her life."

"She was still 18 when she married Jacob." Ross countered.

"I was born four months later, in April 1960, at my great uncle's sheep station in Queensland."

I watched Frank's face. He was not hiding his emotions like he did when he played cards with me. He leaned forward in his chair, with his elbows on his knees, hands in his short straight hair. Then he shifted position, locking his fingers together, resting his forehead on top of his knuckles, rubbing his brow back and forth over them. The tension he was feeling was reflected in the tensing and release of his jaw muscles. In that moment, he looked exactly like his son had when Ross realized in the Bear Claw that Frank knew Jacob Sutherland. I had never seen the physical resemblance before, since Frank had straight dark hair with a different shaped nose and mouth. Where Ross was tall and solidly built, Frank was tall and lanky with slim hips and skinny long legs. He had Ross's broad shoulders but not his musculature. Frank and Ross had the same expressive green eyes. While the two did not resemble each other at first glance, they shared a lot of mannerisms. The better I got to know Ross, the more I saw Frank in him. I caught Ross's gaze and raised my eyebrows in an unvocalized question. Ross nodded slightly in Frank's direction and gave me a brief smile. Ross had recognized himself in Frank's nonverbal reaction. We waited patiently for Frank to speak. After several minutes of massaging his temples, he sat back up and looked directly at his son.

"I didn't know," Frank said while shaking his head, "Mr. Larkin wrote to me in 1962, saying Nora had married and had a new baby. I sent Nora a letter with the Nelson Story book because I was working for the Story Cattle Company over in Paradise Valley at the time. I never heard from anyone afterwards. Not a word."

"Who was my mother seeing that winter, Frank? It wasn't Jacob."

"No, your mother was a good girl, Ross. She was only seeing me."

Ross regarded Frank with his head slightly to one side, his jaw tightening, eyes narrowed. As usual, Ross had taken the chair so his scar was away from Frank.

Frank continued, "Yes, I fell in love with Nora the first time I saw her, but she was very young and I was 10 years older. I'd done two tours in Korea, worked in the Merchant Marines. She was a child and I was a jaded man of the world. I kept my distance. Your mother was persistent. She liked to have a good time and play practical jokes. She roped me into some doozies. First time I kissed her was at her 18th birthday party. Mr. Larkin threw a huge party. Hired a band and all the neighbors brought food. Nora wouldn't dance with anyone, but me. After the dance, she whispered in my ear, 'I'm 18 now, Paddy. I can do whatever I want. I want you.'"

Ross didn't move. The firelight illuminated his face and I could see he had lost that tense expression. He was listening.

"We spent a lot of time together that month. Going out on long horseback rides, laying under the stars, and then I knew I needed to marry her, but she wouldn't say yes. I tried everything I could think of, I could not change her mind. I loved her, Ross. With every cell in my body. Hardest thing I ever did in my life was get on that damn plane. I never would have left, if I'd known Nora was carrying my child. Nobody told me. I never suspected a thing. Not once. All those years, I had no idea I had a son. No idea."

"I've been looking for you for almost five years, Frank."

"Why, now?"

"My sister likes genealogy and she made everyone take a DNA test more than five years ago. I wasn't a Sutherland."

"Damn. Nobody ever told you?

"Nope."

"They must have known."

"Yup."

"Damn." Frank reached across to Ross's knee and patted it. "Maybe I should have tried harder to stay in touch with the Larkins."

Ross shook his head, "Nah. You weren't to know, Frank. Mum rejected you. You did what gentlemen do. You listened to her and moved on."

Frank grunted. He sighed and leaned back into his chair.

Ross broke the long silence, "I always felt at home at the Bear Claw and here in the Madison."

"Did you now?"

"Yes. That's why I came back every August. The odd sense of serenity I feel here and the book you posted kept pulling me back to the Madison." Ross paused before continuing, "None of it made any sense. I followed my gut and it said, know your father's country, maybe you will know your father. My sister saw our Mum cryin' right after David was born. Mum was holding that book you sent about Nelson Story." Ross was choking up, and then he continued, "Ruthie sent the book to me after the DNA test. And the unopened letter from Emigrant. I was in Dakota filming, so after the shoot I rode west. I only had the book and the letter as clues. Nobody in Emigrant knew anything about you, but they suggested I go to Virginia City to see Story's town." Ross stopped. He cleared his throat, "When Cait showed me Evening Star up Bridger Canyon, I couldn't believe it. I recognized the rock from the photo you sent Mum. The more Cait told me about her family, the more I wondered about you and your Aussie greeting, but I didn't want to make a fool of myself, Frank, or dare to hope that I might actually have found my real father, until Cait insisted that *was* you in the photo."

Frank nodded, "I have a grandson, correct?" I couldn't help noticing how Frank tracked conversations. Like his son, Frank didn't always respond in the moment; sometimes he leap-frogged over topics to direct the conversation to what interested him the most. With both men, you knew they were listening to you, but you couldn't predict what they would say next in a conversation.

"David. He's 15."

"He must have been a baby when Nora and Jacob died."

"Yeah, two months old. Mum and Dad never got to meet him."

"Damn, life's a bitch. What's my grandson like?"

Ross shrugged in response and replied, "Honestly, Frank? I don't know. Another man's raising David."

"Hmmm. Is that what you want?"

"Not really. It's just easier. I'm not home enough. A boy needs a man around. A good one. Shelley's husband is a good man. He's a good father to David. What I want doesn't matter. Such is life."

Frank sighed. After a long silence, he asked Ross a question, "Ross, would you ever consider calling me Dad?"

Ross regarded his father for several minutes without expression, but I noticed how much greener his eyes were, and then he nodded with a small smile, "Yes, I would like that."

Frank reached over to pat his son's knee again, "Me too, son, me too."

I poured myself another Scotch. The fire burned on as I snuggled under the throw Frank kept on my favorite chair. The men were silent, lost in their own thoughts. Whatever the future held for Ross and me, at least I had the satisfaction of knowing I had united a son with his father after years of searching, questions, and torment. I sat warm and content in my godfather's home thinking about Frank leaving his one true love, Nora Larkin, in Australia to return home alone. The mystery of the drover—the real American cowboy—had been solved for my friend, Ross. My white martyr—self-described wanderer in the borderlands—had found his truth in the house built by my grandfather in the shadow of our beloved Tobacco Root mountains. I remembered Ross singing me his mother's favorite song the night another fall of rain forced our shared evening of stories and music at the beginning of this Celtic season of matchmaking and harvest:

In tears our last farewell was taken,
And now in tears we meet again.

What a glorious harvest, we had reaped this August. Frank wasn't alone in this world. He had family—a son, a grandson, a niece, a nephew, all blood relatives of his one true love. Frank wasn't a bum lamb after all. And Ross? He had gone to great lengths and expense to tell the story of my country—Nelson Story's epic cattle drive. I felt humbled by my part in the reunion of a father and his son and in the telling of a great Montana story. Perhaps, this was my legacy, not my novel. But as I sat in my godfather's house, I felt a presence I didn't want to acknowledge. A darkness circling, a predator on the edges of our happiness. What had Grandpa had said to me from the grave, *"He's a good man, Cait. He'll keep you safe,"* and yet there was my premonition of sharp turns, my shoulder hurting, and gravel spinning. Why would Ross have to keep me safe? From what? Was my grandfather's gift of foresight a curse and a burden? I felt in my bones the last lines of Nora's favorite song were a warning. Who would need the wreaths of grief and mourning? And why would love have to be half flowers and half chains?

Or how shall I, who love, who bless thee,
Invoke thy breath for Freedom's strains,
When even the wreaths in which I dress thee
Are sadly mix'd — half flowers, half chains?[20]

I pushed back my darkening thoughts and remembered Grandpa's description of our mountain as God's cathedral. Maybe, Grandpa was right, this land does know we are here—Montana summoned Ross, enticing him to tell one of her epic stories and kept seducing him with her wild beauty until he agreed to make the movie, *North to Montana.* Montana performed celestial mass for me in her skies, how could she possibly betray me? Wouldn't Montana keep me safe? She had brought Ross and I together at every turn. A motorcycle flat tire from a freshly graded Montana dirt road had been the stone rolling down the mountain to alter our lives. If I hadn't picked up Ross's copy of "The Greatest Cattle Drive," I never would have seen the black and white photograph of Frank in front of the rock of Evening Star in Bridger Canyon. I remembered how happy Ross had been when I sang Henry Lawson's "Ballad of the Drover" to the tune of the American western song "Little Old Sod Shanty on the Plain."

Across the stony ridges,
Across the rolling plain,
Young Harry Dale, the drover,
Comes riding home again.
And well his stock-horse bears him,
And light of heart is he,
And stoutly his old pack-horse
Is trotting by his knee.

Up Queensland way with cattle
He travelled regions vast,
And many months have vanished
Since home-folk saw him last.
He hums a song of someone
He hopes to marry soon;
And hobble-chains and camp-ware
Keep jingling to the tune.

Beyond the hazy dado
Against the lower skies
And yon blue line of ranges
The homestead station lies.
And thitherward the drover
Jogs through the lazy noon,
While hobble-chains and camp-ware
Are jingling to a tune.

An hour has filled the heavens
With storm-clouds inky black;
At times the lightning trickles
Around the drover's track;
But Harry pushes onward,
His horses' strength he tries,

In hope to reach the river
Before the flood shall rise.

The thunder, pealing o'er him,
Goes rumbling down the plain;
And sweet on thirsty pastures
Beats fast the plashing rain;
Then every creek and gully
Sends forth its tribute flood—
Till the river runs a banker,
All stained with yellow mud.

Now Harry speaks to Rover,
The best dog on the plains,
And to his hardy horses,
And strokes their shaggy manes:
"We've breasted bigger rivers
When floods were at their height
Nor shall this gutter stop us
From getting home tonight!"

The thunder growls a warning,
The blue, forked lightnings gleam,
The drover turns his horses
To swim the fatal stream.
But, oh! the flood runs stronger
Than e'er it ran before;
The saddle-horse is failing,
And only half-way o'er!

When flashes next the lightning,
The flood's grey breast is blank;
A cattle-dog and pack-horse

Are struggling up the bank.
But in the lonely homestead
The girl will wait in vain —
He'll never pass the stations
In charge of stock again.

The faithful dog a moment
Lies panting on the bank,
Then plunges through the current
To where his master sank.
And round and round in circles
He fights with failing strength,
Till, gripped by wilder waters,
He fails and sinks at length.

Across the flooded lowlands
And slopes of sodden loam
The packhorse struggles bravely,
To take dumb tidings home;
And mud-stained, wet, and weary,
He goes by rock and tree,
With clanging chains and tinware
Are sounding eerily.[21]

Before I drifted off to sleep listening to the crackling of the fire and Jack snoring softly at Ross's feet, I thought how odd that in our version of the drover's tale, the men and the faithful dog had reached home under the big sky of Montana and it was the girl—Nora Larkin—who perished without ever seeing her drover again. All I knew for certain was that Grandma was accurate in her admonition—*never give up on hope, Caitlain, never give up on love.* The stories of country, the songs of country, the prayers of country, and a friendly Aussie greeting, "How ya goin', alright?" had all played a part in mending the bonds that had been broken 41 years ago on the sunlit tarmac in New South Wales. Hope and love had persevered for Ross. Would I be able to achieve the same clarity in my search for love and for hope of a better life? Or would I be like the exiles in Merton's poem? Destined to live alone in my grandfather's quiet cabin, listening to Montana skies and waiting? Always waiting for another fall of rain to heal my parched country and to heal my heart and soul? *Never give up on hope, Caitlain, never give up on love ...*

~ Endnotes ~

1. John O'Donohue, "Beannacht," *To Bless the Space Between Us: A Book of Blessings*, (New York: Doubleday, 2008), 10-11.
2. St. Patrick, *The Confession of Saint Patrick and Letter to Coroticus*, trans. John Skinner, (New York: Doubleday, 1998), 79.
3. Patrick Kavanagh, "To a Child," *Collected Poems*, (New York: W. W. Norton, 1964), 9.
4. Wendell Berry, "Water," *Farming: A Hand Book*, (New York: Harcourt Brace Jovanovich, 1970), 11.
5. St. Patrick, *Confession*, 79.
6. Omar Khayyam, *The Rubaiyat of Omar Khayyam*, trans. Edward FitzGerald, (Philadelphia: Running Press, 1989), 51.
7. Patrick Kavanagh, "Wet Evening in April," *Collected Poems*, (New York: W. W. Norton, 1964), 140.
8. Banjo Patterson, "Prelude," *The Best of Banjo Patterson*, Walter Stone, ed., (Sydney: Summit Books, 1977), 31.
9. Hugh Anderson, *The Story of Australian Folksong*, (New York: Oak Publications, 1970), 58-60.
10. Thomas Moore, "My Gentle Harp," *Fireside Book of American Folksongs*, Margaret Bradford Boni, ed., (New York: Simon and Schuster, 1947), 88.
11. Henry Lawson, "Ballad of the Drover," *From the Ballads to Brennan, Poetry in Australia*, T. I. Moore, ed., Vol. I, (Los Angeles: University of California Press, 1965), 117-119.
12. Sean O Boyle, "Bonnie Portmore," *The Irish Song Tradition*, (Dublin: Gilbert Dalton, 1976), 50.
13. Hugh Anderson, *Colonial Ballads*, (Melbourne, Australia:

F. W. Cheshire, 1955), 131-132.

14. John Donne, "Air and Angels," *The Complete Poetry and Selected Prose of John Donne*, Charles M. Coffin, ed, (New York: The Modern Library, 2001), 19.

15. Banjo Patterson, "Clancy of the Overflow," *The Best of Banjo Patterson*, 47.

16. Unknown author, "Blessing," *Celtic Prayers*, trans. Alexander Carmichael (New York: Image Pocket Classics, 1996), 49.

17. Patterson, "The Old Australian Ways," *Best of Banjo Patterson*, 116-117.

18. Thomas Merton, "For My Brother: Reported Missing in Action, 1943," *The Collected Poems of Thomas Merton*, (New York: New Directions Books, 1977), 35-36.

19. Merton, "The Quickening of St. John the Baptist," *Poems*, 201.

20. Thomas Moore, *Fireside Book*, 88.

21. Lawson, "Ballad of the Drover," 117-118.

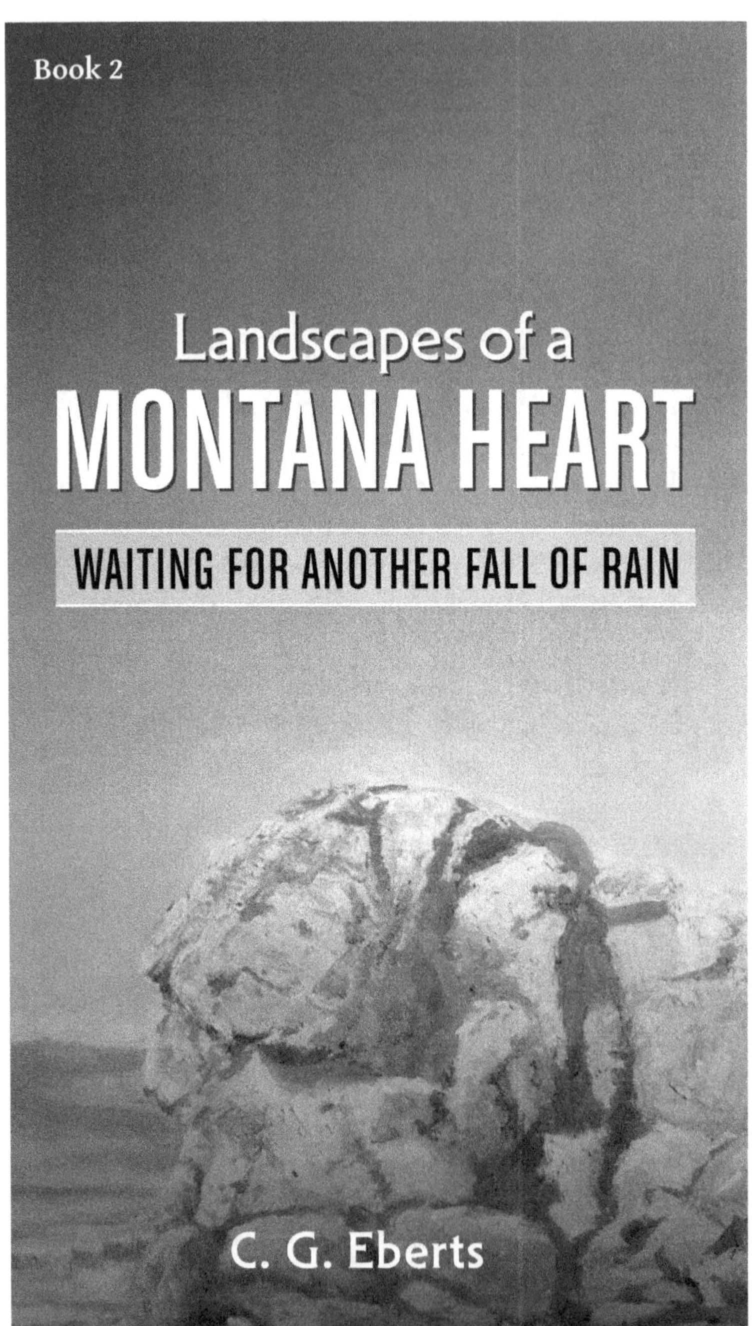

Book 2
Landscapes of a
MONTANA HEART
WAITING FOR ANOTHER FALL OF RAIN
C. G. Eberts

Fire was on my mind, constantly. It was on everyone's mind. Montana was bone dry. After three back-to-back open winters, soil moisture was depleted, streams were running dry, and the aquifer was dropping. Earlier in the week, a rancher who lived on the Broadwater-Gallatin County line inadvertently started a fire with his harvesting equipment in his grain field. A straightforward, manageable fire under normal calm conditions mushroomed into an uncontrollable monster with the 30 mile an hour gusty winds. Within a few hours, 20,000 acres had burned 20 miles north of my hometown of Bozeman. The Maudlow/Toston fire was a problem for my Australian friend Ross, since one of the burnt ranches was a key location for his directorial debut, *North to Montana*. His movie was based upon the famous Nelson Story cattle drive from Texas to the Montana gold fields of Virginia City in 1866. Frank O'Neill, my nearest neighbor and my godfather, suggested moving those scenes down to central Wyoming. Frank's father had been from that area and Frank still had distant cousins ranching the old home place. Ross's immediate problem was solved. For the Montana ranchers the problems were mounting. After three years of drought, pastures that had been in poor condition were now blackened. Donations of hay were coming in from out-of-state, but who wanted to rebuild miles of burnt fencing? Frank, the son of a Wyoming rancher, and Ross, the son of an Australian horse breeder, discussed the hardscrabble economics of living off the land on more than one occasion.

The Beaver Creek Fire had grown, causing safety concerns for residents of Gallatin Canyon. Contingency evacuation plans for the resort community of Big Sky were under discussion. The Bitterroots continued to explode. Every day was worse than the previous. Firefighters were coming up from California with their special fleet of wildfire trucks. Canadians unused to fighting fire in steep terrain with pulaskis were down from Ontario. Australian fire managers were flying up from Down Under to lead the fire crews. Fire was everywhere and so was the smoke. Virtually every county in Western Montana, except for my safe place of Madison County, was incinerating. Even though there were no fires in Madison County, the haze from the surrounding area fires was getting thicker. The winds were blowing additional smoke and ash from the Idaho fires across Montana. Some days I could not see Frank's place from my porch. He was less than a mile away. I was used to seeing vistas of 60 to 90 miles, and the reduction in clarity of familiar landscapes was stifling.

I followed the news with increasing panic. The nightmares were back. As a small child, when I first heard my grandfather's story about his cousin dying with 12 other smokejumpers on the steep slopes of Mann Gulch August 5, 1949, I had nightmares for months. They increased after Frank was nearly killed when a widow maker—a tree whose roots had burned away—fell on him, breaking both his legs and his pelvis, thus ending his career as a hotshot firefighter. I would dream of the sound of the fire roaring like a locomotive, the hurricane force winds of a blow-up, and the searing heat. When I was 13, the nightmares returned. The summer my father started molesting me. Now, Montana was igniting all around me. I thought about my wooden roof, and remembered Frank's comment of last month about re-roofing my cabin. In July, Frank had come over to help me construct a fire line around my cabin due to the increasing fire danger from the deepening drought. I fretted. I worried. I got on my stepladder. I went down to the lumberyard in Ennis and bought the fireproof shingles for my cabin roof, which they promised to deliver that afternoon. I went home and got the extension ladder out from the back of Grandpa's shed. The lumber truck delivering my shingles passed Frank's house as he and Ross returned from a scouting trip. Ever since the recent evening when Frank learned that Ross Larkin Sutherland, the international movie star from New South Wales was his bastard son, the two had become inseparable. After 40 years apart, the two men had a lot of stories to swap.

Frank and Ross strolled over to my place together. Frank looked at me and my bundles of shingles, "What have you got in mind, Cait?"

"Everything is burning, and these cedar shake shingles were a huge mistake. Grandpa never should have used them. I need to re-roof my cabin." A ranting tone was creeping into my voice.

Ross glanced at Frank and Frank grinned back at him, "She's your responsibility, Ross." Frank turned on his heel and headed home. He knew when to evacuate.

Ross put his hands on my shoulders and looked me firmly in the eyes. "Cait, do you know how to roof?"

"No." I admitted reluctantly.

"Have you ever been on that extension ladder you've

got over there?" Ross gestured to the ladder leaning up against my cabin.

"No." I was getting belligerent.

"What the bloody hell do you think you're going to do?"

"Re-roof my cabin before the fires come."

"Why?"

"Because it needs to be done." I thought his was an incredibly stupid question. I was back to ranting.

"No, Cait, I mean why do *you* need to do it?"

"Because I'm tired of living dependent on men. Because I need to be independent." I was feeling defiant and unreasonable.

Ross let go of my shoulders. He sighed and directed his attention to the eagles gliding on the winds off the top of my mountain. All three of them, parents and the young one, were riding the up drafts. Starting at his forehead, Ross ran his hands through his thick curls several times. He walked off a few paces towards the mountain and then turned abruptly and came back to me, taking big strides. He sighed deeply before he spoke.

"Caitlinn Burnett. I care about you, and that means I want to be able to do things for you and you need to open up your heart and let me in. I know you're afraid to be open because you don't want to be hurt again. But you need to let people help you. It's okay to need help, it's okay to ask for help, it's okay to accept help."

"I understand that it's important for you to be independent. I need you to understand it's important to me that you're safe. So," he paused and tilted his head to the right, with his eyes narrowing slightly, "Here's what we'll do. You can fix your own roof, but only under the direct supervision of someone who knows what they're doing. I'll help you. Promise me, Caitlinn, you won't be stupid and muck around on that bloody roof when no one's here to peel you off the ground." Ross said the last few words with a bit of dramatic flair.

The next morning, Ross phoned me, "Cait, two blokes from my movie set carpentry crew are headed your way. They will be removing the shingles and hauling them to the tip. If you want to save any for kindling, you'll have to remove the nails and store the shingles out of the rain. We have to be mindful of nails, as we don't need any more flats. If your roof needs any new sarking boards, they'll replace those too. They've got the magnetic tool to find loose nails. They're good men. They will do right by you. I'm paying for all of this out of my own pocket, including what the shingles cost you. End of discussion."

"Okay." I was too busy wondering what a sarking board was to mount a counterargument to Ross's roofing plan or payment arrangements.

"And Cait, I've sorted my schedule so I'm with you by 4 p.m. this arvo and all yours tomorrow, except for an overseas business call I can't miss. Hope you don't mind, but I asked my dad for help. He's coming by tonight before his shift to get us started. I've done roofing back home, but I don't know much about the shingles you Yanks prefer. Frank does. He thinks you and I can complete your roof on schedule if we work smart. It means a lot to me to have Dad supervise. This should be heaps of fun. See ya at four, luv."

The first evening of our roofing project, Ross fell asleep on my bed waiting for me to make him a late supper. He could fall asleep faster than anyone I had ever met. I covered Ross with an extra quilt and slept in my loft. Next morning, he was apologetic and said I should get him up next time, but I didn't mind. I liked waking to the smell of his freshly brewed coffee. We'd been spending time together since we met early in August at Frank's Bear Claw Bar and Grill in McAllister. While we had grown close, we had agreed to be plutonic friends rather than lovers. I relished those hours spent working together with a minimum of talking. Reroofing Grandpa's cabin with Ross under Frank's watchful eye was a special time for me. I could tell Frank and Ross were enjoying the opportunity to work together—a father teaching his son new skills. During my whole roofing project, I kept reflecting upon my grandparents raising Frank, how indebted Frank felt to a man and a woman not his own blood, and how often Ross had spoken with love and gratitude for the wisdom, kindness, and knowledge Jacob Sutherland had passed to him while knowing that Ross was not his biological son. Jacob had married Ross's mother, Nora Larkin, when she was five months pregnant with Frank's baby. Nora had refused Frank's hand in marriage, claiming she was too young to be betrothed. After breaking the heart of her first love, Nora had asked her parents not to tell Frank of her pregnancy. I had inadvertently stumbled upon vital clues and thus helped Ross discover his true parentage. I felt strongly that the three of us were doing something more than fixing a roof against potential fire, we were building a foundation against future adversity. However, like many of my premonitions it was a disjointed feeling with no clear imagery, leaving me feeling uncertain as to its interpretation.

Ross and I finished the last of my roof as the evening shadows lengthened and the sky changed color. As Ross drove my truck down to the Bear Claw for dinner, I knew he was in a jolly mood, because he was loudly singing Aussie bush ballads the entire way. Sitting at the bar, Ross told me endless jokes, most of which weren't very funny. I never liked jokes dependent upon mispronunciation of words, because I didn't get them. Jokes you have to rehash and explain aren't worth repeating in my opinion. After dinner, his third beer and a string of jokes landing flatter than my grandmother's pancakes, Ross leaned over to speak softly in my ear, "Ya know what a French kiss is, yeah?"

I frowned at him, "Of course, I do."

"Do ya know what an Aussie kiss is, Cait?"

I shook my head, wondering where this was going. Another joke that wasn't funny?

Ross sat up very straight and delivered his punchline with firm authority, accompanied by the now familiar Aussie lilt at the end, "A French kiss Down Under." He looked at me without expression, waiting for my response.

I immediately put my head down on Frank's bar with my hands crossed over my head. I was trying not to laugh. I didn't want to encourage Ross. I didn't want to hear any more dirty jokes. One was enough. How to control my body? I could feel my loins reacting. I could feel my face heating up. I didn't want Ross to see me blushing. *What to do? How was I going to regain my composure and look him in the eye when all I could think about was how much I wanted this man to give me an Aussie kiss? Right here, right now.*

I could hear Frank walk up, with his distinctive cowboy heels echoing across the wooden floor. "What's wrong with Cait?"

"Dunno."

"What did you say to her, son?" It was the first, but not the last time I heard Frank acknowledge his offspring in public.

"I was trying to crack a funny but she didn't find any of my jokes amusing, and then I told Cait a naughty one."

"Didn't your father ever tell you not to tell dirty jokes to a lady?"

Ross snorted, "It's a bit late for that advice, Dad."

"Hmm … . Apparently so."